To Grace
with best wishes
From Rene.

Christmas 1942

EXILES

EXILES

by

WARWICK DEEPING

author of

"SORRELL AND SON"
"ROPER'S ROW"
etc.

CASSELL & COMPANY LTD
LONDON, TORONTO, MELBOURNE & SYDNEY

First Edition	*February*	*1930*
Second Edition	*March*	*1930*
Third Edition (First Cheap Edition)	*February*	*1932*
Fourth Edition	*March*	*1932*
Fifth Edition	*October*	*1933*
Sixth Edition	*August*	*1935*
Seventh Edition	*April*	*1942*

Printed in Great Britain by Butler & Tanner Ltd., Frome and London

EXILES

CHAPTER I

i

SHE had been christened Barbara Irene. But, since the family name was Brown, she had taken to herself in the nursery the more intimate and characteristic name of Bib, and as Bib she had continued to be known until the irreverent affection of a rough and tumble girls' school had named her Billy.

As Billy Brown, aged six-and-twenty, she stood upon the platform of Tindaro, and also upon the threshold of adventure, with a suitcase at her feet, and her fingers searching her bag for a luggage ticket. An Italian porter with the smudge of a three days' beard making his face look yet more swarthy, attended upon her deliberate fingers. A little excited she might be, and travel-stained, and innocently English, but her poise was that of the hockey field.

"I want a taxi."

She passed the man her luggage ticket, but kept hold of her suitcase. She had a way of not letting things go. She followed the slouch of his round figure towards the station buildings, where a solitary electric light made the shabbiness of the place momentarily visible. A little crowd oozed through a doorway. The blue night hung overhead.

She sat in the open car while the porter was collecting her trunk. She was very much on the edge of her adventure, and feeling the thrill of it, and Tindaro, up above there, was like a hill town to be stormed and taken. She had the veneer of masculinity that characterizes the modern young woman,

1

and the phrases of a game-playing generation, but she had much more. A tennis-ball cannot eclipse the moon.

Tindaro, as expressed by its railway station when darkness had fallen, was frankly disappointing, being a collection of shabby sheds and buildings and litter and casual mounds of road-metal and mud. A hideous cripple kept poking a withered arm at her, and assailed her with supplications and an odour of garlic. The driver of the taxi stood and stared with large, round, animal eyes, his lips retracted over strong white teeth. Billy grew tired of the beggar. He was an importunate shape getting in the way of her impressions and symbolizing life as an unpleasant odour and a withered limb. But at last the porter arrived with her trunk, and he and the taxi-driver attached it to the rear of the car with odd pieces of string and much conversation. Billy was to discover that Tindaro was full of such improvisations.

They started. The railway and its clutter fell away. The road rose steeply, and almost the car was like a climbing plane soaring gradually out of the obvious into the mysterious. The sea appeared, and a sudden galaxy of lights like sequins flung by the handful against soft, dark surfaces. The whole hillside glittered, and in the distance there were other swarms of lights that flickered and twinkled. To Billy they suggested pin-points pricked in black cardboard, or yellow burrs on black velvet. Mystery. She sat there conscious of a little inward shiver. Something in her trembled like the lights.

The car went up and up, and not too swiftly. The road ran in great loops and zigzags. It slid along under the walls of perched houses, houses that were dimly grey and white, and under hanging pines, and past sheaves of black cypresses. Green growth foamed over stone walls. The sea became a great black surface. And always there were the lights, and the softer glow of shuttered windows and little mysterious paths and steps going here and there into the darkness. The sky was still a profound blue, and pricked with stars.

The girl sat alert to the adventure. Her face turned this way and that. Her hands were clasped firmly together. She was full of an inarticulate delight in all this mysterious newness, this Italy that unfolded itself upon the hillside. She felt its darkness and its glitter, the peering, elusive strangeness of the unknown. But to-morrow the unknown would be knowable. She had an active spirit. She had come to Tindaro to earn her living.

II

The car, arriving in the Piazza del Duomo, turned westwards along the Corso. The road, paved with blocks of stone, was a chequer of light and shadow. The little cafés and wine-shops were busy, and boy barbers were holding their patrons by their noses and scraping at blue-black chins. The girl saw as much of this new world as the passing machine allowed her to see. There were shops that sold antichità and shops that sold lace, and just before reaching the Hotel St. George she saw a white board on the front of a narrow house—"English Library and Tea Room." She leaned out to get a longer glimpse of that particular house, for it was to be her workshop.

Below the Hotel St. George the car swung out of the Corso into a lane that climbed the side of a hill. The darkness and the scattered lights had returned. The car bumped and swayed, and turning a sharp corner stopped with unexpected abruptness opposite an iron gate. Billy's suitcase toppled over on her toes. The gate was painted white, and carried a wooden panel upon which was the name of the villa—"Villa Vesta."

She had arrived. The driver was down and opening the door, and insisting on handling her suitcase, and leaving her suitcase with him, she pushed open the heavy iron gate and heard it utter a little protesting squeak. A gritty path led directly to the door of a white villa shaped like an oblong box, with two stone lions couchant beside the doorstep.

Someone had been waiting for the car and had heard it stop, for the door opened, and a very tall woman stood erect in the doorway. Her back was to the light, and her face dim, yet Billy's first impression of Miss Julia Lord was by no means vague. She saw the gleam of very beautiful white hair, an uncompromising and upright carriage, and heard a voice that came suddenly and concisely.

"Miss Brown—I presume?"

Billy smiled.   Her smile could be as sudden as Miss Lord's voice, and it was complete and unconcealed.   She smiled with her eyes and her mouth and her teeth, and her short, blunt nose.

"I think so."

"Come in."

On the very doorstep of the new adventure Billy stumbled upon Miss Lord's rock of gravity.   She allowed herself no sense of humour, perhaps because life had given her the choice between laughter and ice, and she had chosen to be cold marble. She offered a hand to Billy, its long straight fingers pressed together, and when Billy grasped it she felt that she was grasping an ivory paper-knife.   Her smile fell back into the pool of herself.

Miss Lord stepped back, and the driver appeared with the trunk.   She spoke to him firmly, calling him by name.   She had lived in Tindaro for nearly twenty years.

"Seppe, carry the trunk up to the landing.   Maria will show you the room."

She turned and walked down a tiled passage, and her shoes made a crisp tapping on the tiles.   Billy followed, feeling somehow that the Villa Vesta was a schoolhouse and that she might find a text in her bedroom.   Miss Lord led the way into a sitting-room that had the air of having been furnished with desultory carefulness for very temporary tenants.   The chairs were as straight in the back as the lady.   The table was laid for a meal.

"I expect you are hungry."

Billy's smile was more controlled.

"I've had nothing since lunch."

"Sit down.   Supper will be ready in a quarter of an hour."

The villa felt chilly, and Billy and Miss Lord sat down on two chairs on opposite sides of that hole in the wall which the Latins conceive to be a fireplace.   Billy could now see Miss Lord's face.   It was curiously unwrinkled and firm and solid, rather like a face that had been kept in ice.   The features were fine and emphatic, the eyes steady, disillusioned and blue.   Miss Lord looked at people very directly and at her leisure, and she was looking at Billy with deliberation and care.

She was asking herself that most important question : What sort of girl was this new girl? Would she be like the previous young women? Would Tindaro play its Circe tricks on her as it had played them on those others? Miss Brown. Undoubtedly Miss Julia Lord had been influenced by the suggestive brevity and the unsensuous plainness of the name. She had had Barbara Irene Brown's photograph sent out to her, and it had appeared to be that of a plain and solid young woman who played games.

But Billy in the flesh was not the Miss Brown of the photo, and Miss Lord was feeling surprised and yet not wholly unsatisfied. She saw Billy as a strong and shapely young woman, obviously very healthy, and with one of those irregular faces that are unexpected and interesting. Billy's brown hair seemed to clasp her head like the young leaves and tendrils of a vine. Her eyes were brown, and of a warm, clear brightness. She looked Miss Lord straight in the face.

Miss Lord made inward comments. Cold she might be, yet her consciousness was not mere glass, but quicksilvered like a mirror. She liked the girl's eyes, and her frank, broad forehead, her blunt nose and her expressive mouth. She liked the strength and the solidity of her, that open-air candour, the healthy whites of the eyes, the texture of hair and skin. Miss Lord's consciousness was not unlike a camera, and she had put her various negatives away, and had grown wise through years of recording and comparing.

She said, "Perhaps you would like to go upstairs and wash. The trains are very dirty."

"I should."

Billy, too, had been gathering impressions. She found herself liking Miss Lord better than she had thought she would. This white-haired woman was definite; she finished all her sentences; she might be rather changeless and like a snow-peak, but you could be sure of her outlines.

Miss Lord rose, and when she stood she appeared like a full-length portrait of herself, dignified, deliberate and complete.

"You are not quite like your photo."

She smiled faintly.

A *

"You look both older—and younger."

Billy's smile returned.

"Well—perhaps I am. We are—sometimes. It depends——"

"I'll show you your room."

"O—by the way—I haven't paid the taxi man."

"Maria will have paid him. She knows. He would have asked you for five lire more than was due to him. You can pay Maria."

Miss Lord led the way up the stairs to a tiled landing, and opened a grey-blue door.

"If there is anything more you want—ask me."

"Thank you."

"Supper will be ready in ten minutes."

III

Billy sat down on her bed and allowed her impressions to revolve and to settle. She took off her hat and gave her head a shake. She looked round the room. It was small and square. It had a red-tiled floor, biscuit-coloured walls, and lace curtains at the one high window. There were no pictures. The furniture included the wooden bedstead, a marble-topped chest of drawers, a marble-topped dressing-table, a wardrobe, two cane chairs and a little black table with a white cloth. It was the kind of room that remains anonymous until some personality takes possession of it and breathes into its staleness an individual perfume. It was as clean as a glass case in a jeweller's shop. It seemed to smell faintly of soap.

Billy gave both the pillow and bed a dig with her fist. Yes, not so bad. She liked a good bed, and preference for good beds is a sign of a wholesome femininity. Maria had placed a jug of hot water in the basin, and Billy rose and unfastened her suitcase and took out her sponge-bag and brushes. A new cake of pink soap lay in the soapdish. One would not have expected pink soap in Miss Lord's villa, but perhaps Maria was responsible for the pinkness.

Billy washed, and she washed with the thoroughness of a young woman who enjoyed it. No mere messing about with a piece of cotton wool and some face-powder. She was active with the towel. She shook and tossed her head like a healthy young animal.

Good business—washing, after two frowsty days in a stuffy train. Yes, on the whole she liked Miss Lord. A little chilly perhaps, but aseptic and knowable. And the lights of Tindaro, and the ascent through that mysterious dark town, and the little shops, and the dimly aspiring cypresses! It was good, jolly good. And she felt hungry.

IV

Miss Lord also was sorting her impressions. She sat very straight in one of the high-backed chairs, and the white and narrow hands in her lap might have been unravelling the skein of a new situation.

Her impression was that she was going to like this new girl. Billy had a freshness, just that breezy April wholesomeness that Tindaro lacked. She was England come south.

But Miss Lord's blue eyes were hard. She was recalling past vicissitudes, and the vagaries of the various young women who had come out from England, to assist in running the English library and tea-shop at Tindaro, and who—in varying degrees—had ceased to be English. Miss Lord had had good cause to remember some of them. Unpleasant incidents! You could never quite be sure how Tindaro would affect people from the north, and how they would behave, or whether they would behave at all. There had been poor little Molly Blake, for instance, who had seen too much of the moon, and had been found dead at the bottom of a cliff. An indescribable and horrid mess! And Betty Backhouse, a dark, full-blooded creature who had had a child by a man from one of the mountain villages, and who had gone native and was living somewhere in the hills in a state of romantic squalor.

Miss Lord knew that Tindaro was not England. It was Italian, Mediterranean, old Greek. It was as though the legend and voice of Circe still lingered here. It had beauty, and there was poison under its tongue, and a perfume that was exotic. It languished; it was lazy; it bred goats and played upon the pipe, and between the blue sea and the blue sky it basked in the heat. Certain things ceased to matter, things that might matter in England or in Boston. A sluggish, satisfied sensuousness became the mood of the hour. Everything was a little tarnished, a little over-ripe, a little sinister. Roses were soon overblown. Men from the north were apt to drink too much, and to be careless about shaving.

Yes, bathing ceased to be a ritual, but Miss Lord took a cold bath every morning. It was the beginning of the day's self-discipline.

And this new girl?

She heard Billy coming down the stairs, and suddenly she stood up with the decisive air of a woman of affairs about to face a public meeting. All her memories of Tindaro were like so many attentive and challenging faces. Should she tell the girl——?

And then Billy came into the room looking so refreshing and firm-fleshed and capable that Miss Lord, the woman who knew, refrained from unfurling the red flag. Why create a suggestive situation? Why spill wine over such obviously clean linen?

She smiled a little thin smile.

"I hope you will be comfortable in your room."

Billy's eyes were bright.

"I opened the shutters just for a moment. It must be lovely—the view."

Miss Lord heard Maria coming with the tray.

"Yes, very beautiful. Tindaro is supposed to be unique. I expect you are hungry."

"Very."

CHAPTER II

I

BILLY opened the green shutters on a cherry-coloured sun rising out of a purple sea, and she stood there in the cold thrill of the dawn, and saw Tindaro and the Tindaric sea as a new world and a new ocean. Over yonder a great headland black as soot seemed to catch the sun's rays and splinter them into an ægis of gold. The hills and cliffs and groves and gardens had a diaphanous softness, and in the deeps below she saw the coastline and the edge of the sea melted together in a haze of blueness. The earth had the air of having just been born; she saw it newly made for her on that Mediterranean morning.

More intimately near to her was the garden of the Villa Vesta, and she was able to say to herself "Orange trees!" Yes, orange trees, deeply green in the hush of the dawn and all hung with fruit. How different from Ealing with its sodden greyness! And Billy, looking down into that surprising garden, and into the terraced valley and the dark bloom of the pinewoods, felt herself on the brim of a new world. Everything was different; she herself had a sense of difference; the very sun burning above the intense blue of the sea was different.

And there were olive trees! She had read that when a wind blew and the olives were ruffled the green lace of the hillside became a silvery grey, but on this morning there was no wind. The cypresses at the end of Miss Lord's garden were like slim spires carved out of black marble. Tindaro itself looped from the hillside to hillside, seemed still silently asleep. Billy could look down on the brown roofs and into the gardens and courts of the white, pink and ochre-coloured houses, and feel Tindaro there to be known and conquered.

9

Her glances returned to the garden. It surprised her. Presumably it was Miss Lord's garden, but it was unlike Miss Lord as a rose-bed is unlike a mason's yard. Its very square-ness had been cunningly concealed. All beauty has a sugges-tion of other dimensions, and Miss Lord's garden—like all inspired gardens—seemed to have something more than depth and breadth and height. Those cypresses towered and yet were unmeasurable. The little formal pool surrounded by blue Iris Stylosa was a mysterious and glimmering hole in the apparent surface of things. There was a pergola scrambled over by roses and vines. There were great earthenware jars like the jars in the tale of Ali Baba. Patches of green growth, very vivid in the slanting rays of the rising sun, would show in the days that were to be tulips, anemones and jonquils. The orange trees kindled their lamps for Apollo. There were loquats and acacias, and oleanders, and a fig tree naked and the colour of stone.

Billy hung poised on the edge of it, with her blue bed-jacket pulled over her throat. Obviously, Miss Lord of the salon and Miss Lord in her garden were two creatures, and yet somehow explaining each other. But what a world, and what a sunrise, and what adventure! Her bed had been a dream; she had slept deliciously; her window opened upon all this, and down yonder lay Tindaro and her job. Billy belonged to a generation that demanded its job.

But someone was moving below, probably that excellent fat Maria with a shape like a pillow, and a moustache on her good-tempered face. And what was that pleasant perfume? Surely it was the smell of coffee, hot coffee? And suddenly three little bells began to jangle in one of the campaniles of Tindaro, and the still, silent scene seemed to take up the vibra-tions. A cheerful clangor.

Billy tossed her head and smiled.

"Good business!"

While she was brushing her hair, and finding it crisp and vigorous, she heard sounds of distant splashings. Miss Julia Lord was taking her cold bath.

II

Miss Lord appeared at the breakfast table wearing a black hat and a dark blue tailor-made suit, and ready for the business of the day. Firm of flesh and white of hair, her hands busy with coffee-pot and milk-jug, she was Britannia in exile.

She asked Billy how she had slept.

"O, splendidly."

The girl looked it. Most certainly she was a very healthy young woman who came down to breakfast with an adventurous face. Miss Lord passed Billy her coffee, and was conscious of a feeling of relief, for Julia Lord was a rather tired woman, in spite of her very straight back. She had lived in Tindaro for twenty years, and Tindaro was not Tunbridge Wells, and Miss Lord's attitude to life had remained aggressively English.

"Two lumps of sugar?"

"Please."

Billy chose a roll, and helped herself to two little twists of butter, and saw that there was English marmalade on the table. Maria's coffee smelt good, and tasted as good as its perfume. And the first day was beginning.

She said, "I got up and saw the sun rise. Rather different from Ealing."

Miss Lord observed her after the manner of a "head" estimating the character and capacity of a new mistress. In Tindaro the tendency was to lie late in bed, but Miss Lord had never allowed herself to succumb to the sensuous, save in the loving of her garden. If you succumbed in Tindaro you succumbed too thoroughly. Physical and mental hygiene were apt to go together, and if Tindaro did call the lady of the Villa Vesta "Miss Cold Bath," it had every reason to respect her.

"There are other differences."

Billy supposed that there were. You could not rush into rhapsodies over Ealing, but Tindaro took your breath and held it.

"I've never seen anything so beautiful."

Miss Lord sat poised.

"Yes, perhaps—never so much so as at the first glance."

She allowed Tindaro its beauty as she would have allowed a certain sort of woman her reputation for good looks, but she was impartial, and Billy took another roll, and helped herself to marmalade, and was sure that there could be nothing amiss with Tindaro when the sun rose like dripping gold out of a purple sea.

"And your garden."

Miss Lord's eyes seemed to soften.

"O, yes, a hobby of mine."

"You made it?"

"I have been making it for ten years."

Almost there was a note of tenderness in her voice. It trembled for a moment like a candle flame, but almost instantly regained its steady brightness.

"Necessary to have interests here. Yes, seriously so. I suppose you play tennis?"

Yes, Billy played tennis. She played the game very well.

"Exercise. And I rather believe in a cold bath each morning. These southern places, not quite like England."

And then, with a matter-of-fact air, she began to speak of their mutual relations, and of the work they were to share.

"I thought it better that you should stay with me for a week. You will soon get the hang of things. I'll show you the bedroom and sitting-room over the library. The women there will cook for you. I should like you to watch the work for a week. The library opens at ten and closes at twelve, and on three afternoons a week we open from three till four. That doesn't satisfy all the old ladies, but it is fatal to give way to grumblers. The tearoom is open at 3.45. We get busier each year. We make our own cakes, and our own jam and marmalade. Also—we sell flowers. I keep a waitress, and two helps in the kitchen—Italians. They need a good deal of supervision. Pilfer anything unless you keep a check on the stores and linen and china."

Billy's brown eyes were attentive and sympathetic.

"What a bore. I can't stand people who pinch. I'll watch things carefully."

"Can you speak any Italian yet?"

"Not much—but I'll begin lessons. I suppose there is someone——?"

"I'll put you on to Winnie Haycroft at the lace shop. By the way—you mustn't mind being told things—to begin with."

"I shan't mind."

"It won't be in public."

Their eyes met in a smile.

"And try and remember faces and names, especially the faces and names of the constitutionally discontented."

Billy laughed. The phrase pleased her, and displayed Miss Lord as a woman of understanding.

"Yes—I suppose that is rather important."

"And suppose we take it understood that when the official working hours are over you do as you please."

Billy finished her coffee.

"Thank you. That's the sort of fairness that one does appreciate."

Punctually at five minutes to nine Miss Lord left the Villa Vesta for the house in the Corso. She and Dr. Burt, the English doctor, were perhaps the only punctual persons in Tindaro, and though the English colony might call this exactness affectation, it was but a part of a personal protest against an insidious, southern slackness. Billy Brown accompanied Miss Lord, and as they descended the lane with its grey walls and terraces planted with vines and olives the notes of a pipe shrilled out like the piping of a bird hidden in a thicket.

Billy's chin went up. She paused. On that morning everything was delightfully and mysteriously new.

"What's that?   Not a bird?"

Had she been looking at Miss Lord's face, she would have seen the firm surface of it momentarily disturbed.

"Someone piping."

"Just like Pan."

Miss Lord seemed disinclined to loiter, and Billy, after looking for the piper and failing to find him, followed her friend. The piper was squatting against a wall some twenty feet above the lane, a bald-headed old scoundrel the colour of a medlar.

A little, yellow dog lay at his feet. He twiddled his two fingers on the pipe, and watched the two Englishwomen, and when they had disappeared he ceased to pipe, and sat grinning. His flat nose grew flatter, and his teeth showed as three yellow fangs.

A herd of goats was being driven up the Corso, brown goats, grey goats, black goats, with a mongrel dog and a goatherd in velveteen trousers and a Joseph's coat at the tail of the procession. The little, pattering hoofs, and the bearded heads with their cold and stony eyes went by in the shadow of the high houses. Billy noticed that Miss Lord kept close to the wall, and she wondered whether Miss Lord disliked goats. But Billy was more interested in all the newness of Tindaro than in Miss Lord's personal idiosyncrasies. This street was a new world with its beasts and its people, asses laden with firewood and vegetables, fishermen carrying baskets on their heads, women busy at shop doorways, little swarthy boys running barelegged over the grey stones. The high, white houses confronted each other with shutters of green, of brown, and of blue. There was a cheerful hubbub. A fat little man in blue trousers was polishing the tops of the tables outside the Café Ceres. The shops were as various as the perfumes, all the tired, warm odours of a southern town.

Overhead wavered the blue ribbon of the sky. It broadened where the Corso joined the Piazza del Duomo, and a hundred yards from the piazza Miss Lord's English Library and Miss Haycroft's lace-shop faced each other. Miss Lord's house was all grey, both within and without, and being referred to by the frivolous as "Our Lord's House," maintained some of the solemnity of a temple. It felt chilly, and smelt of soap. Hands, with the index finger extended, were painted on the walls of the vestibule—"Library," "Tea Room." Dogs were not admitted.

The library was perhaps a little less dismal than the average English library in foreign parts. Certainly it suggested the vestry of a church, and that surplices would be found hanging in one of the cupboards. The cases of books had the usual, dull, flat, anonymous look, for even books in a crowd become less interesting.   Magazines, periodicals, catalogues, and Miss Lord's ledgers were laid out on a long and narrow table.   Spaced around the room were six rush-bottomed chairs.

A bowl full of violets gave to that most utilitarian table a touch of colour and of life, and Miss Lord, after looking round the room, bent down and smelt the flowers.   Obviously, Miss Julia loved flowers, and not as Billy loved them, for Miss Lord's loves were impersonal; they could no longer be wounded.

She pulled back one of the chairs, and its legs squeaked on the red tiles.

"I'll just run through the routine."

But instead of entering upon immediate and practical affairs she opened one of the ledgers, and allowed her eyes to rest upon the bowl of violets, while Billy stood waiting beside her chair.   Miss Lord appeared to lose herself in looking at the flowers.   Her thumb plucked absently at a page.

She was thinking of those other young women who had stood beside her chair to be initiated into the business of issuing books.   They had begun the life much as Billy had begun it, and had developed a passable efficiency until Tindaro had initiated them into other mysteries.   Should youth be warned? Could youth ever be warned?   Miss Lord turned a page, and became practical.

Her system was simple and efficient.   Billy had assimilated the details at the end of two minutes.   Human nature—as usual—was the problem.   The greedy and the selfish and the inconsiderate had to be dealt with in a library as everywhere else.

"There are some people who want all the new books at once, and keep them when they have got them.   No new book is allowed out for more than three days."

"I see."

Miss Lord looked amused.

"But do you?   If we let a new book out for a week it would be touring all over Tindaro, passed on to people who aren't subscribers.   The very wealthy are the worst sinners.   They'll spend ten pounds on a dinner, and try to get a seven-and-sixpenny novel for nothing."

Billy laughed.

"So—I'm to be firm?"

"Always. I don't stand any nonsense."

From the library they went to the tearoom with its pretty loggia, and its panels of blue treillage holding the blue of the sky and the green of the cypresses and the brown tints of old roofs like living frescoes. The tearoom was a cheerful place. Its tables were painted blue. The white basket chairs had covers of English cretonne. The tiled floor was blue and white. Billy felt much more at home in the tearoom.

"It's really lovely. And that view!"

"You'll like working here."

"Rather."

Miss Lord paused in the loggia, with her lips compressed. She was never dull or bored when she was working, but these young things were so temperamental. They did not stay put. They wanted to flutter out through the windows and explore and experiment with life.

Miss Lord's firm lips parted. She appeared to be about to say something personal and intimate, but she changed her mind.

"By the way, we charge extra for home-made jam and marmalade. Now, I'll show you the kitchen and the waitress's pantry. As I warned you—you will have to watch the sugar and the spoons."

III

Billy's first morning in the library added considerably to her respect for Miss Lord. For the best part of two hours the narrow room was full of very large women who appeared to take literature so very seriously that nothing would move them while in search of a particular book. They occupied the library. They stood and conversed, and blocked the gangways on either side of the narrow table. An occasional man ventured in, and became less than a shadow among these large and substantial creatures.

One old fellow appealed to Billy. He was very polite.

"Excuse me, are you the new librarian?"

"I'm helping here."

"I wonder if you could find me Tansley's 'New Psychology.' You have it here. And I have left my glasses at home, and those three ladies are rather set——"

Billy smiled upon him, and saw his trouble, and going to the particular case had to say "Excuse me" twice to the three gossips before she could get to the books. One of the three put up a lorgnette and examined Billy with that staring insolence which is peculiar to women.

Five minutes later Billy was the witness of a combat between Miss Lord and the lady.

"I'm sorry, two days late, Mrs. Sudbury Smith. The book is on the six-months list."

The lady looked at Miss Lord as she had looked at Billy. "I don't think so."

"The entry is here. You owe us five lire."

"Really, it is perfectly ridiculous——"

"O, well—I'll take it out of your deposit."

And Billy realized that Miss Lord feared none of these large ladies, and remained in her chair like an enthroned Britannia, calmly dominating oceans of Bournemouth, Bradford and Manchester. As she said to Billy afterwards while she was locking the cashbox away in the safe: "Never argue. Have your details correctly entered. It is extraordinary how many of these women will try to cheat. And the richer they are—the more careful you have to be."

"Like the lady with the lorgnette?"

"Yes, the Sudbury Smiths are supposed to be worth half a million. Soap—I think."

"But they all seem so very large."

"Just coincidence. It has occurred to me that too much talking makes some women run to fat."

Miss Lord had an air of being pleased with the morning, perhaps because she had used her trident successfully on Mrs. Sudbury Smith. She locked the library door.

"I'll take you across to see the Haycrofts. You'll like the girl. She wants a little knowing."

Billy and Miss Lord crossed the Corso and entered Miss

Haycroft's lace-shop.   Miss Haycroft had lived in Tindaro almost as long as Miss Lord, and had dried up in it until she had the appearance of a skein of grey silk.   Fragile and faded, with one of those narrow and delicate faces, she wore her grey hair all fluffed up so that the thinness of her face was exaggerated, and her tired grey eyes looked like two half-extinguished lamps.   Miss Haycroft had gone to her lunch, and her niece was in charge.   She was recording a length of torchon lace. Her hands were very thin and febrile.

Miss Lord was always direct.

"Winnie, this is Miss Brown.   You two ought to know each other."

Billy's smile came quickly, but Winnie Haycroft's answering smile was vague and hesitant.   She had frightened eyes of a pale, sensitive blueness.   Her hair and skin had a dusty look. She stared at Billy, and blinked rather like a shy and self-conscious child.

"So you've come.   I heard you were coming."

She went on carding the lace, glancing from Billy to Miss Lord, and from Miss Lord to Billy.   Her glances were moth-like in their flutterings.   Before speaking there would be a faint trembling of her lips, for to be articulate seemed to cost her an effort.   And yet there was something charming and inconsequential and naïve about her.   She had a grave, timid gentleness.   Coifed, she would have looked like a nun.

Billy's eyes were friendly.

"Yes, I arrived last night.   It's all rather exciting."

Miss Lord observed them both, but especially Billy.   She wanted Billy to have friends, especially the friends who were necessary in Tindaro.

She said, "I have to look in at Pietro's.   I'll leave you two to talk for three minutes."

She went out, and Winnie Haycroft stood behind the counter, looking at Billy as though there was magic in this other girl who—four days ago—had been in England.

"Did you come straight out?"

"Yes.   London was all fog."

The other girl's lips quivered.

"How lovely—! Fog—and London. Do come and see me. We close at six."

"I'd love to."

"To-night?"

"All right."

IV

Billy had supposed that Winnie Haycroft was applying irony to London and a November fog, but when Billy saw the other girl's room she was made to think of a little England in Italy, Peter Robinson and Marshall & Snelgrove, and Cromwell Road, and Ken Wood on a day that was not a Sunday. Winnie had run down the stone stairs to meet her. She was a little flushed. She had lit a fire of fir cones and pinewood.

"I do hope you will like my room. I've made it as English as possible."

She sat on the bed, and the blessed damosel fresh from England was made to occupy the one armchair. Miss Lord had said that Winnie Haycroft was difficult to know, but Miss Lord and Billy were not of the same generation, and Billy's smile was like England to Winnie Haycroft. Her lips quivered. Her face had lost its look of dustiness. Almost she seemed to draw from the other girl a sudden new vitality, an English freshness, the exquisite sweet pain of April when birds sing. She chattered. Her eyes were suffused with light. She appeared to forget Billy's newness, and all her reticences.

"I suppose you are going to live over the library. I shall like that. There are so few people of one's own age here——"

Billy was an observant young person, and while Winnie prattled she absorbed the atmosphere of Miss Haycroft's room. There were two photos of young men in khaki on the mantelpiece. There were photos on the walls, and Rossetti's "Dante's Dream," and an Annunciation, and Watts' Harper asleep on a Blue Earth. Winnie was true to type in all her details, and Billy's observings completed a mental inventory. White linen curtains with red roses stencilled on them, the World's Classics, a sketch of Salisbury Cathedral, a tennis-racket in a press marked "W. H. Smythe's House, Repstead School." A cretonne-covered box. A photo of an English country rectory with three people sitting in deck-chairs under a tree. Two Toby jugs on the mantelpiece between the photographs. An English flowered almanac suggesting the cover of a seedsman's catalogue.

They talked—though Winnie did the greater part of the talking.

"O, yes, I've been here five years. In summer we go to a little place above Florence. Only Italians. It costs so much to go to England. It's dull."

She would talk of nothing but England, and Billy wanted her to talk of Tindaro, and its people. She shifted the setting.

"What's this place like?"

Winnie's lips became tremulous. She showed a vagueness, an air of having lost the thread of her argument. Unlike Miss Lord, she was easily disturbed and did not complete her sentences.

"O, it's very hot later on. And flies. And smells. I don't sleep very well. You get slack, yes—rather."

"But the people."

"O, the people. Do you mean the hotel people? They just come and go."

"But there are people who have to live in Tindaro, people like us."

Winnie's eyes grew round; they regained their frightened look.

"O, yes, the exiles. That's what I call them. There is Dr. Burt, and his wife; he's dear. And the villa people. Yes, and others. Quite awful, some of them. Quite—— They make me feel frightened."

"Why—on earth—should you feel frightened?"

"O—I don't know. The feel of things. They make you feel that you are not yourself. Perhaps you won't feel like that. You look so strong."

CHAPTER III

I

OSCAR SLADE strolled out into the loggia of the Villa of the Flute and looked at the day. It was an immaculate day, one of those crystal mornings with the cypresses motionless as black obelisks, and the sunlight pouring down through the pines and cedars. Slade had his hands in the pockets of his grey flannel trousers, and a smile on his ironic face. He had breakfasted. He had written two pages of his new novel, playfully mordant stuff.

On a straw mat in a corner of the loggia a sandy cat was diligently licking three kittens that had been born two days ago, and Slade stood to watch the toilet. The mother cat's sandy fur was the colour of red gold, and when Slade spoke to her she took no notice of him, but went on with her licking.

"It's a hard life, old lady."

Stooping, he picked up one of the blind children. He held its funny face against his nose, while the cat's yellow eyes watched. Then she continued her ablutions as though she had complete faith in Slade the man.

Slade replaced the kitten. He was in one of his smiling moods, and his moods were many and variable. There were days when he looked and behaved like an irresponsible boy. At forty-one he could have worn the clothes of one-and-twenty, only he wore them more casually, and with more brim to his hat. His ties had an abandonment. He was both sleek and lean, and out of his brown face eyes of a rather startling blueness looked at life and saw himself in it. He had what Dr. Burt described as "a naked habit of mind."

He went and stood in the sun, for the sun and the south suited both him and his work; his temperament was not English. His cheeks were rather flat; his lower lip protruded slightly;

21

there was just a suggestion of smeariness about his eyes and his smile. And on this November morning he threw quick, faunlike glances at the world, his own particular world, and his nostrils were sensitive to its freshness. He asked for beauty, and sensuously so, purple juices, blue skies, and in the Villa of the Flute he possessed beauty. It had a history, a poignant, human perfume. A long, low, cream-coloured house with shutters of faded green, it lay in the valley above Tindaro, half concealed among its trees. The garden was unique, and Slade had taken care that it should not be too tidy. Fussiness was too English a virtue. He let things riot, and scramble and foam. Water gushed. There was a pool that reflected the sky and the trees, and was as mutable in its moods as Slade himself. From the loggia you could look down on a little classic open-air theatre surrounded by cypresses. Flowers and flowering shrubs grew as they pleased. The place was both hung with shadows and blazed upon by the sun. It was black and blue and gold.

Slade sat sideways on the balustrade of the narrow terrace, and taking off his hat, let the sun warm his face. He approved of the elder Landor's attitude to life, but his pose was less sententious. It was better to be amusing than to be sententious. Slade liked digging the English world in the ribs, especially the English world of the hotels, its old colonels and city fathers and naval gentlemen, and those indomitable and lean women who climbed the hills and lunched on a roll, a hard-boiled egg, and a slab of Gruyère cheese. Nor did the world of the hotels approve of Slade. He was a smirking, supercilious, irreverent fellow. It disliked his smile and his clothes and his books. There were occasions when he used scent.

Slade, having sat in the sun for ten minutes, turned his face to the house and called.

"Lotta—Lotta."

His voice was seductive or ironic when addressing a woman.

"Lotta—I want my stick."

It was brought him, a little yellow cane that was almost like a switch, suited to his lean brown hands and restless movements. The woman who brought it had one of those impassive

Italian faces, and two big black eyes that stared unblinkingly. She was handsome, a dark, sleek cow of a creature, but on this occasion her passivity was sullen. She was the female animal looking mistrustfully at man.

Slade took the stick and made a playful cut at her. The point caught her black skirt, and jerked it slightly to one side. Her face remained expressionless.

"I am going to Tindaro. I shall bring the Signor Frevick back with me to lunch."

"The one who drinks a great deal."

"Is that all that you can remember about him?"

Her stare seemed to relax for a moment.

"They all drink, but not so much as that one."

Slade flicked at a fly which had settled on the balustrade.

"Pagan creature. For Mr. Frevick it had better be whisky. Whisky, Lotta, whisky."

She said with her air of sullen passivity, "I understand."

II

Oscar Slade had used Tindaro for the setting of one of his novels, but as a novelist Slade failed to satisfy, because of his lack of compassion for his characters. He was exquisite and sensual, more highbrow than human, unusually witty, sometimes spiteful. In his books, as in his daily affairs, he might use Eau de Cologne instead of soap and water, but after all, that was only being rather French instead of being English. Behaviour was the bed upon which his psychology reposed. He had amended the text "Man does not live by bread alone," adding to it—"Throw in the wine, the women and the cash, and the whole thing's settled."

Slade had described Tindaro as "histrionic." It posed. It had been so written up and raved over that like some Italian wench who had had her head turned by posing to artists, that it put on a gaily coloured scarf and some cheap jewellery and sat to be admired. It lived on the tourist and the winterer abroad. All that teeming, swarthy, southern underworld looked to the forestieri for the life-giving lira. Slade had written like a Parisian about Tindaro. He talked of its little, bawdy shops, and of its scenic effects that waited like painted women for the confiding tourist. Sometimes he would speak bitterly of Tindaro, as some men speak of their wives. He would call the town a flea-bitten hag wholly and shamelessly unwashed under a picturesque petticoat.

But Tindaro suited him. It allowed him his philosophy of "Do what you please." It did not try to impose upon him a morality that was not of the South, and since he was a man of means it bowed and smiled. Oscar Slade was a person. He was an exile, but not like those other exiles who gathered daily round the tables of the Café Ceres on the Corso, unfortunates who were tied to Tindaro, and who could not go home.

Slade would say that the Circe legend still lingered in this southern town. He had discussed it with Burt the doctor, who knew Tindaro and its exiled English as only a doctor can know them. To Burt, Circe the enchantress and Climate the solvent of souls were synonymous. He could quote history, point to the Normans in Sicily, northerner becoming Orientalized, blazing from a sensual, perfumed pyre into nothing. He would call up the bastard Syrio-Greek decadence of Rome. Tindaro turned some people into beasts, unhappy creatures who had the voices of men and of women, and who were neither good English nor good Italian.

Burt saw them daily in the Corso, sitting at those marble-topped tables, and drinking their little drinks, and watching those other English, the English of the hotels who came and went and were respectable, and Burt was made to think of animals in a cage, gazing with a moody malice and homesick envy at those others.

Burt pitied them. He had doctored many of them, and while doctoring them had tried to talk to them of the fundamentals of health, but Circe was stronger than the healer. They wallowed. They were without hope. They lacked Julia Lord's straight back, and her symbolical cult of the cold bath.

Regularly at eleven o'clock these people gathered at the Café Ceres on the Corso. They came from all the quarters of Tindaro. Frevick the artist, cramming his hat over his eyes and lighting a cigarette with trembling and stained fingers, slammed the door of his small villa in the Via Vittoria, and walked down the weedy path to a rusty iron gate. Old Ponsonby, with a smeary smile and a collection of dirty stories ready under his Panama hat, emerged from his flat and the pocket of his Neapolitan housekeeper. Major Mirleess laced up his surgical boot, and limped out with an air of raddled and blue-eyed insolence, a poor, hard-bitten little blackguard who had suffered from too much vanity. Sir Dyce Duxbury, sleekly globular, trundled down on his short fat legs from his bungalow above the chapel of San Sofario. Sadie Shone, a kind of cosmopolitan American, with the head of a bold and disillusioned boy, appeared in a bright yellow or carmine jumper. The Blaber women arrived from the Hotel Florio. The Baroness von Billing, with eyes like prunes in a chalked face, came sleekly to the rendezvous like a cat after cream. There were others. Tindaro, Italian Tindaro, knew them all by heart, and smiled, and shrugged its shoulders.

Slade thought them amusing, preferring the disreputable to the decorous. They set no standard. He found them more interesting than the untarnished dwellers in the big villas and the hotels, the nicely conventional people who were so afraid of each other. The coterie of the Café Ceres had no illusions as to social prestige, and had ceased to keep up any appearance of being anything but what it was.

"Poor devils."

But, he spoke pityingly. He had seen so much suffering; he had watched so many muddled lives. He had no hard words for these pitiful people, provided that they let youth alone, and did not try to proselytize among the fit.

"Life's eliminating them."

Slade's point of view was that of the realist. He was not interested in mental hygiene. These people amused him. He felt at ease with them; there were no social repressions, no reservations. You could say just what you pleased. It was like playing at the jolly beggar sitting in the sun with a group of unconventional scallywags to laugh at your jokes.

He would tease Burt.

"You'd like to bottle the lot of them in alcohol, doctor, and put 'em safely on shelves nicely labelled.   I prefer to see them alive."

He was Peter Pan, with a difference.   He liked his pirates and his Indians and his Captain Hook and the crocodile, but his Peter Pan world did not include a Wendy or a Tinker Bell.   To Burt he appeared an irresponsible and peculiarly dangerous person, an overgrown and mischievous boy who would have played Guy Fawkes and blown up the House of Convention just for the fun of the thing.

On that peerless morning Slade was early.   He found Frevick alone at one of the tables, and sitting as he always sat, like a sack crumpled upon itself.   His tie bulged; his collar was not too clean; his waistcoat lacked a button, and he had not shaved.   He was a big man, loose and long of limb, with a grey face under a slouched black hat.   There were times when Frevick looked like some big, dumb animal in pain. He had not much to say, but he said it with a kind of swift yet stammering ferocity.   His eyes were the only clean things left to him.

Slade sat down at Frevick's table, and Frevick drew in his feet.   If there was any sympathy between these two it was the sympathy of craftsmen and nothing more.   Frevick could still paint some sort of a picture in spite of his trembling, nicotine-stained hands.   He might have been a very considerable crafts-man but for the Café Ceres and a thirsty heritage.

Slade was playful in a crowd, and one listener could make a crowd.   Also, he rather liked baiting Frevick, who would look at him with those melancholy, brooding eyes, and some-times smile very faintly.

"Anything new, my lad?"

Frevick yawned.

"Would there be?"

"Our Julia might have put on a new halo."

Frevick yawned again, and one end of his cerise-coloured tie escaped from his waistcoat, and Slade, with a neat and playful thrust of his stick, made the loose end more obvious.

"You've had that tie seven months."

"Probably. It comes to hand each morning."

"Why not vary the scenery?"

Frevick yawned again, and replaced the end of his tie.

"Let it alone. One can't sleep in this damned place. It's like lying in a bath—shallow water. One can't get in deep."

"You get in at the wrong end—probably."

"End! There's no damned end to anything. Nothing but infernal sequence of things happening."

"Like your tie, my dear. Just taking it off and putting it on. Why not scrap it?"

"Haven't the courage. Hell—you ought to know that scrapping things means courage."

"I use the waste-paper basket sometimes."

"Might put a match to oneself. Burning paint stinks, Slade."

"I've never smelt it."

The others arrived as habit and the herd instinct moved them. Mirleess always limped straight down the middle of the Corso, looking the whole world in the face with an air of defiant insolence as though daring anybody to call him a broken soldier, a quarrelsome and vain little devil. Old Ponsonby had a stealthiness that was like his smile; you would find him suddenly beside you, and ready with some dirty story, and yet old Ponsonby had his virtues. He had an absurd passion for babies and very small children, and if he met an Italian baby being carried he had to stop and poke a finger at it and make ridiculous noises. Moreover, the babies appeared to approve of his large, round, white face and his noises. Sadie Shone usually was heard before she was seen, talking at the top of her voice, and shouting at the shopkeepers, with whom she was very popular. Her huge mouth was like a hole in a classic mask, and her voice had a torn edge to it. She shouted at everybody; she threw money about; she was disreputable and lavish.

"Say, Papa, where's my little drink?"

She called Georgio, the proprietor of the Café Ceres, papa

and his funny thin face would crinkle up into smiles. She had to hail everybody. Slade called her the "Megaphone."

"Hallo, Archie!—Say, Oscar,—I want you to make me another Limerick. Mrs. Sudbury Smith was a woman of pith! O, my dear, what does one do when your coffee gets spilt over a new frock? Papa—say—papa."

Usually she sat herself down next to Slade, because he made her laugh, and poked wicked fun at the solemn English of the hotels as they passed by, and had no reverence for anything. Like a noisy and bold child she liked to shock people. She had been known to sit at one of the tables wearing Frevick's deplorable hat, and smoking the largest cigar that Papa Georgio could find for her. Yet there were days when her grey-green eyes were shut up, and her large mouth was mute and flaccid.

The others were less spectacular. Duxbury would sit as though silently warming his globular stomach. The von Billing, who could not be trusted at a bridge table, looked at life with oblique eyes, and was careful to count her change. The Blaber woman talked fiercely to anyone who would listen. But the remaining half-dozen were the figures in a chorus that was led by Slade or by Sadie, though Mirleess, if he happened to be in a worse temper than usual, would begin some recitative in an angry and throaty voice.

On this particular morning Billy passed by on her way home to the Villa Vesta just before the Café Ceres dispersed its characters for the midday meal. She was observed. She became conscious of being observed, and glancing casually at the little crowd seated at the round tables, met the appraising stare of Slade's eyes. They were ironic and smiling, and she set her chin straight forward, and passed on.

Someone asked the obvious question.

"Who's the girl?"

Miss Prince, a little sandy woman, who was a subscriber to Miss Lord's library, was able to answer it.

"Julia's new young woman."

Slade drew in his long legs, and observed Billy's departing figure. He spoke to Frevick.

"Strapping young person.   Girl Guide type—I think."
Frevick grunted.
"She knows how to move."

III

In Frevick's ruined face were eyes that could still behold
beauty, sunlight on a bird's plumage, the intense blue of a
wind-whipped sea, the flowerlike face of some young girl.
Though much of him was blurred and sodden, he retained a
streak of that impersonal delight in things, the passion to
paint that which was exquisite and clean.   He saw and enjoyed,
and in seeing and enjoying he possessed, and so was unlike Slade,
who could not see an apple on a tree without wanting to climb
a wall and make the apple his.

But there were days when beauty hurt Frevick, becoming
so personal in its implications, a kind of mirror held before
the eyes of his squalid self, that almost he wished the mirror
broken.   He might sit in the sun, yet the sun would not
warm him.   His eyes would seem to close up in his grey face.
The loose shamble of his long body grew more hopeless.   These
were the days when he was afraid of his razor, and would
appear with grey stubble on his chin, for though he might
long for consciousness to cease, he had a kind of childish fear
of that other darkness.

On these desperate days he drank.

Slade took charge.

"You are lunching with me, my lad."

They went down the Corso together, Slade gaillard and head
in air, Frevick rather like a doomed beast on his way to the
shambles.   He wanted to go home and close the shutters, and
throw himself on his bed in the half darkness, and forget.   The
day was too serene, too full of the might-have-beens, too full
of the face of youth.

At the corner of the Piazza del Duomo he hung back.

"Think I'll be getting home."

Slade held his arm.

"No you won't.   I told Lotta about lunch.   Don't be an
ass."

A vetturino, sitting on the box of his carriage by the fountain, saw Slade's signal, and roused his drowsing horse.

"Get in."

Frevick, strangely dumb and docile, climbed in and sat with his feet tucked up, and his eyes looking at the coachman's back. The fellow cracked his whip, the carriage rolled like a boat in a choppy sea, and Frevick's figure rolled with it. He looked miserable. Slade, with his hat pushed back, and his stick tapping the toe of a boot, had the face of a mischievous boy.

They turned up the lane by the St. George. The old horse took the hill at a walk, blowing heavily, the driver's slouching figure swaying gently on the seat. He had two brown patches on the elbows of his black coat, and his fat back was all creases. The zigzag of the lane took them past the Villa Vesta with its white iron gate through which Billy had disappeared five minutes earlier.

Slade glanced at the board on the gate. It amused him, it always amused him.

"The Vestal's villa! You used to visit there, Thomas."

Frevick looked vacant.

"Used to."

"Let's pause and ask Julia to lunch."

He tapped Frevick's left foot with his stick.

"What about it? And the new vestal?"

Frevick was not to be roused even to the blurting of a "Shut up." He swayed with the lurchings of the carriage. He glanced back over his shoulder.

"O, made that way. Guts. You're as ignorant as sin about some things, Slade."

"Sin? Sinning's knowing—my lad."

"And forgetting."

"Yes, something in that too. But good Julia with her cold-bath cult! How naïve and English!"

"Things you don't understand."

"Not much."

"O—well—leave it there."

The carriage lurched round the next curve, and as the lane

levelled itself here along the flank of the hill the driver whipped his horse into a trot. Frevick, swaying from side to side, his hands clasped between his knees, was remembering things which Slade had never known. They sat side by side, as men and strangers, each slightly contemptuous of the other.

Outside the high green gate of the Villa of the Flute, Slade paid the driver, for that poor devil of a Frevick had nothing to fumble for, and did not attempt it.

"Come back at half-past two."

The Italian understood Slade's sly and ironic look, for the Signor Frevick was always being put into carriages and carted home, and on this occasion the Signor Slade would pay. He grinned and turned his old horse, and the two men went through the green gate and up between the rows of cypresses to the villa. The sky trailed blue between the tops of the trees, and Frevick, walking up that cleft of shade, pushed his hat back and looked steadily at the sky. He was aware of the strangeness of things, their absurdities, their impersonal oddness. That a man like Slade should pay for a carriage! That they should have driven together! That Slade should own these trees. Why the devil should anybody own them? And why should men eat and drink together? And why was he like a sack stuffed with sour wine and infinite wisdom, carried on two servile legs to the house of this scoffer? How was it that he had never struck Slade in the face?

The impulse had been there.

He found himself in Slade's cool salon, with a shaft of sunlight putting a hundred fingers on the colours of a Persian rug. A woman was bringing in dishes, a dark woman with sullen, mistrustful eyes. There were flowers on the table, and the heavy scent of them had the sweet sullenness of the woman's face. And they were as silent.

"Whisky, Thomas?"

"No thanks."

Slade's brown face gleamed with humorous eyes and teeth.

"Just as you please. There's wine."

"No thanks."

They sat down.

IV

Frevick, when completely sober was not a stimulating neighbour, becoming more and more like a melancholy sack into whose dark interior all jibes and playfulnesses disappeared and were swallowed up. He was the Woe of the World, Prometheus with alcohol torturing his liver, a man painfully and acutely conscious of what was and what was not. He would neither laugh nor weep, and Slade had seen Frevick weep, and had not been shocked as he should have been. Psychologically Slade found emotional disturbances interesting.

But Frevick was behaving like a Sabbatarian, and Slade took his coffee and his cigar out to the loggia where a long chair waited for him, and Frevick, looking lost and disconsolate, knew that he was boring Slade. For when Slade became polite to you, you could be sure that he had sucked you dry for the moment.

"Going round your garden."

"Everywhere and anywhere you please, Thomas. If you find me asleep——"

Frevick went out into the sunlight and stood there with an air of not knowing which path to take. There was no particular path for him, and none that mattered. Slade saw the untidy length of him disappear down the terrace steps. He seemed to sink, and vanish into a pool of sunlight, his shabby hat remaining in view for a moment above the edge of a marble step.

Frevick drifted. He was aware of Slade's garden as the pleasance of a man who insisted upon life being sensuous and amusing. The Villa of the Flute! The Pipes of Pan! And Frevick, finding that his legs had carried him into the classic theatre with its marble seats and white pillared proscenium sheltered by its cypress wall, and with the blue of the sky for a velarium, sat down where the sun had warmed a stone bench. He was on the edge of one of these moods of illumination when fragments of the past and present fall into place like the tesseræ of a mosaic.

This Italian sky! But he was haunted by other memories;

yellow daffodils swaying in a wet west wind, the green plaintiveness of an April day, Paris, the Gardens of the Luxembourg,
children playing, Hampstead Heath on a Sunday, a whelk stall,
plumed hats, someone playing a concertina. O, those Hampstead days when he had been young, with a clean eye and a
clean tongue! And now——?

Just sottishness, mental squalor. To sit hopelessly at a
little marble-topped table with other hopeless people; to listen
to old Ponsonby's dirty stories and the Shone woman's screams;
to know that a man like Slade regarded you as a sort of grotesque
study, a pathological specimen, a tragi-comic mask! And to
know that the end was inevitable, and that Burt with his
gentle fierceness had told you the truth.

Frevick put up a hand and felt his chin. He had not shaved.
He had had a morning horror of that bright steel blade.

What a mess!

And Slade scoffed at Julia Lord and her cult of the cold
bath, and at her Englishness, at her stiff back. But Julia
Lord had guts. Vulgar simile, and the expression of Frevick's
eyes changed. He had other memories of Julia Lord, of a
woman whose eyes had looked at him softly until he had made
her realize his hopelessness. She had tried to rescue him.
The absurd, splendid magnanimity of some women.

Yes, wounds. Life was nothing but wounds. You gashed
yourself, and others bled. Life laid a whip across your shoulders
and you shrugged them, and just went on drinking.

But Slade? Slade had never been hurt. He amused himself.
He treated things like toys, and when he was tired he threw
them away.

But surely that was the great sin, to go through life like a
faun, dancing, and piping with a garland of vine leaves shading
your mocking eyes? To give wounds—casually and with a
sort of pagan grace, and to get no wounds. To observe, and
grin and scribble, and not to feel.

CHAPTER IV

I

BILLY wrote home to her mother every week, and Mary Brown, more Martha than Mary, would sit down at night when the work of the day was over, and re-read those breezy, adjectival letters. Billy always had been a consoling person, able to look after her own clothes. She had never been guilty of thoughtless messes, and Mary Brown, with the darning and the mending put away, would give the fire a poke, and light the one cigarette she allowed herself, and try to forget the neuritis in her left leg. She could go to sleep happily on Billy's letters, because they were so full of health and happenings.

Billy wrote breezily of Tindaro.

"This is a topping place. I like Miss Lord awfully. Some people call her a beast, but she's a just beast.

"I've been making marmalade. We sell it to the visitors for twelve lire a pot. You have to watch the Italian cook like a cat. A nice sense of property—when it's somebody else's. That's Bolshevism, isn't it? And she's an ingenious creature. I caught her pouring soft sugar into one of her shoes!

"The society here is really marvellous. You have to catalogue it to understand it properly.

"A. The hotel people. Mostly old. Lots of Sir Somebodies, and Americans. The Elyseo, de luxe, the Bristol not quite so much so. The St. George and the Florio rather fly-blown.

"B. The English and American villa colony. Just so. They give tea-parties. You stand about, and try to balance a chocolate eclair in your saucer, and hear all the

34

gossip.   Rather high-brow and very 'cleeky,' quite in the golf style.

"C.   Us.   The doctor, the lace-shop, the antichità shop, the library.

"D.   Stands for the damned.   I haven't met any of the damned yet.   Except one or two mild ones who came to the library.   Odd people, with lurid pasts or something. Miss L. calls them the exiles, people who live out here always, and can't go home.

"E.   The natives, real Tindaro, and the goats and the donkeys, and the wretched cats.   I haven't been able to make friends with a Tindaro cat.   The dogs are mostly yellow, and spend much time in scratching."

Mary Brown found Billy's letters comforting.   There was a Browning lilt to them—an "All's well with the world" touch. Dear Billy!   Always this brown, vital, lovable child had been Mary's favourite, and especially so in this age of self-expression, a phrase nicely chosen to justify the extremes of a crude selfishness.   Even as a small child Billy had stood up squarely on her sturdy legs and insisted on carrying things, and Mary had been very loth to see her go.   But what would you?   She had four other children at home at No. 19 Braybrook Road.   Eric she had contrived to place in a Bank, but he was in the thick of that uneasy phase when collars and ties are of supreme importance, and the opinions of one's elders dotard's tosh.   Rachel had a job as a teacher of dancing with Miss Gloria Molyneux of Wigmore Street, and Rachel was a little irresponsible.   The two younger children, Mildred and Roy, were still at school, Roy at Merchant Taylors', Mildred at an Ealing academy.   Their fees were paid by an uncle.   Mary Brown could afford only a slip of a servant, and every item in the weekly books had to be checked and considered.   She smoked her one cigarette a day, and bought two new hats at the sales in January and July.

But Billy was all right; Billy was the dark, red rose of the bunch, without a blotch on her petals.   Such a warm-hearted child, and so wise in her way, and Mary Brown would sit and look at the fire, and forget the splutterings and nasal discords of

Roy's wireless in the back room.   What an age it was for noises!
Somebody's orchestra playing, and Rachel trying a new step in
the Yale Blues!   And over there in Italy Billy was making
marmalade, and issuing books, and taking round teatrays to
those fortunate people who had spare cash to play with.   Dear
Billy!   Mary Brown's face softened to the firelight.

Billy herself thought well of her new world.   She had moved
from the Villa Vesta into the two rooms above the library and
teashop, and her sitting-room window looked over cypresses and
olives and old brown roofs to the sea.   The bedroom window
fronted upon the Corso, but Tindaro went early to bed, and after
ten o'clock the stones of the Corso were silent.   Moreover,
Billy was still sleeping an English sleep, and getting up at six
with a sense of adventure, to stand in a tin bath and sluice herself.
She had accepted Miss Lord's clean cult, though she had to carry
up her own water overnight in a great brown earthenware jug.
The Italian women had refused to recognize the necessity for so
much water, and had protested by pretending to forget.

"These English!"

Did not Mascati, who owned and ran the Bristol Hotel, say
that when the Italian season began the deluge of bath water
ceased, and became a reasonable trickle.   Even the Germans
were more considerate.

Moreover, Billy's first week had given much of its energy to a
war of attrition with Maria the cook.   Maria came in daily,
arriving at seven.   She was big and swarthy and raucous; she
had relatives, and a light hand.   And Billy having accepted the
whole job and nothing but the job, had found Maria proposing to
take advantage of Billy's newness.   Billy had smiled, and shown
herself capable of taking care of the flour, and the sugar, and the
baking-powder, and the raisins.   Maria, sullenly and silently
saucy, had met her Caporetto over the sugar.

Actually Miss Lord had laughed.   Billy's picture of Maria's
black-stockinged feet caked with sugar was irresistible.

"She couldn't put it down to the cat, you know."

Obviously not.   And after the incident of the sugar-lined
shoes, Billy had no more trouble.   Maria accepted the inevitable, and at the end of the second week she was breathing garlic

and beneficence upon Billy.   But that bath water!   Neither Maria nor Vanna could ever remember to carry up the monstrous crock.

In the library things went pretty smoothly, and Billy had a way with the constitutionally discontented.

"How is it that I can—never—get the book I want?   I have been a subscriber for three months."

Billy displayed a firmly smiling face.

"It depends so much on the book.   What is the particular book?"

"'Red Ruin' by Ruby Rudd."

"There is a run on 'Red Ruin.'"

"Then you ought to have more copies."

"We have three.   That is our limit.   I'll hold the next copy for you when it comes in."

Even the most crusty had to refer to her as "That nice girl at the library."   Nice was the universal adjective.

Lady Pipp, the leader of the villa coterie, came and saw and approved, and invited Billy to one of her Sunday tea festas. Lady Pipp was a little yellow woman with rimless glasses, long flat feet, and her hair very much in control.   Billy went on Sunday to the Villa Dante, and found herself in a room full of Louis Quinze furniture and much people.   Here were the Sudbury Smiths, the Bromheads and the Landers, Dr. Burt and his little shy wife, and Miss Cramm of the antichità shop, and sundry residents from the Elyseo and the Bristol.   Billy stood in the crowd and tried not to bump people or to get her teacup joggled.   Sir Reginald Pipp was kind to her.   He had a head that went straight up like the sides of a hard felt hat, and was cut off abruptly at the top.   His face was brick red in colour, and his lips precise and thin.   His conversation suggested a wireless operator talking in morse.   Billy heard him talking to Dr. Burt. "Yes, yes, yes.   Indeed!   Quite so.   Most remarkable.   Yes, yes, yes.   Exactly my opinion.   Very late season.   Wind. Yes, yes, yes.   My wife does not like freesias.   Mimosa? Which variety?   Yes, yes, yes.   Dealbata.   Quite so.   Yes, yes, yes."

Billy found herself extracted from the crowd by Dr. Burt,

and led out into the Villa Dante garden. It was a garden after Lady Pipp's own heart, all stone chips and correct paths, and palm-trees, and nicely disciplined borders. It was full of spinous and prickly things, strange cacti which Dr. Burt looked at with a sort of gentle malevolence. Somehow Lady Pipp's garden made Billy think of an Easter egg, but an egg with no frills to it.

Dr. Burt she liked very well. She had met him at one of the bi-weekly dances at the Hotel Elyseo, and she had been grateful to him, because at the age of five-and-fifty he was not among the feverishly eager old men who fox-trotted with bent knees and tantalized you with senile prancings. He did not move in that way. He was one of those men who convey the impression of stillness. The head, and shoulders and bulk of him suggested a wild boar. His bristling moustachios were tusks. He was ugly, grotesquely so at the first glance, but when you had looked into his eyes for a while and listened to his voice, his ugliness was forgotten. He had strangely gentle eyes in a fierce face.

His manner was abrupt, perhaps because he had to deal with so many people who were ready to waste his time, and when he was not doctoring he was hunting—Graeco-Roman antiquities. He was an authority on the flora and fauna of Tindaro and its coast. He tramped the hills in a pair of heavy black boots and grey worsted stockings. Or you might catch him with his coat off, working with the labourers who were excavating in that classic soil. If a figurine, or a potsherd, or a piece of old metal was found anywhere for miles round it was carried to "Il Dottore."

Mrs. Sudbury Smith had said of him, "Burt just blurts at you. No manners. Half the time he is thinking of a Roman pavement or a Greek figurine. I wish he would think more about my figure."

Burt blurted at Billy, but gently so.

"Like this place?"

"Tindaro or the garden?"

"Tindaro."

"I think it's marvellous."

His blue eyes observed her.   She could remember a doctor looking at her with the same intentness when as a girl at school she had developed measles.   Burt's eyes were like two blue slits.

"O, well, that's all right.   You must come up and have tea with my wife.   She'll fix it up.   I don't suppose we shall meet professionally."

They exchanged smiles.

"Ought to say I hope not?"

"Of course.   You are rather lucky in having struck a woman like Miss Lord."

She agreed, and with sincerity.   Miss Lord was so clean cut, not at all smudgy, and when she used the word smudgy Burt's eyes gave her another of those alert glances.   The word was so right, so applicable to much that was human, especially in Tindaro, and he wondered whether she had used it with any complete understanding of its meaning.   She herself had so clear and fresh a surface.   She looked utterly untarnished.

He said, "O, by the way, Bromhead wants you to play tennis. I'll introduce you.   I hear you are pretty good."

"I'm keen.   We had lessons at school."

Bromhead was found, a big, pleasant person with a red face and a ruff of grey hair.   He reminded Billy of the Examiner in "Outward Bound."   He had eyes that were always ready to laugh.

"Miss Brown says she can play."

"Splendid.   I'm president and secretary rolled into one. The courts are a little unsympathetic.   When can we have the pleasure?"

"I'm free on Tuesdays and Fridays from two till four."

"What about next Tuesday?   I'll get a man and a girl from the Elyseo.   I'm rather a rabbit."

"I'd love to."

"Splendid."

He was jocund and kind and clean, and she liked him.

II

Oscar Slade, who had been lunching *en suite* with an American publisher who was staying at the Hotel Elyseo, strolled through the lounge with his hat on, and Slade was a noticeable man, especially in the lounge of the Elyseo. He was aggressively and self-consciously un-English. His hat was broad and flat in the brim; his tie had an air of abandonment, and a black velvet coat and grey flannel trousers were curiously in contrast.

He was noticed.

"Who's that fellow?"

"Haven't the faintest idea. Looks like a Spaniard."

"Me no likee."

Someone leant across and imparted information.

"That's Oscar Slade the novelist. Has a villa here."

"English?"

"O, yes."

"Looks like a dago."

Slade had turned aside to speak to Georgio, the concierge at the Elyseo. Slade bought cigars and other articles through Georgio, who beamed upon him as he beamed upon all gentlemen with money. English eyes watched them both, the tall fellow with his brown, flat-cheeked face and his quizzical eyes, and the little bobbing Silenus in the blue and gold uniform. Slade's was a figure that should have been laughed at by the conventional English, but the laughter failed to arrive. Someone had once called him "An insolent devil," and a confident and ironic insolence does not stand to be ridiculed.

"Got the goods, Georgio?"

"I have, sar."

"How much?"

"Tree undred and fifteen lire, sar."

"Good lord!"

Slade smiled, and put down notes for five hundred lire.

"You're a plutocrat, Georgio, an Americano."

"Thank you, sar."

Slade pocketed two small parcels, and passed out through the glass-doors, and down the carriage-drive of the Elyseo. The hotel was all white and gold; it flew three flags, the flags of Italy, England and the U.S.A. Patches of vivid, autumn-sown grass lay like carpets spread under the palms. People were sitting in the green and blue chairs. Two itinerant musicians were twanging a guitar and scraping at a violin.

Slade arrived on the white and dusty road which was an extension of the Corso, and on the red courts below the road people were playing tennis. A low stone wall separated the road from the Tennis Club, and a few old olive trees growing at the foot of the wall sustained a lacework beyond which the figures moved. Small birds twittered in the olives. A stone pine threw an oval shadow on the white road.

Slade loitered. He was not a player of games; life was his game. But he stood to watch the figure of a girl moving beyond the lacework of leaves, a figure in white, sleeveless, short skirted, moving on a pair of very shapely white legs. It was Billy Brown partnering Tom Bromhead against two people from the Elyseo.

Slade observed her. He was both artist and man in his knowledge of the figure feminine, and as Frevick had put it "The girl could move." When she ran she floated with a kind of long, easy glide. Her swinging racket arm caught the sunlight; her hair danced with her feet. She played the game remarkably well, and in the modern style, running up on her service to volley.

Oscar Slade was interested. So much of life is tentative and bungling, and to watch someone doing a thing supremely well piqued the artist in him. He watched Billy with pleasure, and with Slade a pleasant perception became sensuous and personal. He ran to sex. Women had always been intensely necessary to him; not woman but women.

His sense of humour, stripped of its personal predilections, became a nicely balanced mockery. Old Tom Bromhead supplied Slade with the quizzical smirk; old Tom, perspiring and flamboyant, pounding about the court with a racket that was like a professorial net chasing elusive butterflies. He was vociferous. "Yours, partner."—"Shot."—"O, well played." Billy most obviously carried the game. She was a light-footed Atalanta translating into lyrical phrases the efforts of a galloping and unwieldy centaur.

Slade chuckled. His lips moved. He addressed the inward

word to old Bromhead. "Don't worry, old thing; leave it to her. Just mop and shout."

Such was Slade's reaction, but to Billy old Tom Bromhead, with his fiery face, was a delight and a glory. He was so enjoying himself, the happy rabbit at play. To Oscar Slade he was absurd; to Billy Brown he was a "dear." They won the first set and changed over. Old Tom, wiping his racket hand on the seat of his trousers, said something beaming and gaillard to Billy.

"I'd better keep out of your way."

She smiled and gave a shake of the head, and Slade's face lost its glimmer of mockery. He stared. He was piqued and tantalized by that vigorous head with its sudden smile. How would that smile affect you in a moment of ecstasy, with the shutters closed, and a white pillow supporting a dark head? His stare became brutal.

And Billy became conscious of it just as she was about to return a service. She mishit the ball, and glanced suddenly and half resentfully towards the olive trees. Her eyes met Slade's, and for a moment their mutual challenge held.

"Sorry, partner."

"First you've missed for a long time."

But she foozled the next shot also, and looked grave, and gave a shake of the head. Concentration. She did not see Slade moving away with a faint smile that was too like a smirk. He was intrigued. So Miss Girl Guide was not so solid as she seemed; she could be put off her game by being studied in a particular sort of way. Vulnerable? O, yes, all women were.

III

Billy, running up to her room to change into a black frock and lace apron, found Winnie Haycroft sitting at her window, and looking vague and tired.

"O, you've been playing tennis. I wish I could. I just came across———"

Billy was becoming accustomed to Winnie's unfinished sentences and her general air of mental untidiness.

"Well, why don't you?"

She screwed her racket up in its press, for rackets were precious.

"O, damn, look at that!"

A white stocking had laddered, and stockings were part of the problems of life when you earned some three pounds a week and tried to send spare cash home to your mother.

"Isn't that disgusting! Only worn them twice. I've got to change. Come in."

Winnie got up languidly and followed the warmth and the vigour of Billy into the bedroom, and sat on the bed and looked vague and anæmic.

"You are strong. I can't play here. I get so tired."

Billy dropped her white skirt, and stepped out of it. She was experiencing Winnie's dusty devotion, and liking it, because it was a tribute, and because Winnie made her feel motherly.

"Perhaps it is because you don't try to play. Have to keep fit. I say, hunt me out a pair of black stockings; top drawer, left."

Winnie put a hand to her head and felt for the stockings. She appreciated Billy like a northern breeze.

"It's getting no change. This place—stuffy. I came across to see if you would come to the cine to-night."

"Yes. What's on?"

"That German thing. Rather fine. Shall I call for you at eight?"

"Do. I'm a minute late. Chuck me that apron. One gets jolly hot here."

The pale girl seemed to wince.

"Hot——! Why—later on—I feel I can't breathe. One's like a bit of wet wool."

IV

The Tindaro picture house was a primitive affair. You took tickets for the most expensive seats, because these seats cost you only five lire, and if you sat in the less expensive seats you were likely to be presented with a flea. The building was badly ventilated, and when Billy pushed the curtain aside she met the warm, stale darkness and odours of garlic and of unwashed southern humanity.

She said, "What a fug!"

They had to wait in the darkness at the end of the hall until the lights were switched on at the conclusion of one of those very crude, knockabout products. The place was half empty. No one troubled to take tickets or to assign seats. Billy and Winnie Haycroft sat down in the last row but one, being nearer the door here and the fresh air of heaven. The public was principally native waiters from the hotels, shop men and girls, Tindarese dandies. The lights went down. A piano and a violin began to give out appropriate music.

Billy found the picture boring. It staged the old silly theme of the aristocratic blackguard and the noble laborious fellow and the girl. It played to the mob in the gallery. And Billy had had a hard day, and much exercise in the fresh air, and the hall was abominably stuffy. Her attention fluttered. She glanced at Winnie Haycroft's face, and saw it floating beside her in the dimness as a pale, absorbed profile, like a faded white flower on a fragile stalk. Winnie was absorbed. She had been translated into a world of absurd romance, and like a child she gazed and gazed. Her hands were tense in her lap. Her lower lip drooped.

Billy sat and wondered. What could Winnie Haycroft see in all those very unreal and melodramatic happenings? Such stuff was not life, those hysterical faces with glycerine tear blobs, and noble frenzies, and starched villainies. And there was "the child." Or was Winnie lost in the thing just because nothing ever happened in Tindaro so far as Winnie was concerned? Emotion. Yes, just emotion, craved for and unattainable save in this stuffy, tawdry place.

Yes, perhaps it was that. Or did the happenings on the screen symbolize escape, escape from Tindaro, and exile, and lace and the rather dreary atmosphere of Miss Haycroft's serious shop? Winnie's aunt had a desiccated look, like some pale shred of flesh hung up to dry in a dusty corner.

The noble fellow and the girl were embracing. A little shudder of ecstasy made itself felt in the figure at Billy's side.

Winnie's elbow pressed against her friend's.   Then the lights went up, and Billy saw that Winnie Haycroft's face had a look of hazy exultation.   Her eyes shone.   Almost she had the air of a woman who had a lover, and who had been kissed.

"Lovely.   Don't you think so?"

Billy was kind.   She did not blurt out her opinion, and say that she had found the piece awful tosh.

"Quite up to the average.   The hero was rather funny."

"Funny!"

"Well—such a noble fellow.   I rather preferred the black-guard."

"O, my dear."

They edged into the gangway and joined the crowd that jostled good humouredly out into the southern night.   Billy drew three deep breaths.   She saw stars twinkling.

"Phew—that's better."

She felt Winnie's hand tucking itself under her arm.

"I wish they would have more English pieces."

"But they don't exist, or hardly.   We don't let go enough to have good film faces.   We keep things shut up inside."

Tindaro was black and silent, and the ribbon of the sky between the high houses was spangled with stars.   The Corso with its grey stones lay darkly at peace, like still water flowing between the shuttered houses.   A few footfalls echoed.

By the church of San Domenico three or four dark figures stood as though attached to the old and greasy wall, and Billy felt the sudden pressure of Winnie Haycroft's body.   Her hand clutched.   They swerved out into the middle of the Corso.

"What's the matter?"

"One has to be careful.   One gets spoken to.   Horrid."

Billy's chin went up.

"Well, it needn't kill one."

"Oh, and other things when it's dark."

"Yes," said Billy, "just because it's dark."

CHAPTER V

I

AN Englishwoman from the Hotel Elyseo came into the library and asked for one of Oscar Slade's books, and Billy had to confess that the library did not possess a copy of that particular book.

"We have 'A Middle-class Mélange' and 'Chinese Crackers.'"

The Englishwoman had read them both, and had thought them vastly clever.

"But you ought to have a copy of 'Balaam's Ass.' It is one of the wittiest things of the century. And after all, Oscar Slade is your local celebrity."

Billy supposed that he was, but then Oscar Slade was not a regular subscriber to Miss Lord's library.

"What, you haven't met him?"

"No. I have only been in Tindaro two or three weeks."

"I believe he is rather hard to meet. Not fond of the travelling English. I'm not surprised."

Billy raised the question with Miss Lord, who was arranging violets in white marmalade pots, touching the flowers gently and tenderly.

"A woman has been asking for one of Slade's books. We only have two."

"Which book was she asking for?"

"'Balaam's Ass.'"

Miss Lord went on with the arranging of her flowers.

"No, that book's beyond my limit. I can stand a good deal."

"Dirty?"

"Well, not obviously so. It goes against all my traditions. Clever enough. Besides—the people here don't want Slade."

"No. He's not popular. His books are in most of the time. But he's supposed to be—very much it."

"Have you read one, my dear?"

"No."

"You ought to be able to tell people about books. Still, I won't thrust you into Slade. I believe he has a biggish following in England, and he sells well in America. The critics love him."

"High-brow?"

"Psycho-analysis and pulling things to pieces. Just like a mischievous monkey. You might bring me in another basket of flowers. I left it in the loggia."

Billy felt that she had a duty to perform, and that she ought to be able to advise their subscribers on the wares that were sold, so she took—"A Middle Class Mélange" to bed with her, and was a little perplexed and slightly bored. Strangely enough, the Middle-Class Mélange was an Ealing mixture, and a rather scummy broth at that, but Billy had never dipped a spoon into that sort of suburban stew. She was not guileless and unsophisticated. She knew about most things, but she knew about them like a clean young science student.

Slade made terrible fun of his middle-class family, but he did not know his Ealing as Billy knew it. He saw elevenpence three-farthings posed as the guinea article, and that very nasty person Mr. Smith wearing respectable trousers and uncovering his nakedness behind the scenes. And the young Smiths, horrid young savages who shouted and quarrelled and swanked, and tortured cats, and sneaked away to giggle over dirty stories. A most unpleasant picture and most unpleasantly accurate if you allowed Slade the extremes of suburban behaviour. His description of the Smith family in its car, setting out on Sunday for the Merrow Downs or Friday Street, and accompanied by Reggie Smith and Flossie on motor-bike and pillion, to scatter banana skins and paper and bottles over God's earth, and to flaunt in the faces of the flowers a succulent vulgarity, was richly vigorous and mordant. But Ealing wasn't all Smith; a very large portion of it was Brown, and especially Mary Brown, and Slade was not interested in people who were truthful and honest and clean and unselfish. They were so calculable. They changed their linen regularly, and paid their bills. Your high-brow is apt to prefer a dirty shirt, and something venereal and septic.

Billy ended by dropping the book on the floor. She turned out the light, and lay on her back and reflected upon Oscar Slade's Smithian family, and was quite sure that such people were prevalent and needed suppressing But there were the Browns to be considered. How was it that no one wrote books about the Browns? Dull people—perhaps—who just did their job, but did not get into print.

And what of Oscar Slade himself? A superior person. But rather provoking. No doubt he had his tongue in his cheek.

"I should like to talk to him about Ealing," thought Billy, "and about that Smith family. I could tell him a few things. Yes, plenty of things."

And full of the healthy confidence of her youth she fell asleep.

II

Billy still turned enthusiastic eyes upon Tindaro, and her enthusiasm was as innocent as that of the average tourist, who, having been told by the people who write travel books that you should admire this and that, revels in the same old adjectival stuff. Billy sent picture postcards to her mother. "This is the duomo."—"View of the ruins of the Roman theatre." And her adjectives were there, though modernized. She used "priceless" in place of picturesque, and "marvellous" instead of romantic.

Tindaro was adventure. She saw it in the sunlight between sea and sky. There were the mountains, sometimes grey and sometimes blue. There were dramatic dawns and sunsets, moonlight and soaring cypresses, and the sea seen very blue through the blackness of Mediterranean pines. She liked the strange little streets and the wandering passages, and the stone stairways disappearing into the darkness. Shutters gave such secrecy to the houses. Tindaro was beauty, native and unconsidered. Often about sunset and after her work she would climb to the ruins of the Roman theatre, and gaze and gaze. She could see the ship of Ulysses, and Cyclops on some black headland, hurling rocks. And Calypsos island. And Atlas returning through the purple sea, bearing the golden apples of the Hesperides.

So much for the legendary and the marvellous.

The Café Ceres was reality. It presented its little round, marble-topped tables and its green chairs, and an orchestra that sent forth the tinklings of mandolins and the twangings of guitars. It possessed a gentleman with a goatlike face, who throated forth "Sole mio" and "Funiculi funicula." It supplied strange little drinks, and toothpicks, and bad coffee. It had a window full of cakes; exotic, smeary, pink and yellow pastry swarmed over by numberless sleepy flies. When it rained, an awning was let down to shelter the tables and that odd collection of humans. That they were odd was obvious to Billy. They sat and stared, as though the Corso was a stage upon which Madam Convention trailed a respectable and absurd petticoat. They made obvious fun of all those other English. Whenever Billy passed those tables she was made to think of people sitting round a dancing-hall and quizzing the dancers.

But it was not happy fun. She snatched other glimpses. There was Frevick's sombre and suffering face, and the blue eyes of Major Mirleess, insolent and miserable. Even the Shone woman's huge mouth caught in the midst of laughter was a circle of despair and of horror. One old man seemed to sniff perpetually with an expression of quaint mistrust. You saw faces suddenly slack and naked, fallen in open upon themselves, hopeless with ennui. There were mouths that yawned. Dashkoff the Russian, who was paid to dance with English women at the Elyseo, would sit picking his teeth with an air of profound and melancholy abstraction.

The Café Ceres was not beautiful. It aroused in Billy a sense of something tragic, and a vague feeling of curiosity. She was stared at, commented on. Had she been less whole-some the Café Ceres might have made her shudder.

She was surprised to see Slade there. He appeared to be

one of the regular loungers. His ironic, brown face, with its startling eyes, was always catching her glances. It was as though he waited and willed her to look at him; as though he expected it.

Yes, no doubt the Café Ceres mocked at life. It kept a journal in which its jibes were recorded. It encouraged Slade to produce Limericks upon the local worthies.

> "There was an old lady named Pipp
> Who was a little bit thin in the lip.
> Said her husband—'No thanks.
> I've no use for the branks.
> I suffer too much from the pip.'"

Upon the top of one of the marble tables Slade had scribbled doggerel upon the Lady of the Villa Vesta.

> "There was an old vestal named Lord
> Whose virtue was sharp as a sword.
> When she sat in her bath
> As lean as a lath,
> Jehovah said, 'Julia, I'm bored.'"

Sadie Shone would open her huge mouth and scream with laughter. 'Say, that's cute. Make me one about the new girl, Oscar." And Slade, with a cigarette hanging negligently, had produced a Limerick upon Billy.

> "There was a young lady named Brown
> Who came to this flea-bitten town
> With a smile and a racket,
> And a skirt with no placket,
> A skirt most impeccably brown."

But to Billy it was evident that the little world of the Café Ceres was a world apart, for none of those people were to be met at the Tennis Club or at the villas of the blessed. They remained apart, like the damned or the unclean, drinking their little drinks and talking their little talks. They were rather like the cakes in the café window where the flies buzzed and crawled.

Billy wanted to ask questions, but there were some subjects upon which Miss Lord was not to be interrogated. Anything that suggested gossip made that firm mouth of hers grow yet more firm. There had been an occasion when she had suffered from the idle curiosities and adjectives of the crowd, and it had roused in her such a scorn and hatred of all looseness of tongue that she was silent upon the reputations of others.

Winnie Haycroft had no such reticence. Questioned by Billy as to the antecedents of the Café Ceres coterie she looked both frightened and severe.

"Oh—one doesn't mix—at least—not more than one can help. Though when you meet in the Corso—every day, it's rather awkward."

"I should think it was."

"They keep rather to themselves."

"For reasons?"

"That's why they live out here."

"That little man, for instance, with the angry face and the lame foot?"

"O, Major Mirleess. O, he's really terrible."

"But what did he do?"

"I believe he went about after the war wearing uniform and decorations which he hadn't won. I believe he pretended to be a V.C. And the police—— Yes, a month in prison —I believe. And then they say there were other things, getting money."

Billy looked very grave.

"But what made him do such an utterly silly thing?"

"He's an awfully vain little man."

"Good lord—just swelled head! Well, it might be. Wanting to swank when there was nothing left to swank about."

She asked about some of the others, and Winnie fidgeted and looked uncomfortable.

"The very fat old man?"

"Sir Dyce Duxbury. He swindled people or something. Company promoting. He looks rather harmless."

"Quite. Rather like a white bunny rabbit. And the woman with the big mouth?"

"Mrs. Shone.   O, she's a horrible woman.   She—O—well —she's just horrible."

"I see.   Just like that."

It occurred to Billy to wonder why Oscar Slade allowed himself to be mixed in that mélange.   Was it his protest against the Middle Classes, or a pose?   Or did he find the damned more interesting and amusing than the world's beatified?   Or was it swank?   He might be a celebrity among the uncelebrated, the prince among the beggars.   But she wondered, and without realizing that her frank curiosity had any other inspiration.   She did not use Winnie Haycroft's adjectives; she might dub people rotten or futile, but she did not call them horrible. She had the tolerance of strength, the confidence of youth innocent of wounds.

But most certainly Oscar Slade was not futile.   He had a queer face and queer eyes, and suggestions of audacity that are unexpectedly troubling to the most unexpected of women.   He was sexed, and a woman may react to sex while the rational and educated part of her is pretending that a certain personality is unusual and interesting and arrestive.   Slade's thin, brown, ironic face with its flat cheeks and sensuous mouth and intelligent eyes, was singular and vivid.   In its lighter moods it had a whimsicality, a rather pleasing and mischievous shimmer.   It was so alive.

Billy had also noticed Frevick, sombre and sodden and shabby, Slade's usual vis-à-vis.   The two men were so vividly contrasted. Slade's face was like an edge of light, Frevick's a pit of shadow.

Again, the juxtaposition was intriguing.

III

The Café Ceres came seldom to the English Library, and Frevick was one of the few who ever appeared in that literary tabernacle, and he came seldom and with an air of haste.   He would bang the old book down upon the table, and grabbing a new one rather at hazard, go and hold the book so that the recording angel could write down the title.   He was never conversational; he came and went as quickly as possible.

On one occasion when Billy had been entering up the book

he had selected she had felt moved to glance suddenly up at him, and she had found Frevick's eyes fixed upon her face with a kind of hunger and of helplessness. He had looked confused, discovered.

But Frevick was incorrigible about books. He would keep a book a month, and sometimes the copy when it was returned, was scribbled over. Little savage protests had been pencilled on the margins. "Bosh."—"Life's not like that."—"Succulent slush."—"O, go and boil it harder." Billy had shown one such copy to Julia Lord, and Miss Lord, instead of displaying indignation, had spoken gently. "Oh, it's just Mr. Frevick. Rub it out." And Billy had taken a piece of indiarubber and erased Frevick's scribblings.

Then came an occasion when the artist had held up for three weeks a copy of a particular novel, and the novel was in clamorous demand, and Billy, not wishing to trouble Miss Lord, supposed that a personal collecting of the book was the obvious and most expeditious remedy. She looked up Frevick's address. He lived now in a house in the Vicolo Venito.

Billy sought out the Vicolo Venito, and found Frevick's house, a little, dilapidated pink box set at the end of a strip of untidy garden. It was Tindaro of the Tindarese. A few iris clumps raised green blades above a stretch of dirt. The path was a mere track. The door was almost innocent of paint, though it belonged to the house of a painter; and perhaps because of it. Some washing had been hung out to dry on the bare branches of a fig tree. Billy saw a pair of faded pink pants. There was something pathetic and squalid about those pants.

A rusty chain hung down beside the door. Billy pulled the chain and a bell rang. She waited; nothing happened. She pulled the chain a little more vigorously, and a dog barked.

As she stood looking at the washing on the fig tree the door opened on her suddenly and she turned to find Frevick in his socks, coatless and collarless. His chin was all stubble, his eyelids red. A little yellow mongrel dog with very bright eyes stood with him, and looked up at Billy and wagged a feathery tail.

"What d'you want?"

His sodden abrupt fierceness shocked her. He stood in the doorway as though hiding a secret. The dog sat down, and leaning against his leg, allowed a pink tongue to hang.

Said Billy, somehow feeling that she surprised an animal in the midst of tearing its food—"So sorry to disturb you, but that book, 'Galleons Reach.' So many people are asking for it."

He looked fuddled, bothered.

"Haven't got it, have I?"

"You have had it nearly a month."

She smiled at him, and suddenly the expression of his face changed. His eyes became like the eyes of a sick dog, gentle, helpless.

"Damned silly of me. I'll look it up. Sorry you've had the trouble."

He went to find the book, and the dog went with him like a little sedulous, faithful spirit. Billy saw the red tiles of the passage, and an old overcoat hanging up rather like the figure of a man who had hanged himself. When Frevick reappeared she noticed that he had wound an old silver and blue scarf round his neck, and that his hair had been brushed. The dog waited beside feet that had been thrust into slippers.

"Sorry to keep you. Here it is. Great book. I'll try and be more punctual in future."

She smiled at him and took the book, and bent down to pat the dog.

"I hope you finished the book?"

"Read it twice. There's a man in that book who could take his medicine. Sorry you've had the trouble."

"O, that's all right."

She smiled at him again, and he watched her go down the path, but she did not look back, but opened and shut the rusty gate, and then it was that he noticed the washing hanging on the fig tree. His eyes were both consenting and reproachful. What did it matter? What did anything matter? The dog, getting on her hind legs, was pressing her forepaws against his knee; she gave three little appealing barks, and he bent down and lifted her up, and shutting the door with the toe of a slipper, returned to that frowzy place he called his studio. He sat down in an armchair, with the dog on his knees. Yes, life was pretty hopeless, but something young and gallant had knocked at his door.

CHAPTER VI

I

BILLY was taken unawares.

"Excuse me, I suppose you are in charge?"

Julia Lord had one of her headaches, and Maria had brought a message from the Villa Vesta. "Please carry on." Less than a minute ago Billy had unlocked the library door, and taken Miss Lord's chair and had opened the library ledgers, and had imagined herself alone. She had not heard anyone enter, nor had she been conscious of a presence.

She turned in her chair. Slade was standing slightly behind her, his hat in his hand, looking down at her with an air of amusement, and for the first time she saw him close. She had the impression of a very brown face, of light blue eyes that stared rather disconcertingly, of a purple tie and a blue linen collar. His hair had a waviness; it was complacent hair.

She met the stealth and the suddenness of him with a frank abruptness.

"I didn't hear you. Yes, I'm in charge."

He showed his teeth. The texture of him was velvet. His brownness had an almost golden gloss. When he smiled faint wrinkles showed at the outer angles of his eyes. Her young abruptness seemed to amuse him.

"Sorry. These things are sneaky but comfortable. Good for mule paths and Italian roads. I apologize."

He carried his little stick, and he tapped one of his crepe-soled shoes with it.

"Tried them?"

Billy had the air of a solemn, watchful child.

"No—I haven't."

"Let me recommend them. My name's Slade. I'm only an occasional visitor."

She pushed her chair back and stood up, feeling that she wanted to be more on a level with him, and able to look him straight in the face. And like a child she rather resented his air of talking down to her, his quizzical and half-familiar playfulness.

"You want a book?"

He turned to the shelves and pointed with his stick.

"Well—obviously. Have you read all those?"

"No."

"What an escape. A library makes me feel that I'm in an old clothes shop——"

Her abruptness continued.

"What is the name of the book——?"

He stood poised, ironically considering the interruption. Was it that she did or would not understand playfulness?

"I retract about the old clothes. Miss Lord is the most hygienic person——"

"You haven't told me the name of the book."

There was a pause between them. He walked up the room, looking at the shelves, and tapping the tiled floor softly with his stick. He stooped slightly. In spite of his alert and restless movements he had the figure of a man who sat about a good deal, and took no active exercise. He was both lean and soft. Billy observed him. To her he was unusual, an original type, and she felt the touch of his strangeness, the slight tension of an interested expectancy.

He turned about and glanced at the bowl of violets on the table. His face showed the beginnings of a smile. He put down his hat and stick, and raising the bowl, smelt the flowers.

"No, not old clothes."

His glance was friendly, mischievous. The solemnity of her firm young face appeared to relax.

"No. And the book?"

He replaced the bowl.

"Your attention to business is—admirable. I want a book on alchemy."

"Alchemy?"

She was posed. She had the air of repeating to herself,

"Alchemy, alchemy." She frowned. Her seriousness had a charm.

"Non est?"

His white and brown smile was challenging.

"I don't think we have one."

"Probably not. I chanced it. Scribblers have to poke their noses into strange places. Not all violets."

He had made her smile.

"I'll try the catalogue."

She drew the catalogue towards her, and bending over the table, turned up the A's. The point of a finger travelled down the page. And Slade observed her. Undoubtedly she had a very comely neck. The hair suggested strength, a crisp independence.

"No luck?"

"Afraid not."

"Well, I shall have to bluff or send to England. I suppose you can supply no information with regard to Hermes Trismegistus or Nicholas Flamel?"

She smiled just a little derisively.

"Hardly. I'm not—— But of course, what idiots! We have forgotten the 'Encyclopædia Britannica.' "

He gave her a little, humorous bow.

"Idiots! I agree—in one respect. But you are exempted."

"Thanks."

"You'll find the encyclopædia over there in that case."

"And the fee?"

"Are you a subscriber?"

"No—I pay by the piece."

"I see. I think you might be allowed a free look."

"That's gracious. I will. But I don't like encyclopædias."

"O?"

"They make me feel so abominably illiterate. That I have wasted my time, slacked."

"I don't think that has worried me—ever."

"Wise woman."

Other people arrived, and Billy returned to her chair, and the business of the morning. People brought her the books

which they had read, and she had to mark them off, and take
down the names of the new books that had been chosen. The
long and rather narrow room grew crowded, but her view of
Slade was not obscured, for he had taken a chair at the other
end of the table, and opened the first volume of the encyclo-
pedia. She was aware of the contrasted browns of his hair
and face, and the sudden blueness of his eyes when they looked
at her. They were as of the same blue as his collar.

For the library was not empty of humour. Old ladies came
and asked Billy questions, the most naïve questions. And they
crowded in front of the cases, and got in each other's way, and
gave each other polite and irritable glances. "Excuse me, do
you mind——" "Oh, not at all. I'm afraid I'm in the way."
Some of them would discuss books with the serene sureness of
those who had never written anything but a letter. "Nice"
was the prevailing adjective. A book was either nice or not
nice.

Billy caught Slade's wicked eye. Almost he winked at her.
He did not appear to be taking the encyclopædia with proper
seriousness.

Someone laid a book on the table.

"Not a nice book—at all."

"O," said Billy.

"The first one I have read of Oscar Slade's. It will be the
last. Quite disgusting."

Billy looked at the book, and then at the face of the lady
who had returned it. She dared not look at Slade.

"I suppose it is considered clever——"

"Have you a book of complaints?"

"No."

"I suggest that you ought to keep one. One has a right to
express one's opinion."

"Of course," said Billy, "but need you do it on paper?"

The lady gave her a sharp glance, the kind of glance sixty
bestows upon flippant youth, and went her way in search of
another book. Billy felt the table gently shaken. She looked
instinctively at Slade, and met his ironic, laughing eyes.
His lips moved slightly, and she could imagine him saying

"How priceless! I've succeeded. I love shocking these people."

She lowered her head and tried to appear absorbed in her ledger. She had a sudden sense of intimate, laughing nearness to him. Something had passed, a flash of mischievous sympathy, and realizing it, she felt suddenly serious. She was sure now —without quite knowing how she knew it, that alchemy was so much moonshine, and that his coming had been deliberate and planned.

She felt suddenly hot. She did not look at him again. She attended to business.

But she could not ignore him when he came and stood beside her for a moment.

"Thanks—so much. Sorry you have such a shocking person on your shelves."

Their eyes met. He smiled, put on his broad-brimmed hat, and left her wondering. He perplexed her.

II

Mrs. Burt had been playing the piano. She had ceased playing, and was sitting on the music-stool with that air of abstraction which her husband knew so well. Probably, no one else knew it. Burt called it her "Fourth dimensional look," but his teasing was gentle, and concealed a quiet seriousness, for when she sat like that, as though listening to the shivering of ghostly violins, he felt her strange feyness. She was a rather remarkable little person, with a face like a flower, two very large and expressive grey-black eyes, and copper-coloured hair that was just beginning to go grey. Her face was unlined. She could sit very still like a bird on a bough, listening and looking.

It was Sunday and it was raining, and when it rained in Tindaro the sky let down a grey curtain. Stella Burt's eyes looked at the rain as though she both saw it and did not see it. Two cypresses bent their tops with the wind. A shutter creaked.

Stella Burt rose suddenly from the music-stool. She went out into the hall, and crossing it, opened the door of her husband's consulting-room. Beyond it lay his den where he kept his treasures, those cases of antiques dug from the classic soil, pottery and glass and odd bits of marble, and rusted iron, and beads and implements of bronze, coins, figurines, tesseræ, bones. The inner door was open, and Stella Burt could see her husband's broad back and solid black head. He was sitting at his desk with pieces of pottery spread out before him. It was one of those secret, joyful occasions when he contrived to be shut up with all that dead past.

Stella Burt stood and looked at him. She loved him very dearly; she had every right to love him so. He had given up so much for her sake, a career, children. He had exiled himself in order that she might live. They were very happy together, happy as very few people are happy.

"Jack."

She spoke very softly.

"Hallo."

"Nearly four o'clock. Do you think the girl will come?"

Burt looked out of his window at the rain.

"She's not the sort to mind that. You've seen her."

Stella Burt moved up behind her husband's chair. She saw the pieces of red Samian vase laid out on a sheet of white paper. Her eyes looked very black. Her right hand came to rest on Burt's shoulders.

"Do you remember that day like this just about three years ago?"

"Rain?"

"And something else. It's been haunting me."

Burt drew her on to the arm of his chair.

"Poor little Molly Blake?"

"Yes."

Assuredly he remembered that wet and windy day. Would he ever forget it, and that broken body at the foot of a cliff, its poor face all blood and earth.

"A bad business."

She held the lapels of his coat, and he felt her arms quiver.

"I always felt, Jack—that we ought to have stopped it, but we didn't. Sometimes it haunts me. And that man is still here."

c

"Slade?"

"Well—it was Slade. I had a feeling about that."

"Perhaps Slade has, too."

"Do you think so? I don't. He always makes me think of those little clever boys with no moral sense who pull the wings off butterflies and torture cats—just to see how the thing looks."

Burt placed a big hand over one of hers.

"Well, perhaps. One strikes that sort of man, occasionally, a kind of super-monkey, damned clever, but with no social feeling. A mocker. But what's troubling you?"

"Molly Blake."

"My dear!"

"I've felt her—sometimes—in Tindaro."

"You are too sensitive."

"I can't help it, Jack. It's the way I am made. And I feel all those other people, poor wretches, and then I see Slade with that little stick of his like the keeper of a menagerie poking up the animals in their cages."

"He lends them money, or gives it."

She was looking at the rain, and her eyes were wide.

"Molly Blake. And this other girl."

"I don't think you need worry. She's not that kind."

"I feel I ought to tell her."

"I shouldn't. She doesn't belong to the Café Ceres ménage."

"Are you sure?"

"Well, judge for yourself. I bet you she'll trudge up through this rain. Hardy."

"Yes, English. You are always quoting race, Jack. It is a superstition of yours."

"Not quite a superstition. Breed—white. I happen to know that Billy sends money home to her mother. And by English I mean that mass of decent people with habits of honesty and truth-telling and kindness. It's bed-rock."

"But it's human."

"Quite. But not human as a Greek, or a Gyppie, or a nigger is human. And there's the bell."

His wife slipped off the arm of his chair, and looked at him rather like a bird, and then she kissed him just above the left eyebrow.

"You dear solid thing. I hope the child's not dreadfully wet."

Certainly Billy was wet, but her wetness was superficial. Her umbrella had to be left outside in the loggia, and her rose-coloured mackintosh hung up in the vestibule, where it dripped on the tiled floor. She smiled. She looked at Stella Burt with the air of a sturdy, comely child whose inclination is towards the instant kissing of certain chosen people. "I want to kiss the pretty lady."

Burt stood regarding them both with eyes so strangely kind in that fierce and ugly face.

"Well, why not?"

And Billy did it, and Stella Burt blushed.

"I'm glad you had the courage to come."

"Oh, I wanted to."

"What better reason!"

Burt's boar's tusks were amused and benignant.

They went in to tea, and there were scones and English jam, and Billy gave a shake of the head as though the rain and the wind were still in her hair.

"I do think it's great of you to ask me up here, and by myself, too."

She had counted the cups. She sat down by Stella. She looked at Stella Burt with a kind of fascinated frankness, and Burt was amused. These young things, the wholesome ones, always fell to his wife, and he would stand by and observe the devotion. A very proper position for a married man who did not resent the maleness of him being left very much in the shade. He enjoyed the humanities. He had no children, but sometimes when he came into contact with some of the modern young women, rude, sour, red-lipped, insufferably casual, he did not regret the absence of children. He looked at his wife and was glad.

After tea he lit a pipe, and left them alone together for half an hour, and when he returned Stella was telling Billy's hand, and their heads were very close together.

Billy looked up at the doctor.

"O, she's wonderful.   It's really extraordinary."
Burt agreed.
"Yes, she is rather wonderful."

III

Billy took her job so seriously that it stayed with her every
morning from a quarter to nine till twelve.   She began by being
busy in the kitchen and tearoom, issuing the days stores and
inspecting the spoons and the china, and making sure that glass
and dishcloths were sweet and clean.   Then there were the
flowers to arrange in the tearoom vases, for the Italian women
had not the flower touch, and would cram a clump of blossoms
like a wad of coloured wool into a pot that contained no water.
At five minutes to nine either Billy or Julia Lord had unlocked
the library, and whisked about with a feather duster, and run
a soft broom over the tiled floor.   Miss Lord dealt with the
flowers that were for sale.   She possessed her own small nursery,
and every morning at nine an old fellow with a bald head the
size of a pumpkin and trousers of a heavenly blueness would
arrive with a huge basket.

But Julia Lord had some understanding of Billy's youth, and
of the urge such youthfulness has to be out of doors, and often
at half-past eleven when the library had emptied itself, she would
send Billy out.

"I can manage now.   Go for a run."

Not that Billy ran; no one ran in Tindaro.   But she would
set out to explore the many winding lanes and paths that slid
downwards to the blue of the sea, or climbed towards the more
sombre colours of the hills, and Billy came to know that there
was a Tindaro other than the Tindaro of the Hotel Elyseo, and
of the Tennis Club and of the English Tea Rooms.   The red-
carpeted, white-walled corridors of Miss Lord's establishment
were points of light apparent upon a darker surface.   There
was the Tindaro which the ordinary visitor did not see, for the
well-washed world kept to the Corso and the neighbouring
streets, and did not penetrate into native alleys.   Billy, in her
explorations, discovered other matters.   There were smells;
there were indescribable messes.   Following some fascinating

path you would arrive suddenly upon a heap of garbage. Certain precautions were necessary, for in some of these alleys the housewives of Tindaro still slung their slops out of upper windows. Tindaro was casual as to rubbish. A few old men with barrows and brooms did tidy up the Corso, but elsewhere empty tins, cabbage stalks, derelict boots, rags, discarded bedding, broken crockery, bottles, dead dogs, were shot over walls and into odd and convenient corners.

Billy grew wise. Certain vicolos were to be avoided, for most obviously Tindaro had its own methods. It was southern, and casual. It appeared to regard sanitation as the product of the Americans and the English, busybodies with hypersensitive noses. It had to respect in places the fastidious nostrils of the forestieri, but it cared not a jot for Doulton, and baths, and rubbish destructors, and drain-traps. It preferred sitting in the sun and indulging in ecstasies of scratching to the serious business of exterminating pulex vulgaris.

Such was back street Tindaro, like a handsome slut careless about changing her linen. It adored children and did not wash them; it could be incredibly callous to its beasts: its morals were vague. Occasionally it fought with knives. But Billy, having no mission for the cleansing of Tindaro, passed swiftly down to the sea or up to the hills. There was a delicious little blue bay with rocks running into the sea, and pockets of yellow sand, and she would sit on the sand with her knees drawn up, and bask, and listen to the little chattering waves. Or she would climb up into the maquis, and watch the first yellow butterfly afloat.

For in the main, Tindaro was beauty, though occasionally frowzy and smelling of garlic. The Hotel Elyseo was a shining white temple of hygiene. The Tennis Club exhorted you to exercise. Also, there was the Café Ceres with its odd people and its mandolins and its smeary cakes and its flies. Sitting in the maquis Billy would question the Café Ceres and its humanities.

And Slade! He was a rather attractive person. He perplexed her. She was continuing to wonder why he consorted with those human oddments. Poor devils like Frevick. She was sorry for Frevick, but he had a dog. And the Shone woman with her cropped head, and her mouth, and her straddling legs!

Billy had a feeling that she would like to explore those people. She did not shrink from them as Winnie Haycroft did.

Walking up the Corso at a quarter to twelve one morning, and thinking of something else, she was suddenly confronted with the Café Ceres and its little crowd. Slade was there at his usual table, well to the front, with Frevick brooding over something in a glass. The Shone woman was listening to old Ponsonby. Mirleess sat blue-eyed, glaring at everything and nothing. It was like a stage set with people, and Billy suddenly and vividly aware of it, felt it becoming a setting that was personal.

She met Slade's eyes. He was on his feet. That big, black hat of his was raised.

"Good morning. Come and join those—who sit and stare."

In an instant she was involved. She was being introduced to the Shone woman, who smiled like a bronze boy. "Pleased to know you. Say, sit right down here." Old Ponsonby, grinning under the shadow of his hat, was removed to another chair. Frevick was standing, looking at her with a kind of sombre doubtfulness, as though she did not belong.

Slade had the air of an ironic, glib showman.

"Well, here we are, the people who sit and stare. How are books to-day, Miss Brown?"

She looked at him with her young dignity.

"Much as usual."

A glass was set before her. The Shone woman had made signs and grimaces to the little fat waiter.

"Say, my dear, what will you take?"

"O, nothing, thank you," said Billy.

"But, my dear, you must."

"Well, an orangeade."

Slade slapped a leg with his little stick.

"Splendid! An orangeade. I'll have one, too."

Frevick looked hard at him. Frevick could hate.

CHAPTER VII

I

BILLY heard a voice outside her door.

"Say, Miss Brown, are you inside?"

Billy sat up straight in her chair. She was engaged in writing one of those weekly letters to her mother, with the open window showing the sunset over Tindaro, turning the brown roofs the colour of old copper lustre, and the sea to amethyst. The sky was strange with a rising moon, so that night and day seemed to mingle, and on the sea were pale patches of moonlight.

Billy had a moment of swift self-questioning. The Shone woman! And how had she managed to sneak so silently up the stone stairs? She temporized; she could not make up her mind.

"Who is it?"

But the door opened. "My dear, it's Sadie." There was the gleam of a cerise jumper above a white skirt, and very thin white legs that ended in white canvas shoes. The shoes explained the almost surreptitious advent. Billy sat staring.

"O, come in."

What a chalked face the woman had, and a mouth like a red crayon! And she swaggered. She gave you a sense of perpetual motion; even when seated in a chair she kept rolling from side to side, and jerking her chin and shoulders this way and that. Her large, flat face was curiously mobile. She was always laughing, exclaiming, tossing her head with an animation that was self-conscious and defiant.

"Say—I'm disturbing you.—But, my dear—your room is perfectly lovely. I felt after yesterday that I must get to know you right now."

Billy smiled at her—but watchfully so.

"Do sit down. I'm just writing home."

"Now isn't that sweet.   Mind if I smoke?"

"Please do."

"Have one."

Mrs. Shone flashed a gold cigarette-case at her.

"I-talian—but not so dusty.   Just look at my fingers.   But, my dear, that's life."

Her fingers were yellow, the nails left very long, cut to a point, and tinted red.   She opened her big mouth at Billy and laughed, though there was nothing to laugh at.   She subsided into a basket-chair; she had a way of throwing herself into chairs; she spread her legs; from the neck upwards she had the appearance of a bold and disillusioned boy.

The unexpectedness of Mrs. Shone and the vehemence of her attack had all the qualities of an invasion, and Billy covered up her unfinished letter with a piece of blotting-paper and a book, and became brightly alert.   She felt herself very much in the presence of a person who appeared in your nursery like an overblown and excited aunt, and snatched you up from the floor where some interesting game was in progress.   "My dear, aren't you just terribly lonely here?"   Billy sat like a child, allowing her awareness of Mrs. Shone to sort out its impressions.   Why this thusness, this sudden, loud air of friendliness, this assumption of noisy intimacy?   Gold cigarette-case, and gold in the animated teeth, and legs spread at their ease, and eyes that looked at you as though they saw you naked and unashamed!   Mrs. Shone drove people into corners. The noise and the flurry of her were a little bewildering.

Billy put up her defences.   Very rarely did she go to earth behind barbed wire and sandbags; entrenched she looked forth at this woman who had arrived like a raid.

"Oh—I'm pretty busy, you know."

What did you say to a woman like Mrs. Shone?   She seemed to flop down on you out of another world, a world of cropped heads, and loud nudities, and lip-stick and little drinks, and two o'clock in the morning frenzies.   Possibly she was kind?   Possibly she obeyed natural impulses?   There was so much surface, undulations in movement, and Billy's notions of life were that of a rectangle, or of a figure all square.

Mrs. Shone gazed at her.   Here was something fresh and
vigorous, and young, a sleek spathe, growth that was not overblown, and in Tindaro things were stale, like the cakes in the
window of the Café Ceres.   This tragedy of staleness, of life
sucked and thrown away, of physical excitements repeated and
repeated until both spirit and flesh were flaccid!   Over-
emphasis became a scream.   The shadowy Sadie Shone, trailing behind that noisy, mouthing sensationalist, would open a
shadowy mouth—"O, my god, I'm bored!   Do something;
do anything.   Shout, scream, hunch.   Let's be gay."

The shadow woman in Mrs. Shone gazed upon Billy.   She
thought "O, my dear, you're just like a bit of England in May,
so green and fresh and cold.   My god, to be green again!"

She drawled.   She had a knack of squinting when her voice
became a drawl.

"I guess you're feeling rather raw here.   No?   Well, you
young things make me wonder."

"Do we?   Why?"

Sitting sideways in her chair, her arms crossed on the back
of it, Billy had her share of wonder.   What was Mrs. Shone?
What did she mean, and intend, and signify?   Why was she
sitting in that chair?   Why was she—Billy—feeling so inarticulate and chilly, and perplexed?

"You're so terribly cute.   And you're so terribly hard."

Hard?   Billy's head gave a little lift.

"But how do you mean?"

She was aware of Mrs. Shone laughing.

"O, my dear, what a question!   Isn't that quaint?   Why,
—I might sit here and talk to you for hours and you wouldn't
get my meaning."

Billy was exploring the spaces behind that absurd laughter.
What a funny conversation!   What were they at?

"Perhaps I shouldn't."

"Not more than a nice little college girl——   There, that's
set you on your dignity—I guess."

They observed each other through a little haze of cigarette
smoke, and Billy saw Sadie Shone as a large white face haggardly
vivacious and perplexing.   She remembered Winnie Haycroft's

C*

protest—"O, that awful woman!" And what was an awful woman, and just how was Mrs. Shone awful to Winnie Haycroft? Vicious, demoralized, vulgar, noisy? But people were so queer. Directly you began to catalogue them, you divined qualities that eluded you. There were two people, three people, where you had seen one. There were shadowy selves, shadow after shadow, eyes behind eyes.

She said, "Dignity's a bit out of date, isn't it?"

Mrs. Shone blew smoke.

"How? You're lovely to talk to."

"Aren't we supposed to be more natural."

She was not conscious of having said anything funny, but Mrs. Shone's eyes brimmed over.

"Natural! That's about the loveliest word—— Well, perhaps like a nice little healthy tummy that can take things green and put them away. Why, my dear, life's indigestion, chronic. But what am I talking about? I thought you must be a bit side-tracked in this god-fearing library. You think me queer. Most things seem queer to you English. I'm friendly —that's all."

Billy smiled.

"It's kind of you. I'm not so queer as all that."

"Sure, you're not. You come along to one of our little dances some evening. Once a week at the Ceres. Real Tindaro. I don't suppose you'd had one eye in real Tindaro."

"I don't quite know. I'm kept pretty busy."

"You are that. Literature and buns for the English. You come and dine with me at the Florio one night. Like dancing?"

"Of course."

"English style. I'll introduce you to one or two dagos who dance like—dagos. That's what you call 'em, isn't it? Dagos. What's wrong with a man being south? Besides, on a dance floor.—Well, you'll come?"

Billy sat as though posing for a photograph.

"Some night—perhaps. I'd like to. May I let you know?"

"Sure. No one misses anybody on the Corso. I'm right there—at the Ceres. You can get a close up of me—any day."

Billy nodded.

"Yes, of course I can."

II

The sunset had quenched itself, and the little lights of Tindaro were pricking the darkness, and in Tindaro night was cubist. The roundness of the day had ceased. The angles of the houses jutted out, and triangles of light interlocked themselves with triangles of shadow. Or there were beams of light that slashed like swords, and the darkness whimpered, yet was patient. In the lighted cubes of the barbers' shops little figures were shaving other figures; Tindaro was shaved at night to the shadowy movement of an arm. Most windows were dark, but the little jewelry and trinket shops flashed their tawdriness.

Mrs. Shone, emerging upon the Corso, gave a wriggle of the shoulders. Well, that was that! When you felt about to hate a person it meant that you were afraid. But hatred? No, not quite that. Such a very clean young person, and so apparently sure of herself and her place in the world, and with feet from which the stockings could be peeled without hesitation. Mrs. Shone wriggled her shoulders. A part of her tingled. Another part of her felt in tears.

Slade had said, "Sadie, that girl must be damned dull. Go and dig her out." And she had screwed up her face at him, not to protest, but because she was guilty of being rather helpless. "I'm darned if I will." But she had gone. Man, when sexually inclined, was such a solicitous humbug, but Slade had not solicited her so virtuously. He had no virtue but that of doing what he pleased, and of being able to pay for it in cash, if not in character. He had given her one of his ironical, oblique smiles, like a whip displayed. He held the whip of Circe.

She was feeling furious with Slade, while knowing herself to be snarling behind bars. Frevick would have understood her fury. The faces which you long to smite are the faces that are so immune, polished, successfully insolent, casual. Slade amused himself. He said to life, "Something new, you hag; something new."

She heard the tinkling of a mandolin. The awning was down over the white-topped tables. Lights tinkled like the mandolin. The fat waiter, wearing a white apron, and standing in the shadow, looked cut in half. She saw Slade at his table, all long legs and big hat. At another table some way off Dashkoff the Russian, fresh from circulating heavy cash at the Elyseo thé dansante, sat bored and sullen. What a devil's business it was being hard up.

Some things made you feel sick in the stomach. What of it? The only remedy for the "found outs" was another drink. She was aware of Slade's head cocked at her with ironic expectancy; his teeth showed as a white line; a streak of light touched his blue linen collar.

She sat down.

"Wall—my buddy."

She drawled. Her face looked old, a crumple of lines and of shadows. Her eyes had a dead malevolence.

Slade beckoned to the waiter.

"One brandy—neat, Tommaso."

He was cheerful. He crossed one long leg over the other.

"You look tired, my dear."

She flashed out at him.

"O, go to hell. Tired! Why not? O, go to hell."

His air of amusement was like cold water dashed in her large and haggard face. She opened a bag, and brought out lip-stick and powder-puff and a mirror, but Slade noticed that she did not use the mirror.

She began to talk.

"Fresh as a raw onion. You men are like the legion of swine, only you don't go over the cliff. It's the women who do that. I wonder why we're such god damn fools. I wonder why anything is is. Anything. It's just a yell. Yes, she'll think about it. She's quite a nice child, my dear, and just as white as a bit of codfish. This darned town's got me sick to-night."

The brandy arrived in a little glass on a saucer. She sat and stared at it. She became suddenly and murderously silent. Her face seemed all shadow. She was aware of Slade as the showman, and of what he would say to her if she raged, and of just how he would say it, smoothly, casually, remorselessly. He had the tongue of a clever, callous boy.

There had been other occasions when their respective philosophies had struggled breast to breast. She knew his code. It was wholly his own, removed from the little, fenced enclosures of other men, open country where you hunted as you pleased. He would say, "No one asked me, when I was born, to subscribe to the social compact. I haven't subscribed to it yet. I refuse to be one of a crowd. I don't belong to the universal trade union. I'm an intelligent blackleg. I choose to make my own laws. Society is compromise: 'Don't knife me and I won't knife you. Leave my wife alone and I'll keep my hands off yours.' Compromise, and a sort of cowardice. If you set out to be completely yourself you are anti-social, unmoral. Morality is the code of the crowd. Most men want to be immoral and daren't, or put on sandshoes to sneak round the corner. As for your people you are the fools who have been found out. That's the only sin, the great blasphemy. Belong to the crowd—if you like—but don't get found out. If you refuse to belong to the crowd—you are a society of one. That's the only society fit for an artist and a man of the world."

She sipped her brandy.

She could remember one sultry night, when, after moments of unforgettable intimacy, he had gone and sat at the window, and talked. He had said that life was just behaviour. You lived by behaving, yes, even in those most passionate occasions. Human behaviour was just like the behaviour of a tiger or an ant; you got to know both man and ant by observing them in every sort of situation. But human behaviour was becoming standardized, more machine-like, because modern man worshipped the machine. But if you refused to bow down to the machine, and preferred the symbolism of the winging bird, your behaviour became once more a beautiful, live, and mobile vitalism. There was no shame in behaving like a bird, or like a man who scorned the stupidity of a mechanistic morality. Society put the appropriate penny in the slot, and you produced the proper ticket, but instead of pushing a ticket into society's hand the free man should toss into that servile palm a snail, or a piece of phosphorous, or a flower, it did not matter much which. The important thing was to produce anything but the conventional ticket.

And suddenly and in spite of the brandy she felt tired, hopelessly and unresistingly tired. Her whole body was flaccid. She looked at his lean, brown face, and realized the incorrigible and lustful egotism of him. He exhausted people, just as a persistent and very strong and self-assertive child exhausts the will of its parents

"Oscar, I'm as sick of you to-night as I am of this darned town."

She saw the white line of his teeth.

"That's it. When you feel like a protest—the thing is to go to bed."

She made a rolling movement in her chair. She rose with an air of slackness. Her mouth drooped open.

"That's an idea. That's where your scheme of behaviour comes to an end."

"Not if you snore."

"O, you're hellish clever, aren't you. I'm going."

III

Slade sat on. He had watched Dashkoff get up and follow Sadie Shone. Well, that was as it should be. The discredited shadows of such social vagrants merged beyond the dim edge of society's little artificial glare. The Corso itself was like a piece of life sedulously pretending to be civilized, while on each side of it were little pits of naturalism, surreptitious holes in the social scheme. It was all very amusing. But the Corso looked rather pretty with its scattered lights; it wore the skin of a snake and some of the scales glittered. There was one green light burning in the distance over the doorway of some shop. An emerald on the forehead of the Green Goddess.

But Slade drew in his long legs. Life was on the move, but not as native Tindaro moved. The swing of the skirt was so English. He got up to intercept youth. He stood with his hat in his hand.

"Clairvoyance.   I was just wondering whether I would say something to you."

She paused, and stood with an air of aloofness.

"O?"

"Cheek of me—perhaps.   But I won't keep you standing. If you are walking——"

"I'm going to Miss Lord's."

"Then may I come as far as the St. George?"

"I suppose you may."

"Thank you.   And I'm going to be impertinent.   If you disapprove—say so, afterwards."

Billy moved on, and he walked beside her.   He looked down into her face.

"You are rather new here.   Excuse me saying that.   I'm not; I'm a regular old ruffian.   Mrs. Shone came along to the Ceres half an hour ago.   She happened to say that she had asked you to come to one of the Ceres dances."

He waited, and her silence was poised and hovering.

"I shouldn't if I were you."

"O."

"Not the sort of place, nor the people.   Not for you.   Now, if you think I ought to be kicked——"

They passed a lighted window, and against it he saw her grave young dignity marching beside him.   Her eyes looked straight ahead.

"Thanks, Mr. Slade.   But I'm fairly sound."

"Absolutely.   But that's just it.   One may have a prejudice against seeing sound fruit in that sort of basket.   I can't help that prejudice."

He was aware of her eyes resting obliquely upon him for a moment.

"But you?"

"I?"

"You are a good deal in that basket."

He gave a little laugh.

"Is that an accusation.   But I'm a vagabond; I write books; I see life.   Besides—I'm rather sorry for those poor devils."

Again her glance lay quickly upon him.

"Are they poor devils?"

"Deplorably so. People who have been found out. Now, I'm a bit prejudiced in favour of lame dogs. There are plenty of the people who come to your library who have no more right to spit upon——these—— O, well, the Hotel Elyseo is full of people who haven't been found out. That's about all the difference there is to it."

Her voice was more friendly.

"You think so. But why shouldn't I be sorry?"

"Sorry? O, be as sorry as you please. But don't get mixed up. It can't be done. No, I'm not a humbug. You see, a tough buccaneer like me—doesn't matter. I don't care a damn for the conventions. I'm outside them. But you're not. Well—that's my impertinence."

He looked ironic. He appeared casual and amused, and he himself was the joke.

"Am I supposed to be kicked?"

She was looking straight ahead.

"I don't think so."

"Splendid! That's really very decent of you. I'm quite ready to be on the side of that poor derelict crowd against the whole Hotel Elyseo. And against the Pipp woman—and the Sudbury Smiths and all that they stand for. But then—you are different, a little bit of England all by itself. Explicit. I think I leave you here."

He stood back. It was a gesture.

"Good night."

She put out a sudden hand.

"Good night. I think I'm rather grateful to you."

"O—that's all right."

He held her firm, cool fingers for a moment.

"It's such a dashed stupid, jabbering world. Well—you understand. That's splendid. Good night."

CHAPTER VIII

I

SOMEONE spoke of the Spring. Possibly it was Miss Lord, who, for twenty years, had not seen an English Spring, and yearned for it with a strange and secret yearning.

"It is very beautiful here, but no birds sing."

Strange restlessness, like the stirring of the urge that sends the birds to mate and nest in the green, cold north. To fly with the swallows. Miss Lord, thinking of April in her morning bath, was one of many who felt the qualms of that mute unrest. In Tindaro it might be January, with the sun climbing higher and the sea growing more blue, and the fruit buds swelling and a rank greenness spreading in the gardens, but the thrill of the turning year was translated into English.

Dr. Burt's thoughts went to that country with its vast sky, and great green meadows and thorn hedges, and the towers of Ely, and Kingsley's "Hereward the Wake." His people had farmed in the Fens. Stella's dreams were Cornish; she heard the gulls about Mullion's Cove, and saw the blown orchards, and the stone walls beginning to purple with foxgloves. Sir Dyce Duxbury had a longing for the plane trees in the Carlton Terrace gardens and a seat near the Serpentine. Mirlees even had his urge towards England, Leicester Square on a warm spring night and women and a back bedroom somewhere. As for Frevick an unutterable melancholy overcame him. He thirsted. He thought of the valley of the Test, and the chalk hills above Shere, and Glastonbury, and the Thames at Marlow. The Haycrofts, aunt and niece, seemed to grow a little more dusty and yellow and tired about the eyes. They talked of Cromer and Filey.

Exiles. And they would look with a secret envy at those more fortunate people, the residents at the hotels, who would be going home. A kind of glamour attached itself to the dullest of women who symbolized Bexhill and Bournemouth, Ladbroke Grove, Sloane Square, and the Brompton Road. Tindaro, basking and beautiful, seemed to hatch these instinctive discontents.

As though to console themselves they would speak derisively of the English Spring.

"Three daffodils, my dear, blown flat, and a little green shiver on the hedges."

"Yes, just a raw illusion."

"And those east winds. They always used to give me a bilious attack."

Mirleess, who was subject to sudden rages, would get up from his chair outside the Café Ceres, and with staring blue eyes, curse as he had cursed in the War.

"I'm sick of this blasted place. What! My god, it's like a fried fish shop. I'd like to take a girl down to Maidenhead. What price the Monico or the Café Royal? O, hell——"

Frevick would look up at him with large and sombre eyes. He liked Mirleess for his rages and his cursings. They expressed all that which he had no guts left in him to express.

"Come round to my place and have a drink."

They would go off together and sit in Frevick's dirty studio, and drink with furious, dark gravity.

"O, god damn this blasted place."

"That swine Slade loves it."

"He would. He likes his women greasy. I say—why shouldn't we try Canada, or the U.S.A."

"No good—the U.S.A."

"Not a bit of it. By god—not bad fun being a blasted bootlegger. I'd like to shoot again, shoot men. Ever thrown a Mills grenade in a man's face, Frevick, and seen a red mess that was just like nothing?"

"No."

"By god, I wish the blasted war was on again. There was a little French girl I knew at Amiens. She——"

Truly was it said that Oscar Slade did not hanker for the English Spring. "O, to be in England——" Browning had

been a hairy and ponderous animal. But Tindaro was spiced.
When the almond and the peach were out, and the vines began
to hang up pagan garlands, the world was a very pleasant and
sensuous place. Old Pan played in the midnight of the pines.
You could turn on a fountain and listen to its splashing, and
feel sleek and drowsy and ready for life's delicacies. Slade
liked the heat. It suited his brown body and his brain. He
wrote well behind half-closed shutters, with a shadowy room
behind him, and the strong scent of flowers drifting. He liked
the Italians; they understood the heat of sun and body. They
did not wear frozen shirts. And those little swarthy girls
with plump hips and bosoms like pillows! And the starlight
nights, and the strange, sullen fierceness of Lotta. If the
day was a fiery chariot, the night was a ship of stars.

Nor did Billy miss the English Spring. At Ealing she had
associated it with two depressed looking sycamores coming into
leaf, half a dozen daffodils, and some clumps of arabis and pale
mauve aubretia. Yes, and privet hedges, and the next door
cat that would sit under a flowering currant and watch for
sparrows. Certainly she missed the birds in the early morning,
for even in Ealing back-gardens blackbirds sang, and in spite
of the beastly little boys with catapults and air-guns.

But waking at Tindaro was a pleasant business, an affair of
open windows and scattered sunlight. Billy would hurry out
of bed and take her cold sponge, and remove to the sitting-
room to dress, for this window looked south and was full of the
blueness of the day. Distances were dewy and diaphanous.
Two cypresses stood like gnomons, marking the hours. Below
her window lay the teashop garden beginning to look like a
piece of enamel. A flurry of green growth was in the air.
Red tulips stood erect.

A little narrow path wound between high walls at the end
of the garden, linking up two vicolos. It was used but little,
but every morning about the time when Billy was dressing
some old fellow would pass along it, playing upon the pipe.
He would pause for a minute or two at the door in the wall,
and send up his plaintive pipings. He appeared to play the
same tune, and it became associated in Billy's consciousness

with the blue distances and the incipient floweriness of the world. Every morning she would find herself waiting and listening.

Laughingly she called him "My Tindaro blackbird."

She wondered about him. Was he old or young, and did he come that way to let Maria and Vanna know that the Spring was here. She learnt to whistle the tune.

She whistled it one evening to Oscar Slade when he came to join her amid the ruined red brick walls and broken pillars of the Roman theatre.

"It goes like this."

Slade, sitting on the grass beside her, watched her and listened.

"O, that tune. I don't think they have any names. I gave it one."

"O—what?"

"'The Lament for Adonis.' It belongs to the Spring."

"But Adonis was Greek."

"Asia Minor. Anywhere on the middle sea. As much now as yesterday. The good old padres probably rechristened it 'Salute to the Holy Infant.' Much the same thing."

She smiled vaguely and looked at the sea.

"It haunts me. It makes me feel—like the beginnings of a Wagner opera."

"Not quite so mystical, and yet more so. Adonis still has his Festa here."

"Really?"

"They don't call it that. They call it the Festa of San Soforio. The shepherds, and the goatherds and the peasants come down, and there is a bonfire in the piazza. It means that Spring has come."

"When is it?"

He answered almost casually, "O, next week."

II

Tindaro's most manifest bore was Walter Sudbury Smith. He had hobbies, and he carried them about with him like bad cigars and forced them upon people. He had a room at the top of his glaring white villa in which he kept his wireless apparatus, and his telescopes, and his stamp-albums, a sort of high tower into which he lured the unsuspecting and smothered them with words. Tindaro had grown very shy of Mr. Sudbury Smith, and when he was seen upon the Corso, the people who knew him became interested in shop windows or sought diverticula. His victims came mostly from the hotels, innocents abroad. He appeared so genial. His sharp, red face with its eyes like pale blue glass poked itself intimately into other faces.

"Yes, I got Moscow last night—Bobevitch speaking. And after that—Baldwin—clear as you and I. You must come up to my den."

A den it was, and one of disastrous discords. Walter Sudbury Smith would collect people in chairs, and seat himself in front of his wireless cabinet, and fiddle with it, and let out sudden blaring voices and stutterings and clicks and whistles. "That's Germany. Cologne. Confound that fellow at Genoa. Now—I'll try and get Timbuctoo. Atmospheric conditions bad to-night." He had a raucous voice of his own, and he talked all the time, and fiddled with the apparatus, and fixed the faces of the listeners with his glassy eyes. The sounds he produced suggested the interior of a madhouse with half a dozen wild men trying to orate in chorus. There would be snatches of dance music, the crashings of an orchestra, an operatic voice—very nasal and lonely. But Mr. Sudbury Smith did not approve of continuity; he was always cutting people off, and jamming in plugs and pulling them out again. He was supposed to be very musical.

Also he possessed a telescope. A flat and insensitive blue eye fixed Venus or Mars. He had his little joke.

"You must come up and look at the Man in the Moon, but I'm not sure it isn't a Lady."

He had very white and very artificial teeth, and the kind of smile that seems to associate itself with such dentures, a smile that was perpetual. Someone had said, "I suppose the old fool puts that smile into the tooth-glass with his teeth."

Sudbury's upper room was not unlike a white conning-tower

perched on the top of his villa.   It had four windows.   He
was fussy and inquisitive, and he would amuse himself up there
with his telescope, turning it upon the various parts of Tindaro,
for his villa stood high.   He could spot the tennis courts and
who was playing on them, and the seats and chairs in front of
the Elyseo, and a part of the Corso, and the coast, and the
little blue bay where people bathed.   He was a sort of senile
Peeping Tom.   Again someone had said, and possibly it
was Slade, that "Old S.S. could see everything in Tindaro
except Miss Lord in her bath."   His smirk was genial.   He
was the inveterate Quid Nunc.   And he was afraid of his
wife.

About eleven forty-five one morning the eye of S.S.'s telescope
found the bay where people bathed when the sea grew warm.
It was a blue half-moon clasped by two jutting horns of rock.
The sand was very yellow.   A precipitous island stood farther
out to sea.

S.S. discovered two figures seated on the sand.   They were
very recognizable.   Almost he could study their facial
expressions.

But it was a discovery.   Slade and the new girl at the
library.   They were sitting about two feet apart, knees drawn
up, arms clasped over them.   They had an air of intimate
detachment.   They seemed to be staring steadily at the sea.
Obviously they were talking.

S.S. got a chair and a cushion and sat down.   This was
worth watching.   It was more intriguing than the moon.
It was a double star, and human and surprising at that.

The two figures struck him as being in a very serious posture.
He would have said that they were discussing some subject that
was personal and absorbing, but discussing it at a little distance.
The girl sat very still; she had taken off her hat.   She did not
look at Slade, but S.S. saw Slade looking at her.   He appeared
to be watching her to see the effect of his words.

Slade began to pick up stones and throw them into the sea.
His action was desultory, casual.   Presently he stretched himself and lay on his side, elbow crooked, his head resting on his
hand.   He was drawing patterns on the sand.   Now and

again he would look up quickly at the girl. S.S. caught him smiling.

The girl sat very still. She was both attentive and aloof, listening, considering. Once or twice she gave a little toss of the head. Her arms remained wrapped about her knees.

S.S.'s smile was sly and amused.

He saw the girl move. She glanced at a wrist watch. She put on her hat and rose, and stood a moment. She did not look at Slade, who remained stretched there observing her ankles. And suddenly she walked away out of the picture, but Slade remained with his brown face and his blue collar. He did not move. He appeared to be reflecting.

III

For, on so blue a day, with the little island of the Triton looking no more solid than the air and water in which it seemed to float, the earth renewed itself. Or rather it had vanished in the night, and reappeared as an astral body, ethereal, vapoury, a painted cloud. Time had lapsed. The sea, stroking the sand with little, rippling waves, hid other mysteries. Over yonder on the blue rocks Tritons blew their shells. Neptune would come foaming behind a team of sea-horses. The age of reason had lapsed.

Slade felt the sand warm.

"Ye gods, what a day!"

Billy sat and gazed. Somehow she had a feeling of being in another world, in a present that had slipped back into a legendary but intensely real past. The Golden Age.

"O, to be in England now that January is here."

She said softly, "Don't mock."

That had set him off, touched off the powder in him, for her air of sunny solemnity was exquisite and virginal. Ealing became pagan, and was not realizing the transformation, a white figure on golden sands on the edge of the blueness. A nereid snatched from Tooting. He had to talk, to splash in the new atmosphere like some brown Greek boy playing in the sea.

"Am I mocking? The gods forbid. We are back in reality, the reality of the world before history was written.

History, an old schoolmistress in spectacles. There was no Darwin. The sea was just sea and the sky was sky, and we did not talk of H_2O and protoplasm. London was not. Think of it. No tubes, no motor buses, no Labour Party. If one could wipe it all out."

He provoked her to responses.

"London is marvellous."

"A marvellous mess. Do you know I see it as a great gas bubble that will burst. And New York, too. Some day we'll get back to this. Apollo will fly his chariot over the Middle Sea. This was when England was all east wind and swamp. Life will come back here. Not Birmingham and Brooklands."

"But we can't help it."

"Ealing?"

"It has all happened."

"It has seemed to happen. We are just—manufacturers. Get rid of the absurd idea—of life as a sort of factory and warehouse. Let England go back to swamp and fog and sodden forests."

"But the people?"

"Put the emphasis on the the. There are just people, and the people. Old Shaw has ideas. Another Ice Age would be an excellent corrective. A vast wiping out. The enlightened few would begin all over again in the sun. We should have lost Mr. Cook, and the Inland Revenue, and Poplar, and the too many professors. We'd do what the Greeks might have done and didn't just because they became too damned political. The Carthaginians were too Iky. Rome had too square a jaw. But that fellow Mussolini has ideas. A new civilization and the Middle Sea, Minos over again and better."

She clasped her knees. She felt that the talking part of him did not matter. What did matter was this incomparable day and her feeling of mystery, and the provocation of his almost boyish playfulness. She was less perplexed. This was temperament. It was the first occasion upon which she had experienced temperament, and she found it rather fascinating. He was so incalculable and amusing and mischievous, and if he mocked at things he mocked at himself as well. His eyes were less disconcerting. They seemed to look at her in quite another way. She had become aware of moments of shyness.

But she kept her poise, her point of view.

"And what about your exiles?"

He began to toss pebbles into the sea.

"It would be a much kinder world. There would be no exiles."

"None at all?"

"Well—of course—we should have to exile most of the people who inhabit the Elyseo. The sin would be to try and strangle your neighbour with a rope of conventions. And people who would insist on trying to dress up in humbug."

She looked grave.

"What is convention?"

"Social starch. The product of the north, and smuts, and Puritanism."

"Have the Italians no conventions?"

"Plenty. I'm not talking Italian, but neo-Greek. You see, you are so full of the English idea, of smothering things, of not letting go. Life's self-expression. We seem to have forgotten that."

"Doing what you please?"

"Exactly. And that shocks you."

He turned on his side, and drew swastikas on the sand, but Billy remained gazing at the sea.

"But can one?"

"Of course, if we were all sufficiently civilized. Can't you see it? A beautiful naturalness, kindness. Not suppression. Not the dirty little boy idea, and the schoolmaster with a cane."

She said, "Yes, perhaps on a day like this, with everything like this. The whole world looks washed with light."

"Sunlight Soap!"

He was incorrigible. She protested.

"Well, take Tindaro. It isn't—the sort of town——?"

"You mean it is not English. Why not try and get outside the English superstition?"

"Perhaps I can't."

"O—yes—you can."

"Perhaps I don't want to."

He laughed.

"Now—we are near it. You like to feel in the nice conventional frock. You want your tennis shoes nicely chalked. Well—I've got beyond that. And I'm glad."

She mused.

"I wonder?"

"O, yes, I am. It helps one to be both acutely personal and also impersonal. You can go anywhere and be anything. No one can label you. You can mix with poor devils and help them."

She looked at her watch.

"But you put on fancy dress."

"You think so?"

"You pretend to mock. Is it a pose?"

"No, just cap and bells."

"And underneath——"

"Just man."

She rose from the sand.

"It's ten past twelve. Miss Lord is awfully decent. She pushes me out at half-past eleven—to exercise. Keeping fit's rather important."

He studied her ankles.

"Very."

IV

S.S. informed his wife, or rather he suggested it as a casual gleaning, the picking up of a chance shell upon the seashore. Unpremeditated. "I was trying to find the Island and watch a fellow forking for sea-urchins."

Mrs. Smith, who disliked Miss Lord, and had a penchant for planting burrs, found the suitable occasion.

"I hear that new girl of yours is associating with Oscar Slade."

Miss Lord kept her library face.

"Possibly. You'd like her to. Is that Tindaro's latest?"
Mrs. Smith twisted her lips.

"I suggest—that there have been predecessors."

Julia Lord went home and sat on the seat in her garden
where the cypresses threw two shadows. Shadows? But it
was absurd. These women had raw mouths.

But ought she to warn Billy? Meddling was the resort of
the muddlers. Billy was so sound.

CHAPTER IX

I

ON the morning of the festival of S. Soforio Billy heard Old Pan piping in the lane. She was brushing her hair at the open window, and she paused to listen. O, plaintive sound! The Lament for Adonis. But plaintiveness was not part of the morning; no English blackbird uttered tragic notes in the wet and windy greenness, while an east wind blew. This was no English day, one of those wasted days, sleety and grey, when life stands pale-faced at the window and sees love like a red tulip broken by the wind. O, those English days, dark and deplorable, when you stiffened your lips and pulled through.

The Lament for Adonis! But in England the blood of the youth would have flowed pale and cold, and Venus would have been using a handkerchief. Yes, nose—not eyes.

Billy gave her head a toss, and suddenly the piper changed his tune. The piping had an abrupt, sweet shrillness; the air danced in the sunlight; it came light-footed from the hills.

"Spring is here, Spring is here. The god lives."

Two yellow butterflies played together round one of the cypresses. They went up and up as though weaving a garland.

"Spring is here, Spring is here."

Billy looked out of the window. Her brown eyes had a sidelong tenderness. O, this adorable day, this blueness, young fruit blossom white against sable pines, sunlight on brown roofs, roses like drops of blood upon grey walls. Adonis. She felt full of a sudden joy in life, a delight in the exquisite texture of her youth.

She heard someone singing. It was dark-haired Vanna busy in the loggia with a broom. And Billy laughed, for Vanna's voice was strident and big of bosom, and yet its quality had a vibrant thrill. It was like stroking fur the wrong way, but somehow it thrilled her.

The piper passed on still playing that *gaillard* tune. It was like music passing off the stage, but leaving a bewitched silence behind it, and Billy resumed the brushing of her hair. It stood out like a nimbus; it quivered.

Someone came up the stairs, someone who was surprisingly early. There was a knock.

"Hallo. Who is it?"

"Winnie."

"Come in."

The Haycroft face hung in the shadow of the doorway like a pale pastel. The weak eyes stared; they stared at Billy. The little loose mouth hung open.

"What's the matter?"

"Matter?"

"You look——"

"Spring is here. Didn't you hear the pipes?"

Her hair brush was wielded with a kind of abandonment, and Winnie Haycroft sidled in like a streak of dust, and sat down in Billy's basket-chair, and looked as wide-eyed as a ghost. There was something disturbing in the room, a perfume of violets, the crepitation of brush and crisp bobbed hair, vibrant sunlight. The Haycroft girl seemed to twist herself back into the chair, to shrink into it. The day had too much vigour and glare.

"You're early."

Said Winnie, "I've got a headache."

"A headache!"

"And we're out of aspirin. I sat up doing accounts. It's the sun—too. I wondered——"

"I haven't got any aspirin. Sorry. But you oughtn't to have a headache to-day."

"Why not?"

"It's S. Soforio's day. A Festa. Torches and bonfires. It's going to be lovely."

Winnie Haycroft stared.

"But we never go."

"Why on earth not?"

"It's—so—noisy. And boys throw squibs. It's for the natives. And then——"

"And then?"

"There's confetti. They get so rough and familiar. They try and put it down your neck."

"What—the familiarity?"

"No, the confetti. It's not nice. People get so excited."

Billy began to laugh, but smothered the impulse and gave a last flick to her hair.

"You ought to come. Do you good. Sorry I haven't any aspirin. Look here, I'll bolt along to Julia's. She keeps a store. Had breakfast?"

"No."

"Have breakfast with me. I'll tell Vanna. I'll just shove some clothes on and do a sprint."

"I don't think I want any breakfast."

"Nonsense. Ten grains of aspirin and some hot coffee, and lie down for half an hour. Spring is here."

She whistled, and Winnie Haycroft winced. Billy was so vigorous.

Corpulent Tommaso swabbing the tables of the Café Ceres, saw the English girl go by at a run. He stood to stare, and his stare became a grin, for Billy could run like a boy, and in Tindaro no feminine thing over twelve ever emulated Atalanta. What grace, what legs! Tommaso, being an Italian, had a feeling for such realities. He squeezed out his cloth into the pail of very dirty water, and while swabbing, burst into sudden song. He was operatic. He sang with a kind of fat ferocity about love and moonlight, and beating hearts. Billy, inconsequentially English, took Miss Lord's lane at a loping trot, passing in succession an old fellow with a basket of flowers, a woman carrying a water-pot, and a small boy who carried nothing but a ragged pair of trousers and a shirt. The old fellow and the woman smiled upon Billy and wished her good morning. The boy stared with two very round black eyes.

"Why does the lady run?"

"Because the Spring is here."

Julia Lord was walking in her garden, waiting for Maria to call her in to breakfast when Billy appeared like young Aurora, flushed and just a little breathless. Miss Lord stood to gaze. There was a something in Billy that disturbed her, just as it had disturbed the pale soul of Winnie Haycroft. An elemental something, woman, sunlight, the Spring.

"My dear, what's the matter?"

Never before had Billy heard Miss Lord "my dear" anybody or anything. It seemed part of the day's delicious unexpectedness.

"O, nothing. I've been running. Winnie has a headache, and they are out of aspirin."

"That's characteristic."

"I knew you would let her have ten grains."

Miss Lord looked at Billy rather queerly.

"Of course. I'll get it. Almost I thought the safe had been burgled."

She went in and up the stairs, and her firm face was serious and a little troubled. She too had heard the Pipes of Pan, and could remember a particular morning such as this when the world had seemed to float in a golden mist. But Billy? Woman! Yet Billy had come up to fetch ten grains of aspirin for that anæmic, exiled creature Winnie Haycroft, and Miss Lord felt comforted. She opened the top, right-hand drawer of her dressing-table, found the white glass bottle, and tilted two tablets into the palm of a steady hand.

II

The setting sun dyed the whole west red, and Tindaro, when it saw it, murmured, "The blood of God."

Billy was changing her frock when she heard the women calling her. They had climbed the little wooden stairway leading to the flat roof of the house.

"Signorina, signorina—the lights. They are coming."

Billy joined Vanna and Maria on the roof. The sky was a vast and hollow bowl studded with stars, and Tindaro like a pool of dim and diffused light spreading in the darkness.

The two Italian women were leaning against the parapet, and Vanna was pointing.

"See, signorina, on the hills."

They were strangely excited; they stood close together, whispering and watching, and to Billy their dark figures appeared unsolid and mysterious. She, too, was aware of a tremor of excitement, as though these two southern women had infected her with some old pagan feeling, a troubling of the waters. The night was the mysterious black curtain of an ancient sanctuary suddenly swaying with the wind of the gods' presence. The stars trembled. Strange, old legendary things were happening.

"The lights! They are coming."

Billy looked towards the hills. Visible as dim undulations, their ridges and tops were faintly silvered, and upon one high place a fire had been lit. The blazing brushwood of this beacon burned like a great red flower with petals blown upwards towards the sky, and yet the night was very still, and those flames were mysteriously silent. There were other lights strung together like beads upon black velvet, they moved, and descending, undulating, changed colour. Some had a redness, others were pale yellow.

"Bella, bella," said the voice of one of the women.

The hillsmen were descending upon Tindaro. Shepherds, goatherds, peasants gathered from the villages, carrying lanterns and torches. Somewhere among those lights eight sturdy lads would be shouldering S. Soforio, a gilded, brocaded S. Soforio enthroned in a shrine of gold and of blue. Girls carried garlands and posies of flowers. Down the mule paths S. Soforio rocked and nodded.

Tindaro seemed strangely silent, but Tindaro was waiting for S. Soforio and for a saint older by centuries than S. Soforio. Spring was here; the men of the hills were coming, shepherds, goatherds and girls, men of the vines and olives, men who reaped the corn. Tindaro was at windows and on the housetops, or waiting in the streets. The Piazza, dark as yet, was a place of trembling and expectant shadows. The Duomo was full of hundreds of flickering candles.

Suddenly Vanna held up a hand.

"The pipes."

Distant and strange a thin wreath of sound floated towards Tindaro. It was very faint and gentle, like the piping of birds in some far wood. The notes seemed merged, but as the loops of light descended, each note pricked the silence more distinctly. The sound grew more shrill, more poignant, more disturbing. The Pipes of Pan.

One of the women was breathing deeply, and Billy, who had drawn closer, heard the sighing of those deep drawn breaths. It was as though the dark bosom of the night exulted in the mystery of life and love eternally renewed. And something in Billy trembled. The pipes and the lights came nearer.

III

The Café Ceres had collected its coterie. Frevick was wearing a clean, soft white collar, and a black velvet tie, and his boots had been polished. He sat with his glass in front of him like an overgrown boy, looking wistfully at the people who passed. He was very sad and very sober, because the Festa of S. Soforio had an esoteric meaning for him, and the wine of the day was the blood of a saint. Frevick believed in saints.

The café orchestra was playing "Madame Butterfly." An arm sawing at a violin kept throwing a shadow across Frevick's face. Everybody was talking. Major Mirleess, in the early aggressiveness of liquor, kept asking questions.

"Damn it—where's Slade? Where's Slade? Anybody seen Sadie?"

He was ignored. It was unwise to begin a conversation with Mirleess while he was in the raw beginnings of a red evening, for he would be argumentative and quarrelsome. Later, when well flushed, he would begin to babble about the war, and "Old So-and-so," and French girls, and the various estaminets, and little restaurants in Amiens and St. Omer and Abbeville. No one listened, and it did not matter.

"Where's Sadie?"

"Why—right here."

She came up on the arm of the Russian, possessed and possess-

D

ing. Her black hat had an aigrette set at an audacious angle. Her mouth looked very red until it opened to let out one of her screaming laughs, and then the red lips seemed to disappear and the mouth was a dark cavity.

"Anyone seen Oscar? O, my dear, someone's been telling me a story about an Irish gal and a suit of pyjamas."

"Sit down, Sadie."

"A suit of pyjamas, sleepies. Sit down, Peter. What'll you have?"

The Russian, a little sullen and obscure, reached for a chair, and grimaced at old Ponsonby behind Mrs. Shone's back.

"We'll think about it. Here's a chair."

"Think I can't see a chair, Buddie. I've got to tell my story."

The Russian put a hand on her shoulder.

"You will honour us by sitting down."

And then Slade was with them. He appeared to arrive from nowhere, silently, and yet with the air of the master of the show. His thin face had a smiling edge under the breadth of his hat. He was wearing a red carnation.

"Well, peoples."

He took the chair that always was left vacant for him. There was a moment of silence, and Slade was aware of it and of the sudden muteness of the animals in their cages. Sadie Shone's mouth hung open as though death had touched her in the middle of laughter. Old Ponsonby fidgeted in his chair and smirked like a poor relation. Mirleess' blue eyes glared. "Sneering Swine." He looked it, but dared not utter the words, for he was Slade's client, and Slade was sympatica to the Italian clique that ruled in Tindaro. The Fascisti had abrupt ways. They could have you bundled down to the railway station at an hour's notice, and in twenty-four hours you would be over the frontier and your passport might be dubious.

Tommaso had hurried to Slade's table.

"What can I bring you, sir?"

Slade smiled up into Tommaso's fat face.

"I think—champagne, champagne for everybody, Thomas. Say—six bottles. Write it down."

Tommaso creased himself with an obeisance.

"And take the orchestra a bottle—with my felicitations, and tell them we want the Hungarian Rhapsody. That's the stuff, peoples."

Old Ponsonby pushed his hat back, and had it tilted over his eyes again by Sadie Shone. She got up with one of her screaming laughs. "I want to sit next Oscar." She dragged her chair between the tables, crowding past Frevick who was as patient of her jostlings as a sack. "Oscar's the juice." The voices broke out again; the menagerie gave tongue. The leader of the orchestra, long and flat as his violin, came and bowed to Slade, bow in one hand, fiddle in the other. Slade nodded to him. The tables grew noisy.

Tommaso bustled with bottles and glasses.

"Pop!" said Sadie, and shrieked, "Pop, pop."

Mirleess glared.

"What ho—for the barrage."

But Frevick put a hand over the glass before him, and would not allow Tommaso to fill it. His eyes had a sudden, sombre fierceness. He looked at Slade.

"No thanks."

IV

S. Soforio had come down from the hills, and Frevick sat on alone at his table with his empty glass and his empty thoughts. People had passed, people from the villas and the Hotels Elyseo and St. George, English, Americans, Germans, all hurrying to the piazza, where S. Soforio sat in a kind of palanquin while the bonfire blazed and fireworks crackled. The piazza would be full of shadows, shadows on the walls of the houses and on the grey paving-stones. Frevick's eyes were half closed; he sat all hunched up, his hands in his pockets. The Circe crowd had gone, noisy and intimate and full of the grape. The orchestra had ceased to play.

"Streaks of the brush—just streaks of the brush."

He saw life as a daub, a crudely impressionist picture, a

splodge of light and of shadow, and full of faces that were
unfinished, their mouths like slits cut with a knife.   And in
places someone had used a thumb and dabbed on gobbets of
gamboge, and green, and vermilion.   Splodges of oil, and brush
marks, a mocking mess, a drunkard's joke.   O, God in the
Heaven——!

With an abrupt gesture he pushed the empty glass off the
table so that it broke on the pavement; he sat and stared at the
fragments.   He would have to pay for that glass, and he did
not care.   Yes, he would pay.   Life made you pay.   There
was no escape from the inevitableness of that settlement, though
you might smirk and write epigrams and twiddle your thumbs.
The payment might be made in invisible cash, in coin that
did not pass with the multitude; you paid with the blood of
your soul, with those secret shames and agonies, with the self
stranglings of your craft, the sodden stultifying of your genius.
Beauty and joy took flight.   The perfume was no more.   You
sat at the feet of a fellow like Slade, like a mangy dog going
blind.

"O, God in Heaven!"

Tommaso appeared and gathered the broken glass into the
top of a tin box.   Politely he stood and waited.   Frevick
groped.   He laid a greasy and crumpled note on the table.
Tommaso picked it up, but delicately so, and with a bending
of his fat body.

"Grazie, signore."

It was a gesture, gentle and human.   He had an affection
for Frevick; Frevick was not quite like those others, he had
the eyes of a man; he painted pictures.

"Grazie, signore."

Frevick looked at him strangely.

"The blood of the good saint to you, Tommaso."

"And to you, signore."

They smiled, and the white apron drifted away, and Frevick's
face became suddenly twisted.   "By god, I'll do it to-night.
I'll cut my damned throat.   Sot and pig!   O, God in Heaven,
why am I so lonely?"

He glared, and the glare changed to a slow and doglike stare of surprise. Someone was standing there; he saw a pair of feet and ankles, the edge of a black skirt. His gaze lifted; he seemed to straighten in his chair, he looked tragic, torn, pitiable.

"Julia——"

She touched the table with her fingers.

"I had to come out. You remember. Never since that last night. But to-night——"

He looked up at her, puzzled, questioning. He pulled himself together; he stood up.

"Why——? Yes—I'm all right."

Her eyes looked like two black circles in her firm face. Her voice had a strange softness.

"You'll come. Was Oscar Slade here?"

"Yes."

"I thought so. Tom, I want you to come with me."

He seemed to rock slightly on his feet.

"Anywhere you like, Julia. I'm all right. I wish I had always been all right. My fault."

She gave him a glance of strange and tragic compassion.

They went together down the Corso and for the moment it was an empty street, for all Tindaro had crowded into the Piazza del Duomo, and Frevick was remembering the night when he and Julia Lord had walked down this same street to see S. Soforio in his glory. How many years ago was it? And, after all, life was only like walking down a street; you came to the end of it, and perhaps some strange old saint was waiting for you on the edge of the unknown.

And suddenly he was saying something to the woman at his side.

"You always had plenty of courage, Julia."

"Think so?"

"Why, even to-night—— What is it?"

"I'm worried. It is about the girl. Was she with your crowd to-night?"

"No."

"I'm glad. But not you, Tom. I never think of you as belonging——"

"Thanks, Julia. I belong nowhere. My fault. But has Slade——?"

"Gossip."

"O, probably. That's one of the reasons why virtue is superfluous in a town like this, for no one allows you any virtue."

She touched his arm gently.

"Not true. That's a Sladeism. But this girl, I've grown rather fond of her, Tom."

He seemed to miss a step. He pushed his hat back.

"Of course. Something struck me. What you were like, Julie. I mean——"

"My dear, don't think I'm sensitive about growing old. But you know what Tindaro is, and Slade."

"He's a successful swine. I beg your pardon."

"O, not quite that. He just doesn't care; he has no pity."

"He can't leave fresh fruit alone. He's not white, whatever that means. Like a boy who has always had his own way."

Her face, lit up by the glare of light that now filled the street, seemed both to flinch and to refuse to betray the weakness.

"How crude life is."

Frevick's lips moved silently. "Not crude, my dear, but beautiful, when beauty matters to us more than anything." He stood still. But beauty, beauty should be impersonal, not to be clutched at and torn petal from petal. His eyes softened. He was standing with a woman beside him, beholding beauty, that old brown battered square like a golden box full of amber light. The fire was a mass of glowing embers. The torches had been extinguished, but the lanterns and lamps hung upon poles kept up a constant flickering. Cornices and windows caught the light. The pipes were playing. Clouds of confetti flew, making little blurs of coloured mist. And the southern crowd was happy, and joyous, and good-tempered. It laughed, and its laughter seemed to play upon the old walls like the light. Hundreds of dark heads moved. Hands threw confetti. There were little shrieks and swirls of laughter, and chasings, and little struggles, and a mysterious human thrill. Spring had come. The vines were sprouting. S. Soforio sat in state.

Frevick and Julia Lord stood back against the wall of a house. Their hands touched for a moment.

"Children."

"That's how one should try and see life, Julie."

There was a break in the crowd of figures just in front of them. A woman screamed. Her black hat was awry. She carried a bag of confetti, and she was cramming confetti down the neck of a man who—with his collar turned up—laughed and fled They disappeared again in the crowd.

"Poor devil," said Frevick.

He saw Julia Lord's lips move.

"Where is the child in Sadie Shone?"

"She's all child, my dear. She's never grown up with anyone who cared. I can cast no stones."

She touched his hand.

"I'm sorry, Tom. We're too old now."

The touch became a clasp of the fingers, and the pressure of her fingers warmed him. It said "Look," and Frevick saw what she had seen, the head of a man moving through the crowd with a girl's head very close to it. Slade was laughing, he looked all black and white against the glare, head in air, hat pushed back victoriously.

"Is it——?"

Frevick seemed to lengthen himself against the wall.

"Yes—I think so."

Miss Lord said, "Damn."

And suddenly she turned and moved away, and with an air of discouragement. She looked less tall and sure, and Frevick, following her, was filled with mute pity.

"Julie——"

They were in the Corso again, and their two figures threw long shadows. The glare and the noise grew less; their shadows and the stones became dim, and in the strip of sky above the stars reappeared.

"O, she'll be all right. She's sound. Slade can't fool——"

Her voice broke in.

"It isn't that. It isn't Slade. It's—it's life, the Spring, what we women—all of us——"

"My dear!"

"It's true. Think. Can't you remember——? The first time such a thing happened."

"I can. In the blood, you mean?"

"O, yes. And what am I to do? Meddle? Just tell her what the man is? Sometimes it's so fatal."

Frevick stood still, with the air of a man who had lost his way. His long arms moved helplessly.

"Common sense. What? Leave it to her common sense, Julie. I would. Don't believe in catechisms. He's rotten. She'll—she'll know."

Julia Lord looked back towards the piazza.

"But will she? Rotten men—have a—— Tom, I'm frightened."

He took her arm.

"Julie, I'll see you home. I'd leave it. Common sense, what? But I'm not afraid of the fellow. Look here, I'll tackle him. I'll give him it—full in the face. Either he lets things alone——"

She allowed herself his arm.

"Tom, you are all right. O, my dear, you ought to be——"

He set his teeth.

"Ought to have been. Yes. Rotten—in places. O, let it be, Julie. Some things are too damnable."

CHAPTER X

I

OSCAR SLADE had drawn Billy aside to the steps of the church, and they stood there as upon a little platform jutting out into a sea of heads and of faces. Over the piazza lay a level, yellow light that reached as high as the tops of the houses, and ended there in a velarium of black velvet. All the windows were full of faces. Puffs of confetti drifted like little clouds of smoke. The pipers had ceased to play; they stood in a group near the red ash of the fire.

Billy's face had a kind of sheen upon it, a dusting of yellow light.

"What happens now?"

Slade stood close to her, looking down. His voice was caressing.

"Guess."

"We all go home."

"Not quite that—yet. You'll see something nearly as old as the hills."

She gave him a quick, upward glance. Her eyes, too, had a sheen in them. She had caught the emotion of the crowd.

"Do we sing hymns?"

He laughed.

"Older than that. You don't really think——?"

"No."

"There is some confetti in your hair. It's rather pretty."

He watched her face, and was wise, for he had studied the faces of women, the mystery and the moods of them, those little smiling secret shadows that betray so much, the sudden softness and the sheen, a trembling of the lashes. And Billy was woman, but not quite woman as he had known her previously, a creature of sudden surrenderings, of surprising fervours, of unexpected nakedness. She wore no veil; she used no cunning.

"Gently," he thought—"gently."

Suddenly the pipes began to play with a shrillness that challenged the crowd. The music opened another movement. The piazza seemed to settle into the momentary stillness of expectancy; it was like water that waited to be troubled. Slade touched Billy's arm. "Watch those steps over there, between the houses." She noticed that all the faces were turned towards the dark cleft, between the high houses, from which a flight of grey steps descended into the light. Sudden brown figures appeared upon the steps; there were six of them, men dressed in the skins of animals. With loud cries they leaped down into the piazza. The piping flew upwards to a shrill crescendo. The men in fur were leaping and dancing through the crowd; they carried olive twigs with which they struck right and left, and Billy saw girls and women press forward to be touched by those symbolical wands.

Slade glanced at her face.

"Symbolism. Old as the hills. The gods survive."

"Is it lucky to be touched?"

"It means love—children."

As though moved by some common impulse the whole piazza began to dance, old men and young, women, children, girls. It was like the dancing madness of the Middle Ages, but this Italian crowd was not moved by a fanatical frenzy; it was of the South; it danced because of the human urge in it, for joy, for love, because of the call of the blood. It danced to the sun and the moon and the stars, and to man and to woman. It danced without asking why it danced. It had no melancholy obsessions, no false self-shame. It heard the pipes, and saw those leaping, skin-clad figures, and the heart of it understood. Spring had come. Adonis lived again. The dead rod blossomed. The pipes played.

The men in skins were everywhere; the olive twigs struck hands and arms and shoulders. Jokingly they would flick some old woman. "Salute for the olives of yesterday, mother." Magna Mater! The eternal mystery. Children. Girls were pushed forward to be touched. Young men laughed. There were kisses. One of these skin-clad messengers, leaping upon the church steps, held out his wand to Billy.

"You too, Signorina Inglese."

She gave a shake of the head, and laughed, and then held out a hand, and the man struck it gently with the olive twig.

"Spring has come."

She felt a strange flush go over her. She was aware of Slade at her side; she heard his voice.

"That's lucky. Like an annunciation. These people are wise; they know how to live."

But another voice came to them from the crowd. "Why, there's Oscar! Hallo, Oscar. And Miss Brown! My dear, aren't these satyr boys just marvellous." Her large white face under its disordered hat suggested possible intimacies and embarrassments, on such occasions she would be completely irresponsible; she would scream impossible things, and go off into shrieks of laughter. She had linked up Mirleess and the Russian, had them hooked by the arms, and was dragging them hither and thither with an immense exuberance. They looked rather like two sulky boys who could not escape to play upon their own. She tried to pull them towards the steps of the church. "Come on down, Oscar. Let's go and celebrate. Come on, my dear." She was in the south, but not of it; she was both pitiable and horrible, a grotesque mask, a modern northern fury adrift in a sea of old-world southern symbolism. Billy felt Slade's hand on her arm. He drew her and she followed.

"Some people can't fool decently. They get raw."

His dominance was gentle. It was a gesture which she understood, and as he wished her to understand it, though his grasp was gloved. They were down in the crowd, and moving along the wall of the church, and away from Mrs. Shone, and her appendages. Slade pushed through towards the edge of the crowd, still holding her arm, and she allowed him the rightness of his understanding. She consented, she felt most strangely with him in that southern crowd, with its swarthy and friendly faces.

When they reached the opening of the Corso he released her.

"That's not for you. I think it's about time———"

He glanced down at her with an air of protection.

"Raw spirits. That sort of rawness is the devil. It spoils things. I'm sorry."

He stood close, and she did not appear to question his closeness.

"O, that's all right. I agree. It's rather horrible and pathetic."

"I'll see you home."

The Corso received them. It had a soft and silent appeasement, a shadowy intimacy; it suggested a path through woods, with the stars shining, and all human interference blotted out. They passed up it together with a sense of mutual nearness, though their conception of this nearness differed. To Billy it was sublimated into a more spiritual essence. She felt Slade as man and comrade, as someone who understood life as she herself understood it, but also she felt him as the lover. Well, and why not? To begin with he had perplexed her. She had had other love affairs, but swiftly they had become so utterly inserious, because the men had seemed so very obvious and ordinary, but Oscar Slade was neither obvious nor ordinary. He disturbed her as no other man had succeeded in disturbing her. He had picturesqueness, light and shadow, that indescribable something.

She had begun to trust. And suddenly she had a feeling that she wanted to talk to him about all sorts of things, herself, himself, Tindaro, Mrs. Shone, books and how he came to write them, and what he did when he had finished writing them. She was flattered, but that was the mere flutter of a fan. She was aware of him as man, and almost and romantically as her man, perplexing, disturbing, colourful, touching her to a sudden young tenderness.

She said, "It has been a wonderful night."

The quality of her voice betrayed her to him. He should have uncovered his head to her, to the "Dear Billy" of her mother's thoughts, to a creature of brave frankness and fastidious faith. She stood with Slade on the edge of romance. She was ready to be touched, breathed upon, inspired, to put her hand in his, to see in him man, the boy and the beloved.

He knew. He had moments of exultation. He was accepting this new experience, this most virginal of affairs, as he accepted all that life gave him. Nothing lasted with him long. Things that lasted too long made mediocrity, suburbanism. Love was just a form of behaviour.

"Beautiful."

His voice had a hushed seriousness. Sex can be sacramental in the hour before its consummations.

They came to the door of the English Library, and with her back to it she stood looking up.

"I don't think I quite understood you till to-night."

"Thank you, Billy. That's worth everything. Tired?"

"Not a bit."

He held out a hand, and hers met it firmly and consentingly.

"See you to-morrow—perhaps?"

"Perhaps."

"I want you to come and look at my garden sometime. It's rather a perfect spot."

"I'd love to."

"Splendid. And it has a history. I shall have to write a tale about it some day. Well, Spring has come."

His moment of playfulness was nicely timed. The easy, gentle, almost casual touch was England to her English.

"Good night, Billy."

"Good night."

She turned from him quickly and entered the house.

II

Tom Frevick pursued other thoughts. He had walked on the heels of them up the country lane to Slade's villa, and had come to a pause outside the gates of the Villa of the Flute. They were very beautiful gates, of old Italian ironwork, and often Frevick had been moved to a kind of anger against Slade for being the possessor of such gates. On this night sacred to S. Soforio they were closed, and Frevick, perplexed by the intricacies of his purpose, ran his fingers over the scroll-work like a man trying to trace out a pattern.

What the devil should he say to Slade? For words that can be blurted out in a moment of haste and of heat, may sound crude and absurd when considered in the coolness of reflection. He had come up here to wait for Slade, to waylay him. But supposing that Slade did not come alone? Supposing——? And Frevick stood back and rested his shoulders against one of the stone walls flanking the gateway. Cypresses towered overhead. He could look down on Tindaro as a little nest of lights that gradually diminished as window after window went to sleep. He realized that he might be stuck outside these gates for hours, while Tindaro played at the feet of S. Soforio.

Yes, what the devil should he say to Slade? And would not Slade have every right to resent mere clumsy interference? For man is man, and woman—woman. How did you adjust these social niceties? What was morality? And where—exactly— was a man a cad, and where did caddishness begin?

"He'll tell me to go to hell."

Yes, probably. But what were the realities? Just when were you justified in blundering in and shouldering a man off the path of passion? When someone was going to be hurt? Yes, surely that was the justification. Not the defence of an hypothetical virtue, nor the sustaining of crowd convention, but the prevention of wounds, and especially of those spiritual woundings that may bleed on in secret.

Frevick's fists went deeper into his pockets.

"Yes, that's it."

He had reached bedrock. He who shall cause one of these little ones to stumble, let him be accursed. The caddishness of self, cynical lust, greed, violence dressed up in velvet. Slade had collected women as other men collect pictures or postage-stamps.

Frevick looked down at Tindaro and at its diminishing lights. Life was like that. The house of humanity had its lights; they were lit in childhood, and the quenching or the dimming of one of those lights was sacrilege. Surely?

Suddenly his head went up; he stood listening; he heard

footsteps coming down the path between the cypresses. It was very dark under the trees, but he was aware of a presence, of someone standing inside the iron gates. He could make out a greyness that was a face.

"Is that you, Lotta?"

There was silence. Then one of the gates trembled and gave out a little, metallic sound. Frevick felt two eyes upon him.

"Yes."

"The signore has not returned?"

"No."

She was a monosyllabic creature, but from that inarticulate, dim presence something emanated. She was woman, darkly and mutely woman. She too had come to those gates to watch, and in the darkness Frevick felt her as the shadow of his own thoughts, a human shade that stood to haunt the dealer out of wounds.

"Not at the Festa, Lotta?"

"No."

He could hear her breathing. She seemed to exhale an elemental emotion.

"You wait for the signore?"

"Yes, Lotta."

The gates shook lightly. Her two hands were resting on them.

"He is a bad man. He takes things for himself. He does not pity."

Frevick stood mute. How could you answer such a voice that spoke to you out of the womb of elemental things? He hunched himself against the wall. Reality? He felt an anger that grew, a sense of bafflement.

"Why not go away, Lotta?"

She brooded.

"I say yes and I say no, signore. Is not life like that? Have you not found it?"

He said, "God forgive me, but I have."

He had a feeling that she nodded her head at him. She made him think of some grave, dark-eyed animal caged in, unwise as to her own strength, held in bondage by the fate of her own flesh. Poor Lotta! She was one of those who had given, as the earth gives even though rent by the plough.

He was struggling to find something to say to her. The night seemed so naked; it offered you no ray of illusion, nothing with which to cover up man's physical realities. He pressed his elbows against the wall; his mind felt like an empty sack.

"Lotta."

But she had gone. The greyness of her face had disappeared. He heard the sound of her footsteps ascending between the cypresses.

III

Frevick waited. It was so very still up here among the olive grove and the vineyards, that the night was like a hollow shell held to his ear. He could hear Tindaro as well as see it, and from the murmur that was Tindaro some other sound might detach itself and grow into the sound of a voice.

Frevick felt restless and impatient. "O, hurry up." He wanted the real Slade, not Slade the shadow, the hypothetical enemy who was so elusive, but Slade as a reality with his edged smile and his square yet slouching shoulders, who would be a sufficient provocation.

And then Slade came. Frevick heard his footsteps in the lane; they had a leisureliness. Slade was alone. He carried his hat in his hand, and looked up at the stars as a man may look at them on a clear and fortunate night when the pattern of life is pleasant.

"That you, Slade?"

Slade's feet came together. He stood in the middle of the lane. He could distinguish the darkness of the gateway between the grey flanking walls, but he could not see Frevick.

"What the devil!"

"I thought I'd wait here. Shouldn't miss you here."

"You, Thomas, is it? Funny old devil. What's the matter? Come in and have a drink."

Frevick pressed his elbows against the wall. A drink! Yes, that was the obvious association of ideas. "Frevick, drink."

O, damn Slade!   Putting them through their tricks like a troupe of performing dogs.

He said, "No thanks.   I've come up about something else. You've got a pretty rotten reputation with women, Slade."

That was a shot point-blank fired as from an ambuscade, and Slade's figure seemed to stiffen.

"What!   You're drunk, you old sot."

"No, not to-night."

"Sober.   Well, let's assume the sobriety.   What the devil are you doing up here playing at Balaam's ass?"

"I have a message for you.   Some of us think you had better let that girl alone."

So that was it.   Slade walked forward towards the gates, paused, and put on his hat.

"Since when, Thomas, have you been a professor of moral philosophy?"

Frevick remained by the wall, pressing himself against it as though its solidity helped him to be solid.

"Leave me out of it.   I've no morals.   That's why I can give it you straight from the shoulder.   You have made a mess of one or two lives."

"Specify."

"No need to.   You know it better than I do.   You've never had any decent feeling about women.   And this girl is different.   You'll let her alone."

Slade's head was up.

"O, noble Thomas!   Why, you old idiot, am I such a fool as not to know the difference?   And supposing I feel decently in this case?"

He moved up to the gates and stood close to Frevick, seeing him as a dark mass attached to the stone wall.

"Who sent you on this stunt?   The good Julia?"

Frevick's figure moved.

"Something that's left in me, Slade, something you never seem to have had.   Call it pity if you like, or decent feeling. This isn't a Sadie Shone affair.   You can't do it."

Slade laid a hand on one of the iron gates.

"Idiot.   Well, what next?"

"Someone will tell her just what has happened in Tindaro."

"You are nice people.   And supposing your dear creatures are wrong for once, fouling linen that happens to be clean? Supposing I am going to ask the girl to marry me?"

"I don't believe you."

"O, doubting Thomas!   Yet you stump up here to preach morality at twelve o'clock at night.   Well, you can take it from me that I am going to ask her to marry me.   Sounds rather crude to you—perhaps."

"No, not crude, but impossible."

"Why impossible?"

"You can't take a girl into that house, with Lotta."

Slade had opened one of the iron gates.   He passed through and closed the gate with a clang of metal.

"Lotta!   What do you mean?"

"Just what I said."

"O, you nice people!   A committee of the dirty-minded. You can go to hell, the whole lot of you.   I am going to ask Billy to marry me.   Ergo, I have some decent feeling.   And supposing she wants me?"

"That's a beastly thing to say."

"O, rot.   She's a woman.   Well, and what are all you nice people going to do about it.   Send a deputation to my fiancée and tell her that the man she is going to marry is a blackguard? Sounds rather crude, doesn't it?"

"We might——"

"And supposing she didn't believe you?   Or supposing I could convince her that I'm not quite that sort of sexual beast? O, drop it, you old idiot.   This sort of thing makes my flesh creep.   It's like Sadie Shone when she's on——"

But Frevick's figure detached itself suddenly from the wall.

"Slade—if it's beastly—is that my fault?   You don't under-stand.   Or perhaps you do.   I'm not bluffing.   I may be a rotten devil—but I'm not so rotten as to think it possible that you——"

Slade took him up sharply.   His voice was growing thin.

"Understand that I am going to ask Miss Brown to marry me.   Go and tell the whole of Tindaro, all the old women and

all the old men. And if all you moral people think it your
duty to poison the girl's mind—well—be damned to you.
Good night."

IV

Frevick felt strangely tired, and with this feeling of tiredness
came a sense of discouragement and of helplessness. Neither
the lane nor his legs nor his talk with Slade seemed quite real,
but like the happenings on a stage, woolly and unconvincing.
His face was towards Tindaro, with its dwindling lights and its
fire that was quenched, and its Festa fading away into the night.
People passed him, people who were going home; people who
sang noisily. A fellow was tootling upon a pipe. And something in Frevick felt sick and miserable and voiceless.

He could not think sanely about Slade. The thing enraged
him. Slade, standing there by those beautiful gates, and talking
the sheerest claptrap. Slade of all men! But what was claptrap? Or had he—Frevick—misread claptrap for emotion? for
the distinction is subtle and in the mind of the listener. He
was prejudiced against Slade. O, yes. A swine rooting up
pearls. The thing had nauseated him, made him a blurter of
platitudes, of bunk that had matched Slade's swashbuckling
sentiment. What an occasion! What splurges! "Understand that I am going to marry Miss Brown." It was like the
village green and the village maiden, and the villain and the
squire. O, God in heaven what tosh men talked when they
had lost their temper!

But was Slade serious? If so he was most damnably serious.
And that was that.

"I had better tell Julie."

That was his one live reaction. Julie. Yes, Julie was so
sound; she stood up firm and straight; she did not get carried
away by emotional complexes. And how different life—his
own life—might have been had Julie caught him earlier, before
the sot in him had grown habitual. Habit! The horror of a
habit, a crave that was part of your flesh, a grinning necessity
that mocked at your "Yea and Nay." Yes, Julie.

He turned up towards her villa. He saw it white against

the dark hill-side.   It reminded him of Julie's hair.   He could remember her hair when there had been no white in it.   O, sentimental idiot!   Slade had called him an idiot.   He went round to the front of the villa and opened the gate softly, and looked up at the windows.   All dark.   But her window was on the other side towards the garden, and following the path he descended the steps into Julia Lord's garden.   He knew it to be full of flowers; he felt them, coloured foam, stocks and roses and lilies and wallflowers.   He looked up at her window and saw a light there.

His voice was soft.

"Julie."

She came to the window.   She was dressed; she had expected him.

"Julie, I want to tell you."

She held up a hand.

"I'll come down."

He waited for her on the little terrace below the house.   All these years, and he had never been in Julie's garden, and in the darkness its details were indefinite and mysterious.   There were the two cypresses pointing starwards, and patches of dim foam that were flowers, and Frevick felt strange and awkward in it, and afraid to move lest he should put his foot on some live thing.   Even between the stones of the small terrace, plants had their home, and he had trodden on some succulent, soft cushion, and had winced.

The garden door opened.

"Tom——"

"I'm here.   I'm afraid to move, afraid of treading on things. We're clumsy brutes."

His waiting was like that of a large dog, and her garden became something else to her.

"Anything to tell me?"

"O, yes.   Amazing stuff."

He saw her glance up at the house.   She knew that Maria was awake, and that Maria was woman.

"We'll go down to the lower terrace.   You don't know my garden."

"No.   My fault."

"There are steps here."

He found himself being taken by the hand and shepherded like a child down the steps, and past the water cistern and between the pillars of the pergola.   The tendril of a climbing rose tugged at his coat, and it was like a memory catching him with its thorns.

"I trod on something, Julie, up there, something growing in the stones.   I'm sorry."

He felt a slight pressure from her fingers.

"Never mind; plants forgive."

They came to the seat by one of the cypresses, yet neither of them sat down.   She withdrew her hand, but gently.

"Well?"

"I saw Slade.   We lost our tempers."

"Men do."

"He said that he is going to ask the girl to marry him."

Julia Lord stood as still as one of the cypresses.

"O, not that, surely!   You must have——"

"Perhaps I was heavy in the hoof, Julie.   I——"

"He said that about poor Molly Blake."

"Before——?   But I didn't know.   It's serious."

"Serious!"

Her voice was vibrant with scorn.

"The man's—impossible.   It's too hopelessly crude——"

"Sex is, my dear, isn't it   sometimes.   Well, we lost our tempers, and he let out.   But what the devil——?"

"I shall have to tell her."

CHAPTER XI

I

BUT this was to be one of those rare occasions when Julia Lord temporized and accepted vacillation.

The mood of the night and the mood of the morning were not in sympathy. She stood at her window, brushing her hair, and the morning sunlight lay gently upon her garden like a smile upon a happy face. How clean flowers were, how right and exquisite even in their loves. And this Italian garden of hers was so English, and yet not English in the rhythm of its blooming, for roses and wallflowers were out together, and red tulips spearing up among white stocks, and purple flags raised their standards near to the white trumpets of arum lilies. The perfumes were as various as the flowers, the scent of resida and of roses and of wallflowers and stocks, a mélange of sweet odours. Goldfish were darting about in the cistern. The cypresses were so still and so calm.

Julia Lord thought, "We were getting a little hysterical last night. Yes, a particular night. Things rush back on one. And poor Tom——"

She bent out of the window and looking down at the stones, fancied that she could see the particular plant upon which Frevick's heel had settled. He had been quite troubled about it; he had been troubled about everything; he had looked more lost and loose-limbed than usual, hopeless and sensitive and ineffectual.

But she caught herself up. S. Soforio had made them all a little emotional; it had been in the air, in Tindaro and the Spring, and she resumed the brisk brushing of her hair. This was the morning after yesterday, and her garden had not changed, and Billy was not like poor little Molly Blake, and Slade was an insufferable flâneur. It was more than probable that he had

114

been amusing himself with poor Tom, shaking a red rag. The whole business seemed rather absurd. Yes, they had been a little hysterical.

She breakfasted. Maria's face and Maria's coffee were as usual, and Julia Lord felt grateful. She felt moved to bless those flat and undistinguished and practical faces that fill the frames of the sober and habitual day. If life were one continuous Festa, an eternal Bank Holiday. Horrible prospect! The one, sure, satisfying thing was the work you did.

She walked down into Tindaro. Tindaro was as usual, and so was the Corso and its shops; fat Tommaso was swabbing the marble tops of the Café Ceres tables. Tadeo the barber was having his usual argument with some local citizen, an argument that sounded like a murderous quarrel, and was nothing of the kind. Yes, that was Tindaro, S. Soforio, life, these sudden physical excitements, hot air, dust.

A fisherman passed her with a basket full of prawns, pink and convincing and odoriferous. The library step was white. Miss Lord went in and found Billy busy with a feather duster, a pragmatical and reassuring Billy.

Miss Lord gave her one attentive and anxious glance.

"Finding much dust, my dear?"

"O, plenty. Don't they even water the streets?"

"Yes, sometimes."

Miss Lord sat down in her familiar chair, and felt the books about her and the flowers on the table and the cashbox in the safe, and Billy and her feather duster. Business as usual. Good English. And Billy looked and sounded particularly cheerful, and was actually tickling Ibsen's plays with those feathers. Julia Lord had a quick eye. Ibsen indeed! Rather humorous! And Chekhov and Dostoievsky! Dolorous, problematical people those Russians, finding so much dirt in the world and looking depressed about it, and never making any attempt to use a broom. You just shrugged and said, "O, well, that's life. Why quarrel with what is."

Miss Lord drew a deep breath.

Yes, obviously, Slade was a flâneur. He put all the members of his circus through their tricks, but Billy was not exactly a circus girl. S. Soforio had made all of them just a little emotional.

She said, "Have any of those parcels turned up yet from Simpson & Masters?"

"Yes. They came this morning. I've unpacked them, and put the books out."

"Catalogued them?"

"O, yes."

Billy's face looked as fresh and clear as a new book, and Miss Lord thought, "A messy thing—interference. It doesn't do to read into a tale something which may not be there."

The morning passed as hundreds of other mornings had passed. Books came in, and books went out, old ladies asked questions; old Tom Bromhead appeared with six novels fastened with a strap, and teased Billy, and had his usual friendly difference with Miss Lord. The routine had a reassuring sameness; everything was in order; the wheels of the clock revolved.

At half-past eleven Miss Lord rose from her chair. She had decided to see Tom Frevick, and to tell him that interference might be both foolish and superfluous. Billy was hunting out a book on lace for a visitor from one of the hotels.

"Miss Brown."

"Yes, Miss Lord."

They had tacitly accepted formalism in public.

"Would you mind carrying on till twelve to-day. I have someone to see."

Billy's face was cloudless.

"Of course."

"Thank you."

Julia Lord went in search of Frevick. She both found him and did not find him, for when she rang the rusty bell at Frevick's villa, she was answered by the barking of a dog. And that was all. She rang the bell again and waited, and when no one came she tried the door.

It was locked. She was about to turn away when she thought she heard someone moving in the passage. The dog whimpered, and with something in her heart that answered the dog's whimpering, she turned again to the door and knocked.

"Hallo."

Her firm face seemed to flinch.

"Is that you, Tom?"

"Yes."

She had a feeling that the door could not be opened. She divined its deplorable concealments.

"Tom. I think we exaggerated things last night. I think it would be wiser to temporize."

His voice came to her tonelessly, resignedly.

"All right. You know best. I overslept myself."

"Then you agree?"

"O, yes, I agree."

She hurried away; she wanted to escape from that closed door; it was so like the fatal door that had separated them years ago. Poor, hopeless Tom! So sensitive, so generous, and so deplorable! An exile, the most tragic of exiles, with nothing but a little yellow dog to keep him company. She avoided Tindaro, and hurried back by way of lanes and paths to her villa and its garden, and meeting Maria in the passage, wished that Maria could be avoided.

"I'll have lunch in the garden, Maria."

"The signorina has a headache?"

"No. Just a little tired. It's the Spring, Maria."

She went out and looked for the plant which Frevick's foot had crushed. She found it. She looked at it pitifully. Poor Tom was so like that plant.

II

The library had emptied itself, and Billy was putting the returned books back on the shelves when she felt that other presence. She had closed the door leading into the passage, but now it was open, and from the passage Slade smiled at her, and his eyes and her sudden colour met.

"Good morning."

"You startled me."

"Sorry. Apologies."

He strolled in, closing the door behind him, and with a glance at her that made the act seem as intimate as he meant it to be, laid his hat on the table.   He was dressed for a debonair occasion.

"Tired after last night?"

"Not a bit."

There were still some books to be replaced.   She went on with the work, but her movements were mechanical; her consciousness confronted other incidents, his coming in and closing of the door, the way he sat down on the edge of Miss Lord's table.

"Come out and lunch with me."

She paused with a volume of essays poised in front of a shelf.

"I don't know."

"The St. George.   Why not?   I want you to.   And may I say something?"

She thrust the book into its place and faced him.

"Yes."

"I want you to promise not to believe all that you hear in this fly-blown paradise.   Will you?"

"I'm not credulous."

"Thank you.   I shall appreciate that.   I don't suppose you have any conception of what a place like this can be, and say. I have laughed sometimes.   But you wouldn't imagine——"

"I might guess."

"O, no.   You're too much in the open air.   You have no idea of the malignant fustiness of this backyard.   That's why I live out at the villa.   Well, what about lunch?   I would take it as very gracious of you."

She felt that he was wasting the occasion with a delicate formality.   He was very much man to her, and she stood and considered him and herself, and her young inclinations.   How strangely these things happened.   Meanwhile he sat and smiled as though he understood her and himself and meant her to know just how much and how dearly he understood.   His glances were half ironical, half caressing.

"Be gracious."

She hesitated, and her hesitation went back to the elementals.

Lunching with a man might mean nothing or everything, but lunching with Oscar Slade in Tindaro was a confession of faith, and more than that. She was greatly disturbed. It was the first time in her life when a man had so disturbed her. She knew that he might look at her and utter one word "Billy," and that things would happen, things which to her would be sacred and final. She was woman to his man. She could not say why or how.

She hesitated.

"I'm rather a serious person, Oscar."

He began to look at her with a lover's intentness.

"Be serious, Billy. Isn't life exquisitely serious—sometimes? I want it to be just as serious as it can be."

She stood with hands hanging. Her lips began to move, and in that moment of crisis the door opened on them, and set in the shadows of the passage like a pale cameo, they saw Winnie Haycroft's face. Its eyes seemed to open to a shocked stare; its lower lip drooped.

She blurted.

"I'm—I'm sorry.   I——"

Billy was suddenly and decisively woman.   She laughed.

"Come in, Winnie.   I'm just going out to lunch with Mr. Slade."

Slade had got off the edge of the table.

"Perhaps Miss Haycroft will join us?"

"Yes, come along, Winnie."

The pale girl seemed to flicker like a candle flame. She stammered.

"Thank you—s—so much.   I'm afraid—I can't.   I c— came in to borrow a book.   It doesn't matter."

And she fled.   Slade picked up his hat, looked at it whimsically, and transferred the look to Billy.

"Sheer terror.   Poor kid.   Some people always feel superfluous.   Are you going to be kind to me and put on your hat?"

Her face had a sudden colour.

"Yes."

III

To reach the St. George Hotel they had to pass the Café Ceres, and they passed it with a mutual sense of their especial significance. Some of the habitués were there, old Ponsonby, and Mirleess, and the Blaber woman, and their appreciation of the event lacked fluidity.

Slade saluted them.

"Morning, everybody."

The Café Ceres was momentarily and rigidly self-conscious. Old Ponsonby jerked in his chair, and pulled the brim of his hat. Mirleess drew in his lame leg, but did not rise. The Blaber woman stared like a heifer. Slade and Billy passed on.

His smile had an edge to it.

"Charming people! A bit slow in their reactions. I think I am getting rather tired of those marble-topped tables."

Meanwhile the Café Ceres had regained some of its fluidity. It exchanged glances. It raised eyebrows.

"So—it's on."

"Looks like it."

"Didn't think she'd fall to Slade."

Mirleess reached irritably for his glass.

"Much of a muchness, women. Much the same stockings —underneath. I've had some surprises. It's just a question of cheek."

IV

It was very early when Billy took the mule path down to the sea, so early that the day seemed hers, and the sea and the sky innocent and cloudless. The stealth of the dawn still lingered. So delicately blue was the morning that all that mountainous coast seemed to join sea and sky with an almost equal blueness. The sea was laced with gold, and so were the stones of the steep and winding path. The wild rosemary was in flower. On the hill-sides a smother of fruit blossom showed up against the grey green of the olives and the blackness of cypresses and pines. The shadows in the valleys were the colour of violet.

Billy carried a bag of plaited straw, and in it were her bathing-dress, a light wrap and a towel. She had the face of Aurora, a little mischievous, a little tender, but this beautiful and pagan dawn had other mysteries. Each sea has its song, and every strand a rhythm of its own, and Billy, going down to bathe with her lover, was still a child of the north. The north, in the main flow of its deeper and darker waters, is neither incidental nor fantastic; it goes steadily towards the sea; it seeks finality, a love that accomplishes.

The last curve of the path brought her above that crescent of sand and the horned rocks and the very blue water. Its blueness varied; it was indigo and turquoise; it was both darkly and bluely profound, and exquisitely light and lambent. The Island of the Triton seemed afloat close in to one of the rocky points, an island so unsolid and so vapoury that you could imagine it vanishing like some magical island of the legendary seas.

Billy stood at gaze. She saw a figure on the sands, a white-coated and trousered figure standing close to the inward glide of the little, sleepy waves. There was not another figure to be seen. They had sea and sand and sky for their own.

She hailed him.

"Oscar——"

He turned and waved a hat.

"Hallo—— I beat you by five minutes. Was there ever such a morning."

She ran on and down and he came across the sand to meet her, and his brown face had a kind of vividness. His teeth showed very white. And they stood for a moment looking at each other as though aware of the beautiful newness of every-thing, and of that cool sea and the freshness of the morning, and the mystery of woman and of man.

Slade's eyes seemed to narrow.

"Billy——"

She was desired, and her face had a gentle tenderness.

"Oh, isn't life lovely. And won't the water be cold."

"The first exquisite touch of it, my dear. Your dressing-room is over there. I've chosen my rock."

She looked into his eyes and smiled.   Love—to her—had a rich and generous candour.

"I won't be two minutes.   I'll race you."

"Will you indeed!   It's the island.   Can you manage it?"

"I've swum there before."

"You're splendid."

She was first in the water.   She wore a light blue, and as she waded out and threw herself forward into that other blueness she seemed to become part of its blue flickerings.   Her brown head was the challenge.   Slade went in after her, more brown and more lean in the pursuit, and hastening to match her whiter vigour.   He was a fine swimmer; it was his one active virtue, but he did not draw level with her until they were within thirty yards of the Island of the Triton.

"You young things are too good at the game."

"I haven't been advertised to swim the Channel."

"It's all very splendid—but don't."

They swam the last few yards together towards a ledge of rock that was just awash, the blue water swelling gently over it, and falling back just as gently.

"Mind your knees.   Some of these rocks hurt."

"I know."

He was out first, and turned to help her, holding out his hands.

"Put a foot there and let me pull."

"I might pull you in again."

"You won't."

She came up to him all dripping, but with her brown head crisp and dry.   They were very close.   He slipped an arm under hers, and felt the soft chilliness of her skin.   The early sunlight streamed down on them, and lay in their eyes and in the hollows of the rocks.

Slade looked over his shoulder towards the shore.   The bay was empty of life, its crescent of sand deserted.

"Let's sit in the sun.   Not too long."

They found a flat rock just above the indolent heave of the blue water; another rock screened them from the shore.   Billy sat with her knees drawn up, and her arms wrapped round them. Slade lay sideways, resting on one elbow.

"Well, isn't this good."

She nodded, and gazed seawards.

"Perfect. It's as though the world had just been made."

"And so it has, for us."

"Do you feel like that?"

"Of course. Everything is created over again—for some of us."

He sat up. His arm went round her; he felt the softness of her young body; it was firm and strong, but it did not resist him.

"Billy— "

"Well——?"

"It's the same funny old question. Let's be orthodox. Do you think you could marry me?"

She sat in silence, gazing seawards.

"I've let you touch me. That—means everything."

CHAPTER XII

I

ON one of those occasional and most rare mornings in March, Mary Brown woke early and heard a thrush singing.

"Billy, Billy, Billy," sang the bird, and the voice of the thrush in that Ealing garden on that cold and sunny morning in March, had for Mary Brown a strange poignancy. For she was feeling worried about Billy, though she could not say why or how. It was just a feeling, and it had been with her for days, one of those impressions which arrive from nowhere. Not that there had been anything in Billy's letters to worry her, though that could not be said about the rest of the family. Irene was giving trouble; she had been attacked by the sudden discontents of her age, a passion to possess half Bond Street and to express herself in silk lingerie and decorative garters, and in dinners paid for by elderly persons. Young cynicism with too red a mouth and a peevish self-assurance. Ronald, too, had brought to the house a quite impossible young woman with a pair of feverish legs, a hat over one eye and a most genteel manner.

Mary missed Billy. Billy had been so useful as a family corrective, so wise, so frankly unanswerable on occasions when arguments arose and the family got above itself. It seemed absurd to be worried about Billy, and yet that bird's piping struck a troubled note.

"What an idiot you are."

But Mary Brown was no idiot. When she had a feeling about things she had come to know that mysterious messages do travel. Like Stella Burt she was one of those women who live on the edge of an awareness that is new and yet is as old as time. There were occasions when she could feel at a distance.

124

She sat down and wrote a letter to Julia Lord.

Miss Lord found the letter waiting for her when she returned about six o'clock to the Villa Vesta. She had left Billy to clear up the tearoom; for she had felt tired, and Billy had looked anything but tired. Tindaro appeared to suit Billy. Julia Lord had found herself observing on Billy's face a kind of secret radiance, and Julia had thought, "The girl looks extra-ordinarily happy. There can't be much amiss."

Miss Lord took Mary Brown's letter into the garden. She had seen the handwriting once before, but as a matter of fact, she did not recognize it, and the postmark was blurred. Julia Lord opened the letter as she would have opened any other unfamiliar letter from England, with her eyes and her thoughts on other things. Really the stocks were very fine this year, white and carmine masses, and smelling exquisitely.

But the letter put the stocks out of Miss Lord's mind. Her face became exceedingly grave. She read the letter through without a pause, and then re-read it. It was the letter of a mother who said, "Forgive me and don't think me silly if I have been feeling worried for no reason at all. I have had other worries, and perhaps they create an atmosphere. But Billy and I have always been very near to each other." Miss Lord laid the letter down on the green garden table, but not as though there was anything in Mary Brown's letter that had to be forgiven. On the contrary it produced in Julia Lord's mind a sudden tendency towards self-criticism, a troubled questioning of certain moods and moments, and a renewed aliveness to the world and Tindaro.

Yes, she was troubled. That letter coming from so far away, and speaking with so tender a frankness, seemed most strangely to express her own mood of a week ago. She had accused herself of being a little hysterical, but this letter from England was not hysterical. It had a kind of visionary right-ness. And was it inspired? Had Billy hinted to her mother of any secret tenderness, the beginnings of a sacred adventure? Or was the mother divining things about the child?

Miss Lord reached for the letter, and as she did so she saw the very soul of it standing on the little terrace just where

E

Frevick had stood on the night when he had come back from the Villa of the Flute. Miss Lord was startled, and she was not easily startled. The circumstance was so curious; it was both natural and strange. She slipped the letter away into pocket of her coat.

She made herself look brightly at Billy.

"Hallo. Finished?"

"Yes."

"Come and sit. The stocks are smelling adorably."

And then she realized that Billy's face was strange; it had a curious softness, and yet its softness was but a veil covering something that was to be accomplished. It was the face of annunciation. And again Miss Lord was conscious of feeling startled, and more than startled. She was chilled, breathed upon by some vague yet very real fear.

She said, "It has been a most perfect day" and wondered at her own obviousness, and Billy came down the steps, and with characteristic candour and no prevarication, made her confession.

"I felt that I ought to tell you at once. You have been so very kind to me, and almost it seems like my having taken a job under false pretences——"

Miss Lord was feeling grey. So her emotionalism had been wiser than her logic.

"It only happened this morning. I'm engaged to Oscar Slade."

"My dear——!"

"I hope you don't think I am letting you down. Of course I shall carry on to the end of the season."

Miss Lord, with that letter in her pocket, and more than dismay in her heart, looked at Billy's happy face, and knew that she was expected to say something. But what? She sat there like a woman groping in a bag for some trifle that eluded her fingers.

"It's very sudden, my dear."

"I suppose these things are like that."

Julia Lord felt her face being searched by those brown eyes. Was she annoyed about it, was she going to make a scene? Hadn't she anything human and impulsive to say? What could she say? She wanted to veil her face from Billy's eyes, and go quietly away and think.

"You are not fed up with me?"

Miss Lord forced herself to an air of sudden brightness.

"Good heavens, no. These things will happen. Have you ever been engaged before?"

"Yes, once, only for a month. I broke it off. It wasn't what you'd call the real thing."

Miss Lord winced inwardly. The real thing! And this Slade affair was the real thing to Billy.

Again Miss Lord temporized. She had a feeling that she must hold her breath lest she should blurt out unforgettable and unforgivable words. Never before had she discovered in herself such helplessness, such inarticulate consternation. Slade!

She said, "I'm not much good at congratulations. I'm glad you are not going to leave me till the end of the season. I shall be sorry. We have got on very well together."

She put up her face suddenly and Billy kissed her.

II

When trouble arose in Tindaro it was apt to take itself, not to the English chaplain or to the Venerable Pipps or to the Mayor, but to the Burt's villa. It might place itself on the knees of Stella or in the large hands of John. Even native Tindaro resorted to St. Medico or his lady, and propounded the most unexpected of problems. Perhaps Cesca had been married a year, and no baby had arrived, or Pietro's brother —who was a waiter in London—had written to say that he had consumption and no money, and that he wanted to live or die at home. The Villa Felice was well named. To Tindaro, Stella Burt was La Donna, or a kind of Stella Maris, and native Tindaro was essentially woman and child. The bambino was king, and though Stella Burt had no children, she, too, was woman and child. Tindaro said of her, "She has the blessed eyes," and being childlike in much of its mentality, it laid its troubles upon Stella's knees. Tindaro called Miss Lord La Duchessa, not facetiously so, but with respect. She had so white a mien.

Julia Lord rang Dr. Burt's bell, the doctor's bell. She could hear Stella's piano being played, something of Chopin, but Julia's inclination was towards the man. She wanted the man's grip, something rough and rude laid upon Slade, if such a thing were possible. She wanted the man's voice, "Do this" or "Do that," Burt's tusks, his solidity, his impartial courage.

Julia Lord had plenty of courage, but that letter had upset her. She was feeling acutely responsible, and she was not a woman who shirked such feeling; she pinned it down on a board and dissected it, but on this particular night her hands were unsteady.

Burt's servant opened the door.

"If the doctor is in I wish to see him."

Burt was in his den with a pipe and a tableful of papers and odd bits of pottery and glass. Miss Lord had a view of his broad back and big black head as she entered the room. She gave thanks for his solidity.

"Sorry to bother you."

He had risen and put his pipe down on the edge of the table, and she said, "Please go on smoking. This isn't a professional visit. I suppose that girl of yours doesn't listen at doors?"

This was the Lord directness. Burt understood it, and recollecting his pipe, went to the door and opened it.

"No. Sit down, Julia."

He had a feeling that she had come to him about Frevick; he knew their story, and that Frevick was drinking himself to death, and he waited, standing by the table, and holding the bowl of his pipe in one big hand.

"It's about Billy."

"Oh?"

"She has told me that she is engaged to Slade. It's serious. I've come to you. It seems incredible. She's so unlike—the others. I've got to do something."

Burt remained very still, holding his pipe.

"Good lord!"

"And I have had this. Queer coincidence. A kind of linking up. It's—it's nauseating."

She passed him the letter, and he bent down towards the

table lamp, and read Mary Brown's letter.   He puffed at his pipe.   His forehead seemed to wrinkle up.

"Clairvoyance.   Stella would understand.   How did it happen?"

"How do such things happen?   They just do.   They give one shocks.   But Billy.   So clear sighted.   The man——"

"That's just it.   Man.   There's something about Slade, something essentially male."

"He's impossible.   He's a blackguard.   The worst sort——

"Because he rationalizes."

"What's that?"

"He's logical.   He says—'Man, women, oxygen—carbon. Human chemistry.'   The worst sort of blackguardism unless your woman is like him.   Then it's no more than vital interaction."

She moved her hands irritably, twisting them together.

"But Billy isn't that sort of woman.   She—'s——"

"Exactly."

He returned her the letter.   His pipe had gone out, and he pressed down the tobacco with a solid little finger, and struck a match.

"What's to be done?   That's it?"

"Oh, obviously.   How can I answer that letter?   How can I——?"

Burt sat down in his consulting-room chair, and when he sat his big head seemed to sink nearer to his heavy shoulders.

"No hurry.   But what's the idea?   You see, Slade ought to have been alive in the Ulysses age when the world was full of islands and consenting nymphs.   Life's too stereotyped for Slade.   Besides, I can't see him with a Penelope."

"Oughtn't I to tell her, at once?"

"Just what Slade is, or what we think he is?   But wait a moment, Julia.   It's a major operation, and major operations don't always turn out according to plan.   The girl must be in earnest."

"That's just the horror of it.   She's the sort who will be dreadfully in earnest."

"All the more need for care.   She might resent radical

methods.   You know the attitude, 'I and my man against the world.'

"That's just what I'm afraid of.   That's why I hesitated. Most girls might snivel or sulk for a week—but this girl."

"Yes, she's stalwart.   If one could get at Slade."

"Could you?"

Her face was like a cameo sharply cut in ivory, and Burt gave her a slow smile.

"I'll take that from you, Julia, and from no one else.   But there is nothing."

"Surely?"

"No, nothing.   No septic sore to be made use of.   Besides, if there were—— It comes to this—Slade has put us in a conventional corner with our faces to the wall.   He's got to windward of you.   Supposing I went up to the fellow's villa and said, 'Look here, clear out, or I'll thrash you in public.'"

"I wish you'd do it."

"Wait a moment.   Would it work?   Would it convince the one person who matters?   It might not, you know."

"Then I shall tell her."

"What?"

"Oh, everything.   This man has had dozens of women. I'll point out Mrs. Shone."

Burt made a gesture with his pipe.

"Hold on.   Rather hard on Sadie Shone.   Besides, think of the possible explosion.   Fireworks, emotional fireworks perhaps.   Squibs and rockets.   A doctor has to be a bit of a psychologist, Julia.   When I was young I wanted to punch, use my beef.   I've come to believe that it's better to do things gently.   Modern surgery is not a red-hot knife and boiling tar."

He nodded his big head.

"Some people have the right touch.   Don't take that personally.   Just hold on a minute.   Now—there's Stella. People take things from Stella.   Extraordinarily so.   She's— so—so incorruptible.   How shall I put it?   She's—well——"

"You mean that Stella might——?"

"She doesn't use the knife.   I don't know what the devil

he does use. A wand or a crystal or something. She's
extraordinary. You know. She's been so near to death that
she seems to be able to talk to people like a woman who has
come back from the other side. Supposing my wife were to
tell Billy?"

"Would she?"

"I guess she would. She's not afraid of any mortal thing.
Remember that fellow Nicolo who used to use a goad on his
unfortunate horse? Murderous, violent blackguard. The
police were afraid of him. Stella settled him. The angel of
the Lord, Julia. But look here, no hurry. The situation's
—fragile. Stella has her own way."

"Will you tell her?"

"Of course. She likes to get the feel of things. She'll—
well, I'll keep you posted."

Julia Lord's hands lay relaxed in her lap.

"You are good people, you two. I'm—too—too downright."

"Britannia, Julia, with a trident! Must have my joke.
You're at your best with Mrs. Sudbury Smith. O, yes, I've
sniggered like a bad boy. No one is jealous of Stella."

"I'm not. I felt that I shouldn't sleep. I may now."

"Good. You will. But that fellow Slade. I wish we
could clear him out. It isn't the immoral people who are the
most poisonous, Julia, it is the logically non-moral. People
with nicely oiled bodies who slip impudently through the social
fence. Because—after all—one has to have a fence."

"Exactly."

She rose with her usual air of firmness.

"Discipline, holding tight. The 'Do what you please idea,
provided that you do it gracefully'—is pretty damnable."

Burt knocked out his pipe into a brass bowl.

"The credo's quite simple. Don't hurt people. Hurting
people wantonly or selfishly hurts your own soul. Obviously.
It's all so damned simple—really."

III

It was dusk, and in the vicolo below the teahouse garden
someone whistled the first few notes of the Lament for Adonis,

and Billy, sitting at her window, listened and understood. The dusk was as stealthy and mysterious as the dawn had been, black outlines against a blue profundity of sea and sky. A few stars shone. She rose and turned on the light, and went down and out into the garden.

A wooden door that was kept bolted gave access to the lane, and Billy withdrew the bolts, but with no sense of stealthiness. She had been waiting for her lover, and if he chose to come to her by way of the garden she thought it a good chance. Yes, better than the Corso, and not because the secrecy was deliberate, but because it was theirs.

"Is it you?"

"Adonis."

"Vain man!"

The door closed behind him, and then slowly swung open because of the sag of its old hinges. Neither of them noticed it. They walked up the path between the orange trees until they reached the shadow of the loggia, and there they paused.

"Billy."

She put her head back on his shoulder and looked up at him.

"I'm so happy."

"Splendid."

He held her, and as she moved to the three steps leading to the loggia, his arms wrapped themselves round her, his hands pressing upon her breasts. He kissed her neck.

"You exquisite thing."

"Am I?"

"Well, have you told anyone?"

"That I'm exquisite!"

"If you like."

"I have told Miss Lord."

"And what did Julia say?"

"Not much. I promised to see the season through."

"I'll wager that she hates me."

"Why should she?"

"For stealing. I've brought that ring."

"Have you."

"Rather precious and antique. Old Roman setting."

"Show me.   But I can't see here.   Let's go upstairs."

She freed herself gently.   The intimacy of his hands had made her a little self-conscious; she knew a moment of aloofness, of sensitive reflection.   She went up the stairs and into her room, and he followed her with an air of ironic indulgence. Little wrinkles showed themselves at the outer angles of his eyes.   He was never out of his own field of vision and never out of focus.   He could be light handed.   And Billy, standing by her window, little knew how shrewdly and deliberately such a man as Slade could handle his own hot metal.

Her glance rested on her table.   A writing-pad lay there.

"I was just going to write home, Oscar."

"Why not."

"I'd rather like to do it when you are here.   Sort of feeling that you are sharing."

He was smiling.

"All the dear formalities.   Well, look at this bauble."

He joined her at the window, and with one arm laid across her shoulders, he held up the ring between thumb and finger. It was an emerald in a nest of diamonds, and the setting was a lozenge of reticulated silver.   A beautiful thing.

She took it from him.

"How lovely!   I have never seen anything like it."

Their heads, shoulders, and hands were visible to someone standing in the garden.   They remained in the frame of the open window with the light behind them.   Their heads seemed to touch.

A woman had slipped in through the open garden door, and was standing by one of the orange trees, looking up at the lighted window.   She listened to the two voices.   Her figure had a sombre and sullen stillness.   Her eyes stared like the eyes of some mute animal.

CHAPTER XIII

I

FOR a week Tom Frevick had ceased from sitting at one of the tables outside the Café Ceres. Having broken out of the ring, and defied the ring-master's whip, he had remained at home, and remaining at home meant for Frevick hours of solitary drinking. He drank whisky, for whisky was to be had in Tindaro for sixty lire a bottle, eight shillings or so at the current rate of exchange. He might be seen at dusk, hurrying along close to the houses, and wearing an old overcoat with the collar turned up. His clothes looked too big for him. Slade had to joke about "Old Frevick's elephant legs." In the Corso a Neapolitan kept an Anglo-American store, at which could be bought *The Saturday Evening Post*, soap, patent medicines, liqueurs, tooth-brushes, biscuits, talcum powder, English whiskies, douche-cans, jam, notepaper, and what not. Frevick's loose stride grew longer when he neared this shop. His dive into the doorway was surreptitious. He had the money ready. There was no conversation. The bottle was stuffed into the left pocket of the overcoat, and with this bulge added to his figure Frevick lumbered home.

Thus for a week he was without news. No one went to see him. For hours he lay on his bed and snored, with the little yellow dog curled up against his socked feet. He ate very little, and what he did eat was cold. Cut off from the Café Ceres he did not hear what the Café Ceres had to say on Tindaro's latest romance.

"Damn it, I'm not exactly a prude, but it's a bit thick."

This was Mirleess' contribution. He was a little swollen. He had assumed Slade's chair, for Slade too had deserted the circus.

"Yes, it's a bit thick. I have a pretty good cheek on me. What do you think!"

"Ask Tommaso what he thinks."

"No need.   It means that the girl is pretty badly blown upon. Possibly she's not so new to the game."

Old Ponsonby took up the argument.

"Shouldn't say that.   I should say she's a good kid.   I'd like to see Slade put out."

He lit one of his dishevelled cigarettes, and peered under the brim of his hat at Mrs. Shone.   Mrs. Shone was unusually silent.   Her white face had an air of vacant melancholy; she looked like that when life and too much macaroni had disagreed with her.

"Saying anything, Sadie?"

She came out of her stare.

"Sure.   Slade's yellow.   And the Major's a prize pup. And what are we—anyway?   O, hell!   Sure, someone is going to tell her?"

Mirleess' insolent little red face flared at her.

"You?   Well, why not?   Authentic stuff."

She sat still for a moment looking at him.   Her white and heavy face was all creases.   Then, with a quick thrust of the hand she picked up her glass of vermouth, and slung the brown stuff convincingly in his face.

"Authentic!   Sure, so's that."

The delicate and the indelicate are strangely intermixed. The fingering of fruit rubs away the beautiful waxy bloom that protects the skin, and the fungus can penetrate.   Probably there was no one in Tindaro who wished any evil to Billy, but when Tindaro began to finger her reputation the fine bloom of it was tarnished.   Her happy face during those days counted for nothing; her frankness was mere boldness.   She wore that ring.   And Tindaro was shocked and perplexed. It could understand neither Slade nor Billy.   It mixed up its mads and its bads.   It could not convince itself of Billy's preposterous innocence, of her sincerity, of her Spring mood, while it had nothing good to say of Slade.   It never had.   His new clean linen would not wash.

The serene and the secure people shook their heads.

"The girl must know."

"Of course. She cannot have lived here all these months without hearing things."

"Birds of a feather. But, my dear, aren't appearances elusive! You would have said——"

"Exactly. Quite the last sort of girl. But it's the modern *milieu*. No real decency. I'm sorry for Julia."

Though for the few Billy Brown's bloom retained its waxy blueness. They saw her as she was, and these more human and more deep-eyed people were unexpected in their grouping. Sadie Shone held the same faith as did Stella Burt. Frevick, when he did hear the news, fell into a strange frenzy of filthy language, which was both shocking and right. Old Tom Bromhead wanted to interfere, and was restrained by his wife. "What do you know of the girl—really? You have only played tennis with her." Julia Lord, when questioned, felt the burn of that letter which she carried about with her, and retained a frozen face. She was waiting. She was feeling impatiently towards the two people of the Villa Felice. Stella had done nothing. It was incomprehensible. But then Stella Burt was in some ways an incomprehensible little person. Like the sun in England, you never knew just when she was going to shine.

Julia Lord's silence was an exasperated silence. She said to herself that this thing should not have happened, and she blamed herself as well as a nexus of circumstances. Obviously she should have catalogued Tindaro for Billy's benefit, and placed no less than three red asterisks against the name of Oscar Slade. But then, who could have foreseen the fact that these two would be interested in each other? And Miss Lord, taking her cold bath as usual, was moved to exclaim "O, damn sex! It spoils everything."

Moreover, she was feeling murderous towards Slade. He met her in the Corso and smiled and gave her a wave of the hat. It was the ironic salute of the pirate, Britannia defied upon her own high seas.

For a moment she had conceived it possible that she could turn back and open fire on him, rake him with murderous shots, but she also knew that such an attack would be ineffectual. His ironic, head-in-air parade issued its own challenge. "Well, come along, all you people. I'm enjoying this immensely. Go to, now, and tell the girl that I'm a pirate, a Bluebeard. Turn on the social purity pump. Yes, tell her just what you damn well please. The last word will be mine. You women know quite well that it's no shame to a man to have been a bit of a swashbuckler. It's the rake's picture you hide in your chaste bosoms. What about your Prince Charlies? Your Amelias only marry their Dobbins as a last resource. Oh, I have got you all nicely puzzled."

II

It was typically a Slade conception, a lunch for three in the little open-air theatre of the Villa of the Flute.

"Bring the Haycroft girl with you. I want to show you our garden. Ask her for Sunday."

Winnie Haycroft looked scared. "Oh—I couldn't. He doesn't want me—really. Besides——" With her sentence hanging broken in the air like a boy's kite on a thorn tree, she sat on the edge of Billy's basket-chair, and fidgeted. The chair creaked under her. Her pale eyelashes flickered. This Slade affair had a kind of horrible fascination for her; she could not put impressions into words; she felt herself to be witnessing a cannibal feast, the devouring of Billy. She was amazed at Billy, and immeasurably mute. For, surely Billy would take some devouring, a stalwart creature who looked wholesomely happy and unsuspecting. Surely someone would warn her? But when the voice became personal Winnie Haycroft shrank from reality.

"O—I couldn't. No, really I couldn't."

Billy had been writing a letter, and she was sitting at the table by the window. She spoke over her shoulder.

"Of course you'll come. Why on earth not? Oscar asked you specially."

Winnie's eyes were fixed upon the ring that Billy wore.

"He couldn't have done."

"But he did. I want you to come."

"O, well perhaps——"

"I'll call for you at a quarter-past twelve."

It was a blazing day, but a breeze from the sea blew up the Valley of the Flute and made a little murmuring in the pines. Winnie wore a lace frock; she was just the colour of the dusty road; she carried a sunshade. Billy walked whitely in the southern glare and did not appear to feel it; she had one of those skins that do not scorch, and her eyes seemed to hold the light. They came to the iron gates of the Villa of the Flute, and at the sight of them and the black avenue of cypresses Winnie felt a little trembling of the knees. She suffered from dreams, vivid obsessions; she had dabbled her thin hands in the Italy of the Renaissance, and this was a Borgia business. Red hats, and perfumed iniquity, and palaces, and papal love affairs, poignards and poisoned rings, and little trickles of blood over marble floors.

Where the shadows of the cypresses ceased Slade met them. He stood in the sunlight at the top of the flight of steps that descended to the Greek theatre. He had heard the clang of the gate, and the sound of their voices, for Billy had said, "Aren't these trees marvellous. It's like going up through a temple." But Winnie, thinking rather of the Villa d'Este, had answered, "Rather creepy, I think." And Oscar Slade stood there in the sunlight, wearing an English tailor-made suit of light brown cloth, quite the conventional host, ready for a Sunday lunch. He smiled at them both.

"Well, here you are, punctual people."

He looked less tall than usual, more standardized; his tie was a very ordinary tie; he suggested neither the black velvet mask nor the poisoned ring. He shook hands with Winnie Haycroft, as though he were welcoming a plain and rather shy child.

"Glad you could come. I think we'll lunch first, and do gardens afterwards."

He looked lightly and a little whimsically at Billy.

"I'm sure Miss Haycroft takes white wine."

"Why should she?"

"Muscatel. Now, don't you, Miss Haycroft?"

Winnie's lower lip drooped. The Borgia business was

melting into thin air. Really, the Slade of the Villa of the Flute was a quite unformidable person; he was wearing such a nice suit, and his hair was absolutely English.

She said, "But I never drink wine."

Slade's smile rallied her.

"No, never? O, come now!"

"Once—I did drink Asti—at a picnic in Tuscany. It made me—— But it was a very hot day."

Billy and Slade laughed, and Winnie had to laugh with them. Her laughter was a funny little shrill sound.

"Obviously, Asti, in honour of Miss Haycroft. I think the cellar has some Asti. I'll go and have it hunted out. Will the guests descend to the theatre."

He stood with his hands in his pockets and bowed them down the stone steps. The situation seemed as smooth as silk, and Winnie Haycroft stroked it tentatively. It was all so different from what she had expected it to be. Nothing lurid and passionate and embarrassing. She followed Billy down the steps, and Slade went towards the villa.

The garden of the Villa of the Flute unfurled itself like a scroll, and at the bottom of the first flight of steps a marble belvedere looked out and down upon the little Greek theatre with its sheltering cypresses, and the water cistern, and the terraces and winding paths and masses of foliage and flowers. Camellias were in bloom. Roses and pelargonium scrambled over the balustrades. The *parterre* about the water cistern was packed with flowers. There were statues very white against dark foliage.

The two girls entered the belvedere, and Winnie, with a little sigh, leaned out through one of the narrow windows.

"Isn't it beautiful."

"Yes, just that."

"I've never been here before. Have you?"

"No."

"It makes one feel—you know—there's a story. A duke or somebody was in love with a famous singer, and he built this place for her, the little theatre and everything."

"Did she give up her job?"

"They say so. And she used to sing in that theatre. O, look!"

She pointed like a child, for from the cistern a sudden plume of water shot upwards into the sunlight, and flashed and trembled, and made a cool plashing as the glitter of its falling drops fell back into the cistern. Slade had turned on the fountain. Almost it suggested a playful and aerie question-mark rising and falling in the sunlight.

Winnie Haycroft stood blinking her pale eyes.

"I suppose he used to turn it on for her, the duke—I mean. Did you ever see the fountains in Trafalgar Square? It's just like a silver feather."

Lunch was an alfresco affair. A table had been laid in the orchestra of the Greek theatre, pleasantly in the sunlight, but sheltered by the circle of cypresses. A waiter from Tindaro, hired for the occasion, followed Slade down the steps with bottles wrapped up in wet cloths.

"Asti has been found, Miss Haycroft. I hope it won't be as uppish as the fountain."

It was a very pleasant lunch, with the cypresses throwing a half circle of shadow close to the table. A couple of statues on pedestals shared the orchestra with them, a dancing faun, and a Narcissus. The little waiter scuffled sedulously round behind the chairs. Winnie Haycroft was persuaded to drink Asti, and rather liked it, and was rescued temporarily from her inferiority complex. Slade talked, and he could talk very well, and he talked as much to Winnie Haycroft as he did to Billy. Winnie thought him very amusing.

She had ceased from feeling on edge. Really, Oscar Slade could be a charming person, quite nice and kind, and not the horrible and terrifying celebrity of her imaginings. Yes, certainly Tindaro was a very scandalous town, and people did say such awful things, and you were made to believe them. Perhaps Billy had discovered the real Oscar Slade, the man who owned this delicious garden, and turned on fountains, and was playful and considerate. Those horrible people at the Café Ceres had suggested the wrong atmosphere.

"Luigi, some more Asti for Miss Haycroft."

She simpered.

"No, really—please.   I mustn't."

The fountain continued to play; the dancing faun rejoiced, Narcissus meditated, and from the white belvedere up above a woman looked down upon the luncheon party.   She had reached the belvedere, not by the way of the steps, but by following a narrow path which tunnelled beneath oleanders and arbutus.   It was Lotta.   She stood there with her head pressed against the marble of the belvedere, and her dark eyes had an inward stare.   She kept pulling at her lower lip with a crooked first finger.

III

Burt had been spending half his Sunday up in the hills, exploring the marks of a very early hill-town, and the day had been good.   The spades and mattocks of half a dozen peasants hired by Il Dottore at so much an hour had uncovered the line of a cyclopean wall, and incidentally had thrown out sundry potsherds of primitive and priceless interest.   Burt carried them in the bulging pockets of his working-coat.

He had left his peasants at a wine shop in one of the villages, for those potsherds had produced a litre flask of Chianti.   He had one or two patients to see that evening, and he was expecting Julia Lord, and as he followed the goat tracks and mule paths back towards Tindaro he wondered what he would say to Julia Lord.

For Stella Burt had let a week go by and had not made up her mind, a pause that was comprehensible to her husband, but incomprehensible to Miss Lord.   For the comprehending of Stella was the growth of a lifetime.   You could not catalogue her, or postulate her reactions, or fasten upon her any system of behaviour that was easy and obvious.   She felt things, and until the feel of a particular situation came to her she would be mute and aloof, sitting at her piano or in her garden.   The priestess of Delphi.   Inward seeing has to be waited for; it cannot be coerced.

As a doctor Burt had to employ labels; a definite diagnosis was necessary; the modern and educated patient expected to be treated as a person of intelligence, and Burt could remember a time when he had set out to explain life by means of biochemistry. He had smiled at what he had called the jargon of metapsychics. Clairvoyance, telepathy, spiritistic humbug! Later he had been forced to consider the supernormal in the mental makeup of his wife. For technical jargon apart, Stella Burt had powers which the academic and mechanical psychology could not explain. She did see at a distance, if occasionally; she was like a sensitive human crystal in which other realities became sensuously visible.

A sensitive. A more subtle evolving of consciousness. Nor could Burt use the wise word "pathological." He would have rent any person who had used that word about his wife. She was just strangely sensitive and wholesome, and able in some unexplainable way to gather impressions that were imperceptible to people of grosser texture.

Some busybody had once said to Burt, "I hear your wife's so psychic. She's quite a medium."

It had annoyed him, and it had annoyed him intensely. He had a prejudice against people who talked psychic stuff, but that did not prevent him from realizing that Stella could be fey. She had proved it to him. And she was such a creature of exquisite aliveness, so vital, so sensitive, so lovable, so childlike in some of her ways, that Burt would not have her labelled according to the cant of any particular cult. She was just Stella, a rather mystical but wholesome little person, who had an incomprehensible sensitiveness towards people and things. He left it at that.

He was thinking of the Billy Brown affair when he pushed open his garden gate, and saw Julia Lord coming down the path. Just a coincidence, of course! But he did appreciate the point that Julia Lord was coming away, and that she smiled at him.

"Had a good day?"

She glanced at his bulging pockets.

"Unusually good. Early pottery. I have been hunting for some of this particular stuff for years."

He took out a piece of dull brown sherd, and showed it to her, but his enthusiasm was too technical. To Julia Lord it looked like so much rubbish, but she supposed that to Burt, and to those who knew, it was treasure-trove.

"Very early?"

"Neolithic.   Sure of it.   When old Professor Nitti sees this he'll grow epileptic."

She smiled at him and his piece of brown sherd.   He was so solid and keen and lovable; so English.

She said, "I've had half an hour with Stella.   She has made up that mysterious mind of hers."

"Why mysterious?"

"O, you know what I mean.   It's a term of respect.   She never gives you reasons."

"That, Julia, is why she is so sound.   You can't give any reasons for some things.   Even as a doctor I know that.   We are much less pompous than we used to be.   About the girl, of course?"

"She is going to tell her."

Burt slipped the piece of pottery back into his pocket.

"She is.   When?"

"To-morrow.   She's asking Billy up to dinner.   It's an immense relief to me.   She can do it better——"

"Yes, better than anyone else."

CHAPTER XIV

I

BURT was 'phoned for after dinner. Someone needed him at the Hotel Elyseo, and he left Stella at the piano, weaving improvisations, with the rising moon looking in at the window. He found his patient in a first-floor room, fat, florid and in the late fifties, rather frightened and in pain. "It must be the lobster, doctor. My wife wouldn't eat any." And Burt smiled inwardly and supposed, "So you ate the lot." A very simple case, like the luscious sufferer himself who came from Bradford.

Burt dealt with the gentleman from Bradford and his acute gastritis. "You'll have to starve for a day or two." There were people to whom he enjoyed giving such orders, saprophytic people. Nothing depressed them more than being forbidden to eat. He went down into the lounge of the Elyseo and found it full of bridge-tables and burbling voices and the smothered efforts of an orchestra. The noise was devastating. Old women on perches screaming at each other like parrots. You had to scream to make yourself heard. And not a window was open.

Burt passed through and out into the moonlight. He thought—"Queer way people have of enjoying themselves. All that money. Physical reactions. Too much dinner, too much fug. Go to bed at twelve o'clock chattering and banging doors. No wonder they need me."

He had had a good day up there on the hills, and he was feeling pleasantly tired and sleepy. Thank Heaven Stella did not play bridge, and had no social restlessness, and he was able to go to bed when he pleased, and that was when the flesh willed it. He had had a great day. He had been digging for years to unearth specimens of that particular primitive

144

pottery, rough brown sherds, and he had seen the white teeth of the Italian diggers smiling at him and his enthusiasm. No doubt they thought it strange that a man should get excited about the fragments of a broken pot.

Burt closed the gate of his garden, and noticed that there was no light in the music-room window. He supposed that Stella had gone to bed. He yawned pleasantly, locked the door, and hung up his hat.

"Jack."

He was surprised to hear her voice. It came from the music-room, and he found her sitting at her piano with the moonlight flooding in upon the keyboard and her idle hands. Her figure had a peculiar stillness.

"Anything serious?"

"No. Only a gentleman from Bradford who had eaten too much lobster. What about bed?"

She did not move. Her face and hands seemed to float in the moonlight above the black and white of the keyboard.

"I shouldn't go to bed, Jack."

"Any reason?"

"Someone is coming for you. I've had a rather vivid impression of something rather horrible."

Burt looked at her attentively and then sat down.

"What sort of impression?"

"Something violent and physical."

"The gentleman from Bradford's nausea was that. I'm rather sleepy, Stella."

Her face was turned to him. She loved him for the way he could fall asleep suddenly and happily; it was so innocent; and she loved in him all sorts of things the loving of which might have seemed absurd.

"I have felt it so strongly, Jack."

"All right. You are a strange little person. Like to talk?"

"Go and lie on the sofa. I'll play. And you can go to sleep."

"And you?"

"I feel so very wide awake."

He rose, and going to the piano, bent down and kissed her hair.

"Well, we'll experiment. Imagine the Elyseo trying to understand a doctor sitting up because his wife assured him that she had felt a message in the air?"

"They wouldn't understand it. They eat too much."

"Yes, half humanity is stomach."

Burt lay down on the sofa, with a cushion under his head, and a week-old copy of *The Times* under his feet; he did not take his boots off, and it was an act of faith. Stella's hands began to move over the notes; she was improvising, her head slightly bent, as though she was listening for sounds that passed into her sensitive self, and dropped from her moving fingers. Burt lay and watched her, and wondered. Music, especially his wife's music when she improvised, was like some spiritual solvent reducing materialism to an impertinent absurdity. He heard other voices. Whence, how, whither? How could the merely mechanical explain the creation of music, the rhythm and the mysterious rightness of it, its superhuman something? Or a concerto and the sudden tumult of violins, strings trembling —and with what? Yes, there were people who were unique, and Stella was one of them. If you likened the average man or woman to a drum, then Stella was a violin. She gave what a drum could not give. There was no equality. You had this more sensitive instrument evolving, and something much more than an instrument, a creature of other consciousness, aware of other realities. Humanity was still in the becoming. The trouble was that it sweated furiously after money, and ate too much.

He yawned. He had been out in the fresh air on the hills. Part of him was expectant, part of him wanted to sleep. The music and the moonlight seemed to merge into a melodious mist; his wife became a super-sensuous creature in a world of dreams. He remembered thinking—"The Elyseo. Lobster. Now wouldn't this seem fatuous to Bradford!" and he dropped off, and Stella knew that he was asleep. She withdrew her hands from the keyboard with a gentle, gliding movement. She sat and listened.

Yes, he went off just like a child. Big, solid, boyish, lovable person. The world knew him, and yet did not know him. How little the world knew about anybody. It was satisfied with King, Queen, Jack, Ace. It cherished the Joker. She sat and waited. She felt most strangely alert, and vaguely troubled, and glad to listen to man's tranquil breathing. It was like the sound of the sea on a lonely night.

Suddenly she turned her head; her figure had a momentary stillness; then she rose and stood at the window. She had caught the sound of footsteps; they came to the gate of the garden; she heard the faint creak of the hinges.

"Jack, someone is coming."

II

Burt woke to the flashing on of the light. He sat up, and saw his wife standing by the door, and almost at the same moment there was the clangour of a bell.

He rose to his feet, and passed a hand over his hair.

"Well—you were right. Sleeping long?"

"Nearly an hour—I should think."

"By Jove—I'll go."

He hurried heavily out of the room, and across the hall to the door. The bell rang again, and its clangour was agitated. Burt unlocked and opened the door. A man was standing there, the upper part of him in the shadow, his legs in the moonlight.

"Well, what is it?"

"The Signore Slade——"

"You? No—you're Vanni the gardener. Well——?"

"Come at once, quickly."

The man was breathing heavily; he had been running.

"Slade? Who sent you?"

"Lotta."

"Your master's ill?"

"He is dead, signore."

Burt's deep voice grew sharp.

"Dead! What do you mean? How——?"

The man spread his arms.

"You will see. Come quickly. I do not know who did it. Lotta called me, and I saw. He is in his bed, signore. There is blood."

Burt could move quickly for so big and deliberate a man. He recrossed the hall to his consulting-room, snatched a bag, and returning realized Stella in the music-room doorway. He paused.

"You were right. Something at Slade's place."

She said, "I heard. It has happened as it should happen to such a man. I'm thinking of the girl."

Burt took his hat from the stand.

"Billy Brown! O, that's not—— Good lord! I'll make tracks."

It took Burt twenty minutes to reach the Villa of the Flute. He and Vanni took short cuts through olive groves and vineyards, the Italian carrying Burt's surgical bag, and scuffling along close to the doctor. Vanni was one of those little men with a body like a barrel carried on short, stout thighs. He had been frightened, and he was still very much out of breath, and sedulously keeping his shadow close to Burt's. They did not exchange more than half a dozen words.

"Nothing more to tell?"

"Nothing signore."

Giovanni's silence was accepted for what it was worth and for what it suggested. Burt knew his Italy, or that fragment of Italy which was Tindaro; it could look at you with round eyes and remain stubbornly and sombrely taciturn. They reached the iron gates and the avenue of cypresses, a black cleft into which the moonlight broke in splintered silver. The night was supremely still. Those tall trees did not move a finger; the shadows had sharp and unflickering edges.

Burt knew the Villa of the Flute almost as well as he knew the Villa Felice, for he had doctored people there long before Slade had come to Tindaro. The shadow thrown by the loggia cut the white façade of the house in two. At the top of the steps the door stood open, but there were no lights in the vestibule or hall, and Burt, who had taken his bag from Giovanni, groped his way in. He felt for the switches on the wall of the vestibule, but could not find them.

"Hallo, Vanni, the lights."

The gardener found them for him.

"Which room?"

"The bedroom, the signore's bedroom, upstairs."

"You had better wait here. I may want you."

The staircase was of white marble, and the well of the hall went up to a circular light in the flat roof. The upper rooms opened upon a kind of balcony overhanging the hall, and Slade's bedroom was in the centre and looking south. Its door hung half open. There was a light in the room, but not a very bright light. It came from the pedestal-lamp on a table beside the bed, and diffused itself through a rose lace shade. Burt's footsteps came back to him as an echo from the high ceiling of the flat roof.

Somehow he had expected to find Slade's room empty save for the thing that was Slade, but when he pushed the door back and entered, he saw a woman sitting in a chair between the foot of the wooden bedstead and the window. It was Lotta. She did not look at him. Her eyes appeared to be fixed on the lamp beside the bed. Her face had a strange, stubborn immobility; it was like a mask of white wax with two black motionless eyes.

Burt gave her one glance and turned to the bed. He saw Slade lying there on his back like a man asleep, though the face had a sort of twisted smile. The sheet had been drawn up to the dead man's throat. Burt, with a big hand, turned the sheet back, and stood staring. The blue silk of the sleeping-jacket was all red; something protruded.

For half a minute Burt stood very still, but it was the stillness of a man observing every detail. There was no movement from the woman in the chair. He turned and spoke to her.

"You—— ? "

Her head moved on her powerful neck like the nodding head of a mechanical figure. She did not speak; her eyes remained fixed on the lamp. Burt's face was in the shadow.

"Why?"

Her hands made a movement, clasping each other in her lap. "He was a bad man. He had no pity. It was first one

woman—and then another.   He had told me to go.   He had
had from me what he wanted————"

"And you?"

Her dark head nodded.

"There was to be yet another woman, the English signorina.
I had suffered.   I—too—had no pity."

She ceased, and sat there with her strange, white, taciturn
face, sombrely staring.   Burt had placed his bag on the foot
of the bed.   His shoulders looked all hunched up.   The room
felt horribly still and airless, and it smelt of something.   The
curtains were drawn.   He seemed to remember the moonlight
and the clear night air; he went quickly across the room, and
flicked back the curtains and opened windows and shutters.   The
moonlight poured in.   He stood looking down into the garden.

God, what a business, what a tragic mess!   And that woman,
so strangely like a sullen and stricken animal, sitting there and
staring at the lamp.   She must have crept in and driven that
knife into Slade's chest.   Good god!   What a climax, and
what an aftermath!   He had pushed his big hands deep into
his trouser pockets, and was gripping money and a bunch of
keys.   That room, with its faint and sickly smell, and the
smirk of anguish on Slade's face, and down there the dead
man's garden strangely still and mysterious in the moonlight!

His voice came with sudden vigour.

"Lotta————"

There was no answer.   He turned head and shoulders to
look.   The chair was empty; so was the room.   She had
slipped out with almost incredible noiselessness.   He had not
been conscious of any sound.

"Lotta————!"

He rushed out and looked down the white staircase.   It, too,
was empty.   He hurried down it into the hall, and out into the
loggia, glancing right and left.

"Vanni, hallo————"

The gardener was sitting huddled up on the steps.   His
head rose like the head of a man emerging from dark water.

"Have you seen Lotta?"

"No, signore.   I have seen nothing."

III

Burt was not a man who lost his head. It was too solidly placed between his shoulders, and when he had gone upstairs again to that fatal room, and turned the sheet over the dead face, and recovered his bag, his thoughts had left the Villa of the Flute. The Villa of the Flute would be the concern of the Italian police. Slade might be dead; but like many dead men who have been great hunters of women, he had left behind him the frayed ends of broken affairs. Burt was thinking of Billy. He had begun to think of her at the very moment when he had seen the handle of that knife protruding. Billy was the one person who mattered, because she was just what she was.

He had sent Giovanni off to the police at Tindaro, but the Italian was scared and would not go alone, but followed behind Burt like a dog on a string, and Burt, taking a path that joined the lower road with the lane running past Julia Lord's villa, found Giovanni still the sedulous shadow. He got rid of him at the gate of the Villa Vesta. "I'm stopping here. You had better get on." And he had seen that squat and middle-aged little Italian running on ridiculous, stout legs, like a frightened boy down that empty and moonlit lane. On any other night Burt would have laughed or have felt laughter in him. Giovanni running for his life to take refuge with the police!

Burt turned in at Miss Lord's gate. He was vague as to the time; it was one of those occasions when time became relative, but he supposed that Julia Lord would be asleep. Well, he would have to wake her. He was not sure of her window; he knew that it overlooked the garden, and he went round to the other side of the little white house, and considered. All the windows were dark. He had an electric torch in his bag, and he flashed the beam successively on the three upper windows. The one on the right was wide open. Obviously Julia Lord slept in there.

He bent down and found a small stone and tossed it up so that it entered the window and bounced on the tiled floor of the bedroom. He kept his torch turned on the window. He heard a chair pushed back, and then Julia Lord's voice.

"Who's that?"

He turned off the torch.

"Burt. Sorry to wake you. Something's happened. **Can** you come down?"

He saw her face for a moment.

"Yes. I'll be with you in two minutes."

Admirable woman! Julia Lord would keep her head. And when she came down into the garden she found him standing at the top of the steps leading to the little sunk garden and its cistern. He turned and spoke to her at once.

"Do you mind if we go a little farther away."

He neither noticed the strangeness of her garments, nor the funny old plaid slippers she was wearing; they were English and men's at that. He led the way to the terrace and the cypresses, and put his bag down on the wall. His thinking had become deliberate.

He said, "Slade's dead. I've just been up there. Pretty beastly business. That woman of his—Lotta."

He did not look at Julia Lord, but went on at once.

"Stuck a knife into him. Don't blame her—altogether. But it's about the girl. Rather a problem, rather a ghastly *dénouement*. One of those things that——"

Miss Lord was drawing her dressing-gown round her as though she suddenly felt cold.

"What a deliverance! But my dear man, she'll be——"

"Exactly. A pretty ghastly knock for a girl like her, a girl with character. Nausea. Now, what—— ? "

"She'll have to be told at once."

"First thing in the morning. It wouldn't do to let her hear it from——"

"No. I'll do it. Or would Stella? What do you think?"

Burt looked steadily at moonlit Tindaro.

"Let's leave it to Stella. I'll get her to go down early, and bring Billy to breakfast at our place. Stella has a way of doing things."

Miss Lord stood rigid.

"I might be jealous of your wife if she wasn't Stella."

CHAPTER XV

I

BILLY was up very early, for she and Slade were to bathe. She tucked her blue bathing-dress and wrap into the straw bag, and went out by way of the garden. There was more wind this morning, and the cypresses bent their tops, and the olives on the hill-sides were grey, and the sea itself had a deeper blueness. The Island of the Triton showed a flounce of white foam stitched to its black rocks, and there would be no landing on those rocks this morning.

The wind was in Billy's hair, but the heart of her was untroubled, and when she came to the last loop of the path above the little bay and found the stretch of sand empty she supposed that she was early and her lover late. She turned and looked back up the path, but seeing no one, she went down to the sands, and standing close to the incoming rush of the waves, let herself feel all that fresh and windy blueness. Yes, assuredly life was good, beautiful and good.

But no Slade came, and she had turned and was standing with her back to the sea when the figures of men appeared upon the ridge of rock shutting in one curve of the bay. They came scrambling over the rocks and down on to the sand, and Billy stood at gaze. Two of the men wore the uniform of the police, and Billy knew them by sight; the other three were fishermen. They came along the curve of the sand. They were bunched close together; they were talking; the faces were all turned towards her, and she was puzzled. One of the fishermen, who was bare-legged, was wet almost to the waist.

They approached and passed close. One of the policemen raised his hand to her in a salute. She had a feeling that they looked at her queerly, so very queerly, and when they had gone by the man with the wet trousers turned his head and glanced back. She stood and watched them. She saw them scramble on to the rocks of the southern horn of the bay, and spread themselves as though searching for something. She noticed that their faces were turned often towards her.

She had a sudden sense of chilliness. She felt that she could not bathe with those men there. She had lost her wish to bathe. It was as though the blue sea had suddenly grown sinister. She walked back across the strip of sand to the hill path, and climbed it slowly, expecting to meet Slade. She met no one, but she could still see those five figures searching for something. Had someone been drowned?

She returned as she had come, but the morning had lost its first bloom, and she was more aware of the wind in the trees. She had closed the garden door, and was walking up between the orange trees towards the loggia of the tearoom when she became aware of a figure standing at the window above. She was startled. The morning was giving her nothing but the unexpected. Mrs. Burt! But why? In her room at a quarter to eight! She paused, and stood looking up, aware of the faintly-smiling face of the other woman. And yet the smile was not quite a smile.

"I have been waiting for you, Billy."

"Have you? I went down to bathe."

"So I thought. I came to fetch you to breakfast with us. You'll come, my dear, won't you?"

Billy's face was questioning.

"It's awfully good of you. I'd love to. I shall have to change, and be back at nine."

"You will have time. We breakfast at eight."

Billy passed into the loggia, and through the tearoom into the passage. The unexpected enlarged itself. Of course there was nothing strange in Stella Burt coming down so early and asking her to breakfast, for the Burts were kind people, and yet it was strange. Everything had been a little strange, Slade's absence, those men on the rocks, the unexpected face of Stella Burt, her smile. Billy went slowly up the stairs to find Stella Burt sitting in her basket-chair, and looking over the pages of *Country Life*.

"I'll wait here while you change."

Again that faint smile, and something in the eyes, and Billy passed through into her bedroom feeling vaguely disturbed. Was anything wrong? But what could be wrong? Was Julia Lord ill? No, of course not. Absurd! She might as well confess that she had been a little disappointed in the morning, and at Oscar's not turning up. Just a mood.

She threw her basket of bathing kit on the bed, and got out her yellow jumper and black skirt. She had closed the bedroom door, and was in the act of changing her skirt when she heard footsteps coming up the stairs. There was a sudden movement in the next room, the creaking of a chair; Mrs. Burt was going to the door to meet the person coming up the stairs. Billy stood to listen, her black skirt drawn half way up her legs.

"O—Mrs. Burt——!"

Winnie's voice!

"Yes—I'm here. Billy is coming to breakfast with us."

And then there was a peculiar silence, no more words, not so much as a whisper, and Billy heard Winnie Haycroft descending the stairs. Her footsteps sounded surreptitious; almost she seemed to be sneaking away. Funny! Why that sudden silence? It was as though those two had been making signs to each other.

She pulled up her skirt, fastened it, and going to the bedroom door, opened it with an air of sudden resolution.

"Mrs. Burt——?"

"Yes."

"Was that Winnie Haycroft?"

"Yes."

Stella Burt was in the same chair, reading the gardening notes in *Country Life*.

"Did she want anything?"

"I don't think so. She did not expect to find me here."

Billy stood holding the door and looking at the figure in the chair.

"Mrs. Burt—there's nothing wrong—with Julia?"

"Nothing, Billy. Nearly ready?"

"Yes, I shan't be a moment."

At eight o'clock in the morning the Corso was wholly native, and Billy and Stella Burt saw no English faces. Tindaro was very much in its slippers, taking down shutters, and appearing at shop doorways in bulging dishabille. There were little groups of early newsmongers, especially where a passage or a lane opened into the Corso and brought its casual humanity into the main stream of Tindaro's life, and it seemed to Billy that some of these people stared at her rather unnecessarily. The Italian is a great starer. Outside the Café Ceres Tommaso stood among the tables with his usual bucket and swab, while a man in velveteen trousers and a rather dirty shirt, gesticulated and declaimed. They had their backs to the two Englishwomen. The man in the dirty shirt was obviously excited.

Stella Burt took Billy's arm. Anything to distract the girl's attention from what that fellow might be saying. Yes, probably he was noisy with news.

She said, "This is the time to see Tindaro as it is, before it has dressed up for the forestieri," and inwardly she was saying, "Thank heaven the girl's Italian is rather shaky."

Billy had a perplexed and troubled face.

"Yes. In its shirt sleeves. Does it strike you that people are staring—rather——"

"Are they? Like children. They are big children."

They were close to the Café Ceres, and Mrs. Burt diverged as though to look in a shop window, drawing Billy with her. Stella Burt was listening. Yes, that fellow in the dirty shirt had picked up the news from somewhere, and was displaying it luridly to Tommaso. A shop window offered among other things tortoiseshell and amber, and Stella became suddenly eloquent upon tortoiseshell.

"But we mustn't stop, my dear. Doctors have to be precise people, when they can. I got a lovely little box from that man last year——"

They were past the two men, but Billy, whose face had grown suddenly attentive and troubled, turned to look back. Mrs. Burt felt the resistance of the young arm, and she too, looked back in time to catch the two men staring at them. Tommaso had clutched the shoulder of the man in the dirty shirt. Abruptly, and almost guiltily they turned their backs, and Tommaso began to swab a table.

"Mrs. Burt, what were those two men saying?"

"Really, my dear, I don't know."

"Something about us. Didn't you see the way——?"
Stella Burt drew her on.

"O, gossip."

But Billy had plunged suddenly into the strange and the un-expected as into a dark wood; or like a child playing a blindfold game she felt near to something in the darkness.

"Mrs. Burt—what's funny about Tindaro this morning? What's the matter? There—is—something."

"Why——?"

"There is. Everything's funny. Even the way Winnie Haycroft crept downstairs. And I believe you know."

She was looking into Stella Burt's face, and the face of Burt's wife could not be veiled. She felt the pressure of Billy's arm.

"So—there is something. You do know. Is that why?"
Stella Burt drew her on.

"Billy—there is something. Yes, that's why. But you will have breakfast first. You are going to be brave."

"Is it Miss Lord?"

"No."

"Is it——?"

And then she saw and realized, and seemed to take a little quick breath, and to stiffen herself.

"All right. Don't tell me yet. We were to bathe together, and he didn't come. Has something happened to him?"

Stella Burt nodded.

"You may know that, Billy dear. He died in the night. There is more. But that's enough just now. Remember—you have good friends."

II

Billy followed Stella Burt into the Villa Felice. She was not the kind of girl who crumples; she kept a grip upon herself much as she had kept possession of that suitcase on the platform of Tindaro station many months ago. She remembered the

F

occasion; it came to her suddenly with the smell of hot coffee, and with it the memory of Tindaro as she had seen it and felt it on that first adventurous night. Adventure! But adventure hurt. You felt dumb and a little bewildered.

"Take your hat off, Billy."

She removed her hat just as Burt came in and gave her one quick glance, the physician's glance, searching but kind. He nodded at her. "Breakfast, good business. Glad you could come," and he did not look at her again, but sat down and like a good Englishman ate bacon and eggs. Billy blessed him. These people had the kindness that refrains, a kindness that can appear comforting yet casual. She drank coffee; it was very good coffee, and somehow she enjoyed it, and was vaguely surprised at herself for enjoying it. The rolls were fresh, and the marmalade had come from Julia Lord's preserving pan. Marmalade! It was an extraordinarily silent meal, and yet it had none of the acute discomfort of certain occasions when a horrible dumbness reigns.

Billy found her voice. She made the strangest of remarks.

"One might do worse things—mightn't one? I mean— making marmalade for the poor English in exile."

The doctor accepted her remark with all seriousness. It was symptomatic.

"Very sound idea. Julia Lord's ideas *are* sound."

He looked at Stella, and his eyes said—"This kid has got pluck. I'll clear out now, and leave her to you." His wife nodded at him; they were so much one in marriage that they understood each other without the use of words, especially so when any crisis was in the air. They felt things in the same way.

Burt went off to light a pipe and to prepare for the beginnings of a busy day, for he knew that much of this affair would lie heavily upon his shoulders. It would be both English and Italian, though probably the Italians would not be inclined to advertise the tragedy; it would be hushed up. Burt had had such cases before, obvious suicides which the local authorities had persisted in regarding as accidental. Like snow or bad weather in the French Riviera—such things did not happen. And perhaps in their own way the Italians would be wise. Why allow a fuss to be made over the elimination of a man like Oscar Slade, even though he happened to be a minor celebrity?

Burt lit his pipe, and thought of his wife and Billy. Just how would the girl react? What would she do? Obviously it was the duty of the decent people to rally round her. He heard the opening and closing of a door and knew that his wife and Billy had gone to the music-room, which was also the drawing-room, for that was one of Stella's prejudices; she would not admit a drawing-room into her house.

Billy was standing at the window. How blue the sea looked! And how strange it was to see the sun shining and to feel that dull ache in you.

She said, "You have something more to tell me."

Stella had brought with her her husband's cigarette-box.

"Have one, Billy."

"I think I will."

"Matches—there in the box. Sit down in that chair."

"I think I'd rather stand."

Stella placed the silver box on the window-sill. She had a feeling that Billy did not want to be looked at for the moment, and she went to her piano and sat down, and struck a few gentle and tentative notes.

"Billy, dear, this happened so suddenly. I had made up my mind to tell you something to-day. It was something we felt you would have to be told."

"About Oscar?"

"Yes. You see—you didn't know; you couldn't know— the kind of man he really was. He had a personality."

"Please tell me quickly."

"My dear, he didn't die naturally; someone killed him."

"Who?"

"A woman. You see—there had been many women in that man's life. He was that sort of man. He was very clever; he was what you might call an old hand."

Billy made a sudden movement. She was looking at her own hand, and realizing that she had not worn Slade's ring that morning, because they had been going to bathe together. Then she stood very still, looking out at the sea. She felt strangely numb, and a little sick; she was on the edge of a poignant humiliation.

She said, "I didn't know. I thought—you see, it had never happened to me quite in this way before."

Stella played two or three bars of one of Chopin's nocturnes.

"We understood that. We knew that something would have to be done about it. We were worried. You may call it what you please, a sort of badness in him, a kind of ghastly selfishness. When a woman attracted him he could not say no. Some men are like that. He did not think for the woman. He was like a greedy child. I'm just telling you the truth. It's kinder. You will get over this, dear, and perhaps you will get over it more quickly in this way."

Billy had finished her cigarette, and she dropped the end into a vase on the window-sill.

"Perhaps. It's—rather—horrible. I want you to tell me who the woman was?"

"Must I?"

"Yes, please."

"An Italian woman named Lotta, who kept house for him."

"What has happened to her?"

"They don't know yet. They think——"

"That she has drowned herself? I—I understand now. Poor Lotta. If you don't mind, Mrs. Burt, I'd like to be alone just for a minute or two. I've—I've got to put a new face on life—somehow."

And Burt's wife went softly out of the room.

III

When Stella Burt returned Billy was sitting on a chair by the window. She rose; she held herself very straight with rigid shoulders and back, and Stella Burt was struck by the characteristic inflexibility of that posture. It reminded her of someone else. Who was it? Why—of course—Julia Lord! Just that same carriage of the head, as though on parade, chin well up, not a quiver, the world looked straight in the face. It was as though all the flexibility of youth had melted suddenly out of Billy Brown's figure.

"Mrs. Burt, I am going down to the library now.   I've been thinking.   I have got to show people."

"My dear, I think that's rather splendid."

"You see, it isn't as if I'd been left with something—clean, something that really belonged to me.   I can't just describe how I feel.   One doesn't want to, does one?   But it's like having something killed in you."

Stella went to her piano stool, but she did not touch the piano.

"I can understand.   But don't let it take too much.   He was too utterly unworthy——"

"That's what's so horrible.   I didn't see; I didn't feel.   I thought——   You see I did care."

"Of course."

"But why didn't I see?   It makes one doubt—oh—everything in oneself.   It's like being stripped——"

"No, not quite that.   You looked at him, Billy, with your clean eyes, and you thought that he must be like you.   And now you feel——"

Her hands opened and closed.

"I feel ashamed, naked, as though something had been torn out of me.   But I must hold tight.   Yes, I must carry on.   I'm going down there to work."

Stella sat and gazed at her.   Astonishing, her sudden likeness to Julia Lord, an almost tragic likeness, for life had dealt Julia Lord just such a blow, and that firm white surface had closed over the wound.

"Yes—work.   But Billy, my dear, don't put us and things out of your heart.   You'll understand what I mean, perhaps, later.   I'd like to walk down with you.   May I?"

"Please."

And Billy, with some of the abruptness of a child, crossed over to the music stool and put her face forward.

"You have been a dear to me.   No, I'm quite all right. I'm not going to blub."

Stella kissed her on the forehead, and Billy's forehead felt strangely cold.

IV

Stella Burt and Julia Lord met in the Corso. They spoke with a kind of hushed swiftness, looking into each other's eyes.

"She knows."

"Thank the Lord. Where is she?"

"My dear, in the library. Poor kid, she's rather splendid. She feels like Lady Godiva—but without any of the glory. It has stripped her of something, Julie."

Miss Lord looked fierce.

"What's happened to the woman who did it? I hope she gets away. I'd like to, oh, but I'm letting go. You say that Billy is there?"

"Yes, at her post, carrying on. She's got her head up, Julie. O, my dear, if that beast of a man ever realized——"

"He! He never wanted to realize anything but himself. But I suppose this is best, that she should——?"

"I think it's splendid of her. And you'll know how to back her, Julie; you're just the woman."

"I think I am."

So Julia Lord went on to the English Library, and found Billy in possession, and busy with a feather-duster. Miss Lord closed the door, sat down in her chair at the end of the table, and opened out her ledgers. She was aware of Billy taking books from the shelves and dusting them and putting them back again, and the stout heart of Julia Lord went out to her.

She said, "I don't suppose you want to talk. I know all that needs knowing. In a way it was my fault. I ought to have warned you about that cad."

She made these remarks while turning over the leaves of the library catalogue, and Billy continued to take out books and to dust them.

"You will let me stay on here?"

Miss Lord looked at her sharply.

"What else? We are going to see this thing through together. Of course. I have been wondering whether you would care to come and dig with me for the rest of the season. Just as you like."

Billy slipped a book back into its place, and gave Julia Lord a look that she was not likely to forget.

"You are a sport. I think I'd like to."

The Villa Felice did not see Burt again until half-past twelve. He came in looking tired.

"Billy gone?"

"She went down to the library to carry on as usual."

"Did she—by Jove! Then that kid's got grit. They have found the woman."

"Dead?"

Burt nodded.

"Drowned herself—poor devil. The authorities want to hush the whole thing up. They have been worrying me. But it can't be done. I know the English Consulate people at Rome. I have written to them. I wrote from the Elyseo."

He sat down; he was tired.

"Tell you one thing—Stella, I shouldn't be a bit surprised if a Mrs. Slade turns up from somewhere. I'm glad that girl has grit. Rather a beastly knock. We have got to help her through."

CHAPTER XVI

I

SO, Lotta had turned over a page, or rather she had torn it from the book of Tindaro and thrown it crumpled into the sea. Death is a great simplifier. The formalities gathered and were dispersed, for there was nothing left upon which formalism could spend itself. Slade was buried in the Italian section of the cemetery of Tindaro, and no one went to see him buried save a couple of officials and a busy little English lawyer who had been rushed out from London. Native Tindaro was hostile, though it went in its hundreds to watch the woman laid to rest. It understood the uses and the rightness of a knife.

Native Tindaro watched two Englishwomen come and go along the Corso, Miss Lord and Billy, woman and girl who somehow had grown strangely alike. They strode side by side, looking neither to the right hand nor to the left; their faces were firm. And native Tindaro wondered. These English were strange people.

And yet not so strange. The *Daily Something* had come out with the news—"English Novelist Murdered in Italy," and the Fascist mayor of Tindaro was much angered, and eager to discover the journalist who had dispatched that juicy morsel. The Mayor of Tindaro spoke very good English and was considerably a gentleman. He said to Burt, "Doctor, if your country sends some of its rubbish to us, why should we be pilloried because an Italian woman protests as she has a right to do?"

The Mayor and Burt were very good friends.

"Journalism——"

"Ah, my doctor, we keep our press in order. We do not let any little urchin run around with a pencil and a notebook.

164

If we are not proud of certain things, and we are very proud
in these days, we make it our duty to be quietly rid of unpleasant things and people."

"But you knew Slade. You Fascists should have put him
over the frontier. I would gladly have worn a black shirt for
the occasion."

The Mayor had shrugged wise shoulders.

"Morals—delicate matters. But I object to the headlines
in your newspaper. It is the vulgar touch."

"It is not my newspaper," said Burt.

But this tragedy of the Villa of the Flute produced peculiar
reactions in those who were least concerned with its realities.
Quite a number of people from the hotels strolled up the valley
road and hung their noses over the locked gates of the villa,
and saw nothing but sunlight and shadow and cypresses. There
were others who refrained from entering the English Library
because they disapproved of the girl there.

Lady Pipp was one of the censurers. So was Mrs. Sudbury
Smith, who sent her maid with a list of the books she desired,
and also a note to Miss Lord.

> "I shall be glad if you will select these books yourself.
> I do not wish for books which have been handled by a
> particular person——"

Julia Lord saw red. Mrs. S.S. was just that sort of insensitive person who would assume a hypersensitive fastidiousness
on certain occasions. And this was sheer venom, venom
aimed at Miss Lord. She tore up the letter and the list, and
sent the maid back bookless.

Meeting Mrs. Sudbury Smith full and square in the
middle of the Corso, Julia gave instant battle as was her
way.

"O—let there be no misunderstanding, you need not expect
any more books from me."

Mrs. S.S. was a woman who reared up rather like a snake
when about to strike.

"Quite understood, thank you. We think it perfectly
scandalous——"

"Be explicit."

F*

"The whole of that girl's behaviour. Going back to her work—with an utterly callous air. It proves——"

"Just what?"

"The business was just a low intrigue. She couldn't have cared—one iota—about the man, not as a nice girl——"

Miss Lord mimicked the lady.

"Not one iota! Well, observe, you know nothing about it. It's quite beyond you, utterly beyond you. I am sending you back your deposit. You would never be fit, my dear, to black a certain person's shoes, so please leave her reputation alone."

She left Mrs. S.S. shot through between wind and water, and incapable of producing an adequate retort. Miss Lord passed on and seeing Frevick sitting alone at one of the Café Ceres' tables, she joined him. It was the first time that Julia Lord had sat at one of those tables.

But inwardly she was dishevelled with wrath, a fury with the face of Britannia. She had to tell somebody, let out to somebody, and so she told Frevick. Tommaso, passing near, heard Frevick utter strange words—"That boiled bitch! Sorry, Julie, but that's the sort of woman——" Tommaso, polite and puzzled, and always wanting to do the debonair thing, bent his plumpness into a crease to Frevick. "Did the signore order anything? Something for the lady?" Frevick gave a jerk of the head, and looked at Julia Lord. "Yes, Tommaso, bring the lady an iced orangeade."

For to Billy Brown that was the unkindest thing of all, that she should be whipped for showing courage in the face of humiliation. To begin with she did not realize that there were people who would pass by on the other side. She did not realize it until the Pipps and the Bromheads gave her the cut direct in the Corso. She had smiled at old Tom, and he had half raised his hat, and had been coerced and marched on by his wife, and this act of unfriendliness had hurt Billy rather badly. Did not these people realize how she was feeling, that the affair had stripped her of her youth, and left her secretly humiliated? Was it necessary for them to add to her humiliation? And she was shocked. So that was what they thought of her! She had had the distinction of being the last of Slade's women.

Strange world! But she was profoundly shaken. It was as though she suddenly saw herself as these people saw her, a young woman who was tarnished and had lost caste, and who had become as Sadie Shone. She had not expected this. To a girl of her temper her own secret humiliation had seemed sufficient. Probably there was no one in Tindaro who realized just what Billy suffered. To give generously and to have your giving shown up as folly, and as something worse than folly. To know that you had been no more than a silly little wench who had been played with by a world-wise cad! Yes. the world might have left it at that, and tried to understand the inwardness of her courage in going back to her job as though nothing had happened.

She felt raw, and no doubt her feeling of rawness made her hypersensitive and inclined to exaggerate the significance of certain attitudes and gestures. She began to wonder whether Julia Lord and the Burts believed that she had gone to extremes with Oscar Slade, and were tempering understanding with kindness. Well, even if she had! She was conscious of an impulse towards rebellion. It seemed to her that the blight had spread to the library and the tearoom, and that people treated her with deliberate chilliness. Perhaps some of them did. She began to wonder whether the tearoom was as full as it used to be. Her inward ears began to hear whisperings.

"Really, that girl ought to have had the decency to leave."

There was a day when she felt rather desperate. Someone had tried to be sympathetic, and had succeeded in being stupidly tactless. Winnie Haycroft—of course. But to be patronized by Winnie Haycroft!

"Of course I hear things, Billy, but I don't repeat them. People are so horribly cheap."

Horribly cheap! Just what she was feeling. And she went back to the Villa Vesta and sat at the window of her little room, and thought of that first morning when she had seen Tindaro lit by the rising sun. Horrible town, full of glare and of flies! She felt that something was giving way in her, that she could not brazen it out. And seeing Julia Lord going down to the little terrace with a book, she took her shame in her two hands and made her confession.

"Don't think me hysterical, Julia, but I think I ought to go."

Miss Lord closed her book.

"Go? What do you mean?"

"I shan't do you any good. You see I didn't realize that I should be taboo."

"Taboo! To whom?"

"O, to lots of people. Some of them have cut me dead. And I feel it in the library, a sort of cold blight."

"Do you want to go? I—don't want you to go."

She was aware of Billy's poignant face.

"Some people don't matter, my dear. Very few people matter. There was a time when I had to go through the same sort of thing."

"You?"

"O, yes. People trying to pity you and patronize you and put you in a sweet little hell of their own contriving. Fight them, my dear. Don't go under to the crowd. I want you to stay."

Billy did the most unexpected of things. She knelt down at Miss Lord's knees, and held her hands.

"Julia, you do believe—that I was genuine? To me it was real. I did care. It seems extraordinary now, but I did."

Miss Lord's hands gripped Billy's.

"Of course I believe. I haven't a shadow of a doubt."

"O, you dear."

"Other people believe."

"The Burts?"

"Of course. Even Tom Frevick."

"I'm glad he does. He's rather a dear too, Julie. And then—you see—I haven't told my mother."

Miss Lord sat thinking.

"Good girl."

"Then you think I'm right not to tell her? She has enough to worry about."

"Quite right."

"That's why I'd rather hang on.   It would look so like a licking if I sneaked home.   What do you think?"

Miss Lord looked her straight in the eyes.

"Stay here with me and fight it out.   I know what fighting it out means.   I'm with you, my dear.   I'd rather like to have you as a partner."

"O, Julie, you mean it?   You dear.   That's just the sort of thing I want.   A grip."

"That's it, grip."

II

So, Billy buckled up the straps of her pride, and she and Julia Lord marched shoulder to shoulder between the Villa Vesta and the English Library.   Yet there was a part of the Corso which Billy dreaded.   She could not pass the Café Ceres without being conscious of inward flinching, for a memory sat at one of the tables and looked at her cynically from under the brim of its hat.   So very aware was she of the Café Ceres that she let Julia Lord walk on the side next to the white-topped tables, and though there was no quickening of their pace both women went by it with a sense of haste.   There were more flies in the windows; the cakes looked pulpier and more pink; the same people sat there and yet with a difference. The circus had lost its ringmaster.   It was a little less noisy; it expressed—somehow—a mood of shabby depression; it sat and gloomed; it was less interested in life, and less critical of it.   Its mocking air had departed.   Even the face of Mrs. Shone looked heavier and less aggressively boyish, less chalked, less red about the lips.   She had an air of discouragement. Her laughter did not break forth like water from a burst pipe. Old Ponsonby's hat got tilted more and more over his eyes. Rarely was Frevick seen there.   Mirleess was much as before, but the Café Ceres appeared bored with him.

Burt noticed the change, and so did Stella.   Her impression of the Café Ceres was that of a hollow shadow, as though the awning over the tables hung lower and shut out more light.

"Those people have a lost look."

That was her description of them, and to Burt it was both vivid and subtle. Shadowy people, exiles, under an awning, drinking their little drinks as though habit was dead and sour in the glasses.

Billy Brown's shrinking from the faces under the awning of the Café Ceres lasted until that particular occasion when she happened to pass the place unconvoyed by Miss Lord. She had been tempted to funk, and to diverge up one of the alleys, but she whipped herself on. Frevick chanced to be sitting at his usual table. He drew in his long legs, and stood up, hat in hand. The sombreness of him smiled. He had nothing to say, but his standing there in that attitude as she was about to pass was an act of homage.

She paused upon the impulse, and held out a hand.

"I have been keeping a book for you quite a long time."

"I'm afraid I had forgotten."

"'Precious Bane' by Mary Webb."

Most strange occasion! Other people stood up, Mrs. Shone, old Ponsonby, Sir Dyce Duxbury. The Café Ceres was giving expression to the promptings of an urge. The men took off their hats. Their faces had a sort of sad shyness. Mirleess was the only male who remained fastened to his chair.

Mrs. Shone was holding out a hand.

"Say, it's good to see you about."

There was something in her eyes which puzzled Billy, boldness, doubt, a hesitant appeal. Her heavy face had a shimmery look. And Billy's sudden smile came on. She took Mrs. Shone's hand.

"Getting very hot these days, isn't it?"

Billy could not say why, but the figures under the awning made her think of tremulous leaves.

Mrs. Shone pushed forward a chair.

"My dear, sit right down and have something cool."

Billy's eyes met Frevick's. He seemed to give her an almost imperceptible nod. "Yes, it's all right. We are human."

She sat down; she found herself between Frevick and Sadie Shone. She was trying to make out why Mrs. Shone's face looked different, and then Tommaso appeared, polite and eager to please.

Frevick held up a finger.

"One iced orangeade.   How's that?"

"Yes, thank you, just right."

Old Ponsonby had pushed back his hat and was smiling, and his smile had ceased to be a smirk.   Mrs. Shone sat up quite straight in her chair, with her knees together, and her mouth shut.   She looked smoothed out and tidied up.

Billy found herself talking.   They all talked, and afterwards she realized that she had no very clear recollection of what they talked about.   It did not matter.   She sucked orangeade through a straw.   Mrs. Sudbury Smith went by, and glanced at the group with a surprised malevolence which grew suddenly self-complacent and wise.   An "Ah, I thought that would happen" look!   And that, too, did not matter.   Billy was conscious of a queer little tremor of feeling; the air under the awning seemed to be permeated with a something that the superior people lacked.   And why was she moved suddenly to think of Christ and the publican?

She was aware of Frevick talking about pictures.   Apparently he was going to paint a picture, a fragment of the old Roman theatre with cypresses and blue sky behind it.

And Mrs. Shone was encouraging him.

"Why, you ought to do it.   You have the feel for it, Tom. Do you remember that picture you did of the monastery and the fruit blossom.   Miss Brown, sure, you tell him to do it."

Billy looked under the brim of her hat at Frevick.

"Won't you do it?"

He stuffed his hands into his pockets and seemed to stare into eternity.

"I might.   Depends on Bunty.   That's my dog.   She's a tyrant.   Pulls me by the bottoms of my trousers."

Billy was conscious of her own gentle laughter.

"I'm sure Bunty would be pleased.   Find her a nice place in the sun.   Isn't that the idea, Mrs. Shone?"

Mrs. Shone's eyes looked big and strange.

"Sure.   My dear, you keep him to it.   Why, if I had his

hands—sure I'd be setting to work on something other than my poor old face."

III

Then, at last Julia Lord sat down and wrote a letter to Mary Brown, a letter which was nearly a month overdue. This was the real letter; a previous one had been written to Billy's mother in which Miss Lord had been politely and kindly indeterminate. She began bluntly.

"You are not supposed to know anything of this. I should not be writing to you as I am if Billy had not come through the affair with her head well up. She did not want you to be worried, and now, since there is nothing fatal to worry about I thought it best that you should be told the whole story."

That was a reasonable beginning, but the pith of the matter was to come, and it cost Julia Lord three tentative pages, which were torn up and rewritten. She was a very determined and conscientious letter writer.

The final paragraphs were more facile, because Miss Lord allowed herself to let go a little.

"Billy has joined me here at my villa. She has been perfectly splendid. I can assure you there is no break up, and that there will not be. She has had one of those experiences which are apt to make a woman hard, but I'm not worrying about a little hardness.

I have not said anything about it to Billy, but I think it would be a good thing if she were to go home for a month or two at the end of the season. It can be managed. I usually go to Switzerland for two months. I think that Billy ought to have leisure to consider, a kind of breathing space. I rather think she will come back here. I want her to come back. The business is expanding each year, and has further possibilities, and for some time I have been looking out for a likely partner. I should like Billy to join me.   Capital is not necessary.   I have enough of my own.

So I hope that you and I will understand each other. I have told you the truth, and you will know how to use it.   Billy has a great affection.   And she is big.

Perhaps you will think that I ought to have prevented this.   I was very much worried.   But I mistrust too much interference, and I had faith in Billy.   Then— the tragic business happened so suddenly.   It is over. You must try and make allowances for me.   I can only assure you that I am most determinedly Billy's friend."

IV

Tindaro began to be very hot, and twice a day a rickety watercart trundled up and down the Corso.   Tommaso of the Café Ceres abominated that cart, because he was able to treat his own particular piece of pavement with a watering-can, and the cart was too impartial and splashed tables and chairs.   Flies were growing free and fierce.   The cakes in the window collected a black swarm each day, and Billy, sitting with Frevick or Mrs. Shone at one of the tables, wondered why Tommaso and the *padrone* did not do something about those flies.   But perhaps that was typical of Tindaro, and especially so of Tindaro in the heat.

"Why don't they kill the flies?"

"Flies, my dear!   Why they don't worry about flies in Tindaro.   And sure, if they did, they would be worrying all night.   They wouldn't know where to begin."

But at the Library and at the Villa Vesta war was waged upon flies.   Muslin screens protected the windows, and saucers of formalin and sugar and light beer persuaded the pests to be poisoned.   Also, there were mosquitoes.   Billy reinforced Miss Lord in her assaults upon insectdom; she kept a switch, and occasionally she would use it irritably upon some persistent fly.

"O, get out, you beast."

She was not sleeping very well.   Nor was she looking at herself very critically in her mirror, for mirrors were out of favour, and so she did not realize that she was growing just a little like Winnie Haycroft, faintly dusty and faded. The Tindaro season was drifting to its stale and empty end; villas were being shut up; the hotels were going to sleep.

Winnie Haycroft's plaint was in her eyes. "Oh, if I could go to England."

There was a kind of sadness in Tindaro, especially among those who were exiles; and who sat and watched the hotel buses carrying the English luggage to the station. Green England in May! The Pipps had a house in Berkshire on the river. The Sudbury Smiths went to Surrey. The Bromheads removed themselves to a cottage in Devon. Lucky people. Frevick would sit and stare with melancholy eyes at distant and imagined landscapes, the Weald of Sussex, Amberley, the Dorset hills and the sea at Lyme Regis, Beaulieu Abbey, the green valley of the Test. Mirleess babbled about Northern France, and spoke of Richebourg, and a lane behind Festubert where red may trees grew, and the hill of Cassel. Tindaro was becoming dusty and full of flies.

Billy went twice a week to dine with the Burts at the Villa Felice. Afterwards she would sit and listen to Stella's piano. And on one Sunday, Burt took her with him on one of those digging expeditions in the hills, a long, scrambling day. Billy got very tired and tried not to show it; it was a new thing for her to feel tired. But Burt noticed it.

He agreed with Julia Lord.

"The kid needs a change. That affair has taken a lot out of her. And it's her first season out here."

"Yes, she ought to go home for two months, perhaps for the summer."

"A question of finance?"

Said Miss Lord, "I'm going to make her a present of her ticket. If she comes back she will come back as my partner."

"You are a good sort, Julia. You do keep the flag flying."

"O, I do what I can."

CHAPTER XVII

I

BILLY, standing on the upper deck of the Channel boat, and looking at the cliffs of Dover, was moved to a feeling of wonder and of incredulity. Just seven months since she had seen those cliffs, and if she could say to herself that she felt seven years older that was a mere figure of speech. She did not feel older; she felt different. She had lost and gained. She looked at people and things less personally and with an impartial yet critical aloofness. She was less of the "Dear Billy."

She gazed impartially at the cliffs of Dover, and she thought that they looked rather dirty. May was in one of its northern moods, a grey and lifeless day, when the Spring colouring has a chilly rawness, a touch of the unreal. Red tulips and a north wind! Rather like life. And she had been boasting to her soul about England, and about the English Spring, and English efficiency, and she was met by a north wind and by a something in herself which shrank from it.

The family! Yes, she was going to meet the family, and had the house at Ealing held nothing but a Mary she would have had no qualms. How unexpected life was! Always in the old days she had felt so clannish, so much the sister of Irene and Ronald and the two kids, but now there was no hurrying impulse. Things did not rush to the surface. She was aware of a little edge of coldness in herself, a vague hostility, a watchfulness which looked out at life with more discrimination.

So this was England, her England!

She landed with the crowd. A custom's official was rather curt with her, and she gave him back equal curtness. Confound the man, wasn't she English and back in England. Her smile was much less in evidence. She did not realize it but she was shaping rather like Miss Lord, a young edition, she had dealt

175

with that customs official just as Miss Lord would have dealt with him.

But her porter was English, cheery and kind and reassuring. "Plenty of time for the train, Miss."

And the tea on the train was English, and so was the nice lad who served it. She felt a little less on the defensive, and sat and looked at Kent, and found England rather dim and strange after Italy, like a country with a cold in its head and wearing a grey shawl. A north wind had bleached the greenness out of the grass on the chalk hills, and the whiteness of the thorn trees was cold. She passed a beech wood in young leaf, and it had for her a puzzling and a poignant sadness. The oaks in their spring bronze were not happy warriors, so she thought.

London arrived, and somehow it astonished her. Suburbia! What stiffness! How incredibly ugly it was even with laburnums and lilac in flower! Why did she find it ugly? And nearer London, roofs, chimney-pots, backyards, a universal greyness, yellow brick, slates, a crowded chaos! She sat and wondered; she felt most strangely depressed.

Then Victoria, a sudden tense thrill, a hurrying out, her mother's kisses.

"O, Billy, my dear!" What strange kisses! She warmed to them, and yet was put out of countenance. They hurt her. She wanted to cling, and instead of clinging she stood off and smiled vaguely, and searched for her registered luggage-ticket.

"How's everybody? Oh, I'm splendid. Had a perfectly innocuous crossing."

Was that her own voice? And was that her mother's face, so dear and a little troubled, and hiding something?

"We'll have a taxi."

"Everybody's very well."

"That's good. O, porter, here's my luggage-ticket."

And then began that orgy of inept bustling with which the Southern Railway welcomes those who return home. People stood like sheep, but not quite like patient sheep, while porters bundled trunks out of vans, and dragged them like corpses, and rolled them on end. People waited. When it rained many of them had to wait in the rain. Half an hour went by. A big American behind Billy grew caustic.

"This old country wants a Henry Ford."

Another boat-train came in. Someone explained that no registered luggage could be had until both trains were unloaded. The confusion of trunks and porters seemed to grow more dishevelled.

Said someone, "You see—everything's numbered."

Said someone else, "But you won't find your trunks by the numbers."

Said the American, "Say, this is some transportation. Can't these guys organize?"

Another half hour or so, and then Billy's porter, casual and cheerful, found her and announced the news. "I don't think you're one of the lucky ones, Miss. Your trunk's been left behind at Dover."

Billy's face stiffened.

"But how absurd. When will it——?"

"Can't say, Miss. Might be nine o'clock. You could come down to-morrow morning. They'll store it for you, and you'll find a customs bloke. They'll charge you for storing."

"Charge? When they've left it behind?"

"O, well, that's their way, Miss."

"And I shall have to pay twice on taxis. It's a premium on inefficiency."

"I can't help it, Miss."

Mary Brown was watching her child, and Billy did not see herself as more and more like Miss Lord.

"We'll leave it till to-morrow, dear. You're tired."

Said Billy, "Damn these railway people! Talk about Italy? Why Mussolini would—— Sorry, dear. Let's get home."

But she felt ruffled, and very conscious of her mother, and during the long drive in the taxi, she was aware of herself as making an effort to put things into place, smooth the frayed ends. How different life was from what you expected it to be! Six months ago this home-coming would have been an eager, tumultuous affair. And she was aware of something in her mother, a veiled affection which had felt rebuffed, and watched her with careful eyes. Did her mother know? She could not know unless some friend had written to her. Meanwhile there was a kind of poignant and frustrated silence.

The taxi arrived. The two young things had been on the watch. They came hustling out, and captured Billy before she had entered the gate.

"O, Bill."

"Bill, darling."

She hugged and was kissed, and it occurred to her to think that these youngsters were spontaneous; they had not been hurt; they had not had to close doors; their faces and eyes were open. She felt better, as though the congealed streak in her had melted.

"Where's your box?"

"The nice Southern Railway forgot it."

"Mustn't it have been the French?"

"I don't think so."

"I'll carry your suitcase in. Same old room. Oh, I say, Irene's quite sick because she's had to turn out. Do her lots of good."

"Yes, Irene's awful swollen."

They went in, all bunched together. There was the same old door-mat, and the tiled hall, and the red carpet going up the stairs, and an engraving of one of Leader's pictures, and the family coats and caps and mackintoshes. Supper was laid in the dining-room. And Billy, passing through to the drawing-room, found Irene negligently arranged in an armchair, reading *Vogue*, and trying to look sophisticated.

"Hallo, Bill."

She had developed a slight drawl. She did not get up. She gave her elder sister a cursory and inattentive glance.

"Had a good journey?"

"Very."

"Pretty poisonous weather. You look a bit thin, old thing."

Billy moved past her to the window and looked out into the garden. The deal fence and the privet hedges, and the rather ragged turf were just the same. And there were red tulips and blue forget-me-nots in the round bed.

She said, "Where's Ronald?"

"O, Ronald's got a girl. Three yards of pink leg, and a genteel voice. Silly ass."

A thrush was singing, "Billy, Billy, Billy." Probably it was the same thrush which had sung to Billy's mother. There was the heartbreak of the English Spring on a grey day in the bird's singing.

Said Billy, "I think I'll go up and take off my hat."

II

Yes, life was a competitive affair, and a small house in the suburbs rather like a nest full of fat and hungry squabs, nor did it take Billy long to discover that when once you have vacated a corner and the rest of the brood has spread itself out, the return of the native may mean the recrowding of others. It was the recrudescence of the elder sister. Another personality reinserted itself into crowded occasions, and came into too close contact with youth at its most egotistical period.

Irene had vacated the room which had been Billy's; Mary Brown had insisted; but Irene, very much the young woman of the world and with distinct views and red-lipped appetites, had resented the re-intrusion of Billy. It was a bore. She had all her private possessions nicely arranged, and she had had to remove them to that rather stuffy little room with a dormer window; a servant's room. Irene had very much grown up; she was an exacting young person; she had been spoilt by a number of elderly and foolish gentlemen who were feverishly juvenile.

Nor was Ronald a consoling person. He had become aggressive and dogmatic; he was in the collar and cuffs stage; he lunched out at Lyons' tea shops, and talked as though he frequented Claridge's. He corrected and patronized his mother. He argued and squabbled with Irene. He was an inflated and thoroughly selfish young ass.

"Hallo, Billy, old girl, how did you like the organ grinders?"

At breakfast he gave them a little lecture on Mussolini. He approved of Mussolini. Though a very junior clerk in a branch of one of the Big Five, he was ready to criticize the financial views of the very distinguished gentleman who was the brain of the Bank. He referred to him as "Old So-and-so. A bit prehistoric but quite solid, you know." He had a way of strolling home in the evening and taking the armchair which had always been his mother's, and Billy having observed this intrusion on two successive nights, made it her business to remove him.

"Now, then, my lad, mother's chair."

"Hallo, joined the Women Police, have you?"

"Come along out."

And seeing him inclined to sit she had taken a hank of hair between thumb and finger, and resolutely so.

He was very annoyed; his dignity rebelled.

"Shut up! I say, you're——"

"Get up, Mussolini."

"Oh, all right, all right. You are a bit bossy these days, young woman."

May produced some days of inspissated gloom, and yet Billy reacted to the raw flavour of England; there were no flies as yet, and an abundance of work if you looked for it. She saw her job in the tired eyes of her mother, and in the exactions of those very crude young people who expected so much and gave so little. Billy went to Kew and to Hampton Court, but she took her mother with her, and Kew was "all blue" as the papers put it, bluebells and green gloom. At Hampton Court beds of azaleas protested vividly against the north-east wind and the blighted sky. Billy and her mother wandered down the high walk between the wall and the old pollarded elms to look at the river. It oozed by like liquid lead.

Billy had a moment of meditation. She said—"Funny old climate—this. But it does help you to get down to realities. Quite incalculable. Doesn't flatter your pet picnic. Suppose that's why we English get things done. Contemplation isn't exactly encouraged. Have to get busy and hit a ball."

Her mother was exploring the new Billy. It was a rather sad adventure. The little, impulsive girl had disappeared, and in her place stood the young woman who had lost her romantic bloom, a very capable young woman, but betraying signs of an incipient hardness. Mrs. Mary felt rather sore about it. Her beloved Billy. O, bother that beast of a man! He had rubbed the bloom off the soft and virginal surface.

And would Billy ever confess to her, sit at her knees and have her hair brushed as in the old days? Mary Brown thought not. The face of the new Billy was set rather sternly towards practical things. She would shrink from caresses.

"Yes, but England's kind, my dear. And it does give us contrasts."

"Yes, I suppose it does. But do you think it is as kind as it was?"

"Much of a muchness."

Billy was thinking of Irene and Ronald. Irene's attitude to life was really that of an amateur mondaine. She wanted everything to be provided without any personal exertion. Having powdered her nose and used lip-stick she expected the walls of Jericho to fall. "Yes, I want a car, but not a Morris Cowley, thank you. What, lunch in Soho? Not this child. The Berkeley, thanks. And a frock from Wardour Street? I don't think. Some silly old ass will hand out the necessary." Nor was Ronald any less egocentric. He, too, demanded a car. He had his eye on a secondhand sports model into which his young lady could insert her long pink legs. Life owed him a car. Obviously! Supervising the details of other people's banking accounts had given him inflated ideas as to value, the value of Ronald.

Billy had to suppose, "O, mother's spoilt them. She's been too easy, given too much of herself. I'd like to put Irene in a laundry for six months. That sort of vogue. Catch me spoiling people. No, life's got to be half and half."

At the end of a week she was being energetic in the house on behalf of her mother. Irene was informed that she would have to make her own bed, or find it waiting for her in dishevelled naturalness. Ronald's boots were left to his own ministrations. A most ungentlemanly job, but he did it and did it very badly to begin with.

Billy twitted him.

"If that's your idea of polish, my lad!"

Ronald and Irene agreed that Billy was rather a beast.   Tindaro had not improved her.   But the two young ones loved her; they still had spontaneity.

With the housework adjusted, Billy set herself other tasks. She took lessons in shorthand and in book-keeping.   She was a fairly expert typist.   She played some tennis; she could give her brother fifteen and beat him 6—3, which, no doubt, was good for him, but after three such lickings Ronald lapsed.   Miss Long Legs was more accommodating.

III

Mary Brown had wondered whether Billy would go back to Tindaro, and there were occasions when Billy asked herself the same question and answered it in the same way.

"Of course I'm going back.   I'm not afraid of the respectable people.   If they think I'm beaten—well—I'm not.   I don't know that I really want to go back; part of me does, and part of me doesn't, but I think I know which part of me is going to win."

She wrote to Julia Lord in Switzerland.

"I'm learning shorthand and book-keeping.   Do you remember saying that quite a lot of secretarial work could be done for the hotel and villa people?   My idea is to develop a new side to the business; I shall have the time. And I suppose you would have no objection.

Has it ever occurred to you that we might run an English Club?   I dare say it has.   Don't think me bossy, but if you take me on as partner I would like to bring activities of my own into the show.   I don't want to be a sponger."

Miss Lord's answering letter was sympathetic.

"Quite.   I have had the idea, but one's energy is limited.   You will supply a double quantity.   We might start what we could call an 'English Agency,' and run it with the library.   We have no Cook or American Express here.   Quite a lot of work could be done.   I think I could get the ground floor of the house next door."

Billy became seriously interested in these new possibilities. When next she travelled to Tindaro it would be no sentimental journey, but the final quest of a career. Like Young Italy she was becoming a pragmatist, vigorously practical, out for the accomplishing of things. She supposed that she would find self-expression in her job, though she did not put it so precisely into words. She would take her stand beside Julia Lord.

Her imagination became practical. She remembered that she had never seen fly-papers in Tindaro. Why not import fly-papers? She chuckled over the idea.

As for any personal confession, it was not made, and Mary Brown understood that she might never be told by Billy's own lips the tale of her first winter in Tindaro. Billy spared her mother and she spared herself. The Pipes of Pan might sound, but her ears would be stopped against them; she had landed on her enchanted island and had found it false and fatal. Never again. She was a resolute young person, and in a mood to look at man with cold and impartial eyes, seeing him for what he was, often a rather inefficient person, plausible, vain. She excepted men like Burt and Frevick, because Burt was interested in one woman and in his work, and Frevick was a poor, hopeless dog with a head to be patted. Her reaction was characteristic and inevitable. She would loathe the type of man who was interested in women only as a sex product, the type of man you could see any day in Regent Street, the ordinary, sensual middle-class cad. No doubt she exaggerated her type, and there was a wise wilfulness in the exaggeration. Inevitably she was developing into Miss Lord's predestined partner.

The house at Ealing soon ceased to fill her day, and at the end of June she managed to obtain a temporary post as secretary to Dr. Christopher Hazzard of Welbeck Street. Dr. Hazzard's secretary, who had been with him for seven years, had had to go into a nursing home, and he needed a substitute. Billy owed this piece of good fortune to Dr. Burt, who was a friend of Hazzard's. The Burts were in England for two months, staying in a furnished cottage down at Marlow, and Billy spent a week-end with them. She was rather full of Hazzard, for her enthusiasms remained, though the inspiration was more impersonal.

"He's a wonderful man. The very way he looks at you. And his white head."

Hazzard's hair was quite white now. His snow-cap had arrived in autumn.

"Easy to work for, Billy?"

"O, quite. You feel the whole time that it is the job which matters, and nothing else. Of course I was a bit raw at first, but he was so jolly patient. I have to write rather technical letters, about streptococci and things. And Mrs. Hazzard's a dear. She knows quite a lot. Sometimes when I'm stumped I bolt up to her."

They allowed her her enthusiasms. Assuredly Hazzard must be supremely refreshing after a highly scented excursion into the Slade world. And Burt told her the story of Christopher Hazzard as he had heard it from a mutual friend.

"There is not a man in London who has had more prejudice to overcome."

Billy was up in arms.

"But surely in a thing like doctoring, it's the work and not the man? You mean they tried to suppress his discoveries?"

"Men are jealous beasts, my dear."

"But how dastardly! Well, anyhow, he has climbed over their heads. Dr. Burt, I don't believe that women would try to smother a genius."

Burt looked at her humorously.

"O yes they would."

"I don't believe it. We are out to put the job first. At least, I am."

"Probably. Life can be a bit of a scuffle. What about a trip in the punt before dinner?"

To Stella Burt, Billy talked a little more intimately. She was both naïve and sophisticated. She said that men like Burt and Hazzard were the only men worth considering, because you could work with them like a man, and that seemed rather rare. The ordinary male was such a rotten, physical creature. He got upset so easily, and knocked off his perch.

Stella was delicate with Billy, realizing that Billy was very much in her new harness, a Julia Lord Billy. She had kicked against pulling the chariot of the emotions.

She said, "Life's so relative. I hate generalizations. But I do agree that I have no use for a man unless he is something of a fanatic where his job is concerned."

"Yes, just like Dr. Hazzard. He really is great, and I believe he is great to his wife."

"I happen to know that he is."

"Well, isn't that splendid."

Stella Burt's eyes glimmered.

"Billy, I believe that if the post could be permanent you would be digging yourself in in Welbeck Street."

Billy's denial was quite definite.

"O, no, it has been a sound experience. I'm going back to Tindaro and to Julia. My job is there. I shall have things to fight over there."

"You Amazon!"

"No, not really. But it seems that one has to fight for one's job, the woman's job. I'm rather looking forward to it."

CHAPTER XVIII

I

ON the night before Billy left for Tindaro she sat with her mother at the open french window of the drawing-room. It was a warm, autumnal night, and they had the house to themselves, for the two young things had been packed off to bed, and Irene and Ronald were out upon their affairs. Between mother and daughter there was the silence of an acknowledged sadness. Billy had switched off the lights, and the room was as dark or even darker than the strip of garden, for the upper back windows of the house in the row opposite were all lit up. People were going to bed. Somewhere along the row a wireless installation kept up a nasal bleating.

Mary Brown sat and waited. She had been waiting all those months for Billy to tell her a particular thing, because Billy was Billy, and more precious than any other child. Mary Brown wanted to be told. She had watched the evolving of the new Billy, but in her heart she cherished the Billy of a year ago. Not that she suffered from the exactions of the sentimentalist, but in the soft gloom of that autumnal night she felt that she wanted to hold in her lap the soul of Billy, just as in the old days she had held Billy the child.

Said Billy in a voice which sounded casual, "That loud-speaker's pretty awful. What a pity you can't come out and spend two months with us."

"Not to be thought of."

"Well, perhaps some day. As a matter of fact, I'm getting rather ambitious. If the job out there goes as I want it to go—yes, some day."

She sat forward in her chair, and in the dim light her mother saw her as a figure set in an attitude of alertness towards the future. She had put away self-pity; she did not wish to speak

186

of the intimate things which had happened; she spoke only
of things which might happen.   Her mood was not retrospective.   She had no thought of lying in anybody's lap for the
sake of sympathy, and yet her mood was full of sympathy
towards her mother.   On this last night she was not moved
to lean upon Mrs. Mary, but to sit beside her as woman by
woman.

"You have had a pretty hard time with us.   Queer things,
kids.   It must be rather queer being a mother."

Mrs. Mary made no movement.

"O, yes, full of the unexpected."

"I should think so.   I've often wondered——"

"So have I, Billy."

"Whether it was worth while, whether it seemed to you
worth while."

"Some things happen."

"Us.   Five of us.   Yes, I suppose things just happen.
Afterwards you make the best of them.   But what is the
best in Irene and Ronald?   That sort of modern attitude—
'I mean to have a good time.'   And what just is—a good
time?"

Her mother, watching the windows of the house beyond
that other back garden, saw a window grow dark.   A light
had been switched off, and the sudden darkening of a window
always reminded her of a night when she had pulled down a
blind and stood very still, realizing death in the bed behind
her.

She said, "Everything is so new to the young.   It's a kind
of adventure.   It's natural, isn't it?"

Billy's voice was decisive, like a quick firm line streaked in
under a signature.

"Quite.   But one gets through that.   What I mean is—
one's idea of a good time changes.   One isn't out after the
same things.   But what amazes me is—that one seems to pass
through periods of blindness.   Take Irene, for instance.   She
doesn't see further than next month's new frock.   She's right
in the middle of things which shout to be looked at, and she
doesn't see them.   She doesn't see you."

Mrs. Mary's hand made a little groping movement on the arm of her chair.

"One mustn't expect it. Some of us do learn not to expect——"

"But it's rotten. I'm not putting on side, mater, but I do see certain things now, what your job has been, and what it has to be—— You have stuck to it—so jolly pluckily."

"Life, my dear. What else?"

"O, that's all very well, but you must have felt pretty sick and lonely sometimes. Kids can be so rottenly selfish. I'm sorry I'm going to-morrow, and yet I do feel——"

Somehow she seemed to divine that hand waiting to be touched and held. She held it and held it hard.

"You have always been such a dear to me. O, yes, you have. You have never fussed and interfered too much. That's why I feel that the job out there has a meaning. I shall be able to help a bit."

Mrs. Mary sat very still.

"Your own life, Billy. You mustn't——"

"O, there's nothing to worry about, nothing at all."

And for the best part of a minute they sat in silence, and Mary Brown was feeling that though Billy the child had grown too big to be nursed, Billy the woman was just as adequate and lovable. She understood. How suddenly your attitude might change! An hour ago she had wanted to be told about Oscar Slade, and Billy had not told her, because Billy was something better and bigger than a child. She understood.

Mary Brown rose and bending over Billy, kissed her.

"You have always been—such—such a help to me, made things worth while."

"Dear."

"I think I'll be getting to bed now. I'm coming to Victoria with you."

"Splendid. I'll wait for the others, and lock up."

II

Mary Brown could remember walking up and down the same platform with Billy a year ago, a far more youthful and impulsive Billy, to whom Tindaro had meant the unknown and adventure. She could remember the look in Billy's eyes, and her air of sparkle and excitement, and those last quick kisses. Yes, that had been a very different affair, and Mary Brown had felt troubled and responsible, yet glad of the girl's courage. "Don't worry, dear; I'm going to have a lovely time. I'll write directly I arrive."

There had been more smile in those days, the shimmer of a happy illusion. Billy had asked questions and allowed herself to be treated rather like a nice child by an elderly porter; the boat-train had been more than a mere string of coaches, but on this autumn morning Billy walked up and down the platform with the air of a young woman very much in touch with the realities. Her manner was more abrupt and more impersonal. She had watched the weighing of her registered luggage, and had stood at one of the windows while her baggage-ticket was being made out.

"Fifteen and sixpence, please."

Billy had argued the point.

"What for? I'm only a few pounds over weight."

The clerk had explained the figures to her, while her mother had stood and watched her daughter, and realized that the new Billy was taking nothing for granted. She was just a little combative.

"I brought the same trunk home with me from Italy, and the Italians charged me about half what your Southern Railway is charging."

The clerk was sarcastic.

"Probably, Miss, we are more accurate than the Italians."

"I wonder!"

She had folded up the yellow ticket and tucked it away in her bag.

"I'll see the box into the van."

Yes, undoubtedly Billy was taking nothing from life for granted. Her very smile was different; it expressed a challenge and a question, and a frank scepticism with regard to particular things and particular people. Especially was she moved to challenge the male's assumption of infallibility, his air of polite patronage where a woman was concerned. Almost she had snubbed her porter, a young and superior porter. She had carried her own suitcase and had found her own corner seat in a second-class carriage.

They walked up and down, and Billy, remembering that she was a book-merchant, stopped to look at the books on the platform bookstall. She looked at them critically as merchandise and not as literature. She spoke to the young man in charge.

"Do you sell much of that—'The Satin Slipper'?"

It was an unusual question, and the clerk looked at her as though he suspected her of being the mother of that particular book.

"O, pretty fair. It's a bit of a thriller."

"Yes, easy reading, I suppose."

She turned again to her mother.

"Have to study trade."

Her smile had a touch of irony. She looked so much more solid and self assured. The texture of her was tougher. Even books had a different meaning for her, and she would read them far more critically, with a slight attitude of suspicion, and an eye on the look out for "tosh." She was a little hard, and well washed, and abrupt. The surface of her had an efficient lustre. She observed and considered the realities.

She said, "You have to think of your public. Our public —at Tindaro—likes things rather succulent. It's amusing."

That was yet another facet, an aspect of humour, polished and crystalline. She had begun to find certain things amusing, and her smile was self-conscious. Life could be rather absurd.

"You'll take a taxi back?"

"No, a bus, Billy."

"I'll pay."

"I prefer a bus."

Billy's eyes softened suddenly.

"You would do. Dear old unselfish thing."

Each of them was aware of a feeling of tension, emotion suppressed and held in control. They stood by the open door of Billy's compartment. A whistle blew, and suddenly their two faces seemed to wince like two surfaces played upon by broken light.

"Good-bye, dear. Next year—perhaps—I'll be taking you out with me."

"Billy."

They kissed.

"Now, don't be too unselfish to those two."

III

Tindaro!

Out of the darkness came a little whispering wind from over the sea, and as Billy walked down the platform looking for a porter, she remembered the Island of the Triton and the sunlight and the blueness of sea and sky, and suddenly the wind felt chilly. The same porter took the yellow luggage-ticket in his grubby fingers and went in search of the same trunk. There were the same lights upon the hill-side, and the same stars, but they had ceased to be mysterious.

She expected no one to meet her, Julia Lord would not arrive till the Saturday, and the Burts had broken the journey in Rome. Carrying her suitcase she walked along the platform to the station buildings and the little crowd of Italians who were trickling out by the light of a very decadent lamp. A whiff of garlic drifted to her, the smell of a foreign country. Most strangely it intensified her sense of exile, and the feeling of loneliness which had seemed to be waiting for her on the platform. She had felt all right in the train, but in leaving it she had been touched by a chilly breath, the ghost of an associated memory and its tinge of emotion.

Silly! Her hand tightened on the handle of her suitcase. She was coming back to Tindaro with a different grip upon the realities. That melancholy and draughty little wind, and the coldly impersonal stares, and the odour of garlic, and the grubby station, were realities. She had a feeling as of squaring her shoulders. She surrendered her ticket to the official, and passed through into the narrow and half dark waiting-room and booking-office. She was aware of people, Italians, and she did not look at them. They were mere anonymous figures.

"My dear, it's real good to see you."

The voice startled her. It was like a voice forgotten, and yet poignantly familiar. It made her feel suddenly and strangely raw. But it was real, and so was Mrs. Shone, an unexpected and welcoming presence, a human shape with live hands.

"I heard you were coming to-night. I had to come right down and meet you."

Strange consummation! She saw Mrs. Shone's face and knew that she was glad. She, too, was glad.

"I say, how sporting of you."

She found herself kissing Mrs. Shone. It just happened. The large white face had loomed up against hers. She was surprised at the softness of Sadie Shone's lips, and the cleanness of her breath. But what a thing to notice!

"I grabbed a taxi for you. Say, my dear, I've been so bored."

They went out together almost like old friends.

"But it wasn't being bored that brought me down here. I've been seeing your face for days."

"It was kind of you to come. Who's here?"

"O, the same old gang. Isn't life a blurb."

Life, the unexpected, repeated some of its formulæ. The cripple with the misshapen arm came and stared at them and made animal and appealing noises, and Billy's trunk was attached to the grid of the open taxi by a length of old clothes-line. She challenged the clothes-line and gave a lira to the cripple.

"Haven't you a strap? Do you think that's safe?"

"Si, si, signorina."

She followed Mrs. Shone into the taxi, and found the cripple trying to kiss her hand. Hurriedly she withdrew it.

"Same old Tindaro. Bits of string and garlic."

"Same as ever was."

Yes, life was unexpected even when you set about to reduce it to vulgar fractions. Mrs. Shone was unexpected, and so was her own reaction to Mrs. Shone. The Café Ceres had come down to meet her, and she had been glad of its coming, and in the kissing of Sadie Shone she had not thought of little drinks and pink pastry swarmed over by flies. Did they still tinkle mandolins up there, and was Tommaso as fat and as debonair as ever, and did poor old Frevick slouch in his chair like a crumpled and half empty sack? How pathetic! It touched her, hard young woman that she was in the making. The Hotel Elyseo would never touch her. It had too much money, and too much money produces a fatty decadence of the soul and complacent dullness. The Hotel Elyseo had not to jump for its food and its job. It was like a fat old white cockatoo in a cage, uncertain of temper and overfed.

The stars and the lights of Tindaro, and that chilly wind from off the sea, and the dark cypresses bending their tops! The Island of the Triton would be wearing a petticoat of foam. White lace? No, Billy was prejudiced against the white lace tradition, and the petticoat parade. Why petticoats? She had returned to Tindaro with the severest of "shingles." An Eton crop was a little too masculine, and her tendency was towards the neuter.

She became aware of Mrs. Shone as a plumpness swaying towards her as the car took one of the sharp curves. A year ago she would have sensed Mrs. Shone as a large white tuberose or camellia, too heavily scented, but to-day she was feeling sympathetic towards Mrs. Shone. They were women together.

"How's Old Frevick?"

"My dear, he's grown very thin."

"Poor old Tom. Been here all the time, has he?"

"Mostly. But he is painting again. He went up to the mountains for July and August, and took the dog with him, that little yellow dog."

"I'm glad he is working again. That's the only thing worth while. What about the others?"

"Old Pon has a new hat. The Baroness has gone to Algiers to cheat a fresh crowd. The Mirleess man disappeared in June. Owed too much money."

"No loss. He was a beastly little cad."

The car ascended, but Billy was more conscious of Mrs. Shone than she was of Tindaro, for Tindaro was not the Tindaro of a year ago, and Mrs. Shone was something other than Mrs. Shone. She was less restless, less noisily self-expressive, more of a blend of America and England, less red of mouth. She would break abruptly into Italian, and when she spoke Italian her voice had a gentler quality.

"Are the Pipps back yet?"

"Si, signorina. Bella Pippa. And old Tom Bromhead."

"O, old Bromhead."

Billy realized while uttering the name of Bromhead that she had no further use for the Bromheads, and all the rather superfluous silliness of such male optimism. It was so physical, so digestive. She would like her man to be either a Frevick or a Burt, and even then her liking would be candid and dispassionate, a rather chilly comradeliness. She had her job. She was quite sure that she would want to slap any man who tended to be sentimental and who tried to talk the God and dear little children stuff to her. She had uses for a man like Hazzard. She could tolerate the reality of Frevick's crave, and feel tender to him because of it. Doctoring and drinking were realities, and the man who drank and painted pictures was a live figure. The potterers, and the sentimentalists, and all the world's Pipps were like the conventional novel, or the Primrose League, or Societies for the Prevention of This or That. They ceased to convince her. Just conventional pottering.

She said, "It's something to have a job. It keeps you from being slushy."

Mrs. Shone gave Billy's arm a little prod.

"Sure, you'll be growing just like Julia."

"Well, and why not? Julia's staunch. No flies."

"O, sole mio! Find Sadie a job, my dear."

"Well, why not? Why don't you take over the Haycroft lace shop. They were talking of going. You could do it."

"My, that's an idea."

IV

Mrs. Shone did not invade the Villa Vesta. In the days of her "experiences" her loud laughter and a redness of the lips had appeared conclusive to the conventionalists, and yet nothing is so inconclusive and short-sighted as the conventions. Mrs.

Sadie supposed that Billy was tired, and would want to get unpacked and washed and to bed. And she, too, had divined in the new Billy a younger sister of Miss Julia Lord. No messing about, thank you, no gushings, no emotional insincerities. Mrs. Shone had taken herself off while Billy was paying the taxi-driver. "So long; see you in the morning."

The driver of the taxi made no immoderate profit out of Billy. Fat Maria, broad bosomed in the doorway, was put to immediate use.

"Help me up with the box, Maria."

Supper and Maria's coffee could wait, and Billy's trunk went up the stairs without bumping either the walls or the banisters, and into Billy's little room. Maria was out of breath, Billy not at all so.

"Will you have supper? Yes, in ten minutes?"

"In ten minutes," said Billy, looking to see that there was a jug of hot water in the basin—"I want to wash."

Maria's slippers and bulkiness redescended the stairs, and Maria was thinking that Miss Brown's reappearance resembled exactly the reappearance of Miss Lord. Immediately they washed. Lack of hot water would be the most flagrant of omissions. The English were so very practical.

Billy's washing was an efficient business, more especially so after two days in the train, and second-class at that; her cropped head went into the basin, and while towelling it afterwards she stood at the open window and saw the lights of Tindaro looped across the soft bosom of the night. She rubbed her wet head and gazed. The wind from the sea made a little restless stirring in the orange trees, and the cypresses by the terrace were not asleep. There were lights on the hills, flickering silver dots. And over there in the valley lay the Villa of the Flute with its white statues and its theatre and its shadows.

Billy's hands were still for a moment. She was conscious of inward qualms, a tremor of emotion, but she suppressed these uncomfortable feelings. She resumed the drying of her hair. She thought, "Orange trees! Last year I was quite excited about orange trees. They might just as well be eunonymus. Of course."

V

On her way to the library next morning in the sunny breadth of the Corso she came upon Tom Frevick sitting at his usual table outside the Café Ceres. He was alone. Tommaso, in his shirt sleeves and apron, was busy with the inevitable pail and swab, cleaning tables as though at that hour life was all slabs of marble. He sang.

Billy diverged towards Frevick. He stood up. He looked thinner, less of a sack, but his pallor was extreme. His melancholy eyes had a shyness.

She said, "You are early," and sat down, and found Tommaso bobbing and smiling at her, and holding the swab like a bouquet of flowers.

"Good morning, Tommaso."

"Felicitations, signorina. We begin the season. It is good."

Frevick, with an air of abstraction, stood looking down at her, and then resumed his seat.

"Yes, early. So is the sun. You are going down to the library."

Obviously. She smiled at him vaguely.

"Plenty to do. Open up, dust, check crockery and everything. Take nothing for granted."

"No."

He looked at his boots as though he felt that she was not to be looked at too closely. She had a different surface, and her voice was deliberate and purposeful. It marched. She had lost the tentative and virginal explorings of youth, and somehow he was sorry.

"Julia's coming back soon?"

"Saturday. I hear you have been painting."

He glanced at her cautiously.

"Daubing. Who told you?"

"Mrs. Shone. She came down to meet me last night. Rather decent of her."

"O, she's not a bad sort."

"Yes.   I'm learning to grade people rather like books and apples.   How's the dog?"

"She keeps me in order."

He gave a kind of melancholy chuckle.

"Men—yes, want it.   A dog to keep you in order.   Funny. Yes, rather like a blind man on the end of a string."

CHAPTER XIX

I

A NORTH wind was blowing and Frevick was wearing a woollen scarf. He came down the Corso from the direction of the Hotel Elyseo, for he had a minute villa now, a little white box, beyond the Elyseo and overlooking Capo Moro. He walked slowly, like a man not too sure of his feet, and in his grey overcoat and light trousers he suggested a long, thin candle carried against the wind. The flame of him was growing feeble. He used a stick. Betty, the little yellow dog, marching daintily at his feet, would turn and look up with a pair of bright black eyes which observed the face of the master. Occasionally she would let out a little protesting yap. "Come now, how slow you are! We women have to be patient." And Frevick would stand still, and regarding her with tolerant affection, reply to her protests, "You Little Thing, you—very—Little Thing. No, I won't be managed this morning, you little schoolmistress." And she would give another little yap, and put her fore-paws against his knee, and perhaps take the slack of a trouser end between her teeth and tug.

She did this on this January morning, and Frevick tapped her head very gently with the end of his stick.

"O, yes, greedy one. It is because someone keeps lumps of sugar in a drawer. Disgraceful!"

He quizzed Betty with a kind of frail chuckle. Raising his eyes he could see the white sign of the English Library and Tea Rooms, and beyond it a second sign projecting from below a first-story window. It displayed light blue letters on a white ground. It had a polished and bright distinction. It was like a shield of honour hung there for all the world of Tindaro to see.

"THE ENGLISH AGENCY
LORD & BROWN."

Like his little yellow dog that sign moved Frevick to a frail chuckle. It had for him something ironical and pleasantly humorous. Messrs. Lord & Brown! Two women, and two rather remarkable women. Yes, women who did things for you, all sorts of things, and did them with efficiency. They would cash your cheques—within reason, insure and forward your baggage, let you a villa, hire you a car, recommend servants, view rooms for you at any of the hotels and arrange terms, provide you with a temporary secretary or a stenographer. Yes, and they would bury you, buy you your niche or slip of soil in the cemetery of Tindaro among the cypresses and roses, and have you laid to root. Always Frevick was piqued by that proposition. "Rummy thing, Julia burying me! But she'll do it some day. And Billy will brightly overlook all the necessary details. Good business."

He pottered on and entered the doorway of the library, and Betty began to bounce on her four legs and emit excited yappings in that solemn literary vestibule.

"Tsss—quiet, little greedy."

He opened the library door, and saw Julia Lord sitting in her usual chair. The hour was barely ten o'clock, and the library was empty. Miss Lord, pen in hand, turned to look at Tom Frevick as she always looked at him as at something that was both very near and a long way off. She wore a hat, the same sort of hat, with a brim and a feather, the hat of an eighteenth-century duchess.

"Julia, apologies for the dog."

It was his perpetual greeting. He looked at Julia Lord with a little, crinkled, devoted smile. He stood there rather like a long, thin awkward boy who paraded with washed face and brushed hair. Betty had her paws on Miss Lord's knees and was snuggling her black muzzle into a firm white hand.

"Disgraceful creature."

His gentle chuckle sounded. He watched Julia Lord open a drawer in the table, and take out a lump of sugar, and hold it between finger and thumb.

"Sit up—like a gentlewoman."

Betty sat up, and made appealing dabs with her fore-paws.

"I suppose one has to spoil something" said Frevick, "even if it is good canvas.   Well—well!"

He knew that he had not very long to live, perhaps six months, perhaps a year, and the prospect of dying had caused him to pause and look at death as he looked at his little dog. Absurd little creature, absurd climax to the state known as individual consciousness.   He was not in the least afraid of death.   What to him was extraordinary was that life should have passed so rapidly and that he should have made such a mess of it, for he could remember so well the days when he had believed in his power to paint pictures.   Quite confidently he had supposed that he would leave some sort of reputation behind him.   And then, so imperceptibly he had begun to muddle his life and his colours.   He had got into a London set, in among the clever people, who talked themselves into a fatuity of complacent chatter.   As to his craft it had become a pot-boy to his stomach.   Extraordinary process!

He watched Julia Lord and the dog.   He had found himself gently resigned to the watching of such things.   His crave was dying, and with it his thirst for life.   He was gently amused at himself, at the mess he had made, and at all the foolish hungers of humanity.

Miss Lord, taking up Betty into her lap, asked him one of the usual questions.

"Vanna took your bread up yesterday?"

"Yes."

He had special bread made for him in the Lord-Brown kitchen, and he was supposed to soak it in milk.   He could take very little food.

"How's the picture?"

"Haven't done anything to it for three days.   Doesn't seem worth while, Julie."

She reproved him with tender severity.

"You mustn't say that."

"It's not a pose, my dear.   You see, I have finished, and I know that I have finished.   Quite placidly.   I just sit on the edge of the sea and dream.   Comes a time when the only pictures you paint are dreams."

"Old or new?"

"Both. New worlds and old. You sit and wonder. What's on the other side of the eternal sea; is there anything? I'm conscious of curiosity."

The dog, after looking up into Julia Lord's face, jumped suddenly off her lap, and sat up at Frevick's feet. She appealed to him with eyes and paws. He eyed her whimsically.

"Well, what now, you very little thing? Are we going to cash a cheque at Miss Brown's? But she doesn't keep sugar in a drawer."

He wagged a finger.

"Some young women don't approve of sugar. Miss Billy doesn't. Does she, Julie?"

Miss Lord was examining her finger-nails.

"Why should she? We are business women, Tom. Besides, all her sugar——"

"Goes to England. I know. Not wasted on men and dogs. Anyhow, we do appreciate a little sugar, Bettykins, don't we? Come along, you very little thing; I hear the footsteps of the literary people."

He smiled at the woman in the chair.

"You really are a unique person, Julia."

She glanced at his scarf.

"That's right. Keep covered up. It's treacherous to-day."

"O, that!" and he seemed amused at her and at himself; "it's simply that I don't want to cause trouble. Come along, you very little thing. Mustn't cause trouble."

For that very reason Frevick did not make use of the private door between the Library and the Agency, but passing out into the street and under the blue and white sign, entered the Agency like any unprivileged mortal. It was a big, airy, well-lit office, with a tiled floor and two white Corinthian pillars supporting the ceiling. A girl clerk was clattering away on a typewriter. Billy had her desk in the far corner, facing obliquely towards the door, and when Frevick entered she was interviewing an American who wanted to buy a villa in Tindaro. Frevick sat down on one of the leather-covered chairs, and fastened the end of a leash to Betty's collar. The office walls, distempered a warm yellow, were placarded with useful information.   There was a little wire-caged *caisse* into which Billy entered when financial affairs were under consideration.   In the centre of the office a polished wood table offered the latest magazines and timetables and leaflets dealing with steamers and motor tours.

Frevick sat and listened to Billy's voice.   It was pleasant and deliberate and impartial; it dominated the office, it had the quality of bright steel neatly dissecting the question in hand. Her smile was less seen than in the old days, and especially so by men.   Her dark hair was glossy.   She showed to the world a bright, compact surface, and an imperturbable good temper that was founded upon indifference.   It was her business to advise people, to do certain things for people, but there her responsibilities ended.   So much of her life was "office," and the office was efficient and successful and quite fascinating in its developments, for Billy was ambitious.

Frevick's glance trailed to the corner where a few of his pictures were on show and for sale.   They appeared to amuse him.   Messrs. Lord & Brown sold an occasional picture for him, and refused to take a commission, for he and Burt were the privileged children.   To others the notice was there for all to read, "No nonsense, please."

The American was on his feet.   He needed a large villa, and no large villas were available, and he was proposing to try Capri or Taormina.   He said, "Some live man ought to take a grip of this place and build."

Billy, tapping her chin with a pencil, nodded slightly.

"That's so.   It's a possibility.   We have it in mind."

"Question of dollars?"

"Partly.   I suppose you would not care for me to put you a proposition."

"But I want a house right now.   Mrs. Joshua P. Blaney and the young women——"

"I'm sorry.   I think the Villa of the Flute would have suited you, but it has just been sold."

"Well, I'm much obliged to you anyway, Miss Brown. This office is right there.   I'm going over to Mrs. Sadie's; Mrs. Blaney is there buying lace."

Frevick stroked Betty's head.   He had heard Billy speak of the Villa of the Flute as though she were referring to a packet of envelopes.   No emotional twinge.   No, the Billy of the English Agency had no emotional twinges.   She had grown absurdly like Miss Lord, or what Miss Lord appeared to be outside her own garden.   And sometimes Tom Frevick would wonder whether Billy had a garden of her own, a secret place where she peeled off that brightly efficient surface and let herself dream.   All women should dream.   Office furniture and files and cheque-books were so palpably male and so final.

Meanwhile Billy was at his service, or very nearly so, for when he made a movement to leave his chair, she smiled across at him.

"Do you mind waiting just one moment?   I have a letter that must catch the next post.   Miss Soulby."

"Yes, Miss Brown."

"Take down this letter, please."

The typist produced a pad, and Billy dictated her letter in a voice which was level and deliberate.   She did not hesitate; her sentences went over the net like cleanly driven tennis balls. Betty, lying at Frevick's feet and watching Billy with bright black eyes, seemed to know that in the English Agency a lady had to be on her best behaviour.

Billy, having finished her dictating, unlocked a drawer, and taking out an envelope, held it up for Frevick to see.   He nodded at her and smiled, and crossed over to her desk.

"I was going to ask you to cash a cheque."

She held out the envelope.

"Someone from the Elyseo bought a picture.   Ten guineas. She paid in cash."

"No need for a cheque—then.   Which picture was it?"

"The one of the ruins of the Roman theatre."

Frevick chuckled.

"Always seems to please 'em.   I have repeated that thing at least a dozen times.   What one would call enlightened pot-boiling."

The dog was gazing solemnly at Billy as though observing a very remarkable and significant specimen of the sex, and Billy addressed her brightly.

"Well, how's Betty? Had her sugar as usual. Come and say good morning."

Frevick's little yellow dog walked solemnly round the desk to have her head patted by the junior partner of the firm of Lord & Brown.

II

The Café Ceres was still the Café Ceres. Its little drinks and its flies and its cosmetic cakes and its mandolins continued, and so did its clientele, but with a difference. Sundry of its shabby intimates had disappeared, to be replaced by other figures, seedy cosmopolites, other exiles. Old Ponsonby was dead. Sir Dyce Duxbury and the Blaber woman had got married and had transferred their mutual shadinesses to some other Italian town. Sadie Shone ran the Haycroft lace shop and with a large measure of success, and in thorough sympathy with Messrs. Lord & Brown. Her cry of "My dear, I'm bored," somehow had developed into the pragmatical persuasions of the saleswoman. She had ceased to be interested in any sort of man who trailed his maleness up and down the Corso. "Aw, cut it out." She, too, was Lord & Brown, and very full of her job, and finding life much less an affair of powder and lipstick and loud laughter. She was able to talk of "Billy, Julia, and Sadie." Burt called them "The Three Musketeers," warriors all of them, tolerating the doctor and the artist and the artist's dog. He asserted that they ran Tindaro, and were secretly allied with the local Fascisti, and were called into conference by the Mayor, and gave the Roman salute to Mussolini.

For the Café Ceres had lost both Frevick and Mrs. Shone. The loggia and the garden of the English Library had become the rendezvous of the older exiles. Frevick toddled in there each morning when the sun happened to be shining, and sat at a round green table, and drank just one glass of vermouth, and drank it very slowly. The little yellow dog had her eyes upon him, and so had the Three Musketeers. Sadie Shone would bustle over for ten minutes, and take Betty into her lap, a very capacious lap, for she was growing stout. She drank Vichy water. Miss Lord preferred milk and soda. Billy drank nothing at all, and was there less frequently than the others, being very much the young protagonist, the builder up of new business. Besides, Miss Soulby was but a poor creature to be left in charge, a nice myopic thing who blinked amiably at clients through high-powered pince-nez and was far too persuadable. Miss Soulby made an excellent subordinate to Billy the autocrat.

Occasionally Stella Burt joined the circle, but she was a little mute and aloof in the presence of the Musketeers when Billy happened to be present. She and Billy disagreed, but in silence. They had ceased to be able to compare attitudes. Possibly Billy thought Stella Burt "An absolute dear, but rather mawkish." Billy was shy of soulful people. They tantalized you. Tindaro was a box of bricks, and not a day of dreams.

As for the new crowd which sat at the tables of the Café Ceres Billy had no use for it at all. Frankly and emphatically she spoke of these as rotten people, slimy, a little sinister, ambiguous. Burt described them as quite a nice collection of perverts and cosmopolitan cads, and strange women. The Café Ceres had a very sexual flavour, something Sapphic and scented.

Billy passed it as Julia Lord had passed it in the old days, with the air of a young man who had other and wholesome affairs to attend to. Not that she was a self-congratulatory prig. She had come to understand and to share Julia Lord's stoicism. When life dissolved beneath you into a glucous and emotional mess, the only thing to do was to get a grip on some solid purpose and to hold tight. The people who let go were the flabby and the unclean.

To Billy these people seemed so much more unpleasant than the old crowd, perhaps because her grip upon life had grown harder, and tolerance may suggest insecurity. She was bluntly outspoken.

"Beastly people."

Miss Lord was less emphatic. She had absorbed a tinge of Frevick's resignation. "Poor devils, all of us, especially the poor devils who can't say no."

To Billy she displayed an austere tolerance.

"Why worry about them? Some things and people can't be helped. In these backwaters you are bound to get——"

"Dead dogs."

"My dear, don't be too sure!"

"Sure! Take those two females who live together, the woman who dresses like a man, she calls herself Alec Collingwood I believe, and that frowzy, smoky-eyed creature. Well— you know! They're notorious, absolutely septic."

"Possibly. Leave them to the psychologists. What has it to do with you?"

"O, nothing. But that crowd's a kind of challenge. Ask Sadie."

"I don't want to ask Sadie. Besides, she understands—in a way. The old crowd used to write Limericks about us. I dare say the new crowd does worse."

"I know one," said Billy; "Sadie told me. It was about you in your bath. There is one particular cad there whom I would like to take by the collar, and cuff, a smeary beast with a permanent wave and a little moustache and the sort of eyes——"

Miss Lord laughed.

"Probably he was born so, potentially so. But why worry, why feel aggressive about it. The Café Ceres doesn't matter —now."

Billy gave a toss of the head.

"Fools, yes, but I can't stand nasty fools."

III

Yet Tindaro retained its beauty for those who had the inward eye to see it, and to such people as Stella Burt and Frevick it was full of the mystery and sadness of beauty. Colour, and cloud effects, and shadows over mountain and sea. The sweet chilliness of the dusk and the first scent of the mimosa. The grey ghosts of headland and mountain on a rainy day. Tindaro retained its nature mystery, and at night, with a full moon, rising, it sometimes made Frevick see a white shape unveiling, dropping a dark garment at its feet. Or the moon was the curve of the bosom of a Madonna leaning from behind a black cypress tree to look at the eternal babe in the cradle.

Frevick had lost the urge to set it down in colour just as he had lost the crave for drink.   The flesh in him was very feeble. He was all eyes.   He seemed to see more than he had seen in the days of his fierce interpreting, because he saw it so impersonally, and without the desire to put it upon canvas or upon paper.   He saw the soul of it shining through, the soul of the moon in the pepper trees, the soul of the flowers in almond and peach and apple.

To him the Café Ceres had ceased to matter.   It might be fungoid, but it was a form of growth, and as such inevitable. People grew fungoid faces and blotched souls.   Or like Billy Brown they ceased to flower, or sent up a little spike of hard white blossom.

He agreed with Stella Burt as to Billy.   He was often at the Burts' villa now; he liked to listen to music.   It did not come from the stretched wires of the piano, but from the beyond, from the other side of a seeming reality.   It was celestial sound dropping through the obscuring curtain of consciousness.

He and Stella Burt had spoken of Billy.

"It is a pity she has grown so hard."

Frevick agreed.

"Yes, you cease to see things when you grow hard."

CHAPTER XX

I

DR. BURT walked into the office of the English Agency, to find Miss Soulby clicking away at her typewriter, and Billy's chair unoccupied. Miss Soulby's hands remained poised above the keys, her very round blue eyes innocuously staring.

"Miss Brown out?"

"Do you want to see Miss Brown?"

That was the kind of question Miss Soulby asked.

"Yes, and I'm in rather a hurry."

"O, Miss Brown has just gone into the library. I'll tell her."

Miss Soulby left her chair and disappeared through the door that communicated with Miss Lord's department, and Burt walked up and down, and looked at Billy's desk, and the *caisse*, and the pictures on the yellow walls. The office of the English Agency was very much new woman, asserting an almost meticulous efficiency, and reproving the human untidiness of the male, and Burt, observing all its details, saw his own den as a badly organized and amorphous apartment. Yes, no doubt Billy Brown and her agency were admirably efficient, and yet Burt had a personal preference for the Billy of three years ago, nor was it a mere question of prejudice. Billy the girl had been more human than was Billy the business woman, and Burt liked his women to be gentle. Unfortunately the competitive process made some women brightly and briskly insensitive. Your business man might be a hard person in his office, but usually he became quite a different person in his home. He left his job and its leather coat behind him. The trouble with a working woman was that she lived with her job all the time.

Then Billy came in and smiled at him, and sat down in her

chair.   Yes, she was so confoundedly official these days, always enthroned behind her desk.

Her smile asked, "What can I do for you?" and Burt remembered that he was still wearing his hat, and removed it as though it had trespassed upon the Lord-Brown etiquette.

"By the way, is that villa of Strozzi's still to let?"

"Yes."

"Good!   I think I shall want it."

"Season or permanently—more or less?"

"O—more or less permanently.   What's the rent?"

"Seven thousand lire a year."

"Rather a lot "

"O, not so very stiff.   Seventy pound or so.   Who's it for?"
Burt rubbed his chin.

"Remember Dr. Hazzard?   He is sending a man patient of his out here, a fellow who has to live abroad.   He wrote to me to see if I could do anything."

Said Billy, "I have had one or two people after the villa. If your man wants it he had better make up his mind quickly."

Burt looked at her consideringly and said, "Quite so," and realized her as the complete business woman.

"How long can you give me?"

"Two days.   You had better wire."

He nodded his big head.   Some of these young things did dot your i's and cross your t's for you.

The telegram was dispatched, and when Burt received the reply he called up the English Agency on the 'phone and spoke to Billy.   He said that Mr. Isherwood would take the villa, and would Billy put the business through with Strozzi.   Billy, with a "Hold on a moment, please," reached for a notebook and scribbled down the necessary details as Burt gave them to her over the 'phone.   She wrote down the name "Thomas Isherwood" without being moved to any curiosity.   Her attention to business was final.

"O, just a moment, Strozzi may ask for a deposit.   If so, I suppose Mr. Isherwood could wire us credit?   Or his lawyers or his bank would?"

"Probably.   You have his address."

"No. 7 Hexham Gardens, Holland Park.   Correct?"

"Quite."

"Very well, if Strozzi wants a deposit we'll wire Mr. Isher-wood.   Meanwhile we will get on with the business, and I'll keep Mr. Isherwood informed.   Any idea when he is likely to come out?"

"Almost at once."

"Righto."

So the English Agency proceeded to put the business through. Signor Strozzi was a citizen of Tindaro, who, some twenty years ago, had emigrated to South America, and having made money there, had returned to Tindaro and had built himself a villa.   He was a little man of energy and ideas, and he had bought land, and had built half a dozen other villas to be let or sold.   Strozzi spoke both English and German.   Billy had done business with him previously.   She liked Strozzi; she liked his bright little eyes, and his smile, and his air of dry keenness. He had clean hands.

These new villas of Strozzi's had been built in an old olive garden above the Villa Vesta, six or so white little houses with very red new roofs and turquoise-blue shutters, doors, and win-dow-frames.   They had been a source of offence to some of the elect, but the Tindarese thought them a part of new Italy, and so they were, neat and new and cocky little places, white faces set towards progress.   Strozzi was his own architect, with limitations.   He had toured the French Riviera, and brought away with him a belief in the persuasive virtues of colour-wash and bright blue paint.   Certainly the sun frizzled your paint, but Italian pleasure resorts ought not to be outpainted by the French.   Moreover, Strozzi was of the opinion that the new world liked its artiness to be bright and blue and cheerful, or all aluminium and red, like a sports-model car.   A faded, sweet melancholy was out of sympathy with the new world's prag-matism.

Billy went up and viewed Mr. Thomas Isherwood's new villa.   It stood a little apart from the others.   It had a little brick gateway crusted with tiles, and a yellow gate with the name painted in green letters "Villa Byron."   Signor Strozzi had a partiality for historic titles. There were the Villas Garibaldi, Mazzini, Savoia, Cavour. Six young cypresses had been planted between the yellow gate and the bright blue door of the Villa Byron.

Billy inspected the house. She was not concerned with its æsthetics; she was not very conscious these days of Tindaro's æsthetics, or its lack of them. She did not see its cypresses or its sea, or the midnight of its pines or the shadows between the old houses, as she had seen them three years ago. Her world was limited by the bright, straw-coloured walls of her office. She worked early and late. She sat up till eleven typing the manuscript of Dr. Burt's history of Tindaro. She was very strong, and kept herself fit; she walked hard for an hour each evening, and played tennis three afternoons a week.

Billy assured herself that the Villa Byron was in order and ready for occupation; that the water taps and the lavatory functioned properly, and that all the builder's rubbish had been cleared away from the back garden. She saw the back garden as a stretch of reddish soil shaded by three magnificent, old olive trees. Well, the back garden would be Mr. Isherwood's affair. Her attitude to the unknown Isherwood was impersonal and uncurious. She had not bothered to visualize him. Probably she supposed that he was an elderly invalid, one of those faded exiles who had to live in the sun. She did not trouble to wonder about him, or whether he would approve of the yellow gate, or the gilded radiators in the rooms, or the friezes of brilliant blue iris and purple grapes and yellow lemons. The Villa Byron was up to date. Strozzi was all for progress. He splashed colour about lavishly.

Having relocked the blue front door, she descended the very new and raw road which zigzagged down the hill-side to join the Villa Vesta lane. As of old, Pan was sitting under an olive tree, playing upon his pipe. Bald headed and fat, with his yellow dog at his feet, he piped the Lament to Adonis.

Billy did not hear it. The pipes of Pan had no personal note for her.

She returned to her chair and her desk and the music of Miss Soulby's machine, and interviewed a succession of clients.

One of them wanted to bury a pet dog in the cemetery of Tindaro, in a nice little niche among the Catholic humans.

Billy explained that it could not be done.

Really, people had amazing ideas! Billy had had to bury old ladies' husbands, but never their dogs.

She suggested the garden of some friendly villa. Or, why not one of the wild hill-sides under a rosemary bush? It would be quite a fragrant resting-place for poor Fido.

II

The man arrived at Tindaro by the morning train. He looked as though he had not slept well in the train, and had found life not worth a morning shave. His eyes were very blue in a very brown face, one of those squarish and rather flat faces which remain maturely boyish. He wore tweeds and a greyish overcoat and a blue and white scarf, and the brim of his brown felt hat was turned down all round, giving him, with his country clothes, an air of out-of-door casualness. He had dressed himself for Tindaro much as he might have dressed himself for the Test or the Dart.

He stooped, and was slightly round shouldered. He moved slowly and with a suggestion of carefulness, as though he carried upon him a label marked "Fragile." Quite suddenly, and for no obvious reason, his eyes would grow frightened and set themselves in a round, blue stare. His age might have been anything between thirty-five and forty.

No one came to meet him, and he walked slowly along the platform carrying a brown leather suitcase. He looked for a porter, and meeting the same swarthy person who had handled Billy's luggage, he thrust the baggage-ticket at him. The name upon the luggage-ticket was "Isherwood."

Apparently, he had no Italian, not a word of it. He was the typical Englishman, inarticulate abroad, just capable of asking "How much?"—"Give me change."—"What time is dinner?" To the porter he uttered the one word—"Taxi."

He and his luggage were put into a taxi, but he appeared to have forgotten the necessity for giving an address.

"Hotel Elyseo?" asked the driver.

His blue eyes looked startled.

"No, Hotel Flora."

The taxi-man gave a faint grimace. All the English who wore English tailor-made clothes went to the Elyseo or the St. George. The Hotel Flora was frowzy and cheap; its table-cloths were changed only once a week. If you spilt your soup you had to live with the sinful stain for seven whole days.

Isherwood's way of sitting in a car was reminiscent of Frevick's sack-like slouch in a chair. He seemed to crumple up; his waistcoat was all wrinkles and his tie bulged. He did not look at this new world with any obvious interest, but was carried along like a tired child whose round blue eyes fixed things with a perfunctory stare. They did not brighten or change their expression. They accepted the sea and the mountains and the sky and the cypresses and the garden, and the old battered, sun-blistered walls, as a disillusioned dramatic-critic's eyes might accept a new play. Life was just a panorama which differed in its minor details. The atmosphere was the same.

The Hotel Flora was kept by a Maltese who met all complaints with polite indifference. His hotel smelt of sour bread, and Beelzebub was its deity, but when his patrons complained, the Knight of Malta smiled upon them truculently.

"Yes, madam, but my terms are so very reasonable. Nowhere else in Tindaro will madam find accommodation so very reasonable."

Which was true. The Maltese knew his public, the people who were hard up and had to buy their sunlight as cheaply as possible, and who could not afford to stay either at the Elyseo or the St. George. His hotel was always full, and he had assumed the indifference of the monopolist.

At the Hotel Flora, Isherwood was shown a room on the third floor. Its window looked north, and its furniture was very shabby.

"But I ordered a south room."

"We are very sorry, sir, but all the south rooms are occupied."

"O, all right. I'm staying only a couple of weeks. I have a villa here."

He accepted that scrofulous room. He was tired, and his

tiredness had developed into a perpetual resignation, and the little Maltese, having attempted his usual piece of bluff, closed the door on a man who could be made to accept the worst room in the hotel. Had the argument continued, and the Englishman shown any aggressiveness, another room would have been offered at higher terms. The Maltese despised people who did not turn and snarl when a tail was twisted.

Isherwood took off his scarf and overcoat, hung them upon a peg behind the door, and sat down on the bed. His face looked tired and rather grey; he was one of those men who lose their colour quickly, not only as to the skin but also as to the soul. He had his moments of pathos and his moments of petulance. He looked at the cheap wardrobe with its door hanging all awry, and at an eczematous and peeling patch upon one of the walls, and he knew that he had been weak in allowing himself to be pushed into this room. But did it matter? Did anything matter? Why have a row with a little, oily dago over the hutch you were going to inhabit for fourteen days?

He got up and looked at himself in the mirror, and his self-scrutiny was both appraising and apprehensive. A day's beard did not add to his beauty, and he turned away from the glass with a little, inward shrinking. Yes, he was pretty rotten physically, and life was a sucked orange. But he opened up his suitcase and took out his razor and sponge-bag, and rang the bell for hot water. One had to make some sort of effort to keep up appearances.

A valet opened the door, and Isherwood stood in the middle of the room, trying to remember the Italian for hot water, but failing, he had to use English.

"Hot water, please."

The valet had much more English than Isherwood had Italian, and the hot water was brought in a white enamelled jug, and Isherwood removed his collar and tie, and proceeded to lather and shave himself. Both the light and the mirror were bad. They made him look grey and old, or he thought so, and as he scraped at his chin he was assailed by a sense of the fatuity of things. Why travel a thousand miles or more and exile yourself in order to drag out a perfectly fatuous existence? Why

scrape your chin daily when there was not a person in the whole
darned world who cared whether you scraped your throat or cut
it? He was out of the fight. He had gone under. Nothing
that he could do or say or think mattered.

But he shaved and washed himself, and brushed his hair, and
noticed that he was growing grey at the temples, no new discovery, but one that was remade whenever he felt in the mood
for it. He unpacked some of his things, languidly, and with an
air of resignation. Happening to glance at his watch and
hearing the sound of a gong, he realized that the luncheon hour
had arrived. He supposed that he would have to go down and
eat something

He went. They placed him in a little dark corner behind
the door. The dining-room was all soiled white paint, and
shabby gilding. Sleepy flies buzzed and settled on the bread,
and the coarse cloth, and on your head. The place seemed full
of old women, sinister and sad old women. There were
vegetable soup, and spaghetti, and veal, and one tinned apricot
on a little pat of sickly sweet rice. Isherwood ordered a flask
of Chianti. He felt chilly and lonely and strange, and even the
crudest of wines offered a contrast. He drank two full glasses
of the acid stuff.

Afterwards he went upstairs to his dismal room, and took off
his collar and shoes, and locked the door and drew the curtains.
Sleep, yes, sleep was the supreme escape. You eluded your
wretched ass of a body, and shed your loneliness and your sense
of the hopeless finality of things.

Isherwood lay down on his bed, and slept till three o'clock.
When he woke his coat and his hair were crumpled, and his blue
eyes—so like the eyes of a child—seemed to resent the com-
mands of consciousness.

III

Billy was helping Julia Lord in the tearoom when Miss
Soulby came to say that she was needed in the office.

"It's Mr. Isherwood."

"Isherwood? O, yes, the man who has taken the Villa
Byron. Ask him to wait ten minutes."

The ten minutes became twenty, for the English Tea Rooms were growing more and more popular in Tindaro, and three Italian waitresses had to be supervised, and the old loggia had been added to the tearoom and a new loggia built in the garden. Billy and Julia Lord prepared the trays, and made out the bills, and kept careful eyes upon all the details.

Meanwhile Tom Isherwood sat on a bent cane chair beside the table, with the collar of his grey overcoat turned up, his brown face in a brown study. His elbows rested on his knees, and he twiddled a stick with its ferrule on the tiled floor, and its handle just under his chin. Miss Soulby, busy at her type-writer, threw at him occasional glances of short-sighted interest and sympathy. He looked so resigned to things, even to wait-ing upon the coming of Miss Brown. His blue eyes, staring at nothing in particular, seemed to suggest that nothing that was visible could be particularly pleasant to him. Also, he looked quite young according to the standards of Anglo-American Tindaro.

Then Billy came in briskly through the communicating-door, and glanced with businesslike directness at the seated figure. He appeared for the moment to be unconscious of her presence. He was twiddling his stick. His hat lay on the table beside a pile of magazines. He looked inexpressibly forlorn and melan-choly, a lost man-child, and something in Billy was surprised in an impulse of vague pity, but the English Agency did not deal in pity, and the emotion was suppressed.

She said, "I must apologize for keeping you waiting."

Startled, he came out of his stare. He looked at her, and stood up, and laid his stick on the table beside his hat.

"My name's Isherwood."

"Quite. The Villa Byron."

Her briskness and her compact self-confidence seemed to confuse him. He became self-conscious.

"Yes. Arrived this morning. Putting up at the Hotel Flora. I haven't seen my place yet. I thought you might be able to tell me."

His face was both vivid and vague.

"Thought I had better call on you. Don't know my way about yet. I suppose you have a key?"

Billy opened a drawer and picked up a key with a label attached to it.

"Here it is. But you won't know the way."

"I'm afraid not."

"I'll send Miss Soulby with you. Miss Soulby, would you show Mr. Isherwood the way to Strozzi's villas?"

Miss Soulby left her chair and her machine with eager alacrity.

"Certainly, Miss Brown."

Billy closed the drawer, and stood observing Isherwood while the typist put on her hat.

"Anything we can do, Mr. Isherwood——"

"O, thanks. You see, I suppose I shall want some furniture. I suppose there is furniture to be had?"

"Yes. Rather dear—though."

"Well, I shan't want very much. Perhaps you could tell me where——"

Billy smiled brightly. She was thinking that this new exile was a vague and helpless kind of creature, the sort of child to whom you said "Come, pull up your socks." She felt tolerantly dominant towards him. Meanwhile Miss Soulby had got her fluffy head inside her hat, and was beaming through her pince-nez upon the adventure.

Said Billy, "Come and report to me if you don't find everything in order. The house is quite new and up to date, though the garden is a little ragged. We represent you. It's our business to look after your interests."

He gave her a queer, unreadable smile; at least—to Billy it conveyed nothing of his feelings or his thoughts.

"Thank you."

Picking up his stick and hat he gave Billy a shy nod, and prepared to follow Miss Soulby out into the Corso. He was thinking, "Some young woman—this. Modern efficiency. Hard as a bit of glass. She'd soon frighten me to death. A bit formidable. Good lord——!"

IV

When Miss Soulby returned to the English Agency, Billy, who was writing letters at her desk, looked up and asked a question.

"Mr. Isherwood satisfied?"

Miss Soulby's little bud of a mouth pointed its lips.

"Well, partly.   He is not the sort of man to say much, but then, you see——"

"No, I don't see.   What's wrong?"

Miss Soulby was very much of a creature of sentiment, and Billy would not tolerate Miss Soulby as anything but a secretary and typist.   Miss Soulby liked to weave garlands.

"Nothing's wrong—exactly, Miss Brown, but then—you see —Mr. Isherwood is an architect."

"O!   Is or was?"

"Was—I suppose."

"So he grew historical?"

"I think Strozzi's idea of colour was rather a shock.   The gate—for instance, and——"

"A man does not live on his front gate.   Strozzi's places are much more sanitary and workable than some great dirty and romantic old barrack.   Had Mr. Isherwood any serious complaints?"

"O, none, I think."

Miss Soulby removed her hat and returned to her table in the corner.   Obviously Miss Brown had no feeling for the artistic temperament, or whatever you chose to call it, but Miss Soulby was more sympathetic.   Why shouldn't the poor man be shocked by Signor Strozzi's verdant greens and blues and yellows?   Her further silence was a sentimental protest against Miss Brown's lack of understanding.

CHAPTER XXI

I

FOR Billy had had no opportunity of observing qualities in Isherwood that had touched the woman in Miss Soulby. The ascent to the Strozzi villas was somewhat steep, and Miss Soulby had found Isherwood lagging. He had paused near the top of the hill with a look of distress in his eyes. She had been aware of his quick, shallow breathing.

"Sorry, but I haven't been tackling hills lately."

Miss Soulby had observed him anxiously.

"It—is—rather steep. Can you manage?"

"O, yes. You see—I have had a chest. That's why I'm here."

Miss Soulby was soft hearted. Really, Dr. Burt and Miss Brown should have exercised more forethought, and not sent an invalid to live at the top of a steepish hill. And Miss Soulby's soft heart was wrung by the pathos of that panting chest. A man in distress was as appealing as a sick child. He—was—a sick child. And Miss Soulby discovered an added pathos in her appreciation of Isherwood as a man who was young and who looked as though he had been strong and healthy. He had a skin which tanned quickly. His blue eyes were of the open air.

She did not pass the cup of her compassion to Miss Brown. She kept it to herself, and cherished it, and was ready to wish that the English Agency might place the ordering of Mr. Isherwood's affairs in her hands. The Hotel Flora was such a squalid place. And the poor lad wanted furniture, and the Italian who kept the furniture shop in Tindaro was a veritable brigand, and obviously Mr. Isherwood had not too much money. Also, who was going to look after him in that hyper-coloured little box of a villa? A man was so helpless.

Yes, helpless as a baby.

Moreover, that was Burt's feeling about Thomas Isherwood when the new exile called, and placed himself in Burt's hands.

"I feel very glad you are here, doctor. Dr. Hazzard advised me to see you at once."

"I'd like to examine you."

"Of course. One lung was rather badly touched, but Dr. Hazzard assured me that it had healed."

So Isherwood was made to strip to the waist and to sit with a rug over his shoulders while the big man percussed and listened with deliberate thoroughness. Isherwood's eyes were anxious, and Burt noticed their anxiety. The man had been badly frightened. But that was natural.

Burt folded up his stethoscope.

"Right. You can dress. I can find no signs of any active trouble."

"Good."

"Coughing or spitting at all?"

"No."

"What about your weight?"

"I put on ten pounds at home."

"Excellent. Put on another ten pounds. You can carry it. I should like you to be weighed once a month. I'll weigh you here."

Isherwood was fastening his collar.

"Doctor, I'd like to know the truth. Have I been sent out here to die?"

Burt looked at him kindly, tolerantly.

"No reason why you shouldn't live to be seventy. Those new villas are well up in the air and sun."

"Rather a climb."

"That won't hurt you. Take it easily, and very soon you won't notice it."

Isherwood tied his tie, and Burt noticed that he looked at himself anxiously in the mirror.

"There are several things, doctor."

"What things?"

"I shall have to get fixed up with furniture and a servant. I'm rather raw out here."

"Get the Agency to help you."

"That Miss Brown?"

"Yes."

"She seems rather a hard young person, doctor."

"So much the better for you, in a way. She gets things done. She'll see that you're not done."

"O, perhaps so. I'm awfully obliged to you, doctor. It's pretty rotten having to be a desultory wash-out."

"You'll find interests. An architect, weren't you?"

"Yes. And I paint a bit."

"Plenty of material here. Come and dine with us on Friday, and meet my wife."

"Thanks. Awfully good of you."

"Eat well and keep in the sun. Not much alcohol."

"May I smoke?"

"Within reason. Keep cheerful."

That was their first interview, and afterwards, Burt, in describing Isherwood to his wife, spoke of him as a rather helpless person. "Been badly frightened, poor devil. We've got to be kind to him. There are parts of the fellow that remind me strangely of poor old Frevick."

II

Isherwood had a history. That is to say he had never been either slave-merchant or slave, but always the rather original child wanting to play his game, and to play it in his own particular way. He had been born under the sign of Gemini. But to be able to play a game in his own particular way a man needs not only originality, but fierceness of purpose, belief in himself, perhaps a touch of arrogance, and a skin that is not easily rubbed raw. Isherwood had had too sensitive a skin.

Also he had possessed ideas, and had developed them rather prematurely, and the commercial world of the day is very critical of the young man with ideas if he wears them too much like a halo. At the age of twenty, Tom Isherwood had gone about exclaiming, "Let's do something new. To hell

H

with the old stuff. Can't we create?" So flamboyant and radical an enthusiasm may be excusable in a student, but when your duly qualified professional man joins himself to a solid and conservative firm, he may be about as welcome as a Chinese cracker let off in the middle of a parish missionary meeting.

As a designer of houses Isherwood had worshipped the abstract to the exclusion of the concrete. He had had his Gothic phase and his Classic phase, and they had been followed by a period which had been wholly and supremely Isherwood. He had said, "I am going to dream something new." The office of Churt, Hanson & Isherwood had had its chuckles over Tom's dream-houses. Certainly they were damned clever, so clever that old Churt who had a jealous disposition, had waited and waited like an old man with a club. Damned young fool, he'd catch him. Then had arrived that plan of Isherwood's for "A Gentleman's Pleasure House overlooking Beaulieu River," and old Churt had been able to ask—"What about the drains, my lad?" Yes, what about the drains? Isherwood, supremely and hotly the artist, had not forgotten the ideals of sanitation, but had merely extruded them for the time being.

He had said, "That's a study. If I draw you a picture of a beautiful woman in the nude I don't give you a sketch of her internal arrangements, liver and tubes and kidneys. One takes them for granted."

Old Churt had replied, "Oh, indeed! You had better not take your drains for granted. We plan houses in this office; we don't paint pretty pictures. Your plans should show every damned tap and electric-light switch in the place."

Both Youth and Age had gone red in the face.

"I prefer to show a man a picture of his house before I introduce him to the closets, sir."

Old Churt had felt himself insulted. Besides, the weather had been hot and thundery at the time, and Europe had been feeling oppressed. July, 1914. There had been other explosions, and Isherwood had rushed in among the first hundred thousand, and his "Mad houses" had changed into dug-outs.

The war tore him rather badly both in body and soul. He

had a leg smashed at Hooge, and was gassed on the Somme. The inadequacies of a sensitive temperament accumulated, so much so that he finished the war in retreat at home. The prevailing restlessness assailed him. He did not return to the office of Churt & Hanson, but being the possessor of a small private income, he set up on his own. He had some success until his war-chest played him false and left him a broken man with scars in his left lung.

The war and its crudities had left other scars. He had not emerged from it feeling like a hero. He had learnt to drink and to smoke too much; he came out of it a little coarsened, and with more than a tinge of cynicism. He had seen other things besides men and houses blown to smithereens; something in his sensitive, mobile self had been exploded; his will to accomplish and his belief in the fineness of accomplishment had slackened. And finally, six months before his illness, he had happened upon a love affair with a little woman with red hair, who was a saleswoman in a fashionable West End furriers. Hard as a piece of ivory, with her cream-coloured face and bright bobbed head, she had taken as much out of Isherwood as she could get, and then—in the midst of his physical defeat —she had thrown him over.

Another dream-house gone.

Though Isherwood still dreamed dreams, he dreamed them differently. They were the melancholy phantasies of surrender. He had come to think of himself as a man who was out of the fight, a guttering candle, a valetudinarian. He had grown careless. He had moods of slovenly pessimism. He was bored with himself, and yet afraid of dying.

For a man with such a temperament to write the word "Finished" over the door of his house of dreams meant the surrender of everything that mattered. Your artist must either be dreaming or dying. He cannot be made to turn a wheel in a cage; he lacks the stolid, digestive cheerfulness of the habitual man. He is so much the Peter Pan. With him resignation slides towards decadence. He asks much from life, and finding the mystic fruit snatched from his hands, he may be too easily discouraged.

Isherwood had accepted discouragements. He was like a bored child who had ceased to be interested in his toys, but he was much more than a bored child. He had begun to cultivate a fatal self pity. He lay too much in bed, and felt his pulse too often, and looking at the tongue of his soul found it furred. He accepted its furriness. It was part of the Isherwood fate, unescapable, brutal, pathetic. He had come to regard himself as one of those futile and tragic figures, misunderstood, misdirected, balked. He would always fumble at life, and life would have the laugh of him.

As Burt had said, "A rather helpless person."

III

Isherwood and Tindaro began to know each other. That is to say this tallish, stooping figure with its lost blue eyes under its casual hat, became seen upon the Corso, for Isherwood was still at the Hotel Flora, where two or three of the old vultures had tried their sympathetic claws on him. But Isherwood, like many men who have been sick and mortally afraid of dying, shrank from old women. They were so much like the birds upon a battlefield, waiting to pull you to pieces even while your blue eyes still looked at life. The Hotel Flora made him think of a dark aviary smelling of dead things, in which a number of grey old birds sat grimly upon perches, each with a piece of flesh tucked away under a clawed foot.

Isherwood preferred the sunlight. It was more pleasant to dream dreams in the sunlight, even though they were the dreams of a valetudinarian. Besides, the Villa Byron was providing him with a sense of occupation, and with reflections upon Signor Strozzi's soul. The old olive trees were gorgeous, and so was the view, but the villa itself had the hectic face of some little madam waggling her hips in Shaftesbury Avenue.

Isherwood's first domestic purchase was a little wooden stool which he bought at a shop on the Corso and carried up with him to the Villa Byron. He placed the stool in front of the blue door and sat on it, and contemplated. The sun shone. A troup of very small birds twittered in the olives. The other villas were sufficiently far away and did not interfere with Isherwood's moods. When it was not being sat upon the stool lived in the vestibule of the Villa Byron.

Isherwood sat upon it every morning and made the same resolve.

"I must see about furnishing this place."

Obviously so. The Hotel Flora was impossible. But Tindaro had a soporific effect; it exaggerated his sense of the to-morrow; it soothed and encouraged his melancholy indolence. He sat on his stool in the sunlight and looked down at Tindaro and the sea and the rocky coast, and the Island of the Triton. Something in him proposed to do nothing but sit on a stool in the sun, and stare blue-eyed at blue horizons.

Then the weather intervened. Rain-clouds arrived over Tindaro, and when rain set in over this Italian coast a grey curtain was let down and remained dismally unfurled for days. The hill-paths became little muddy watercourses; the steps in the steep vicolos were small cascades. The Corso became a street of puddles, and when a motor passed, those who did not wish to be mud-splashed made for the doorways. The Café Ceres withdrew its tables, and huddled them under a sagging awning, and Tommaso, emerging periodically with an old broom, would give the awning a prod and send a squelch of water splashing upon the pavement. Even the sleepy flies responded to the wet gloom, and slept upon the cakes in the window or crawled torpidly upon the walls and tables.

Two days of rain damped Isherwood's indolence. The Hotel Flora had offered him the alternatives of the stuffy lounge or his dismal bedroom. You might get up late and go to bed early, and indulge in an after-lunch siesta, but ennui, the sudden sadness of such days in an Italian town, followed you from room to room. The sea was grey as lead. A wind whipped the cypresses. The Corso was empty, save for the figures of a few energetic and elderly English, protesting in mackintoshes against England in Italy.

On the third day one of these wet figures appeared in the office of the English Agency. It wore an old brown trench-coat, and was the worried possessor of a wet umbrella. It appeared to feel responsible for the umbrella and its tricklings upon the floor.

Billy, seated at her desk, gave this rather forlorn figure a dispassionate glance, and a brisk good morning.

"Rotten weather. How is the Villa?"

Isherwood smiled at her disarmingly.

"I want to ask your advice. What do I do with this?"

Said Billy, "Miss Soulby, please take Mr. Isherwood's umbrella, and put it in its proper place."

Miss Soulby had compassion. The proper place was a big earthenware oil-jar near the door, where umbrellas could leak at leisure.

"You had better take off that raincoat."

"Perhaps I had."

"Hang it on the back of that chair."

She saw him as a very helpless person, and she had got into the way of treating people as she found them. An efficient and arbitrary frankness saved time and tissue. She pointed with her pencil to the chair on the other side of her desk. And Isherwood sat down, and looked at her rather like a whimsical small boy in the presence of a governess.

"It's about furniture."

"Furniture? For your villa?"

"Yes."

"Haven't you done anything about it yet?"

"No."

Her brown eyes considered him. It occurred to her to wonder how it was that some people hovered and hesitated, and why Tindaro appeared to attract these very helpless and flabby figures. Exiles. People who let go, whose grip was limp, people who flopped and drifted.

"What's the idea?"

Miss Soulby, who had returned to her corner, saw him look at Miss Brown as though he were being questioned by an examiner.

"I wondered whether you could do it for me?"

"Furnish your villa?"

"Yes. You see—I haven't much Italian, and a man's

rather lost—isn't he—about kitchen things and towels and sheets? Of course, you may think it—rather undignified. And of course—I'll pay you a proper commission."

Billy's smile appeared.

"Undignified! Well, not exactly. We set out to be universal providers. So you have nothing."

"Not a stick. Just a wooden stool."

"A wooden stool!"

"I bought it to sit on in the garden. But when the rain began——"

"You were driven inside with the stool."

"Exactly. And the Hotel Flora——"

"Yes, I know the Hotel Flora."

There was a moment of silence, and it held suggestions for an incipient friendliness, the sort of relation that may be established between a capable woman and a dog.

"So you wish us to do the best we can?"

"Please."

"Very well. I'll draw out an inventory."

"Please make it—as—as simple as you can. I have to be careful."

"I understand. We'll go through the inventory together, and then I'll tackle Calabria."

He looked puzzled, and she explained.

"O, Calabria is the local furnishing store. We call it Calabria because——"

His blue eyes lit up.

"I see. The local brigands. Better leave them to you, had I? Yes, obviously. I shall be awfully obliged."

"Supposing you let me have the key of the villa. I'll go up and look round."

"Thanks awfully."

She was as Olympian as a college tutor, or as one of the urbane gentlemen who furnish for you on the hire-purchase system. "You provide the girl, sir. We——" Isherwood smiled at Billy, and there was a something in his blue eyes which made Miss Capability Brown think of Tom Frevick.

IV

Billy went up to the Villa Byron in the rain.   She despised umbrellas.   Russian boots, a good masculine mackintosh, and a red rainproof hat satisfied all her requirements.   There were no facial frescoes to be damaged.   She found the new road leading up to Strozzi's villas, a yellow and adhesive squdge.

The wind troubled the wet foliage of the olive trees, and their trunks were very black.   The young cypresses on either side of the path leaned away from the wind and the rain, and for the first time felt a little critical of Strozzi's idea of what a garden gate should be.   It suggested a cheap and sticky wooden toy.

The turquoise-blue of the front door was blurred and softened by a film of moisture.   She brought out her key and opened the door, and standing in the vestibule she saw Isherwood's little wooden stool.   It looked so small and solitary, and so much the only piece of furniture in that very new house, that she was aware of a twinge of compassion.

"Poor little thing."

She smiled.   But she was Miss Capability Brown.   Her boots were distinctly dirty, and she pulled them off, and went and washed her hands under the kitchen tap, and dried them on her handkerchief.   She had brought her notebook with her in an inner pocket of her mackintosh, and hanging the latter garment on the rail of the stairs she set about making her inventory.

She wrote a headline on each page.   "Drawing-room"— "Dining-room"—"Kitchen"—"Stairs"—"Bedroom No. 1 —" —"Bedroom No. 2."   But at this point it occurred to her that Isherwood would not need two living-rooms, or more than one bedroom.   Economy and the conventions ran in double harness.   It would be much better for him to have a woman in by the day.

She went upstairs, and found herself standing in the middle of an empty room, and looking through the window at a grey and blurred landscape.   It was all wet as with tears.   And suddenly she was conscious of the house's emptiness; it had never been lived in; it was so new and raw. Her impression of it came to include the man who was to live in it, and suddenly she felt sorry and vaguely troubled.

"Poor devil."

Almost she felt about him like a man. Her compassion was bisexual. He looked such a very helpless creature, such an exile. She was reminded of his likeness to Frevick, an air of lost and detached resignation, an inability to stand up against the world and against the ennui of a melancholy self.

Tindaro was rather fatal to such people. In Frevick's case. But she frowned, and began to write with a firm hand.

"Bed and bedding. Six sheets—single. Three blankets. Toilet set. Washhand-stand. Drawers. Rugs or carpet ——"

CHAPTER XXII

I

TINDARO accepted Thomas Isherwood.

But there were degrees of acceptance and of recognition, and varying ways of feeling sorry for gods and for men, and the cup of Stella Burt's compassion held other wine than did the chalices of Lady Pipp and Mrs. Sudbury Smith. Isherwood could listen to Stella Burt's music, and not feel torn and challenged by it, for it was neither a sea chantey nor a hymn. At the Villa Dante a reprobate might still hear the distant strains of "Onward, Christian Soldiers," and Isherwood, having gazed into Lady Pipp's little yellow face all buttoned up like an old-fashioned bodice, had declined from grace and lapsed into paganism. He wanted to lie in the sun and to do nothing and be nothing. There were occasions when he felt about people as a sensitive and fastidious child feels about fat meat and vinegar and earth worms, and the type of female hand that is hard and skinny and liable to chilblains.

Tindaro had so many faces and such varying moods. It could be Roman with Messrs. Lord & Brown, or neo-Pauline with the Pipps, or Dionysian with the Café Ceres, or it could be just Tindaro, a faded, sun-baked Italian town with no northern urge toward the virtues of an irritable pragmatism.

For Tindaro was very tired and old and tolerant. It had known Greeks, Etruscans, Romans, Frenchmen, Spaniards, Austrians, and it would let a man go to the dogs or the devil in his own way. Even Fascist Tindaro could not alter the faded colours of Tindaro's philosophy. It accepted the sun and the dust and the flies, and man's urge towards woman, and woman's willingness to clasp the man, and the graciousness of the grape, and the virtues of garlic. It did not fuss, and it knew not ethical dyspepsia. A man might die of drink or of dysentery, and be held free from all responsibility. Tindaro could sit and sun itself. It had not to get busy like an English town that is moved to keep itself warm most of the year, both inside and out, by various restless activities. Its cry was not "Let's do something." It was content to do nothing. It was old and faded and sunny and resigned. The English and the Americans were so young.

The trend of Isherwood's mood was to do nothing, and to be nothing. He had written "Explicit" over the gate of the world of action. He did not want to run about after a ball, or climb mountains or play with pieces of pasteboard. He had surrendered. He had the tiredness of the artist who had lost the urge to express himself in sounds, words or colours. He was empty of ambition, he had ceased to be the slave of his male urges. He was out of the eternal scuffle.

Tindaro and he smiled at each other and proposed to lie down together in the sun.

For so far as Isherwood was concerned the furnishing of the Villa Byron had not lacked a sense of humour. It was the English Agency that lacked humour, and was pragmatic and purposeful. Miss Capability Brown had made the new exile sit down in a chair and go item by item through her inventory.

"Don't want to furnish two bedrooms, do you?"

"No."

"Quite unnecessary. Or two sitting-rooms. And stained floors and rugs would be cheaper and cleaner."

He was so much more subtly aware of her as Miss Capability Brown than she was of him as Tom Isherwood the vale-tudinarian. To begin with, she amused him. She attended so decisively to business, and Isherwood's inclination was to do everything but attend to business.

"You will want a woman to look after you."

His blue eyes smiled at her tolerantly. He allowed her her dominations, as he would have allowed a doctor his dogmatism.

"Yes, I suppose so. It's awfully good of you to take all this trouble."

"Not at all. It's business. Saves trouble to call a thing by its right name."

She compelled "Calabria" to realize that Mr. Isherwood was not a person to be exploited. She moved him out of the Hotel Flora, and bundled him and his furniture into the Villa Byron. She was capably kind and coercive. Her direct brown eyes and her smile and her vigorous hair were positive, while he, in his faded, negative blond blueness was amused and submissive. She found for him a middle-aged Italian woman, who had warts and a moustache, to cook and clean and bed-make. She made him feel pleasantly helpless, and old and wise. "Now then, buck up—pull your socks up. Let's get this job finished."

To begin with, he was not challenged by her philosophy of action. She was England, the new Nordic woman, domiciled in Italy, and he had left England and its weather and its "sports-model" culture behind him. She was just a jolly good sort, hard and capable, and kind in her own way, kind in doing things, but not so much so in feeling them. He looked at her with his wide, blue eyes, like an intelligent and lazy child, a child who somehow felt himself to be so much more delicately civilized than his nurse. O, yes, let her fuss about soap and water and tooth-brushes and the whiteness of a collar. It was just the English tradition, the Bible in Brixton, and cricket, and nice white tennis shoes, and Queen's Hall, and Mudie's, and a well-brushed head of hair, and the sort of assumption that people ought to be good.

But what the devil was "being good"? Tindaro had other standards. It liked garlic and oil. Morality may be a matter of climate and appetite, and both are relative.

II

Because there was an air of innocence about Isherwood which was both pathetic and absurd, to Stella Burt he appeared as a blue-eyed boy, a most transparent creature even when regarded as a valetudinarian. Being sad he was very, very sad. He gave Burt's wife the impression of having lost himself, and without realizing that he had lost himself. He wandered about looking at life with those boyish eyes in a man's face, and to Stella Burt they were dumb with the eternal question. "Where am I? What does all this muddle mean?"

Isherwood had dined with the Burts.   He had talked music
to Stella, and Minoan art with Burt.   He had one of those
slow, pleasant, sleepy voices, and when Stella Burt had played
Schubert to him and listened to his voice she felt that she knew
a great deal about Thomas Isherwood.   He liked Schubert's
music and was not ashamed to say so.   He had a rather delight-
ful candour, and none of the self-conscious caution of the man
who is too carefully clever.

Stella Burt was not a woman who could be sentimental about
a man or a child just because they had rather frightened blue
eyes and an air of innocence.   She felt people and their essential
ugliness or beauty just as Isherwood felt them, and perhaps
that was why she understood him.

"Have you noticed his eyes?"

Her husband had.   He said that you often saw that sort
of secret distress in the eyes of people who had had trouble
with heart or lungs.

"Do you think Tindaro is going to suit him?"

"It should do.   Chests do quite well here."

"I don't mean physically.   You see, he is a Gemini."

Burt smiled at her as she sat at the piano.

"You and your astrology!"

"There is something in it, Jack."

"Yes, you are a bit of a witch.   And what of your Gemini?"

"When Gemini loses his enthusiasm it is apt to slop rather
badly.   No wings left.   Rather tragic when a Gemini is
stripped of its wings.   Besides, he has a sort of innocence."

"Yes, I think I know what you mean.   A boy with a
temperament.   Has to be looked after."

"He reminds me so much of poor Frevick.   Tindaro gets
that sort of temperament and reduces it to—well—to its
elementals."

"Yes.   The old Circe legend.   Quite."

Isherwood's desultory figure was seen upon the Corso.   The
Café Ceres observed it, and made observations upon it, but as
yet Tindaro had not yet introduced the new exile to the Café
Ceres.   It was Isherwood's first glimpse of Italy, and the
beauty of it was not to be questioned.   Isherwood explored.

He pottered about the town and the hills and the shore. He was seen sitting among the ruins of the Roman theatre making a sketch of the broken walls, darkly red against the blue sea and the sunlit coast. Frevick chanced upon him there one morning, with a pad on his knees, and a box of water-colours on a stone beside him. Frevick had met Isherwood at Burt's; they had sat and listened to the same music.

Frevick loitered. He knew that it bored him to have anyone standing behind his back when he was at work, and he would have left Isherwood alone had not Isherwood looked up and nodded.

"Morning. I don't annoy you, do I?"

Frevick looked at Isherwood's face as though he was more interested in the man than the picture.

"How do you mean?"

"As the amateur. I suppose you have often sat here."

"Yes, pretty often."

"Looks so easy, and isn't. I can't get that sky. What do you think about it?"

Frevick moved round behind him, and looked down at the water-colour study on Isherwood's knees. The fellow was strangely ingenuous, rather like a nice boy asking you how you liked his piece of poetry. But Frevick was supposed to be studying Isherwood's attempt to render the old red brickwork and that Italian sky, and to behave as the artist and not as the man.

He considered the work. It was not so amateurish as he had expected, but the sky was wrong, and Frevick knew just why it was wrong.

"You wash in?"

"Yes."

"I belong to the other school, the blot school."

Isherwood looked first at the sky and then at his study of it. There were clouds about.

"Yes, too washy, is that it?"

"Probably. Depth—you know, and those bits of shadow."

"Wish you'd show me. Would you? I know the blob idea is the thing, but I have never been able to manage it. Line of least resistance—I suppose.   I could resist all right over houses."

He got up, and looked at Frevick with those friendly blue eyes.

"Don't think it cheek of me?"

"Hardly."

Frevick took the pad from him and sat down, and chose a fresh brush from the box, and making a wet mélange of certain colours began to impress upon Isherwood's washy sky a series of bold splodges.   Isherwood, bending forward, watched his hand at work.   It was the hand of the master.

"Ah—that's it.   I haven't the touch.   What's more, I don't suppose I see all that you see."

"Matter of practice, furious trying.   That's the difference——"

"Quite.   But I don't suppose I should do it.   I haven't that in me which makes it worth while."

Frevick appeared to be struck by those last two words.   The hand of the painter was arrested.   He sat quite still, looking at the sky, and his response was that of man to man.

"Oh, it depends.   I used to think it worth while.   One of the tragedies when you lose the feeling."

"But you haven't lost it?"

The older exile's face had a sudden fierceness.

"I?   O, lord, yes.   I lost it years ago.   My own fault—of course.   Always is.   After that life becomes just messing about with paints or words.   Sit down and have another shot."

But Isherwood had grown silent, and absorbed in some more introspective study.

"O, not now.   Some other time.   I think I'll light a pipe. You smoke?"

"Too much.   One of the drugs, my dear chap.   That's all the philosophy a man may have left.   But don't you take that as final."

But to Isherwood during the early days of exile nothing was final, because he felt that he had passed beyond finality.   His acceptance of Tindaro as a place in the sun designed for desultory dreaming signified the acceptance of his desultory self.   He was sorry for Thomas Isherwood and gentle towards the same Thomas Isherwood. He understood what Frevick had meant by the feeling that the doing of things had ceased to be worth while, and that when you had reached that state, life became a mere messing about with idle words and colours. It implied that a man had ceased to respond to the fierce challenge of life. He did not leap up when the Roman trumpet sounded, and put on his brazen helmet and grasp his Spanish sword.

Isherwood breakfasted in bed. Certainly he did emerge at seven to unlock the door for Maria of the warts and the moustache, but he got back to bed again, and took his coffee there. Maria was large and Italian and kind, and she treated Isherwood rather like a large child. Women felt moved to compassion by his air of half-whimsical lostness. His shaving and his dressing were as desultory as the rest of his day. He pottered about his bedroom, and smoked cigarettes, and threw the ends out of the window. Often he would forget to pull the bath plug to let the water out of the bath.

Also, he was capable of treating himself humorously, and of regarding his premature nothingness as a gentle joke.

"One just sits in the sun, you know."

And yet he escaped from appearing completely futile. If the world of Tindaro spoke of him as "Poor Isherwood" it did so with the conviction that he had not always been poor Isherwood, white trash, if rather nice white trash. The personality of the man followed him like a shadow, or looked out of his blue eyes. The ghost of his youth still haunted him, and was sometimes apparent to those who could see.

He became a familiar figure to Julia Lord. He was in the English Library every other day. His choice of a book to read was as desultory as his reading. He would wander about and stand in front of the shelves as though nothing on them piqued him. His indecision hovered and could not perch.

He was less shy of Miss Lord than he was of Miss Brown, for Miss Lord was becoming less urgently capable and less of a reproach to an idle man. He had little conversations with her. And Julia Lord noticed that he glanced rather often at the door that communicated with the English Agency.

"I say, I suppose you haven't seen my garden gate?"

Miss Lord had not seen it.

"The colour. Like a cake of yellow soap. Also, I don't feel at all Byronic. That furious fellow—Byron. I wonder if Mr. Strozzi would object if I changed the colour and the title?"

"You had better go and ask Miss Brown."

Isherwood's eyes rested upon the communicating door. His hesitation was obvious. Probably he was a little afraid of Billy, that capable, brown-headed, steel-bright young woman. Possibly she disturbed his sense of repose, and challenged his inclination to find a sunny corner and to lie in it. There is no doubt that she did disturb him. He had not wanted to admire her, and yet there was a something in him which grew troubled and self-conscious when she looked at him. He felt so much less than he was in her presence. His slumbering virility seemed to stir and to be vexed with life because of her.

"I'm always bothering Miss Brown about something."

"It's her business to be bothered. She has acted as your agent."

"All right. I'll go and ask her."

But he went out into the Corso and approached Billy by way of the official door. He smiled and looked shy. His air of irresponsibility appeared exaggerated. Even his clothes seemed to hang on him rather helplessly.

"I always seem to be bothering you, but it's about my gate."

"Something wrong with the gate?"

"The colour. Rather jaundiced. I wonder if Strozzi would mind if I had it painted."

"I don't suppose so."

"And the name. I'm not much in sympathy with that furious fellow Byron."

And suddenly she was moved to remember that Byron had been an exile, and in looking at this other exile she was conscious of a curious compassion. His disillusionment was so different from the unhappy stormings of the author of "Don Juan." Byron afraid of growing fat! And Isherwood was bothered by the colour of a gate. What children men were! And somehow she realized both the man and the child in Isherwood.

"Shall I ask Strozzi? I don't suppose he will object."

"I could paint it myself, you know."

"Splendid. What colour?"

"O, just white, something harmless and unprovocative!"

She carried those words about with her. Harmless and unprovocative! But what words for a man to use before he had touched the meridian of forty! Such tired words, so full of the spirit of surrender. It was quite wrong. A man should not feel harmless and unprovocative.

Some days later, being moved by a vague curiosity, she climbed the road to Strozzi's villas and looked at Isherwood's gate. Yes, he had repainted it. It hung there a mild and innocuous white, and upon the upper bar he had lettered in a new title.

"The Crater."

She was puzzled. Why "The Crater"? There was nothing of Etna or Vesuvius about poor Tom Isherwood.

CHAPTER XXIII

I

BEYOND the gardens of the Hotel Elyseo where Tindaro ended in a scattering of villas, vineyards and cypress groves, Capo Moro thrust a dark wedge into the sea. It was all plumed with pines against the blueness, and scattered over its plateau were olive groves and orchards and warm seams of reddish soil where grapes ripened early. Capo Moro was still peasant property. Tindaro had spread no further, the white bulk of the Elyseo, standing there like finality, or like the angel of the Lord barring the way to any little commercialist mounted upon an ass.

But Billy had gazed upon Capo Moro. Beyond the wall of the Hotel Elyseo an old mule path climbed circuitously into the maquis, and here the hill-side remained virginal. When the sun warmed it this hill-side could smell sweet. It was a bundle of live herbs. Rosemary lit its little blue lamps. The tree heath grew in white masses, with cistus—white and pink, and yellow broom. Arbutus made a green glittering. Small birds twittered, and grasshoppers shrilled.

High up on this hill-side some understanding person had erected a wooden seat. It was a very old seat, and lovers had carved their names upon it, and sometimes about sunset or earlier Billy would climb the mule path to this seat and sit there with Capo Moro tongueing out into the sea below. Capo Moro would lie there burnished by the slanting splendour of the sun. The green gloom of its fringe of pines made the blue of the sea more intensely blue.

A ruined tower stood in the centre of the Capo Moro plateau, rising from the grey green foam of a grove of old olive trees. There were a few scattered cottages, their old tiled roofs brown as the soil, and vivid patches of green where the peasants had

239

sown maize or lupin.   But to Billy the beauty and the innocence of Capo Moro had inspired the dreaming of other dreams.
Probably she had never heard of Cap Ferrat or Cap Martin,
but Capo Moro was what those other capes had been before
the rich had sought places in the sun.   Billy looked at Capo
Moro with the eyes and the imagination of Miss Capability
Brown of the English Agency.   She saw Capo Moro as a
property to be developed, a magnificent site for the spreading
of a new Tindaro.

But late one afternoon she found another person on that
solitary seat, Tom Isherwood rubbing a sprig of rosemary
between his palms just for the sake of smelling it.   Nor did
it occur to her to wonder how Isherwood saw Capo Moro.
More than half the seat was hers, and she took it.

He had risen and given her a lift of the hat.

"Gorgeous place—this."

Obviously so.   Nothing can be so platitudinous as the picturesque.   He sat down again.   He had dropped the sprig of
rosemary, and in place of it his half-whimsical shyness suggested
an olive branch.   Not that they had quarrelled.   Their differences were temperamental and in their attitude towards each
other these differences were subconscious.

He had not realized her as one who might come to look at
Capo Moro under the edge of the sunset, while she was aware
of him as a careless child who had come out without an overcoat.   The air grew chilly when the sun set.

She remarked on it.

"I suppose Dr. Burt warned you?"

"I believe he did.   Another ten minutes.   Apollo is still
suspended."

Her brown eyes observed him.   Was his language part of
his trifling or did he really think of things in that way?   Apollo,
and Pan, and Proserpine?   The more modern deities should be
Property, Purpose.   He was prodding the ground with the
point of his stick.

She said, "I suppose you came here for the view?"

The question caused him to smile.   He countered her
question.

"And you?"

"O, perspective."

"To see Capo Moro in relief, or like a cameo?"

She was a little puzzled. Almost his smile seemed directed at her.

"Depends how you see things, doesn't it?"

"Or what you want to see."

"We are getting rather subtle."

"O, no, not subtle. But what I see in Capo Moro, and what you see in it may be—relative. I have to do something, so I just stroll up here and stare."

"Nothing else?"

"What else is there?"

He seemed to shrug. He was smiling, but his smile was different. It suggested a tolerant self-pity.

"When you have finished with life—or rather—when life has finished with you, you just sit and stare. Perhaps you don't understand that. I hope you don't."

She glanced at the setting sun. He was between her and the sun, and it seemed to throw into relief the round-shouldered resignation of him, the faded smile of his fatalism. And somehow it shocked her. To her vital courage such a surrender appeared so wrong. She was conscious of a twinge of contempt, but almost before she was aware of it that little cleft of scorn had widened into a feeling of compassion.

She said, "Aren't there any things you want to do?"

He may have felt the implication of her pity.

"No, not now."

"Isn't that a rather terrible confession?"

"Of failure?"

"I did not say failure."

"Let's take it for granted. And what is failure? One can fail in all sorts of ways, emotionally or as a good citizen. One may fail to make money, or to turn one's own particular sand-pie out of the bucket. Besides, may there not be something in the Eastern idea, contemplation?"

"Or vegetation."

"The plant or tree as opposed to the squirrel in a cage. What is modernity and all this progress but an absurd fuss. The same hole in the ground is waiting for the fusser and the philosopher."

He tapped with his stick, while she sat looking at the ruined tower on Capo Moro. She wondered whether he had the same feeling as she had about this sudden confessional. It was as though she had opened a door and surprised him and herself, and the occasion had called for the use of concealing words. They were pretending to discuss life impersonally, while the poignant personal urge listened behind the curtain. They differed, because the urge in them differed, or rather because she was vital and vigorous, and he a tired, sick man, content to sit in the sun.

"But there was a time when you wanted to do things?"

His smile was retrospective.

"O, yes. I believed that I was going to be a devil of a fellow. Conceive and build something great. Like those two splendid kids Gilbert Scott and Ralph Knott. When you're young all things seem possible."

"You talk like an old man."

"I am an old man. Finished. And you despise that sort of thing."

She felt herself put upon the defensive. The suggestion was that she was young and hard, and that she had all youth's scorn of people who had ceased to be physically successful. Nor was the accusation groundless. She wanted to express herself by doing things, not by sitting and thinking about them. But she felt herself most strangely involved with him in a problem that was personal and becoming more intimate.

"One ought not to despise anything unless one understands it."

"But may I suggest that if you understand life—completely —you cease to despise."

"Do you think so?"

"I've experimented. You may feel inclined to despise yourself, but when you realize that your self cannot help being what it is, you chuck troubling."

She was in arms again against this philosophical flabbiness, this contemplative fatalism.

"I think that's damnable, quite damnable. It means that you accept what is—because it is."

"Well, doesn't one?"

"No. Does one accept flies and dirt and foul drains?"

"Not even in Tindaro?"

"Not even in Tindaro."

"You have kept very English."

"I have."

He glanced at her with his smile of amusement and of surrender, but her face was not to be smiled at. He met her brown eyes, and something in him winced from their resolute steadiness. Yes, obviously she was a young woman with ideals, though her ideals were practical and Western. She believed in keeping the world clean and fit. She would not allow you a sweet, succulent melancholy. He and she were temperamentally opposed.

He said, "Obviously, you think me a rotter. I can't play the game, the good old English game."

It was her turn for inward wincing. She was self-accused. It was as though she had given a hard and pragmatical slap to a child who needed comforting.

"I'm not quite so crude as that. People are so different, you and I. The I in me seems to you—fussy, and to me——"

"Yes, flabby."

"No, not quite that. You don't want to fight things. I do. I've had to."

And for some moments there was silence between them, the silence of two people groping through temperamental contrasts to an understanding of each other. Billy was looking at Capo Moro. She saw an edge of shadow cutting sharply across the sunlit surface. The sun was sinking behind the hills.

Abruptly she rose from her seat.

"Sunset. You ought not to stay here."

He looked up at her before rising, and the act of looking up had other meaning.

"I suppose not. But why should you trouble?"

"I don't know."

II

Being honest with herself afterwards she had to confess that she had troubled about him because he attracted her. Yes, she supposed it was that, just physical attraction, a silly sexual something. And she was angry. Oscar Slade had inoculated her against the sexual illusion, and the reaction still held good. She meant it to hold good. She was not going to make a fool of herself over some fellow because his physical make-up happened to pique the female in her. What rot it all was! Life was so much more efficient if you kept your emotions in cold storage.

Also the Slade affair had made her most horribly proud and fastidious. She did not regret it. She had come to think that it was rather a good thing for a girl to get through the slushy period, and having washed her feet in the waters of wisdom, to plant them firmly on the path of accomplishment. She had a career. She was ambitious. She had no intention of tolerating sentimental interference.

But had not a man like Isherwood any pride? Were some men such soft, facile creatures, who threw up their hands and surrendered, and went meekly into captivity.

Yes, she supposed in a way that she understood Isherwood's case. Tindaro was a tower for those who had surrendered, for the clever people whom life had bored, for the easy fatalists, for the little whimpering boys, for the decadents. But what a rotten business! It was poor Frevick and all those various sorry exiles over again, people who had no grip, people who let go. There were moments in life, beastly and agonizing moments when you could not let go; you had to set your teeth, and clutch something. Yes, she knew; she had been through it.

But why had he no grip? Was he made that way? Was he just a sick man who had some right to be humoured, and who could be left to sit in the sun? He was not a fool. O, by no manner of means. He had a sensitive quickness, a delicate appreciation of the ironical and the ridiculous. Yes, perhaps too much so. He was too sensitive, too soft-tempered.

He shrugged and smiled when he should have flown into a rage, and let out at life with fists and feet like a strong and determined child.

She happened to be spending that particular evening with Julia Lord, for they dined together once a week at the Villa Vesta, and discussed the affairs of the firm. It was a kind of weekly board-meeting. Messrs. Lord & Brown were finding in success many of those satisfactions that make life both more exacting and more a matter of routine. Absorbed in controlling their separate jobs, they found themselves seeing less and less of each other, though nothing but a deal door separated them. Billy's passion for keeping fit had to take its tennis and its swimming and its climbing when it could, while Julia worked in her garden.

On this particular night a full moon shone, and they put on coats and carried their coffee-cups to the terrace. Miss Lord allowed herself to smoke three cigarettes a day. She still practised economies and self-repressions, but her inspiration was more human. She kept it secret, even from Billy. It was she who had bought Tom Frevick's villa, and after sundry persuasions let it to him at a perfectly absurd figure.

Billy did not smoke. She stood by the terrace wall, stirring her coffee, and confronting the full moon. Probably her conception of life was that it should be rounded and polished and complete like the full moon. She was not concerned with seeing a man in it. Even eclipses were calculable phenomena; one could look them up in the almanac.

She said, "I wish we could make something of that Capo Moro idea. But it's an idea without money."

It was. The financier was lacking, some person whose capital could be persuaded to assist in the development of Capo Moro.

"Too big for us, Bill."

"It shouldn't be. It's rather exasperating to have to sit and wait until some other fellow comes along, and sees your idea and sneaks it. Capo Moro is simply asking to be built on."

Julia Lord, being some twenty-five years older than Billy, was more content with Capo Moro as it was, and less eager to

cover it with villas. Moreover, she happened to be thinking
about Frevick. Poor Frevick could not last very much longer;
he was a house whom death would pull down.

"We haven't much to grouse about."

"I know. Our figures have nearly doubled in a year. But
I do wish we could get that land, Julie. We could sit on it
and wait."

"Roads," said Julia, "roads, and drains and a water supply."

"O, yes, I know. I have got it all down on paper. We
should have to sink thousands in purchase and development."

She looked at the moon. She let herself drift into a pragmatical monologue, while Miss Lord smoked her cigarette.

"My idea is a syndicate. Some of us could get together and
put up the money. I believe the Mayor would come in, and
it would be just as well to have Italian interest in the scheme.
It would smooth things for us. We should have to have a
competent architect for the general lay-out, and for the houses.
I have thought of talking to Strozzi about it; but I don't think
he has much more money to play with, and I don't want to
present him with the inspiration."

Miss Lord savoured her cigarette, and Billy's feminism.

"You'd prefer a petticoat syndicate."

"Well, wouldn't it be rather intriguing. If you and I and
Sadie could have put up the money."

"With a ready-made architect to hand."

Billy's stillness was the poise of one whom some unexpected
voice had surprised.

"You mean Isherwood?"

"Of course."

"He's perfectly useless."

"Is or was?"

"Well, both, I should say. He might draw you out a nice
arty plan, but I should think he would be hopeless on detail.
We should want a man with some guts, able to stand up against
contractors and people like that."

Said Miss Lord, "Burt did tell me that Isherwood had had
a sort of reputation, that there were people who believed in him,
and that he might have done big things."

"But he didn't."

"No. The war and his illness."

"I don't believe he had it in him."

"Oh, one can't dogmatize. The poor lad's rather broken."

She looked at Billy standing there beside one of the cypresses and with all the straightness and strength of a young tree. There were times when she saw herself in Billy, the Julia Lord of twenty years ago. Billy had grown so self-sufficient; she wouldn't bend to a breeze, and Julia Lord had come to realize that whether one wished it or not, there were certain emotional strains that swayed one. You might keep your roots in the ground, but you felt the pressure of human winds.

"I think it is one of the most pitiful things."

"O—what?"

"A man cut off from his job. Don't be too hard on men, Bill. I know it is one of the modern tendencies."

Billy put her cup down on the green table.

"Am I hard? O, well, perhaps. I haven't much use for men, except men like Burt and Dr. Hazzard. I'm rather off sensational man. He can be such a messy, mischievous little beast. Meanwhile, I suppose one is building Castles in Spain."

"Or a second Cap Ferrat. I'm not quarrelling with the idea, Bill. But as things are it is rather beyond us."

"As things are. But not as I want them to be. Dash it all, I wish I had the money. But one hasn't, and that's that."

III

Billy had returned to her flat over the English Agency, but Julia Lord remained in her garden, because the night was so gentle, and because her thoughts were edged with melancholy. There were nights when life seemed as round and as clear as the full moon, and the horizon limitless. The little parochial landmarks of the day's routine were blotted out, and the world appeared in its astral body.

Julia Lord walked up and down the paved path between the water cistern and the terrace. The stones were familiar to her feet, and yet the path itself had all the strangeness of an unexpected and mysterious mood. She felt wakeful, vaguely uneasy, like a woman waiting for something, she knew not what.

She found herself thinking about Billy.

"Yes, a woman must make a fool of herself about something. Men too, I gather. The supreme wisdom of being foolish."

The moonlight, and the dim depths of the moonlit vista beyond the cypresses were like a hollow space which memory filled with its weavings. Threads of black and of silver. Billy was so sure that she would never commit the supreme folly. Yes, and she herself had been just as sure, appearing to the world of Tindaro as an upright and a downright person, erect as one of those cypresses. The crowd's consciousness was all surface. It did not allow for those terrible moments when your self lay prone at the feet of your own soul.

Miss Lord paused on the terrace, and then turned her head to listen. Surely she had heard the ringing of her bell? And Maria had gone to bed.

She walked up the garden, climbed the flight of steps, and walked round the white villa. She saw someone waiting in the shadow by the door. The vague and wakeful melancholy of her mood had divined the patch of shadow and the waiting figure.

"Yes, who is it?"

"O, Signorina, it is you."

"Cesca! Mr. Frevick——"

"Yes, he is ill. He was out yesterday in the wind. He will not be careful. He sent me——"

Miss Lord stood in silence for a moment.

"Go back, Cesca. Tell Mr. Frevick I am coming."

CHAPTER XXIV

I

AS she sat beside Frevick's bed and listened to his breathing, there came into Julia Lord's mind a little crowd of memories, memories of Frevick as she had known him. They were part of the man who lay there, part and parcel of his battered humanism, poignant and vivid. She saw him as man, a strangely imperfect yet lovable creature, both sordid and splendid, and yet somehow and always the artist. Her compassion sat and contemplated him in all his human nakedness, and loved that which was good, and forgave all that which had hurt her.

Yes, it was amazing how easily one forgave when one came to understand and to pity. In the old days she had not been able to forgive. She had been too much Julia Lord. Like Billy she had carved for herself an idol out of ivory. But now she could sit beside the bed of this man who was dying, and see him just as he was and as he had been, and feel towards him as woman.

These memories crowded upon her like children. His funny ways, his whims, his queer æsthetic ferocities. She saw him as the drunkard, and understood and forgave She recalled the way he sat and walked, the pathos of his exile, his air of fierce melancholy, his old clothes, his very hat. That poor old hat! How he had torn and humiliated her pride! And it was just because she had let her pride walk carefully on ice that the tragedy of him had happened.

And he had forgiven her.

She looked at the little yellow dog curled up asleep at the foot of the bed. How deeply dogs understood. Or was it that they loved so much, and set up no self-created, exacting "I" against the reality of man's humanism? They accepted.

They demanded no hard, ethical standard.   Their paws reached for a man's knees; their eyes looked up into his face.

And Tom Frevick was dying, and dying so very gently. He had made no fight for it; he was just drifting towards the revealing darkness, undistressed, tranquil.   It was like the fall of a leaf, or the coming of night; gradually, gently.

She saw his eyes open.   He drowsed a great deal, but when his eyes opened they showed an unclouded consciousness.   His left hand made a little movement.   Her right hand went out to clasp it, and to rest with it on the bed.

"Still here, Julie."

"Yes."

The dog, raising its head, and looking at Frevick with a kind of mute and tragic wisdom, crept up and lay with her head resting on his right shoulder.

Frevick caressed her feebly.

"You Little Thing, you Very Little Thing.   Dogs do stay with one, Julie."

For a moment she felt anguished.

"Yes."

"You'll look after her?"

"Of course."

He lay there, vaguely smiling.

"Even a battered old sot like me."

She pressed his hand.

"No.   Never that.   And for the last two years———"

"The crave died out of me, Julie.   Perhaps, because— Funny mix-up, life, silly sort of muddle.   It's one's damned fool body that will go and play in the mud, just like a kid. I wonder if they give us a fresh start over yonder?"

She said softly, "So, you believe in the over yonder?"

"Somehow, yes.   Otherwise this would be such a futile show, and I have a feeling that it isn't a futile show."

He closed his eyes, and she sat very still, thinking that he was drowsing off again.   The dog lay and looked fixedly into his face.   And then he sighed and opened his eyes.

"Exile.   Sorry for exiles, people cut off from their jobs. There's that fellow Isherwood."

"Yes."

"I have seen a good deal of him the last month. Rather derelict. I should like him to have my paints and things. He ought to dabble more seriously. Shouldn't give up."

"You want me to tell him?"

"I think I'd like to see him for a minute. The fellow understands. But he has chucked in his hand. Shouldn't do that."

"Are you strong enough to see him, Tom?"

"O, yes. Doesn't matter much, does it, if I knock five minutes off the time table?"

She was shaken, but she did not show it.

"Shall I send for him?"

"Yes. Stella has been here. She's the nearest thing to the other world. And I'd like to see Billy. Poor Billy."

"Why poor Billy?"

"Ask Betty, my dear. You Very Little Thing, you know."

So, Tom Isherwood was sent for and found, and he came and sat alone beside Frevick's bed, with the afternoon sunlight filling the room with a quiet glow.

"O—Isherwood, I'm leaving you my paints and brushes and things. Use them."

"My dear chap, I can't use them—like you."

"Try. Don't chuck. Doesn't do to be without a job. That's the only sort of scallawag sermon that I know."

When Billy's turn came Frevick lay and looked at her for some moments in silence. His eyes had a kind of tragic, far-seeing kindness. He moved a hand to and fro over the red coverlet.

"Well, I'm going over. You'll back up Julie. You always have done. There's a thing I should like to say."

Her face was the face of Billy of three years ago, and he smiled at her.

"That's it. You look more like you used to. Don't grow into a graven image, my dear. Such a pity."

She looked at him questioningly, and with a sudden stark self-consciousness, and then bent over to stroke Betty's head.

"Is it a pity?"

"Of course. Make allowances. I know. Some people have made allowances for me. Like the Little Thing here. Doesn't do to be too hard."

He put out a faltering hand.

"Shake. Say I'm forgiven."

She bent and kissed his forehead.

II

They buried Tom Frevick in the cemetery of Tindaro, not very far from Oscar Slade, and at high noon one tall cypress threw a shadow across the place where Frevick lay. Isherwood was there, with Billy, and Julia Lord, and Mrs. Shone and Stella Burt. The day had a blue and an ethereal stillness; the women had brought flowers; it was a very simple occasion.

They stood there in the sunlight with their various and secret thoughts and emotions. Isherwood felt lonely, for in Frevick he had lost someone who had understood him, and to whom he had been able to talk as one craftsman to another. Frevick had had no pose, no carefully curled vocabulary. He had possessed the great secret of the craftsman, and had known that a thing may be done exquisitely without the craftsman being able to tell the world just how the thing did itself. Yes, Frevick had been without any subtle slaver. Isherwood found himself looking at the faces of the women. Sadie Shone wept and was unashamed. Julia Lord had a face cut out of white marble. Billy stood as though thinking hard about some particular problem of her own, with a little frown on her forehead. Isherwood did not know that she had a lover lying near, and that some of the shadows of three years ago had drifted up. She both confronted and shrank from a memory.

Afterwards he found himself with Billy, walking down the steep and winding road from that high-placed garden of the dead. Julia Lord had hurried on alone. She had whispered to Billy, "His dog, I must go back to his dog," for Betty was shut up in the little salon of the Villa Vesta, inconsolably wailing. Stella Burt and Mrs. Shone followed at a little distance, strange contrasts, yet able to share their thoughts.

Isherwood, incongruously formal and casual in a black coat

and his brown felt hat, made no attempt to talk to Billy.   She
looked so much more sleeked to the occasion in her chaste
black suit.   Her eyes and her lips had a stillness.   The dusty
road wound this way and that under the overhang of pines
and olives, sometimes striking towards the blue of the sea, and
sometimes towards the grey and the green of hillside and valley.
Tindaro spread its pantiles below them.   The campanile of
the duomo seemed to keep changing its position.

Billy was silent because she was feeling things.   It was one
of those occasions when one's consciousness is like a fresh keen
dawn, a little raw and poignant and strange, and tinged with
a wondering melancholy.   She felt insecure, on the edge of
things, sensitive to sounds and scents and glimpses.   The sky
seemed more blue.   And the complex of her emotions included
Sadie Shone's tears, and the wailing of Frevick's little yellow
dog behind the closed shutters of the Villa Vesta.   She knew
why Julia Lord had hurried home.

Also she was more aware of Isherwood, or she was aware
of him differently.   His very clothes suggested Frevick.   It was
as though Frevick in dying and being buried, had left them
alone together.   Each consciousness seemed to grope and touch.
They walked with questioning eyes on life and on each other.

Said Billy suddenly, "You got to know him a little, didn't
you, before he died?"

Her voice had a softness, and so had her eyes, and Isherwood
glanced at her as though some unseen quality in her had
discovered itself.

"O, yes.   There was something big about Frevick, a sort
of raw and Promethean humanity."

"Why raw?"

"The wrong word—perhaps.   What I mean is—he knew
about all the raw things of life.   He'd been torn and crucified,
he'd had the spongeful of hyssop against his lips, and yet—
somehow—he was never quite beaten."

She reflected.

"Yes, I think that's true.   He had something to say, something that mattered.   After all—the respectable people have
so little to say."

I

"And if so—it's mostly hearsay. They don't know."

"Haven't experienced things?"

"No, not like Frevick. I suppose he was one of the vast failures, and quite wise about it, and that little dog of his didn't care a damn about his failure."

"But he did."

"Oh, a man like Frevick would. He could be fierce with himself. Some men can."

His voice ended on a note of resignation, and in glancing at him she realized the sadness of his eyes. He walked down towards Tindaro as though returning to some idle corner in the sun, and to a discontent that was helpless and submissive.

She said, "He left you his paints and brushes."

"Yes."

"Why don't you use them?"

His smile was whimsical.

"But he didn't leave me his hands."

III

Isherwood's inheritance included some old sketch-books of Frevick's, dating back to the days when the urge of his craft had been proud and strong in him, and on some of the pages were jottings in the dead man's liquid, cursive writing. There had been no tremor in those days, no sense of defeat. Julia Lord, who with Burt had gone through all Frevick's possessions and papers, had glanced at one or two of these books, and not being able to bear the intimate reality of them, had put them aside for Isherwood.

Had she been as methodical in her handling of these relics as she was in the checking of her library books Julia Lord would have discovered that one of these little books contained a diary. But she had a horror of too much sentiment, and especially was she temperamentally hostile to the "Victoria and Albert" tradition, and Isherwood, sitting in a deck-chair under the olives behind "The Crater," and allowing himself a desultory interest in the dead man's technique, came upon this diary. It dated from the days when Tindaro had had only one hotel, and the English Library had contained less than five hundred volumes, and women had worn blouses, and straw hats perched well back on buns of hair, and the waist-line had not gone the way of theology.

A faded slip of red ribbon led Isherwood to open the book at that particular place, and upon the right-hand page he saw a pencilled sketch of a woman sitting on a rock with a wrap over her shoulders. Underneath the sketch was written in Frevick's hand—"Julia after Bathing." Also he had added some notes on the atmosphere and colour, intimate personal touches. "Much turquoise in the shallow water. J's wrap silver and blue. Get that amber glint in her hair." Both sketch and notes suggested that Frevick had made a rough study of Julia Lord, and that he had meant to paint a picture of her sitting on the rock above the sea, combing out her wet hair. Yet further on Isherwood came upon a little pastel of the same woman—"Julia looks at Tindaro." Thereupon Isherwood closed the book, and laid it aside.

So, that piece of faded red ribbon marked a page in the lives of those two. And Miss Lord had been a very comely woman of five and thirty with amber gleams in her hair! "Julia looks at Tindaro." Isherwood, somehow feeling that he had made an innocent intrusion into the secret of two people, went in and routed out a piece of brown paper and some string, and made a parcel of the book.

He put on his hat and descended into Tindaro. In the Corso he passed the Café Ceres, with its little crowd that was new and yet the same. A woman smiled and nodded at him. She had very full blue eyes and a suggestion of plumpness, a well creamed throat and chin. She was a Mrs. Marrish who occupied one of Strozzi's villas, and who had appeared in the little world of Tindaro as an easy and pleasant bouquet of flowers to be smelt and enjoyed. She had a red mouth which always looked a little moist, like fruit freshly peeled.

Isherwood raised his hat to her and passed on. He was not in a mood to be conscious of a vacant chair and of the dish of cream which was woman. He did not enter the English Library, but went in through the glazed door of the agency, and saw Billy's brown head bent over some papers on her desk.

Miss Soulby was clattering away on her typewriter, and the keys were suddenly and expectantly silent, but Isherwood did not look at Miss Soulby.

He approached Billy's desk. He was aware of her fine head with its aureole of hair, her firm chin, and the gracious strength of her shoulders. Something in him yearned suddenly and strangely and was inarticulate. He was so very conscious of himself as the valetudinarian, the man who had ceased to matter.

He said, "Excuse my troubling you, but I have brought something——"

She raised her head. Her face had come to suggest to him white light, a steady and luminous surface. The very directness of her gaze made him feel unsure and self-conscious. She was so complete, and in opposition to his flickering incompleteness.

"What is it?"

He held out the brown paper parcel, and she noticed that it was a very untidy parcel, and that he had knotted together two odd pieces of string.

"I found this among Frevick's things. It looked like a sketch-book. I just glanced at it. I think it should belong elsewhere."

He nodded meaningly at the communicating door.

"Rather you handed it over—if you don't mind."

She took the parcel, and her smile had an inward quality. It was less superficially bright and capable.

"Yes, I will. Thank you. I understand."

He seemed to hesitate for a moment, and then turned rather awkwardly about, and brushing against the table in the centre of the office, passed out through the glazed door.

Miss Soulby's head was down again over her typewriter. She seemed to droop like a frustrated flower unvisited by the winged messenger. She felt that she had a grievance against her pince-nez. They disparaged you so cruelly.

Billy had laid the parcel down on her desk, and was gazing at it, but not as though she saw it as a mere parcel. It was a part of Isherwood, rather eloquent of his fumblings and of his odds and ends of string and insolvencies. He had brought her something of Frevick's, something that should belong to Julia Lord, and he had brought something else of Frevick's, little, funny, pathetic incoherences that he and the dead man shared.

CHAPTER XXV

I

THE mantle of Sadie Shone had fallen upon Mrs. Marrish. To the Three Musketeers Mrs. Marrish was that other sort of woman who will always be found at the side of and in the pocket of a man. She was a bundle of appetites, prettily gowned and nicely perfumed, a creature of natural curves who was blown hither and thither like a puff-ball, or like a soft burr attached itself to some likely situation. She was a pretty woman who could sit up playing bridge till two in the morning, and then snuggle into bed and meet the young day with an air of complete freshness. Her prominent and very blue eyes did not vary their expression. They had a kind of innocence, the candour of a healthy appetite that is always ready and unashamed.

There was much of her. Her amplitudes were all swansdown and cream. She set up no standards, but smiled life into her salon and made it sit on her sofa, and offered it cocktails and cigarettes. Like Catherine of Russia she had immense capacity, but she was not an empress. Men liked her; she was so easy with them, and her ethics travelled from place to place packed up with her frocks and her perfumes. She had a wonderful skin, white and soft and fragrant. When the flesh of her was pinched between thumb and finger it was found to be nicely cushioned.

Billy had let one of Strozzi's villas to Mrs. Marrish, and had thought no more of her. Mrs. Marrish might be Pipp, or Elyseo, or Café Ceres, or all three of them rolled together. She would be popular with the Reginalds and the Toms until such a time as the ladies of the household put down their feet.

Sadie was more alive to the implications of Mabel Marrish, for Sadie knew life more intimately than did either Billy or

Julia Lord.   Having come to feel an angry disgust for the
eternal treacheries of sex, for all its stale falsities and traitorous
repetitions, she was all the more wise in her appreciations of
a woman like Mrs. Marrish.   She knew her and knew the
whole of her from the moment that lady appeared in the lace
shop.

She called her "Mrs. Snuggle."

For she was all snuggle as to voice, manner, and movement.
She was like a cushion floating about, a cushion with a pair
of inviting blue eyes, and dimples, and a soft white throat.
She had that sort of woman's infinite capacity for physical
satisfaction, and she would be troubled by no spiritual loyalties.
Being sensational woman, she understood the sensational man
from alpha to omega.

Mrs. Marrish had speedily discovered the Café Ceres.   She
had a partiality for saxe blue, and her speedwell eyes began
to observe the Corso like the eyes of a greedy, insatiable and
cunning child.   She was very much the woman of the world,
and a widow.   She was a little point of bright colour in the
Café Ceres crowd, which happened to be a rather dingy crowd
that season, not doing credit to Circe.   There were leopards,
but they were rather ragged of fur.   Fat Tommaso regretted
the Slade, Shone, Frevick days, for he was doing less well as
to tips.

Had Tommaso's summing up of the more habitual patrons
been translated into English, it would have run much as
follows.

Mr. Botterel: A little chattering man with a hot black eye
and a greasy skin.   Horsey and bad horsey at that.   Pushes
his lower lip out when he looks at a lady.   No good.

Mr. Warner: A gentleman with a very yellow face.   Said
to come from India.   Grey flannel suit creased and rather
dirty.   Always tries to let the other patrons pay for drinks.
Never has a match or a cigarette.   No good.   Even less good
than Mr. Botterel.

| Mrs. Collingwood Doucy | Bracketed.   Rather a puzzle to |
| Mrs. Dance | Tommaso who had never heard of the Lesbians. |

Miss Lanchester: A fierce, black and white lady who smoked as though she had Vesuvius inside her.

Little Cobb: Rather like a sparrow. An impudent little creature who had been made to cease from being a solicitor, and who now solicited other favours.

Mrs. Marrish was like Tommaso, she had an eye for the human values. She saw Mr. Botterel as a useless and unappetising cad. Warner was all together too yellow, and had the eyes of a dead fish. Little Cobb had the eagerness of a monkey, and she disliked that sort of man. Circe's leopards were shabby animals.

The Café Ceres had descended. There had been days when it could split a straw cleverly, but now it only sucked them. It was not even picturesque in its decadence; it challenged no compassion. In passing along the Corso, Billy had almost ceased to be aware of the Café Ceres, and its tables and its crowd. As for Julia Lord, she passed by on the other side, not like the Pharisee, but because she was mourning for Frevick, and rather absorbed in Frevick's little dog and his diary and her garden. There were two Frevicks in her consciousness, and one of them still sat huddled in a chair outside the Café Ceres; a long, loose, melancholy figure with empty, burnt-out eyes. That figure of Frevick accused her of having somehow failed as a woman.

Mrs. Shone looked attentively at the Ceres whenever she passed it, and smiled her huge smile at Tommaso. No longer had she any desire to sit at one of those tables and be pawed by such creatures as Botterel and Little Cobb. She had subscribed to the Lord-Brown creed. She had developed a queer passion for lace, and the selling of lace. It was clean and lovely stuff to handle. She had gone over to the cause of those women who preferred to handle life as a clean job and to express themselves in it. She understood their fastidious prides, and was astonished at herself. "Me, Sadie, selling lace! Prohibition Sadie! Beats the Belle of New York! But my buddies are good buddies."

Burt, who continued to know Tindaro as few people knew

it, looked at the Café Ceres with the eyes of an alienist and
a physician.   It had gone to the flies.

"What a set!"

He had a large compassion, but it could not swallow that
new old crowd.

"Rotten people."

For in the old days the Café Ceres had had a sort of cachet.
It had known Slade's wanton wit and his colour.   It had
known Tom Frevick, that poor Prometheus, who, from the
tearing of his vitals, had produced words of wisdom.

II

Some cynic had allowed Isherwood three months of sitting
in the sun, and that same cynic knew Tindaro intimately, and
its effect upon the blue-eyed, high-coloured type from the north.
The old Iberian stock could return to the shores of the middle
sea and lose no shred of its vitality, but upon the long-headed,
fairer man, call him Nordic or what you will, the transplanting
had its reaction.   Something in him wilted, unless, like Burt
or Julia Lord, he lived stubbornly according to the English
will, and had work to stiffen him.   Tindaro was both Circe
and Calypso.   It played upon the pipes of Pan.   It had a
strange, gradual, otiose smile.   It shrugged its shoulders and
settled itself against a sunny wall, and whistled softly.   "Why
worry?   What is life after all but sunlight?   You lean, red
people are always catching flies."

This observer of the effects of climate upon behaviour had
noted down certain signs and symptoms.   The male exile began
to be less particular about his person.   He shaved irregularly,
or grew a beard.   His hair and his clothes shared in a casual
untidiness.   He loafed.   His attitude towards the stringencies
of life became apathetic.   His tolerance was the tolerance of
a slovenly inertia.   Mentally he became a dilettante, unable
to concentrate his attention upon any subject, or to will himself to do the thing that was difficult.   Very often he drank
too much and continued to drink more than too much, or he
became native in an unmentionable way and was lost for ever
to the world of the habitually clean.

I*

Mrs. Marrish, passing the gate of "The Crater" on her way to the town, observed Tom Isherwood and his potterings. She saw him sowing flower seeds in the front garden of the villa, or making a desultory attack upon a vigorous crop of young weeds. She was friendly.

"You—are—energetic."

He was nothing of the kind, and she knew it. He might be in his shirt sleeves, but that was for the sake of atmosphere.

"One has to do something."

He drifted towards the gate to talk to her. Mrs. Marrish was easy to talk to; she was easy about everything.

"I don't agree."

"No?"

"A matter of temperament, isn't it. I'm hopelessly lazy. I don't play any games."

"Or garden?"

"I loathe gardening."

She cultivated her own *parterre*, the lobelia of her eyes, and the geranium of her lips. Gardening was for the woman who had no physical exteriors that were worth cultivating.

"Constitutionally lazy?"

"I am. And why not? Being energetic is just like being political or pious, part of your make-up. And the energetic people are so horribly cocky about it."

"They are."

"I really don't see why one shouldn't be complacent over a pleasant laziness. These east-wind people——"

She amused him. She was in sympathy with the Isherwood who was for surrender, though the other Isherwood had been making an effort to be pragmatical. There was that in him which had realized the necessity for effort. He had been conscious of a slipping down towards seedy slackness. He had been thinking a good deal of Billy Brown, more than was comforting to his self regard, for Billy was not a cushion but a challenge.

Mrs. Marrish asked him whether he played bridge.

"Not too grimly, you know. And I hate post-mortems."

"I always revoke."

"I'm sure you don't.   One can go down to the Elyseo every evening.   I haven't seen you there."

"I haven't danced for three years."

"Why not take it up?   They have a really spruce little orchestra down there.   You must have been rather good."

"Nice of you, but why?"

"You look like it, nice and loose in the shoulder."

She passed on, having allowed her blue eyes to leave the invitation of "Blue Danubes" and "Girl Friends" behind her, sentiment and syncopation.   "Come and dance with me." She was not abrupt and coercive.   She did not advise a man to buck up and adjust his sock-suspenders.   She trailed a lure; she flattered and was friendly, and left behind her an aroma of roses and warm bath, and cigarette smoke, and face powder.

Isherwood remained at his gate, leaning his crossed arms upon it.   He was bored, and just beginning to realize his boredom.   He was not a little tired of contemplation, and of contemplating Tindaro in all its various aspects.   He had explored it to repletion.   He had slacked on the sands and stared at the sea, and scrambled aimlessly about the hills, and been shaved by Italian barbers, and ridden on a donkey up to Eryx, and bought the *Continental Daily Mail*, and tracked interesting and romantic alleys to blind ends and almost visible smells.   He had just missed receiving the contents of a crock emptied out of an upper window by a Tindaro matron.   He had been solicited at night by sinister and slimy youths upon the Corso.   He had watched the tennis at the Tennis Club.

He had seen Billy playing tennis there, and, like Slade before him, he had been attracted by the way she moved and by the easy rightness of her movements.   White light hitting a ball. But unlike Slade he had not answered the challenge.   Somehow, Billy's vigour had depressed him, and he had not confessed to the rightness of the feeling.   She made the incipient slacker in him feel old and tired.

"I couldn't live up to her."

He had allowed himself that lapse into an urge that was thrown back like a wave from a rock.   He had not considered the alternative, the living down to a woman like Mabel Marrish.

He was unhappy. There was that in him that asked to live up to Billy, to that sudden smile, to the gracious, comely strength of her, to the breeze in her brown hair. He was tantalized by Billy. To begin with, he had felt rather repelled, and no form of repulsion can be more significant. She was no mere cake with iced sugar on it. She challenged. She was young Atalanta, only she would not be fooled by mere man dropping a silly apple.

There had been that day of Frevick's funeral.

He had felt suddenly near to her, and to a something which was essentially clean and exquisite, firm flesh and firm soul, and he had flinched. He had gone home reflecting, "Damn it, don't be an ass. You haven't the stuff in you. You're too old, too finished."

Also, he was very lonely. He had been able to talk to Frevick, but the man who had understood the shabby, discouraged craftsman in him, was dead. He could not talk to Burt. Even the gentleness of Burt's eyes accused him of being poor white trash. He had listened to Stella's music, only to find that it made him more unhappy. It tantalized; it had the voice of his youth, the mystery and strange, sweet splendour of those days when he had believed in youth. It spoke of all that he had dreamed of doing and had not done.

He rather shrank from going to the Burts. He was beginning to shrink from so many things.

III

But the nights! Stars and lights and loneliness. He was made more unhappy by the multitudinous lights of Tindaro, the eyes of other lives, bright and glimmering and satisfied. They were like the eyes of women looking at him from high and half-shuttered windows.

It was when the sun had set that he felt so much an exile. No one had need of him. No one cared whether his door remained closed or open. A great silence seemed to descend, or there would be a little, moaning restless wind from the mountains. There were nights when he sat down to read some novel, and in the midst of his reading he would be attacked

by this horror of loneliness and isolation, and he would get up
and open the villa door, and sit with both doors open.   It was
a mute invitation to life, or as though he felt less cut off from
the world with the doors wide open.   He would sit and listen.
Perhaps someone would come?   But no one came.

There were occasions when he snatched hat and coat and
rushed out into the night.   He could not bear the solitude of
that bright little bon-bon box of a villa.   It was so final and
so futile.   He would walk and go on walking, until his very
loneliness felt tired out, and he could go back to "The Crater"
and tumble into the blessed forgetfulness of sleep.   He blessed
sleep.   It saved him so many empty hours; its very dreams
were not like his day-dreams, tantalizing and retrospective; it
was like a soft hand closing gently over the painful pulsings
of a distressed heart.   It was more blessed than any drug.

He began to be afraid of ceasing to sleep, and directly that
fear was born in him his very approach to his bed became
tentative and self-conscious.   Inevitably he began to sleep less
well.   He lay awake with this new dread beside him, his fear
of insomnia and all that sleeplessness might imply.

After a week of such restless nights he went to see Burt,
but even his confession was a little shamefaced.   It was like
confessing to another frailty.

"I'm not sleeping very well.   Anything I can do about it?"

Burt was not a "drug man."   The essentials of health are
so simple.   Health is like fruit waiting to be gathered, and it
was Isherwood's misfortune that he had to gather no fruit.

Burt looked at him consideringly, and knew that he ought
to tell Isherwood just what he had to tell so many of his patients,
"What you need is work, a job, something a little more interesting than your dinner, something that justifies your dinner."
The overloaded stomach and the sodden mind.   Such places
as the Hotel Elyseo were full of fat carcasses.

"Sleeping badly?   But just how badly?"

"I lay awake for five hours last night.   And sleep here
seems so shallow."

"That's not abnormal.   People do with less sleep here.   It
is a different climate."

"But it worries me, doctor."

"You mean—you are afraid of it?"

"Yes, that's it."

"The more you worry about it—the less well you'll sleep. Vicious circle. Try a walk last thing and a glass of hot water."

And then Burt's natural brusqueness, his hatred of euphemism and all medicated soft soap, caused him to blurt out the obvious.

"What are your interests? Have you any?"

Isherwood met the question with a self-conscious and wincing smile.

"Yes, I suppose that's the trouble. I haven't a job. I'm a loafer."

"Can't you make a job? You paint."

"O, damned badly. My job was creating houses, and I did not do that so badly. You know, doctor, some of us can't get interested in bungling. It's boring, exasperating, shameful."

Burt nodded his big head.

"That's why I don't prescribe soft soap and something in a bottle. Hitting a ball has saved many men's souls. I suggest to you, Isherwood, that you paint and paint—until you cease to bungle. Fight something."

"Yes, I expect you are right."

His rather hopeless shoulders seemed to carry the burden of Burt's wisdom out of Burt's consulting-room, consentingly, but with no air of eagerness. Words of wisdom? But wisdom might cease to be wisdom when a man ceased to care.

IV

There came a spell of heat to Tindaro, spring in winter, golden days, and each morning very early, Billy went down to bathe. The Island of the Triton seemed to float like vapour on another surface of vapour which was the blue of the sea. Old rocks warmed themselves like sea-monsters heaving up craggy snouts and backbones. The sand was quivering gold. Billy, wearing a light blue bathing-dress, would throw her raincoat on the sands, and kick off her shoes, and swim out towards the rising sun. She did not think of the Slade days. Life carried her on, not back.

But one morning she found a man sitting on the sand close to the sea. Little, loquacious waves were gliding in, and he sat and stared, and did not so much as pick up a pebble. Even his old grey felt hat had a depression in it which he either had not noticed or had not troubled to remove. The sand silenced her footsteps, and she was able to look hard and attentively at him, and at the negligent melancholy of his attitude.

"Hallo, come down to bathe?"

He looked up at her over a rounded shoulder. She had surprised him, and yet he was not surprised, for he had been thinking of Billy at the very moment of her descent.

"I'm not allowed to. Rotten—not being allowed to do things. Possibly they might permit me to paddle."

She sat down by him on the sand and unbuttoned her shoes. She supposed that it did not comfort a man to be able to indulge in self-mockery.

"Bad luck. I'm going in."

"I'll be a good dog and watch your shoes and coat."

She smiled, and then the smile died away. She was suddenly and strangely sorry for him, and as a woman is sorry for a man only when she is moved by him in other ways. He looked so forlorn, and lost, just like an exile sitting at the edge of an alien sea. Even his little attempts at humour were deplorable.

She said, "But—probably—you will be able to do things later. Anyhow, you managed to get out of bed at six o'clock and come down here."

"The lesser of two evils. I couldn't sleep. But I'd like to watch you swimming."

She rose and threw off her coat and wandering in, threw herself forward against the bosom of a little wave. She felt the cold, clean lift of it, and the saltness of it on her lips. She felt other things, as though the surrender of her body to the blue embraces of the sea symbolized other, elemental urges. She struck out strongly, as though the capable, self-sufficient creature in her protested.

Poor devil! He reminded her somehow of Winnie Hay-croft, who had made her think of a tired and faded flower, unable to sleep or to close its petals. But he was a man. There was a part of her that despised him, while yet another part of her turned fiercely upon her facile scorn. Perhaps some things could not be helped, but you might have the courage to bear them, just as the sea bore you up on this most perfect morning.

CHAPTER XXVI

I

BUT to watch Billy Brown swimming or playing tennis tended to emphasize the coloured and perfumed indolence of Mrs. Marrish. A lame man may watch Atalanta running, and turn away sadly from the swift white figure of her youth, and meeting Voluptas all scented and rosy outside a wine-shop, go home with the more accommodating lady.

Even the office-boy can talk about the inferiority complex, and Communism is the self-same complex viewed in mass production, but Isherwood's sense of inferiority was a more simple and yet a more subtle product. He was tempted by easy virtue, because the more difficult ascent tantalized and hurt him. Being suddenly and deplorably in love he became like the old-fashioned figure in an old-fashioned novel, a kind of Sydney Carton ascending the scaffold, and surrendering all illusions to the impossible lover in himself. His complex was complicated by an absurd sensitiveness, by an introspective melancholy. Like a man who goes in terror of top-hats and all the pompous publicity which the top-hat implies, he chose to wear a cloth cap and to wear it desperately.

Mrs. Marrish, passing by on her way to the Café Ceres, and finding Isherwood hanging on the lip of "The Crater," collected him.

"Come and join our show."

She could drawl amusingly. She explained to him that she regarded the Café Ceres as a sort of puppet show, Tindaro's "Little People." Her use of adjectives was characteristic. Things and people were "Quaint"—or "Stuffy" or "Septic" or "Marvellous." She flowed like a river through rich, fat country, and at a pace that was easy and pleasant, and Isherwood flowed with her.   He was feeling rather deplorable, and any warm, human presence suggested sympathy.

She said, "I'll introduce you to the Rag and Bone men. They really are rather furiously disreputable.   Mr. Botterel, Mr. Warner, Little Cobb, Shem, Ham and Japhet, or the Abednego crowd.   Disreputable people are so much more amusing."

He did not ask her whether she included him among them, he didn't really care; he was feeling emotionally disreputable.

"Rather a fly-blown place?"

"Yes, rather—rather.   But does it matter?   That's the charm of these bastard places.   You really do see a bit of life as it is, not dressed up for Kensington High Street and the sales. I think Tindaro's lovely."

"As life or scenery?"

"Both.   It's like a musical comedy, only better.   One just chuckles.   One doesn't chuckle sufficiently.   We haven't any curate here, but there's that priceless person who runs the English Library.   Know her?"

"Miss Lord?"

"O, Lord!   Yes.   And Miss Brown, Miss Capability Brown.   She makes me think of a commandant or something of Girl Guides with a nice little silver whistle."

Inwardly Isherwood winced.

"Yes, she's very capable."

"I should say so.   Utterly modern and all that."

As an artist Isherwood could not but be conscious of Mrs. Marrish's clothes.   She was sort of woman who could wear bright blues and greens and cerise and yet refrain from looking crude.   Her throat and shoulders seemed to rise pleasantly out of a coloured spathe.   Her eyes were both sensual and roguish.

He was so wanting someone to be kind to him, because he wanted the kindness of Billy, and her compassion soared far above him like a snowy peak.   How could he expect her to come down to his valetudinarian level, his slough of surrender?

He said, "I suppose you travel a good deal?"

"Obviously.   An English winter is too sanguinary.   And you?"

He hunched his shoulders.

"Oh—I'm an exile.   I just travel round Tindaro.   Chest, you know."

Her blue eyes seemed to enlarge themselves.

"O, poor man!   But you look quite well, nice colour."

"There's nothing active now, but I'm not allowed to go home.   I just mooch about, and get bored.   Do you ever get bored?"

"Hardly ever.   I have a splendid appetite and a splendid digestion.   Look at my skin."

He did look at it, half daring and yet not daring.   Yes, she was very appetising.

"Peach blossom."

She laughed; she had a pretty laugh, jocund and a little sly.

"Made that way.   Thank the lord, I do enjoy life.   It's a chocolate box.   I'm kind to myself.   Some of you people are so crusty with yourselves.   You are always taking your soulful innards out and examining them.   So English.   I don't believe in too much self-inspection."

He rallied her.

"Not even in front of a mirror?"

"O, that's part of the cult."

"Quite successfully so."

"Thank you."

So, Isherwood was crowned with the Marrish garland and led along the Corso to the Café Ceres, where Voluptas exhibited her capture.   He was introduced to Messrs. Botterel, Warner and Cobb, and also to those two strange women, Mrs. Colling-wood Doucy and Mrs. Dance.   He did not realize how innocent he was and how innocent he looked to these damp and peeling people.   Little Cobb could be very amusing, especially when he was thirsty and hoped that someone would stand him a drink, and when he had been stood a drink he was even more amusing.   Mr. Warner borrowed Isherwood's matches and forgot to return the box.   Mr. Botterel's black eyes fixed themselves hungrily on this piece of new meat, for Botterel was very like a blow-fly.

Tommaso sailed around with a tray full of glasses. Yes, assuredly the new gentleman would pay, and Isherwood did pay, and Tommaso felt sorry for him, and wanted to nudge Isherwood and whisper, "Some people are sponges, signore, just sponges. You understand?" Mrs. Marrish's blue eyes were jocund and watchful. She observed Isherwood. Yes, he really was rather a pet. He had such well-shaped ears and a tinge of brown in his skin, and the eyes of a boy, and a suggestion of shyness, nice shyness. She rather liked that sort of man. They handled you with an air of innocence that made you feel new and fresh and virginal.

Julia Lord, passing up the Corso on her way to the Villa Vesta, saw Thomas Isherwood seated at one of the round tables between Mrs. Marrish and Little Cobb, and she was startled, for Isherwood happened to be sitting in the very place which had been sacred to Frevick. Extraordinary and poignant coincidence! Julia Lord was disturbed by it. She was always seeing Frevick in Isherwood, and the likeness prejudiced her.

She passed on. She could remember Frevick's capture by the Café Ceres and its crowd in those days of long ago. The Café Ceres was much the same, but to Julia Lord its crowd seemed more smirched and sinister. Rotten, insolent people, complacently tainted, and making a mock of those who used spiritual soap! How she had loathed that café with its little drinks and its flies and its tinkling orchestra and its smeary cakes.

So, a second Frevick had joined the Ceres crowd. She was sorry, and she was troubled, and somehow she felt responsible. She found herself wondering if Billy knew, though it was no concern of Billy's. And yet, at the same time, Julia Lord had a feeling that it did concern Billy. The English Agency! The thing did concern all women who knew Tindaro as it was and as it could be, tragic Tindaro, debauched Tindaro. Messrs. Lord & Brown traded in Tindaro. They had built up their own particular tradition both as women and busi-

ness women.   They believed in holding on tight to certain
cleanlinesses, certain decencies.   They had confronted the
realities.

Julia Lord was sorry for Isherwood.   He was a sick man,
a tired man without a job, and Tindaro waited at its dark
corners for such people.   It beckoned them in to its stuffy,
secret little holes and corners.   Isherwood was too good
for that sort of thing.   He was rather like a trusting child
whom some sot of a woman would abandon on a doorstep.

And that afternoon Julia Lord told Billy.   She did not tell
her as though she had any suspicion that the news would be
emotionally important to Billy.   She had no such suspicion.
She announced the fact as though she were commenting upon
the loss of a library book.

"I see Isherwood has gone in with the Ceres crowd.   Rather
a pity."

Billy's face had a sudden white gravity.

"Sure?"

"Well—I saw him——"

And Billy was silent, self-defensively silent.   She had come
into the library to get change for a five-hundred lire note, and
with an air of preoccupation she went on counting out the
money.

"Silly ass."

She closed the cashbox and returned it to the safe.   If a
crack had opened in the clean, hard surface of her consciousness, she did not betray it to her partner.

II

Mrs. Marrish's contention that the disreputable are more
amusing than the reputable was certainly a point to be argued,
but Isherwood did not argue it, nor did he ask Mabel Marrish
to define for him what was reputable and amusing.   He
strolled back with her to Strozzi's hill, still wearing her garland, and listening to her seductive voice.   She had piquant
things to say about the Café Ceres crowd.   She advised him
not to lend money to Mr. Botterel or Mr. Warner, and not

to confer on Little Cobb the freedom of his whisky bottle. And Mrs. Collingwood Doucy and Mrs. Dance were best left in cold storage.

"But they really are rather priceless, bits of life in the raw."

She paused outside the gate of "The Crater," and looked at Isherwood with her jocund, sensual eyes.

"I suppose you never paint portraits?"

"Very badly. I've tried it."

"Modest fellow. Usually I tea at four. Stroll along—if you feel like it."

She gave him one of her gaillard smiles, and left him wearing her garland.

Isherwood's introduction to the Café Ceres crowd was in a sense an introduction to the Café Ceres in himself. These people were so accommodating. They set up no standards; they cultivated no inhibitions; they did not ask to see your moral passport. They cadged from life, and accepted any of the trifles life cared to toss to them.

And to a man who felt rather desperate about life, and who, each morning after a restless night, fumbled at the collar of his feeling of inferiority, the Café Ceres offered compensations. It proffered a sponge soaked in wine, forgetfulness—if there can be such an escape by way of forgetfulness.

Isherwood began to develop the Café Ceres habit. He wandered down to it about eleven o'clock each morning, and sat in the sun, and ordered his little drink, and became more and more aware of the easiness of Mrs. Marrish. He found a welcome here. Fat, kind Tommaso bustled about, and dusted your chair. Little Cobb had endless funny stories; they might be more than a little dubious, but Isherwood found himself laughing. He wanted to laugh at something or anything, because there were times when he felt so near to rotten tears. The oleaginous, yellow Warner cadged his matches and cigarettes, and was full of a genteel servility. Botterel tried to persuade him to play poker, but Isherwood was not such a fool as to allow himself to be fleeced by a man who looked like a nasty, dissolute little jockey.

And there was Mrs. Marrish. She, too, was luxuriously

unexacting. She suggested the intimacy of a cushion inviting you to repose. She smelt like a white lily.

Yet a part of Isherwood resisted, and each morning he traversed the same vacillations.

"I'll go for a walk. I'll not go down to the Ceres this morning."

Perhaps he did start out to walk, only to find himself alone with himself and his unhappiness. He was so bored with himself and his own futilities. Also, up on the hills among the pungent brushwood, he found himself thinking of Billy, of that impossibly complete and confident young woman who challenged his tired and submissive self. Besides, Billy was so aloof. She sat most of the day in that bright, yellow walled room, and when she was not working she was bathing or playing tennis. Her pace was beyond him, and to sit and watch her was too damned tantalizing.

He declaimed at his dreaming self.

"What an ass you are, what a futile ass! Hankering after a young woman who thinks you a soft rotter. Do be a little more sophisticated."

Mrs. Marrish was near at hand. She was nicely and charmingly sophisticated. She waited for a man on sofas and at little tables, and in the lounge of the Hotel Elyseo.

She persuaded Isherwood to go to one of the gala dances at the Elyseo, and they drank champagne and wore paper caps, and threw fluffy balls at every possible stranger, and blew whistles, and made a cheerful uproar. It was not so cheerful as it seemed, and the dancing was indifferent. The gay old people would crowd the floor like a troop of dancing bears.

Isherwood drank too much champagne. He found himself going home in Mrs. Marrish's taxi, and the sensuous part of him was a little silly and inflamed. Her nearness was soft and scented and intimate. He felt his knee touching hers.

At her gate he kissed her hand, and she patted his head.

"Nighty-night. You've been quite a nice boy. Do you good."

"Rather."

He walked back along the dusty road to "The Crater," and found himself full of sudden argumentative impulses and reflections. He was half pedant and half Pan, and rather vinous and emotional.

"Good! What is good? She's a jolly attractive woman. She understands a man. What a lot of rot one talks about chastity. Why not let go? It's just life."

He closed his gate with a slight swagger, and then stood to look at the diminished lights of Tindaro. Silly, sleepy town! And somewhere down yonder Billy would be asleep, very much herself in her chaste, clean bed.

He turned away.

"O, damn!"

His latchkey made several attempts to insert itself into the keyhole.

"O, damn! Damn all good women! When they're not bloody sweet they are so bloody superior."

III

Billy had called Isherwood a silly ass, but she never quite came to think of him as either a silly ass or a rotter. And thinking and feeling about people are as different as reading about tragedy and experiencing it in the flesh and the spirit. There was that strange resemblance between Isherwood and Frevick, and to Billy, Frevick had been one of the most moving of figures, like a blind man groping to touch a flower because the scent of it had drifted to him in the darkness. Frevick and Isherwood had been drawn towards each other. Apparently they had understood each other, and that sensitive unlikeness to the crowd man. But Frevick was dead, and Isherwood was taking to drink.

Sadie Shone told her.

"My dear, it's just like poor Tom all over again."

Billy, feeling strangely shocked, and shocked by her own way of feeling this particular thing, demanded facts.

"Who told you?"

"That little creature called Cobb. And I have eyes. Tom

Isherwood was at the Elyseo the other night with Mrs. Forget-Me-Not."

"Mrs. Who?"

"The Marrish woman. She's just like Myosotis. And it was not the first time. I know the blue of that sort of eye. Sure, it makes me think of the old song, 'Drink to me only with thine eyes,' but she doesn't sing it in that way, my dear."

Then somebody came into Mrs. Shone's shop, and Billy walked out of it, feeling both hot and cold. Also, she was angry with herself for feeling in that way, and almost angry with Isherwood for being able to make her feel in that way. It was perfectly absurd. What cause had she to get mushy-hearted about a silly ass with frightened eyes who was going about with the Marrish woman and drinking more than was good for him. Dash the Marrish woman; dash both of them. The association was sufficient to damn all sentiment. She wanted to be contemptuous.

But, life—somehow—wouldn't let her be contemptuous, which was exasperating and futile, but a fact. She could say, "You allowed a man to make a fool of you three years ago and it taught you to be pretty well fool-proof. What about it? Don't be an idiot." Yet this most sensible self-invocation proved itself inadequate. What you said and what you felt were utterly different things, and it appeared that you could not help feeling in a particular way about a particular person. It was as though life in some of its aspects had an overwhelming appeal. Billy had felt like that towards Frevick, rather like a capable, sensible young mother, but she did not feel quite like a mother to Tom Isherwood. That Marrish woman! And then she was furious with herself, and suddenly cold with a fastidious and frozen pride. She was not going to let Tindaro play nasty, emotional tricks with her.

Because she was so very fit both in body and mind, and very much mistress of her own job, and emotional interference could be an infernal nuisance. It so dominated a woman; it might upset all her nice calculations; it compelled her to make certain surrenders, and Billy had no intention of making surrenders. She was much more keen on making a success,

for success meant money.   She was not a little proud of her
show.   The English Agency was her own creation, a memorial
built over the grave of a romantic illusion.

She confessed to no one.   She was a little ashamed of her
weakness.   She cast her eyes upon Julia Lord and claimed
Julia as her exampler, though she did not see herself as a second
Julia Lord.   Nor did she know just how life had torn Tom
Frevick and Julia Lord nearly twenty years ago, and that the
Julia of those days had refused to stoop and touch the man
who had fallen.   Julia Lord could have told Billy many things,
that compassion cannot go about in a starched petticoat and
remain—compassion.   There must be some soft fabric about
a woman.   Julia Lord had been left with a dead man's dog
and a memory.

Billy rallied herself.   She had other plans for the future.
When Ealing and the family were disposed of, her mother
would be free to come out to Tindaro each winter.   Mary
Brown was a very tired woman, but not too tired to be loved,
and that was the kind of love that Billy would allow herself.
She could express herself in it without being a fool.

She happened to be thinking of her mother when she swam
back from the Island of the Triton a few days after her own
referring to Isherwood as a silly ass.   She stripped, and dried
herself behind the usual rock, and put on her clothes, and
feeling vigorous and fresh and cool-headed, she started to climb
the mule path back to Tindaro.   The morning was blue and
serene, the broken sea caught the sunlight on a myriad watery
facets.

Half-way up the path she came suddenly upon Isherwood
sitting under a stone pine.   Her impression of him was instant
and unwilling.   She thought he looked rather red about the
eyelids; also he had not shaved.   She resented his unshaven
chin.   Also she resented the rather frightened look in his
eyes.   A man had no right to be caught like a scared and
abashed child.

He made a sort of scrambling movement from the ledge of
rock under the pine, and stood on the edge of the path.   He
both looked at her and flinched from looking.   She had the

feeling of being asked some question by a man who was inarticulate, and acutely conscious of her as something that he was not. The very timidity of him affected her, and she did not thank him for making her feel self-conscious. She was fresh from the sea, and ready for the day's work.

It was she who spoke.

"Early again. Topping morning."

The words were as casual as her voice. She let her eyes rest on his unshaven chin. A man should not be caught like that, however decadent he might be feeling. Yet, it was obvious to her that he winced as though her glance had too cold a brightness.

He spoke. He said, "You're always so splendidly fit," and she was surprised to get the impression that he was reproaching her. Accusing her of being fit! Well, really! She had paused under the shadow of the pine, and her eyes had a brittle darkness.

"Well, it's of some value, isn't it?"

"Of course."

"Part of my plan of life, keeping fit."

She caught herself in a defensive attitude, and she resented it. Was she expected to justify her fitness to this unshaven exile. She wanted to say to him, "Why don't you shave before showing yourself." And he stood there regarding her with eyes which reminded her of Frevick. She noticed one of his hands fiddling with the flap of a pocket. He looked so hesitant, suspended there in the strong sunlight, yet somehow questioning her, and watching her face.

"O, yes, you're to be envied."

She gave a slight and restive shake of the head.

"One has a philosophy. Depends what you do with it. Coming up to Tindaro?"

And suddenly his face ceased to be a mere face. It was like a mist, vague yet illumined by many inward emotions. He sat down again on the edge of the rock, and she was made to think of him sitting on that little wooden stool.

"No. I'm staying here."

"Right. I'll be getting on."

She left him and went up and on with a sudden, angry flush. Absurd emotion! He might have been a blind man, a creature groping at life, and it was as though he had put out a tentative and appealing hand, and she had ignored it. She was angry.

CHAPTER XXVII

I

THE English method, or what was supposed to be the English method of keeping the proud flesh washed and in order, may prove economical and efficient provided the stresses are not too severe. Billy, like a capable and determined young schoolmistress, might plaster her walls with textual exhortations, "No nonsense"—"Such things are not done," and yet not reach finality. She might assert that sex is a nasty and untidy business, and that the sooner it is eliminated from life the better it is for the world's work. It behoved you to concentrate upon your job, and sex is a dissipation of energy. But the core of the whole problem is touched when, having asserted that certain things are not done, Miss Efficiency goes on to assert that the same things shall not be felt.

For even Paul made another shipwreck here, and the good Puritans might plaster humanity with red A's and remain blind to the inevitableness of Charles II. Since the days of the fig-leaves man has felt and quarrelled with his feelings, and listened furtively for the voice of God in the Garden. The serene naturalness dreamed of in Arcady has eluded priests and philosophers and yet may be attained by the ploughboy and the harlot.

Meanwhile, Billy felt certain things as a woman feels them, and either smiles a secret smile or stiffens her lips. Also, she seemed to know that Isherwood also felt certain things, and felt them about her. She had caught glimpses of herself in the mirror of his male consciousness. He desired her, but she did not know quite how he desired her. It might be like a monkey or a lascivious boy, and she would fight furiously against such desirings. She could not say whether he desired her as a

281

thirsty man in the desert craves water, or a blind man music and sight, or an artist beauty, or as a magnanimous lover the exquisiteness of her surrender. The fibres of her were still too tense to tremble to the exquisiteness of surrender. She had got into the way of giving advice, but not her lips.

Besides, there was the Marrish woman.

For Billy did not realize that Isherwood was in danger of a surrender that could not be called exquisite. Drink and an accommodating lady with sensual blue eyes. Mabel Marrish did not worry over how she felt about things; she was satisfied with feeling them, and therefore according to her own standard she was wiser than Billy. She could be sorry for Tom Isherwood.

"Give the poor man a drink."

She was so easy. She believed in having a good time, and she was quite ready to share her good time with other people, so long as they pleased her. She was as easy in her discardings as she was in her pickings up.

Yet neither Billy nor Mrs. Marrish understood the real Isherwood. To Mrs. Marrish he was just a man with nice manners and appealing eyes, a man who would be rather shy and unusual as a lover, and therefore, all the more refreshing. She had had so many lovers, and there were occasions when she tired of the bull man. And Isherwood was strange fruit to Billy's hard young hand.

How could she know how such a man felt, as man and artist, and sot and demi-god? He was as complex as Tindaro, and much of Tindaro she stubbornly and blindly ignored. How could she know that such a man as Isherwood sometimes felt himself full of a legion of swine, and was moved to rush down some steep place into the sea? Or that men kill themselves out of weariness, and in a moment of tired disgust, because of the little, sordid shames of a wearied self? The world seeks a motive, and often there is no motive, but often a last flaring of the will in the guttering stick of disillusionment.

"She doesn't understand."

That was his inward cry when she left him. She had seemed blind to his signals of distress. She understood neither his unshaven chin, nor the Marrish woman, nor his sleeplessness, nor his horrible sense of futility, nor his self-disgust, nor his struggles. She was not made to understand him. She had no temperament. Or perhaps she was one of those women who shrank from understanding life too thoroughly, and who was sufficiently strong to go striding along straight pavements without looking at agonized, sodden, or stupidly tragic faces. She was so self-sufficient.

And yet—to him—she was so surprisingly splendid. His youth rose up in the body of his tired maturity, and yearned to her. She made him feel both alive and dead. She was so impossible and yet so desirable, as a beautiful statue may appear desirable to a man capable of appreciating loveliness of line. She was not merely Miss Billy Brown of the English Agency. She was so much more than that, a creature who somehow convinced him, a beautiful building surely set on strong foundations, white stone, a tower, a Pharos, woman as he had never quite seen her before. Also, he could not move her. She stood in the midst of things as in the sea, and let them wash about her feet, and was unheeding. She did not understand that a man's troubled essence could be like the sea.

He sat and stared.

"You silly ass! She neither understands nor cares, and if she understood she would not care. Feeble and fatuous. There's nothing in you to convince her."

He left the shadow of the stone pine and the spread of the sunlit sea, and trailed heavy feet up the steep path. The steepness of it tired his chest. He was conscious of a feeling of intense despondency, of physical and spiritual abasement. Nothing mattered. Why strive and fret and yearn and suffer? His breath seemed to fail him on the steepness of the ascent. He sat down again and looked at Tindaro, all white and brown and yellow, with the morning sunlight lying upon it, and the cypresses very black against the old walls. It was both vivid and dim, a tired town, not quite as old as the hills, but sufficiently old to understand an indolent cynicism. Why had they sent him to Tindaro? He might just as well have completed the tragic farce in England. England was the land of the farcical, of the vulgar knockabout comedy which passes for humour.

He got on his feet again and trailed on. He remembered that Maria would provide him with shaving-water and hot coffee. Good Maria with her warts and moustache. She neither tantalized nor reduced you. Certainly he would shave, but he did not feel like breakfasting. He entered Tindaro by the sea-gate, a grey tunnel showing the brilliant colours of a flower-stall against an ochre-coloured wall. He glanced vaguely at the flowers, carnations, stocks, iris, violets. The pavements of Tindaro were very tiring; they hurt the feet as Tindaro seemed to hurt the soul. Yes, it was a very tired town, in spite of all its vellum-skinned, swarthy people. He went slowly up the Corso and past the Café Ceres, where Tommaso was swabbing the tables.

Tommaso was singing.

He uncovered white teeth to Isherwood.

"A beautiful morning, signore."

"O, very beautiful."

Fifty yards farther on he met Miss Lord, accompanied by Frevick's little yellow dog. She gave him a sudden, wide-eyed look, and seemed shocked by something, the vision of a dead man walking. She stopped.

"You are out early."

Obviously! But her meaning was less obvious. He looked deplorable, shrunken, but Betty did not appear to see him thus. She sniffed at his trousers, and then put up her paws.

Isherwood caressed her. His eyes felt hot. Frevick had felt like that.

"I think I must get a dog."

Julia Lord's face still wore that shocked, illumined look. Yes, he was so pathetically a second Frevick.

"Yes, I should. You have never been to see my garden."

His glance was almost deprecating. This woman and the dog were kind.

"No. May I?"

"Of course. Any time after half-past five. But that's rather late just at present. Come and have tea with me on Sunday."

Isherwood coloured. He wondered how she had managed to forgive him his chin, for she was a particular person.

"Thanks—awfully. Next Sunday?"

"Yes. About four."

She passed on. She was asking herself a question. Was there no one to rescue this second Frevick?

II

Billy was in a bad temper that morning, though she had neither swum too far nor climbed too fast, and she was terse with Miss Soulby over a clerical error in a letter. Miss Soulby had her inaccurate days when her pale eyes dreamed behind her pince-nez, and she and her machine were detached from each other or at cross purposes.

"I wish you would cultivate accuracy. Do you always spell 'passport' with a *b*?"

Miss Soulby apologized.

"I'm sorry; I have one of my headaches."

"You seem to have them pretty often."

The secretary returned mutely to her machine, feeling towards Billy much as Isherwood had felt. "O, yes, you're so strong. You don't understand people making mistakes. You don't make allowances." And yet Miss Soulby was devoted to Billy, for Billy was exacting in the office and demanded a high standard, and exacting people appear to be able to command the devotion of the humble.

For Billy was a builder. She had her plan, and her passion for the last three years had set itself towards the steady and sure completion of her plan, though she was still working on the foundations. She had chosen to regard life as a scheme on paper drawn to scale, and not as a jumble of brass pots floating in a swiftly running stream. Yet inherently she was as much of a brass pot as Miss Soulby, though of stouter metal, and when this other pot which was Isherwood jangled against her she gave out a responsive note. Disturbed, she attempted to regard it as a discord, for all human and inevitable sounds may be regarded as discords, the wailing of a child or the hysterical screaming of a woman. Undisciplined emotion! And yet

K

this discordant clash of human metal upon metal had set other elementals vibrating.

Half-way through the morning Miss Lord's door opened. Billy had been interviewing a fussy person who had been purchasing antiques and was worried about the freight and the insurance. The Italians were such thieves. Billy had defended the Italians. She had said that she had travelled hundreds of miles on the Italian railways and had never lost so much as a cake of soap, but that on one occasion she had had a mackintosh stolen from a trunk, but that had occurred between Waterloo and Woking.

Said Miss Lord, "I have asked Mr. Isherwood to tea on Sunday. Are you coming?"

Julia Lord's voice was casual, but to Billy it seemed to slip a surreptitious suggestion—like a hastily scribbled note—on to her desk. Her response was abrupt.

"No. Afraid not. I'm playing tennis with Captain Booth and the Ormerods."

"All right. I'll ask Sadie."

Julia Lord's door closed, leaving Billy accusing the morning of presenting her with a series of irritations and interruptions. Why should Julia ask her to meet Isherwood? And in the face of her refusal why should Julia revert to Sadie? Did this spoilt man-child need amusing? The sleek, pragmatical surface of her felt the rub of an interfering hand. She hated interference. She would not allow her sense of soreness to be serious. It was a mere patch of erythema, scarcely skin deep.

She spoke rather sharply to Miss Soulby.

"Take down these letters, please."

Miss Soulby reached for her shorthand pad and pencil, and looked at Billy a little protestingly. She wished that Miss Lord had asked her to tea on Sunday at the Villa Vesta, but Miss Soulby was one of those women whom no one asked out to tea.

III

Isherwood shaved himself, and despite the fact that he was using a safety razor he cut his chin. He looked pathetic over it, as though it was another trivial disharmony added to the other disharmonies, white lather stained a rusty red.   Shaving was a peevish business, and could be deleted by the growing of a beard, a nice, lazy, devil-may-care crop of hair.   He was feeling acutely miserable, shabby and submissive, and even the blob of red blood on his chin seemed less red than the blood of other men.

He thought, "I'll get a dog.   A dog doesn't expect too much from a fellow."

But the issue broadened.   Why stay in Tindaro at all? Why not go back to England and allow the fog to choke one? There were other fogs and other chokings far more distressing and poignant than water vapour and smoke.

He heard Maria carrying his tray of coffee and rolls up the stairs.   Like Julia Lord's Maria she made excellent coffee, but Isherwood had no stomach for it.   He heard her knock and put the tray down outside his door.   In some ways he was an absurdly sensitive creature, too afraid of hurting other people's feelings, and he did not want to hurt the good Maria by not drinking her coffee.   He carried the tray in and put it on the table beside his bed, and mixing some milk and coffee in the cup, drank it without sugar.   Its bitterness had his sympathy.   As for the Italian bread, he left it untouched.   It knew the tiredness but not the beauty of Tindaro.

Having done his duty to Maria as a fellow craftsman he sat on the edge of his bed and lit a cigarette.   He had begun to fear and to hate his bed.   It invited him to sleep in it, and yet when he lay down it could not give him the sleep that he desired, hours and hours of utter forgetfulness.   Such sleep would have helped him to kill the night, but his nights were becoming like his days, a kind of acute and wakeful soreness, a restless melancholy from which he could not escape.   For it was from himself that he wished to escape, from that load of personal consciousness which weighed upon him more and more, and crushed him with its mental oppression.

He got up suddenly from the bed, and stood looking at it. The crumpled pillow showed the mark of his head; the clothes lay as he had thrown them back, and he received an impression of frowsiness, of something stuffy and crumpled. His own unmade bed somehow disgusted him.

He went downstairs and out into the garden. It too had a kind of unmade, morning hopelessness, an unfinished futility; it could not be called a garden. The path was full of weeds. He had made an attempt to sow some grass seed, but it had come up in patches, and the lawn was like a half-bald head. It suggested to Isherwood an arid pate upon which some enthusiast had used a fantastic hair-restorer. He saw it suddenly as a ridiculous mottled patch of soil and sickly grass, and he was moved to equally ridiculous laughter. What futility!

Meanwhile the whole day lay before him, and he had nothing to do but kill the hours as they came. Yes, nothing to do but to go down to the Café Ceres and sit there and drink and listen to gossip and Little Cobb's stories. There seemed to be nothing left for him to do, none of those things that a man does with furiousness and passion and a sense of the breathing of God. He fetched out his stool, and planting it in under one of the olive trees, he sat down and brooded. The little chocolate-box of a villa had become very full of Maria's activities; she was half Swiss, and her Swiss heritage moved her to shake and smack things with earnestness and vigour. Every morning she thrust his bedding out of the window, and let it air in the sun, blankets, sheets and duvet, an immense red and white flag announcing to all the world that Isherwood was up. He rather wished that she would not be so thorough in the airing of his bedding. It was rather like having one's trousers hoisted on the front lawn, but then Maria was in authority.

He yawned. Maria was thumping his pillow. He found himself wishing that something would happen to distract his attention and to break this crust of oppression. Something did happen. He saw a figure outside his gate.

"Hallo——! Anyone at home?"

He got up quickly from his stool. She had appeared like life at his gate in a light blue jumper and white skirt; she looked both slim and mature. The blue of her body had a lissomeness, and under the silk the curves of her breasts showed. He was excitedly glad of her.   She seemed to open the gate to distraction and escape.

"Hallo——"

She waved.

"I've got a car to-day.   Going to Pomonium.   Care to come?"

His eyes had a brittle brightness.

"Rather.   What's it, a party?"

"Do you want a party?"

"Well, not exactly."

"Call it a coupé day."

She laughed.   She looked very handsome and so alive and so jocund.   She nodded her head at the bedding protruding from the window.

"Your woman does air you thoroughly.   Mine's French. She thinks a bed should be left with a sort of warm smell of Quelques Fleurs."

He laughed with her.

"Point of view.   The couch of Aphrodite.   What time?"

"The car's coming at eleven.   I'm taking a luncheon basket."

"Splendid."

IV

Pomonium revealed itself as an old grey temple, lonely against the intense blue of the sky.   They walked to it across a surge of wild grassland.   A herd of goats grazing on the skyline unfurled the suggestion of a frieze.   They carried the luncheon-basket between them, having abandoned the chauffeur and the car at the little white *osteria* in the valley.

A light wind blew.   It seemed to pluck with invisible fingers at the wires of the grasses and to make mysterious music, and the trembling of the grasses emphasized the solidity of the Doric pillars.   Where the sunlight played upon them their fluted strength gleamed out against the shadowiness of portico and cellar.   In the architrave Heroes and Amazons struggled together.

Isherwood stood and gazed.

"God," he said—"those old people? Does anyone die after building like that?"

She looked at him tolerantly, possessively. A man had to be allowed his rhetoric, for when men declaimed things their words were for the ears of some woman.

"Almost do for the new Regent Street, or Selfridge."

He came down from Olympus, but protestingly

"That wasn't commerce."

She laughed, and her blue eyes were pagan.

"O, no. But I hold some drapery shares. They pay me rather well. I'm Philistia, I suppose. O, yes, I have heard of the Philistines, but in these days——!"

"Philistia—the universal. Besides—their detractors were the Jews. The Philistines came from Crete, Minoan refugees —probably."

"What a lot you know."

She gave her side of the basket a little shake, and a faint jingling came from it. She proffered the present in place of the past, red wine and pâté sandwiches and coffee in a thermos, and herself.

"Where do we lunch?"

"In the sun."

"It's almost like a hayfield. And not a cloud."

"No, all blue."

His glance fell from her blue eyes to the blue silk that sheathed her shoulders and bosom. In her way she was shapely as that temple, yet somehow suggesting the Madeline and Paris and the Rue de la Paix and Auteuil. She was like a basket of blue and white flowers in a Paris street on a perfect day in April.

They sat down in a little grassy hollow with the basket between them, and unpacked its contents with an air of sharing other intimate things. She handed him the wine and a corkscrew.

"Your job."

He noticed that the glasses were blue, like the Tindaric sea off the island of the Triton. He was conscious of a sudden pang. How she—Billy—had snubbed him on the path that morning.   Unshaven rotter!   He drew the cork, frowning, teeth set, and picked out one of the blue glasses.

"One ought to begin with a salute to the gods."

Bending forward to reach for something she smiled up at him.

"Which god?"

"The blue goddess, Anadyomene."

"Anno Domini?   Don't be rude?"

"To the Blue Goddess."

"That's me!   Or are you being puckish?"

"To the Lady of the Sandwiches."

Afterwards they lay in the grassy hollow, hidden, save from the big blue eye of the sky.   It was a sleepy eye.   An old grey goat came silently down from the brow of the hill, and seemed to gaze at them before turning wisely away.   The Doric column stood up straight and strong.   Everywhere there seemed to be the soft, sly whispering of the wind in the grasses.

CHAPTER XXVIII

I

ON the Sunday Billy played tennis with Captain Booth and the Ormerods, and she was off her game. She was mistiming her shots and finding herself caught on the wrong foot, nor did she seem able to mend matters by concentrating on her strokes. The fact was she could not concentrate, and did not care sufficiently about the game to concentrate. A part of her was aloof and away, and seriously disturbed and dissatisfied.

Captain Booth, one of those correctly good-looking young men cut out of cardboard, with a little ginger moustache and a hot colour, quizzed her like the superior male, and she was not in the mood to be quizzed by a young fellow from India who was given too little competition in Tindaro.

"Feeling a bit off to-day?"

"No. It's the wind in the olive trees."

He looked at her with his flat eyes, eyes which could sight a bird or a ball or a leg, and little else.

"You mean the shadows? Not much wind—really. They ought to cut those trees down."

She looked bored.

"O, would it be worth while?"

When they had played three sets she said that she was sorry, but that she could play no more. She said that she had promised to drop in at the Villa Vesta for tea or after tea. Captain Booth looked at her with his neat little smile and wondered whether her whimsies were personal. He supposed her to be the sort of girl to whom you could tell a funny story—"No nonsense, you know," but she seemed to be peeved about something; her game; or himself? He was extremely self-centred. The sun's rays converged upon him.

She went.   She had slipped her racket into its case; rackets were precious in Tindaro, and especially so at post-war prices. She allowed the wired door of the enclosure to swing back behind her with a clang.   She felt distraught and on edge, and acutely aware of Booth as a complacent and comely fool.   Probably he and the Ormerods would think that she was peeved, because she had been off her game, but did it matter what people thought? She had had to face much silly curiosity and censure on those tennis courts.

Also, though she might try to explain away her unrest she was aware of its inspiration.   She had been troubled about it all day.   The thing had shocked and humiliated her, and she had been still more shocked by her own feeling of humiliation. She had realized its significance.

The news had come to her through Sadie Shone.   Tindaro and the Café Ceres had seen Isherwood drunk at six o'clock in the evening.   It had seen him lifted from his chair, and placed in a hired carriage by Tommaso and the vetturino, and driven away up to "The Crater."   Sadie herself had witnessed the incident.   She had described Little Cobb as adjusting Isherwood's crumpled hat upon his lolling head, and getting in beside him with a comic bow to the Café Ceres, to see Isherwood home.

Abominable farce!   And still more abominable had been her own feeling of humiliation.   But why?   She had been conscious of a kind of trembling chilliness, anger, astonishment. What was happening to her?   Why did she feel torn and distraught, and unable to fix her thoughts upon her work? She had determined that they should be faced, and she had sat bolted down at her desk, only to find those restless thoughts vagrant in Tindaro.   They had haunted the Café Ceres, and "The Crater."   They would not be localized or restrained. They were like the distraught movements of a creature in pain.

She had not meant to go to the Villa Vesta, but now she was going, drawn thither by a force which was stronger than herself.   Or perhaps it was herself, compassionately curious, and flinging off all those careful and artificial restraints?   She went

K*

there, protesting, angry and yet shaken, pitying and despising both man and herself. Her reason said nay, but the yes in her was like the beginnings of a tumult. She both delayed and hurried.

She found herself at the familiar gate. She pushed it open and walked round the white house to the garden. She supposed that they would be in the garden, having tea on the terrace, for such was Julia Lord's custom when the sun shone on her name-day. The garden was beginning to be very beautiful, with colour added to the green of its trees and the grey of its stone. Julia Lord loved her colours massed and contrasted, red and purple anemones, white and rose stocks, blue iris, wallflowers, roses, narcissus, flaming tulips. The orange trees were hung with fruit, and something in Billy paused and stood still. She seemed to draw a deep breath and hold it. Her hands went to her bosom and clasped her breasts. She was aware of beauty, beauty in the sudden swelling of her emotions, and in the flowering of this garden. It was like the garden of an annunciation. She was touched; she was conceiving an infinite and poignant tenderness; she was being reborn as woman. Her flesh was flesh.

She went down the steps and along the path past the water cistern. She saw a tea-table and an empty chair, and Julia Lord sitting in another chair with a book in her lap. She had on her reading-glasses; she took them off when she became aware of Billy slowly approaching. The cypresses stood very still, and the long shadows trailed away from them into the flower-beds.

Billy moved to the wall of the terrace, and laid her racket on it. Her movements had deliberation, mystery.

Julia Lord closed her book.

"Had tea?"

"No. I don't think I want any."

"Maria can make some more."

"O, don't bother."

The vacant chair was obvious to both of them, and neither of them fell to the obvious. But Billy sat down in it. So, he had not come, and her consciousness was fraught with ques-

tions. Why had he stayed away? Was he incapable of
coming? Did he not dare to come? Was he hiding up there
and feeling as shamefully as she felt about it? But why should
she feel that there was shame in it? Possibly he did not care;
he was on the edge of an insensitive and sottish apathy; he had
fallen into "The Crater," into one of those foul war-holes full
of smeary water and indescribable remnants. He was the
tragedy of tragedies, a man smothering in his own surrender.

She felt that the silence was unbearable. She looked askance
at Julia Lord.

"Had your tea?"

"Yes."

"I got rather bored with tennis and the Booth man."

Her very breasts felt painful. They seemed to be swelling
with the milk of her emotion. It was damnable. For she
had begun to think of that Marrish woman, the other woman.
She seemed to see things as she had never seen them before.
She knew without knowing how she knew, and without caring
how she knew. Isherwood had been with Mrs. Marrish.
The way of her knowing was like a flash of red light.

She moistened her lips, and spoke.

"Isherwood did not come."

"No."

Julia Lord's face was marble.

"He may come. I kept the things here."

She was remembering how Frevick had suffered with her
in the same desperate evasions, but Billy knew that Isherwood
would not come.

II

Isherwood's lapse had been very sudden. Like a man slowly
descending a flight of rotten stairs, and coming to a still more
rotten step that had given way under his feet, he had floundered.
The whole world seemed to smell of Quelques Fleurs and
cigarette-ash, and face-powder, and whisky, and somebody
else's scented bed. He had experienced the full opulence of all
these intimate incidents; he had been clasped and had clasped;
he had given and received unrestrained kisses. He should

have been able to boast to himself of the adventure, and have written lyrically of southern nights, but instead of this he had emerged like a conventional April out of March winds. Reaction—no doubt, but he had felt more than virtue to go out of him. For what is virtue as understood by lovers? Probably he had never felt more miserable than after the passing of this spasm of sensationalism. He came out of it shivering, like a man who had stayed too long in the sea.

Being unable to sleep, and going down half-dressed into the garden just when the rim of the sun emerged as a red arc out of the sea, he stood in the chill of the dawn, and wondered at life and at himself. After all, why this dejection; this feeling of having sinned against the nature of things? He had embraced nature in the arms of a natural woman. It had been a mere physical incident. And yet he knew that it was no such thing, and that his sour mouth and his sense of shame were realities. Just because he was rather futile and hopeless and wanted to forget he had behaved like a man who goes up to London and gets drunk and then ends the adventure with a woman.

With his raincoat buttoned loosely, he opened the gate of "The Crater" and wandered along the new road towards these other villas. The light of the rising sun threw into relief the roughness of the road's surface, its ruts and heaves and hollows. It was very raw and very new. Mrs. Marrish's white villa met the dawn full face. The green shutters were closed. A young mimosa in flower raised a golden plume. Isherwood stood and looked at the villa, and suddenly he knew that he hated it and the woman who was sleeping in it, for she had helped him to this last failure, the degradation of the lover in him.

He faced about and going to the edge of the road, looked down through the olive trees at Tindaro. He saw it laced with the leaves and gently mysterious under the edge of the dawn. The coast-line was flushed with a faint, rosy light; the Island of the Triton floated like a cloud in the pale, silvery blue of the sea. The dawn had the hush of innocence.

Beauty? Yes, he knew that he—a craftsman—had sinned

against beauty.   He had chosen to do the botched job instead
of burning with fasting and prayer to perform those other
sacred and mysterious rites.   Life could be sacred.   Certain
things which were in man were sacred, the love of beauty, the
love of one particular woman.   And with a feeling of strange
childishness he looked at Tindaro and the mountains, and the
sea, and felt a desolation of loneliness just as a child feels it,
with a kind of wondering, innocent and deplorable poignancy.

He turned and walked back towards "The Crater," and looking at its painted gate and blue shutters, he saw it with the eyes
of the eternal symbolist.   A crater, a hole blown in the ground,
a pit; and suddenly he was afraid.   He had gone over the edge
of the pit.   He was like a fly struggling helplessly in some
sticky liquid, a Café Ceres fly, an insect pushing its proboscis
into smears of spilt wine, and sucking at the sugared cakes
softening in the heat of the sun.   He discovered a sudden
horror of the Café Ceres, and of the faces of its people.   Botterel's saturnine servility, Warner with his yellow face and
yellow teeth, that libidinous monkey—Little Cobb.   And the
women, and the atmosphere of faded, sweetly scented, fly-blown
nastiness!

He turned about again towards the sea.   He saw it as
something eternally old and eternally new washing the feet of
Tindaro, and the words came into his head, "Wash and be
clean."   He thought of Billy swimming in the sea, and coming
forth from it fresh and renewed.   Why was it that he desired
her as he did, so hopelessly, and with a sense of self-abasement?
Was it not her strength, her cleanness which appealed, a quality
of steadfastness, a courage that held and did not let go.   Illusions?   No, be damned to such cynical snuffling.   He had a
feeling that if she cared she would not fail a man, and in caring
a man would not fail her.   Life was not one vast, glutinous,
flypaper to which all silly dreams stuck, to be quizzed by
pessimism squinting through its spectacles.   Man lived and
dreamed and willed.

Yes, but the will?   How could he will that thing, being
what he was, and with the smell of the other woman in his soul
and in his hair.   He—an incipient sot—whom Little Cobb

had helped to push into a carriage! Yes, sin was just what the older folk had called it, sin. A tolerant, wordy, passionless science might talk it into sublimations, and complexes, and associations of this and that, but sin was a wounding. Blood flowed, man's mystic blood, and perhaps the blood of others. It might be so final. There might be no stanching of the stream.

He went in and shaved and washed himself. He even tied his tie with a particular care. He was going down to the sea. It drew him. It was like sleep, a deep, blue-black sleep into which forgetfulness sank and was glad. He was conscious of a vague feeling of exultation. Wash and be clean. Sink and forget. He smiled as he closed the door of the villa, and in him was the knowledge that he might never open it again.

III

Billy, too, was sleeping the sleep of Tindaro, sleep which was so shallow, and no more than a film of water covering the upper consciousness. There was no deep, satisfying submergence. Such sleep was broken and dispersed by the slightest sound.

She, too, woke just when the sun was rising out of the Tindaro sea, though what had roused her she could not say. Someone had passed down the vicolo at the end of the Tea Room garden, and had opened the gate, and had stood looking up at her window. And perhaps the sound of Isherwood's footsteps had ruffled the shallow surface of her sleep, and made her open her eyes to the daylight ribbing the shutters.

She got out of bed, and opened the shutters. There had been a dew, and the garden was wet with it, but she, unlike the garden, was unrefreshed, and at the beginning of another restless day. But how absurd it was! That she should be so oppressed and distracted by an emotion that she had not sought, but had fought to thrust it out into the world of forgotten, dead illusions. It was as though she had conceived, and the child stirred in her, a child whom she had not desired.

But the morning had clear eyes, and she thought she would make of the day what all her other days had been. She dressed herself quickly, and took her bathing-dress and towel, and pass-

ing out by way of the garden she went swiftly down towards
the sea.   It called to her.   She asked for its cold, impersonal
challenge, for its resistance, for its buoyant wrestling with her
strong body.   It was both beloved friend and enemy; its saltness lay upon your lips; always you had to strive with it or
surrender.

For Billy was very modern, yet no more modern than Julia
Lord.   She believed that life could be controlled or ought to
be controlled.   Her case against man was that he had grown
rather careless and untidy and otiose, but she did not go on to
discover that such an attitude might be vulgar man's protest
against a bureaucracy, against all the fussy Old Women in
London, Moscow or Rome.   She herself was on the edge of
being a bureaucrat, though she swam in the sea.   The man-
child protested against too much washing, too much bumping
of brooms and whirring of carpet-sweepers.   His cry might be,
"O, do give life a chance.   I know you are damned efficient,
but I don't want to live in a sort of sterilized lab.   A little
more dust, and less flapping of dusters, and I should be much
more comfortable."

She did not understand these things, at least—not yet, for she
was resenting the very untidiness of love, its moods, its unprac-
tical evasions, its disturbances.   It could not be pigeon-holed,
or card-indexed.   It was so turbulent.   She had thought of
tearing the thing out like a page out of a ledger.   She confronted it as she confronted that seductive, subtle, incalculable
sea into which she meant to plunge.

She swung down the zigzags of the path with the morning
sunlight first on one cheek and then on the other.   She could
see the olive and lemon groves in the valleys, and here and there
the flush of an almond tree in flower.   The coast dwindled
into a diaphanous dimness, but the sands and the sea edge of
the little bay where she bathed were hidden by the cliff.   She
had no view of the half-moon of sand until she came to the
last ramp of the steep path, but when she came to it she paused
with suddenness and stood still.   Life laid a hand on her
throat.

For down below there she saw a man, fully clothed, standing

up to his knees in the sea. He had his back to the shore. His hands, hanging limply, almost touched the water, and it seemed to her that he stood there like a man who had heard the voice of some sea goddess. The lure of the blue deeps was upon him. And yet, most human of touches, he was wearing his shabby grey felt hat, and she saw the sway and swell of the sea moving the legs of his trousers.

She did not call to him, but she picked up a biggish stone and threw it so that it thudded on the sand behind him. She was aware of the startled turn of his head and shoulders, and of his face looking up as she descended the path. She did not hurry. She went deliberately down to the sands, but her very deliberation was willed. He was still standing in the blue water, rather like a child caught paddling in some forbidden pool. A spasm caught her. Yes, how like a child he was! Almost she wanted to chastise him.

Before her feet had touched the sands he was wading out. He looked foolish, tragically foolish. It was as though the fabulous Tritons and all the young nymphs of the sea were laughing and blowing their shell trumpets. His wet trousers clung about his knees; the sea squelched in his shoes.

They looked at each other. Was it farce or tragedy? But his eyes betrayed to her the deeps of his humiliation.

She said, "Paddling isn't very safe here. There are holes in the rocks."

His face was a sudden redness.

"Thanks. I can swim."

The words, blurted out, seemed to strike her bosom. They hurt. She dropped the basket which held her bathing-dress and towel.

"O, then—it's all right."

There was no need for her to glance at his wet trousers and oozing shoes, or to remark that it was unusual for a sane man to bathe in his clothes. The implications were obvious. They shocked her, but she would not allow him the comfort of knowing that she was both scared and shocked. She wanted to be both hard and soft, and as it so often happens on such tense occasions her hardness was the more apparent.

His redness had gone. He seemed to be trembling, or was it merely her impression of him as a wet and unhappy dog, mute and consciously ashamed? He stood, accused of futility even in the face of death.

He said, "I suppose one can buy bathing togs in Tindaro?"

She nodded, as though someone had jerked her chin.

"Yes, at 'Calabria.'"

"Thanks."

There was a silence, and something writhed in her, because he looked so boyish and forlorn and foolish. She wanted him out of that attitude. She struck.

"Hadn't you better go home and change? Not very wise for an invalid, is it——?"

Again she was aware of that red flush. His eyes grew very blue and round and staring. A moment later he was white.

"Does it matter? Besides—I shall be dry before I get up there. And salt water."

"That's rubbish. Look here, you'd better go behind one of those rocks and use my towel."

His eyes said, "Keep your damned towel." And she was aware of her own eyes falling before him. So, he could be angry. He had that virtue left in him, and she was glad.

"O—all right. But it won't be good for your trousers."

He walked past her up the sands.

"Well—they are my trousers."

"Quite."

CHAPTER XXIX

I

BILLY bathed, and went back to her breakfast, and the day's work. It was to be a day of other distractions and excitements, and they began early, and while she was smoking her after-breakfast cigarette in the Tea Room garden. The telephone rang, and she went to answer it.

The voice was English.

"Hallo—is that Miss Brown?"

"Yes."

"Jevens speaking. By the way, I have been thinking seriously of that business proposition, Miss Brown."

"Capo Moro?"

"Yes. My Italian partner happens to be coming down from Turin for a couple of nights, and I'm going to take him to spy out the land. What I want to know is, have you any figures?"

"You mean details, possible costs?"

"Yes."

"I know how much land there is, and the average price of land in Tindaro. Yes, I have quite a lot of stuff on paper."

"I wish you would come up and dine and meet Savelli. And bring your figures."

"To-night?"

"Yes. Say eight-thirty."

"Right. I will be with you, Mr. Jevens, at eight-thirty."

She hung up the telephone receiver, and leant against the wall, for she was feeling a little breathless. Extraordinary coincidence! She was going to dine at the Villa of the Flute with Mr. Jevens and his Italian partner, and to talk business with these men. She felt intensely excited, and conscious of the need of a clear head. Things seemed to happen so suddenly,

302

and she was being assailed by those other distractions just at the moment when concentration was called for.

But Jevens—of all men! She had met Mr. Jevens for the first time about a year ago. He was what the journalists called a "Captain of Industry," and no man could look less girt and harnessed. He was very tall, and of the thickness of a piece of plywood, and of much the same colour, and out of his sallow and emaciated face a pair of blue eyes gazed mildly. Elbows, shoulders and knees protruded. He was slightly hesitant in speech, and was partnered and supported by a little, thick-set, bull-throated wife who wore lurid jumpers, and clenched her fists and swung her red forearms when she walked. Jevens was a tired man who suffered from asthma and bronchitis. He had the high, strained shoulders and the anxious eyes of the asthmatic. He had bought the Villa of the Flute, and his wife gave vast and flamboyant parties in the garden where Oscar Slade had left the memory of an amorous and faunlike face, but the Villa of the Flute had become respectable. Pan had no chance with sturdy little Mrs. Jevens, who spoke her English with a tinge of Lancashire, and who always referred to her husband as "Mr. Jevens." She had caused some of the more enigmatic statues to be removed and decently hidden in an outhouse, but not being a classical person she had preserved Leda and the Swan. Certainly "Mrs. Leda" was a little undressed, but then the lady was being so nice to the dear bird.

Mr. Jevens had made much money in cotton before financial gloom had been added to Lancashire's industrial, grey melancholy. Also he was in artificial silk and very successfully so, for those pale blue eyes of his had vision. Billy had pictured Captains of Industry as big-headed, full-throated and rather truculent men, with pronounced chins and well-developed masticating muscles, and here was Mr. Jevens rather like a tallow candle which had been compressed under a board. She had wondered whence his energy flowed, and how that frail body of his could produce such strength. At his wife's parties he wandered about like a ghost in a panama hat. Socially he was inarticulate.

She had spoken to Mr. Jevens of Capo Moro, without
expecting him to be usefully interested. She could remember
him fixing her with his pale blue eyes, and rubbing his chin
with two long fingers.

"Bricks and mortar in Italy! H'm. Give Mussolini
another year."

That was all he had said, and it had sounded repressive, but
Billy did not know Mr. Jevens. Also, she did not know that
for the best part of a year Mr. Jevens had been acutely bored,
and especially so in Tindaro. His tallow candle of a body
carried a flame which should have belonged to an arc-lamp.
He had a restless spirit. It was said that he spent two hours
a day in sawing wood. He manipulated a super-wireless
installation. He owned the biggest Fiat car in Tindaro,
and sometimes drove it himself and with a kind of pale and fero-
cious recklessness that scattered children, hens and goats. Such
activities could not exhaust him; they were the etceteras of life.
He wanted something more.

Billy walked up the Corso to meet Julia Lord. The news
was clamorous, and yet not so clamorous as it would have been
a month ago, for neither Capo Moro nor Mr. Jevens held the
centre of her field of vision, all the time she was seeing Tom
Isherwood standing in the sea like some quite craven and
futile Atlas whose heart had failed him. No Apples of the Hesperides! And he had been furious with her, and sick and
ashamed.

A month ago she might have thought to herself, "Silly ass.
Do him good." But her easy, follow-through philosophy had
become like her tennis, rather cramped and self-conscious.
She was not sure that she wanted good doing to Isherwood.
She had slipped past the social fence and its notice-boards, and
was in the wilderness where strange things happened. She
rather wanted them to happen. She knew now that she could
have stood up to her knees in the water with him, and felt the
sea playing with her skirts. She could do the most ridiculous
things with him, and they would cease to be ridiculous.

Just beyond the Café Ceres she met Julia Lord and the
dog. Billy had looked full and steadily at the marble-topped

tables, and at the window of the cakes. The flies were feeling the spring; she had seen dozens of them actively crawling and with a sort of inevitableness, and almost she had felt consenting towards the flies. Woman was woman, and Tindaro was Tindaro.

Frevick's dog yapped a good morning, and Billy bent down and caressed the creature. A light had come into her eyes.

"I have had a piece of news."

"So early."

"Mr. Jevens just rang me up. The Capo Moro idea seems to have intrigued him."

Miss Lord, who had seen the light in Billy's eyes, was moved to answer, "Is that all?" For Mr. Jevens and the English Agency and a gamble in real estate were not sufficient, nor had the English Library and Tea Rooms been sufficient to Julia Lord.

"You mean—he is going to put up the money?"

"I don't know yet. I am going up to dine and meet his Italian partner. They make artificial silk somewhere in the north. I'm just a bit excited."

Billy spent the morning in getting out figures for Mr. Jevens. She retired to her room, and left Miss Soulby in charge of the office, but distractions were not to be dealt with by the mere shutting of a door. She had made a little plan of Capo Moro, and marked on it the existing roads and peasant holdings, but it was obvious to her that Capo Moro would have to be surveyed and all the measurements scaled. She could foresee roads and sewers and water mains and electric cables, and play with them on paper, but she had not the technical knowledge to carry the thing through. And Isherwood, thrust outside the door of her consciousness, stood and knocked as Isherwood the architect as well as Isherwood the man.

Of course! She supposed that he had been trained to survey as well as to construct, and it was probable that he had the very knowledge which was needed. She sat and stared and tapped her chin with her pencil. She thought, "If only he had the grit. But he must have. But then old Jevens isn't the kind of man. O, lord, life's difficult."

Billy passed a restless, worrying day, and at half-past six she put on her best frock, knowing that even men like Jevens prefer a woman to be comely as well as capable, and with a little self-accusing quirk of a smile she acknowledged the lapse, the sacrifice offered to the old, heathen gods. The Christian maiden before the throne of Cæsar! O, rot, she could hold her own with old Jevens. She had ordered a carriage, and she drove up to the Villa of the Flute in the cool of the evening. The hills were the colour of lavender, the sky like a great opal.

The iron gates of the Villa, rusty and musical in Slade's day, had been painted a bright blue, but the avenue of cypresses towered too high for Mrs. Jevens's red and interfering hands. Billy should have liked Mrs. Jevens, for she was a downright person who thumped you, and let it be known that she stood no nonsense, but Billy was prejudiced. She preferred Stella Burt, which was rank heresy according to the creed of the pragmatist. Mrs. Jevens was rather like a restless cow deprived of its calf, she would not remain in any particular field.

Billy foresaw Mrs. Jevens making trouble. Her hostess was the first person whom she met, active in the formal garden below the loggia with a big, red watering-can, and dispensing dew. She looked at Billy's fur coat and the frock beneath it, and she said what she thought.

"You need not have bothered about war-paint. When I'm gardening—I'm gardening."

Obviously so, in a pair of slippers and a rather tashed cretonne frock. And to Billy it seemed that the large red can was part of the lady.

"Sorry. It doesn't matter."

She supposed that she had better humour Mrs. Jevens.

"Your nemesias are lovely."

"Yes—but that rogue of a gardener thieved half my seed. Sutton's. Had it sent out specially. Mr. Jevens and Savelli are putting on shirts."

Billy understood that Mrs. Jevens thought her overdressed, but Mrs. Jevens was that sort of woman. If you put on flesh-coloured stockings she would inform you that she pre-

ferred black ones.   She was superfluously frank and candid.
And then Mr. Jevens himself appeared on the loggia, and looked
whimsically at his wife, and her watering-can, and smiled a
faded smile at Billy.

"Always punctual, Miss Brown."

She gathered that he approved of her cerise-coloured frock.
She had taken off her fur coat, and Mr. Jevens offered to put
it away for her.   Then Savelli joined them, one of those tall
Italians with a gentle and ironic head, and a courtesy that was
not artificial silk.   He bowed to Billy, and looked as though
he would have liked to kiss her hand.   He had kissed Mrs.
Jevens's hand, which was like saluting a hot red brick.

They went in to dinner, Mrs. Jevens abandoning her can
at the very last moment, but bearing sundry splashes down the
front of her skirt.   Mr. Jevens had no social dilatoriness.   He
arrived at Capo Moro with the soup, and before the fish had
left them, they were in the thick of Capo Moro as a financial
adventure.

Mrs. Jevens protested.

"Well, I call it silly, Fred.   What do you want to bother
with more work for, and just when the doctors sent you down
here for a rest."

Billy sat calm and mute.   Confound the woman!   Yes, she
had expected that Mrs. J. would be difficult.

Her husband gave her another whimsical look.   There were
occasions when he drove over his wife as he drove his big Fiat
over a protesting hen.

"Must have some amusement, Beatie.   Doesn't suit me to
lose my edge."

Savelli, smiling gently, surveyed the pair of them with an
air of faded yet complete sagacity.

The discussion proceeded, but it was Jevens himself who
mentioned Isherwood.

"That architect chap, ready to hand.   He might be of some
use in surveying and estimating."

Mrs. Jevens was waiting with her watering-can.

"Don't be silly, Fred.   Why, everybody knows that the man
drinks.   He was half drunk at the Elyseo the other night."

Billy's face had a sudden, white stillness.

She said, "I don't think that's quite true.   Tindaro always tells the worst about people."

II

A man can survive being called a drunkard, or a scoundrel, or a dissolute person, but convict him of being a futile fool, and he wilts.   Therefore, Isherwood, mounting—perhaps a little self-consciously—the steps of tragedy, and finding himself told to go home and change his trousers, had felt that the final ignominy had touched him.   Even the dawn and the Tindaric sea, a gorgeous stage for a tragic gesture, had allowed him nothing but futility.

He returned to "The Crater," but he did not change his trousers.   He sat in a deck chair in the garden, and let those ridiculous garments dry in the sun.   He was much more wholesomely savage than he had been since the days of the war, sore and savage, and wanting to break out and run amok.

While he was sitting there a maid brought a note from Mrs. Marrish.   She used french-grey notepaper and blue sealing-wax, and her hand was soft and round and indolent.

"DEAR PIP,

I want to go to the Elyseo to-night.   I've booked a table and I'll collect you at 8.30.   Remember—it's tails and a white tie.

MABEL."

Something in him raged   Dear Pip—indeed!   How these women treated a man like a dog to be patted or smacked, or led him out to some social occasion!   He got up and went into the villa, having told the maid to wait.   The reaction was surprising.   Having had his pride badly thrashed by one woman he should have hurried to the other to have it healed, but he did nothing of the sort.   Mrs. Marrish's sheet of paper enraged him, and anger was not the only component.   He was conscious of self-disgust; he felt like a man who had been too much fondled by a sly and persuasive hand.   He had been submerged in woman like Clarence in his butt of malmsey. Life smelt of Quelques Fleurs and hot bath and warm pillow and cigarette-ends. It was stuffy and sensual and smothering.

He wrote his reply.

"MY DEAR MABEL,
Sorry, but I am suffering from an attack of morals. Please excuse me.

ISHERWOOD."

He sent the maid off with the letter, and probably he was too sore and reckless to realize its finality, or to be aware of it as a crude gesture of the unregenerate male. It corresponded to the black eye dealt out by the Bill Sykes man to the woman who pestered him when he was feeling murderous. Isherwood did not pause to reflect, but taking his hat and an old ash-stick, made for the hills above Strozzi's villas, where vineyards and olive groves melted into the grey-green maquis. The path led him above Mabel Marrish's villa, and he paused and sat down on a bank that was starred with purple anemones. On the terrace below him a young Italian was at work with his clumsy mattock, but the tool was not clumsy in his strong brown hands. It bit into the green and weedy soil and pulled it down into a rich, red tilth, and there was something in the steady, stolid inevitableness of the work which fascinated Isherwood. The peasant was a handsome fellow in blue trousers and a loose white shirt; his skin seemed to mix gold and bronze; he had big, black, rogue's eyes.

Isherwood watched him for a while, and then strolled on, to pause again higher up the path, where a twisted pine spread a fan of shadow. He saw the Italian still hacking at the soil, a figure half blue and half white, with the sun on the gloss of its oily black hair. Lower still the very red roof of the Marrish villa looked like a large red cloth laid out to dry on the green of the hill-side.

Isherwood reflected. He thought, "Now, if I had a back and shoulders like that Italian fellow." But the roof of the villa stared at him redly, and he went on to wonder what Mrs. Marrish would make of that letter. Possible she would

think him a peevish fool, a temperamental idiot. It was more
than probable that she would come in her car to collect him
at eight-thirty, and be ready with a half-playful and reproving
pat. Such women were not easily rebuffed, unless they were
ripe for the rebuff.

But he was out in his estimates. Mrs. Marrish had read his
rude note and had torn it up, and dropped it into the waste-
paper basket. She could be as swift and sensational in tearing
things up as she was in the clutching of them. Her air of
easiness was fallacious, and like a cat on a cushion she purred
only when she was pleased. For Isherwood's curt, quick note
had stung her; it was the sort of note that a clever man writes
in a stupid moment to a woman who is neither quite a gentlewoman nor a pretty lady. Its self-conscious rudeness carried
the most intimate of insults.

Her response was, "Very well, my lad, you can go to hell,
or come round and lick my shoes. And if you do—I may
kick you."

She was not sufficiently fastidious or sensitive to feel profoundly hurt. Moreover she had compensations. She was
a little Catherine of Russia. If one man did not please her
she found another. The young Italian of the blue breeches,
when he was not busy with his mattock, cut the grass and
weeded the flower beds in the Marrish garden. She had cast
her blue eyes upon him. Undoubtedly he was Pan.

III

Maria left "The Crater" at six o'clock, for she had a husband
and a family in the background, and of necessity Isherwood's
last meal had to be a cold one, unless he chose to heat up the
soup which Maria left on the stove. Those chilly suppers
taken in an empty house lay heavy upon his soul, and on this
particular evening, when the opal of the day was changing to
jet, Isherwood felt like a man abandoned to the emptiness of
self. Maria always closed the back door of the villa with a
firm hand, and the thud of it had finality. It was like the
rap of a hammer on the nail of another day. The light would
fade and the night close in, and he would sit confronting hours

of loneliness and of sleeplessness, idle hours, when he would sit and stare or dawdle through a book.   He was afraid of the nights and afraid of his bed.   What a helpless creature was man when no woman had the mothering of him.

He had stood at the window and watched the flush of the day dwindle from the hills.   He had seen the taxi pass on its way to Mrs. Marrish's, and he had wondered whether it would stop at his gate on the way to the Hotel Elyseo.   Almost he had wished that it would stop.   Almost he had regretted that sudden peevish letter to her.   He felt so very lonely.   There was no living thing but himself in the house.

Almost he had forgotten the self-shame of the morning, or had it dwindled to a feeling of ineffectualness?   A ridiculous occasion!   Futility standing up to its knees in the sea!

What a fool Billy must have thought him!

He saw the Marrish taxi go past on its way to the Elyseo, a black silhouette against that afterglow upon the hills.   No face showed at the car's window, and he felt abandoned.   But it was his own fault, and yet he felt petulant about it, and ready to cry out, "No one cares."   But why should anyone care for a wretched, moody valetudinarian?   What was there in him that could provoke Billy to care?   Nothing.

There would be dancing at the Elyseo, bright, brisk, syncopated sound, live men and women, movement.   And he felt rather like a forgotten and unwanted child shut up in an empty house.   What a fool he was, what a weak, purposeless creature, as unconvincing to himself as he was to Tindaro.

On the table behind him Maria had left his supper, slices of cold ham and tongue, bread, butter and cheese, bottled cherries in pale pastry.   He felt choked.   He had no stomach for the meal, cold food in an empty house.   An impulse pushed him towards the Café Ceres, lights and the nearness of his fellow humans, for the Café Ceres possessed a little salon and an Italian chef who could cook ravioli.   Afterwards, after the wine and the pungent, native cooking, he could sit at one of the little tables on the Corso and drink coffee and brandy, and smoke, and watch the night-life of provincial Italy.   Other men would be there, even if they had to be Botterel and Warner and Little Cobb. He wanted men, any sort of men. He was sick of women.

So he put on his hat and his overcoat, and leaving that cold meal to Maria and the morning, he went down the hill towards the lights of Tindaro.

CHAPTER XXX

I

A MOON had risen, and the cypress avenue of the Villa
of the Flute was itself a flute, piping moonlight with
a round and silver note between each tree. Mr. Jevens, walking with Billy to the iron gates, and rather like a cardboard
figure with its long legs attached by wires, joined his dry voice to
the night's mystery.

"Yes, I think we can do something about it. You might
make tactful inquiries. Savelli's no fool."

He opened one of the iron gates for Billy, and raised his
panama hat. That hat and Mr. Jevens were inseparable; it
had to enjoy with him the moonlight.

"Pity that fellow Isherwood isn't employable. I'd prefer
an Englishman, even though he hasn't all the local knowledge.
You know where you are with a Britisher."

There was something tentative and questioning in the cock
of his head.

"I suppose he is a washout? Or—is it——?"

Billy folded her fur coat over her frock.

"No, gossip, partly. He had to come out here for his health.
I believe he had quite a reputation at home."

"As a practical man?"

"I gather so. You know, Mr. Jevens, a man is apt to go
to seed without a job, especially in Tindaro."

"That's understandable. Same here. There's something
muggy and slack about these places. Well, we'll think it over.
Good night."

She heard him close the gate behind her, and the faint clang
of it had an inward, personal echo. She was excited, strung
up; even the moonlight was tense and tremulous, and the rough
road velvet to her feet. Mr. Jevens's dry voice still seemed to

follow her. What a dry stick he was, but a sound stick, not cut out for gestures and gesticulations, but good ash. She liked the man. He had a thin, quiet, forcefulness, wisdom, a whimsical yet kind look for his wife and her watering-can. And he, too, had discovered the Circe in Tindaro, and realized the perils of the place for men of blue eyes and pale skins. In Tindaro work and hard, lean living were as potent as Miss Lord's cold bath.

Billy saw the lights of Tindaro; they blinked at her like sleepy eyes, cats' eyes. They were neither sinister nor beautiful; it depended upon your mood. And she felt strangely strung up and excited and compassionate. The moon was like a dot to the question mark of the night. If—if——! But why would her thoughts persist in trailing a question? Why had they ceased to be celibate and self-centred? A man and a little stool, a man foolishly wading out to her from the sea. How idiotic and inevitable it all was!

But she thought, "I must tell Julia. It's not a castle in Spain. Old Jevens doesn't indulge in castles in Spain."

She paused for a moment close to a wayside shrine with its gaudy Madonna and pink Child, sheltering behind a panel of wire-netting in the plastered niche. The new and the old were mingled; the Holy Virgin had to be protected from the infant and educated Italy which threw stones. Yes, that was just like Tindaro, our Lady of the Peach Blossom, and the flies of the Café Ceres, and wire-netting for the salvation of saints. She was aware of life and herself as a most extraordinary mixture. There lay Tindaro in the moonlight between the mountains and the sea, and she was wise as to all its beauty and its ugliness, and her affection for this faded, odorous Italian town. She had loved it and loathed it, and now she had come to love it again, because it was like life, something that could not be helped, and had to be lived in and worked in, whether you wept or laughed.

She went on down into Tindaro. She followed one of the dark little vicolos, steep as a mountain stream. It led her into the Corso, and much of the Corso was asleep. The shops had closed their little, tired eyelids; only the barbers were busy shaving and chattering into the night. But the Corso had mystery, with the moonlight aslant upon it, and one side of the street all shadow, the other banded with lights, its balconies and shutters sharply etched upon the white walls. Here and there a waiting figure filled a dim doorway or the mouth of an arch or passage; or some prowling youth walked the streets unsatisfied. To Billy every house was familiar, and yet remaining secret and aloof. The sign of the English Agency saluted her, and she lingered for a moment, looking at it with an upward and half-whimsical smile, a Jevens smile. The office of the English Agency had been her *lararium*, and in it she had offered her sacrifices to her gods; Efficiency, Accomplishment, the I Will and I Can in herself. But there were other gods.

She passed on. The smudge of light which was the Café Ceres came into view. Tented by the white awning, the little white-topped tables and green chairs were still awake, and the melancholy and faded tinkling of its orchestra was like the music of ghosts plucking and scraping at ghostly strings. Tommaso's white apron bulged in the doorway. Billy's head went up. She had a feeling of tension as she drew near to the Café Ceres; it was as though she set her shoulders and walked resolutely. He might be there, and she was no stooping lady. She was aware of a little group of men, but Isherwood was not among them. She gave the group one full-eyed, steady glance, and glances came back to her, surreptitious, sinister, mocking.

She passed on. She heard a man's voice, Little Cobb's.

"Didn't know Miss Capability did street-walking."

There was laughter, silly sensual laughter. She felt the whip of her scorn tingling. What silly, cheap fools some men were, idiotic beasts! And he consorted with such creatures. But was it because he wished it, or was it because of a kind of weariness, because he felt so desperately lonely and finished, because the other smug people hurt him? She remembered how Frevick had stuck out his long and melancholy legs under one of those tables. Did a man surrender to Circe because he was unhappy, and because no one cared whether he fought or died? But if someone cared, then the urge of life might again become sacred.

II

She had turned up past the Hotel St. George, and was beginning to climb the hill where the lane ran between two high white walls, when she saw a man's figure in front of her. The moon was shining along the lane, and the high walls and the surface of the road were like the sides and bottom of a long and narrow box, and the figure ahead of her gave her the impression of something dark and alive, a drugged insect blundering in a collector's case. When she first saw him he was leaning against the left-hand wall, like a patch of shadow or some dark object attached to the moonlit surface, but at the moment of her pausing to stand at gaze, she saw the dark patch begin to move. It seemed to be feeling its way along the wall, rubbing against it with one arm and shoulder. It needed the support of the wall.

Isherwood!

She knew it without knowing how she knew. She was conscious of a sudden pang, a sense of tension as though something in herself was being drawn taut to the point of tearing. She could feel her heart-beats quick and hard under her left breast. The white walls had a dense glare. They shut her in with her crisis.

She went quickly on. Nothing was deliberate or willed; she was just a white-faced, angry impulse, though anger was the mere froth on the surface. As she overtook his unsteady, laborious figure he seemed to become aware of her footsteps. He paused, and turning slowly with his back propped against the wall, he stared at her. His face was both vacant and infinitely wise. The legs of him were more fuddled than his head.

"O, so—it's Miss Brown. Good evening, Miss Brown."

She felt the flare of her impulse. His face was a white surface asking to be marked. It was like a white page upon which she had to scrawl a passionate protest.

She said, "How beastly of you, how utterly beastly."

He just stood propped against the wall and stared. His hands hung down. Did he understand, or was he too bemused and sodden? She felt and knew that he had to understand.

He did understand. He had the reckless clarity which comes to some men in their cups. He had lost his inhibiting self-consciousness. He saw himself and her as two naked souls shut in between two high walls.

"Does it matter?"

The challenge had been thrown back, and she stood off, breathing more quickly.

"Is that for me——?"

He caught her up with sudden fierceness.

"Why should it be? Who the devil cares? Can't one go to the dogs in one's own way? It simply doesn't matter."

For the moment she could think of nothing to say. Nor did she look at his face, but at his hands, which were pressed with spread fingers against the wall. Almost she could feel them pressing against the wall.

"Oh, as you please. If you must be——"

"Who asked you to preach. You women who are so damned superior——"

There was silence. She felt that something had struck her, and that she was numb and a little bewildered. This ferocity ——! She was aware of his feet moving with a kind of clumsy carefulness, as though they were not to be trusted. He was sliding away from her along the wall.

"You let other people's souls alone. No bloody right to interfere. Besides——"

She stood still; she felt him going; something seemed to struggle in her, to clutch and strive towards the surface out of the deeps of her feeling. For a moment she could not move. He was passing away like a shadow along the wall. She wanted to cry out.

III

She did cry out, but her voice was strangely smothered. He had gone less than ten yards when the articulate woman in

L

her tore its way to the surface.   Her movement towards him
was like the quick gliding of a shadow.

"Tom, don't——"

He stood still.   He appeared rigid, his arms pressed against
the wall.   His eyes stared.

"Don't—don't drink.   I can't bear it."

The stare seemed to go out of his eyes.   He was profoundly
astonished, as though the moon had fallen out of the sky and
rolled at his feet, but astonishment was the mere edge of the
cloud.   His face seemed to darken; it ceased to be like the
wall, a glaring, defiant surface.   He was trying to say something,
and no words came.

"I'm sorry."

She looked ashamed, confused.

"O, it's all right."

"I wonder!"

"Yes—I'm afraid I——"

But he was supremely sober now, and more than sober.
The white walls were surfaces of illumination.   He seemed
to be standing with her in a fierce white light, but behind her
was the softness of a shadow.

He said, "I'm sorry.   I've got to ask you a question.   I
hadn't the insolence to believe——"

He gave a kind of shrug, but his hands were no longer
pressed against the wall.

"What I mean is—I'm not quite the sort of beast—Well,
it didn't seem to matter.   I've got all crooked, and yet it didn't
seem worth while to straighten things out.   But if—what you
said just now——"

His voice had a sudden gentleness.   The crude, white glare
had gone.   He was the man who loved her, and was ashamed,
and yet had found a kind of courage.

"If what you said just now——"

She was looking at his hands.

"Yes, I said it.   I meant it."

She let her eyes meet his.

"I'm sorry.   It was forced out of me—somehow——"

"Sorry!"

"No. Not in that way. You see, it does matter."

He looked at her with an air of profound stillness, but within him there were other and profound movements.

"Good God—it's I who am sorry."

He was standing clear of the wall now.

"You see—a man couldn't realize, could he, not the sort of man that I have been lately? I mean—some things seem so impossible. One wanted them—and they seemed like that moon. There's so much that you couldn't possibly understand."

Her face seemed to float. It had an expression of tender whimsicality.

"Sure?"

"You're too clean."

"O, I don't know. I had a sort of hardness. But when things hurt——"

Again he was silent, looking at her, and she suffered him to look at her in that particular way. It was as though he touched her, tentatively and wonderingly. It was as though he could not believe it.

"Things hurt. You—— But could I have been anything but a blind beast? I was a beast—because—well, it didn't seem possible that it could matter. But—that—too—was a rotten sort of cowardice. One was so damned lonely, and I thought——"

He seemed to grow inarticulate. Some things could not be said; they were too deep or too difficult. Also, he felt himself recoiling from mere words, from the dreadful facility of the insincere. What could you say when a woman like Billy tore out her heart and showed it to you? And there was the same moon which had suddenly ceased to be a sot's lantern, and had become the face of the eternal mother.

His right hand made an awkward gesture.

"It can't be said—somehow. You have done a rather wonderful thing to me. I'm feeling down in the dirt."

"Need you?"

"For the good of my soul."

And then the solitude was broken from them by the voices

of men, peasants who had been drinking at one of the little wine shops in Tindaro and were returning to the hills. One of them carried a pipe, and as they came up the lane he piped a little plaintive tune tremulous in the moonlight.

They looked at each other, and in her eyes he read the question.

"Can you?"

"Yes, now."

He walked quite steadily, and they went up the hill together in silence, with the piping and the voices following. They came to Julia Lord's villa, and here Isherwood paused as though he knew that the night had brought them to the parting of the ways.

She said, "I am going in to see Julia."

He replied with a consenting movement of the head.

"Great woman—Miss Lord. Some women make one—— Yes, you have."

She held out a hand.

"It's reality."

He raised her hand and bending, touched it with his lips.

"That's how a man may feel. There are no words. But— reality."

"Good night."

"Good night."

IV

On this most warm and gentle night Julia Lord was sitting in her garden. She had put Frevick's yellow dog to bed in her basket in a corner of the bedroom, and had gone forth into the moonlight. A very sleepy Maria, opening the door to Billy, was yet sufficiently awake to look appreciatively at Miss Brown's fur coat. Maria wanted to stroke it.

"In the garden, Mees."

"Right. I'll go round the house."

She found Julia Lord on the terrace, between two of the cypresses. There was a vacant chair, and she sat down and remembered that she had set out for the Villa Vesta for the purpose of telling her partner about Mr. Jevens and Capo

Moro, but for the moment that project was as far away as the sea, a kind of glimmering background. She knew now that she was going to tell Julia Lord about Isherwood.

"Well—what luck?"

Billy sat at gaze.

"I think he means to fall to the scheme, though Mrs. J. tried to drown it with her watering-can. But I came here to tell you about something else."

Her voice sounded tired.

"You may think me a fool. I found him in the lane down there. He had been drinking. Well—I let go."

Her face caught the moonlight, though the edge of the shadow of one of the cypresses lay across her knees. Her whole figure had a stillness.

"Isherwood?"

"Yes."

Miss Lord moved restlessly in her chair.

"How much did you let go?"

"O, rather badly. You see—it kind of rends me to see him going to the devil. Funny world. I thought I had finished with that sort of thing."

Julia Lord seemed to hold her breath.

"And what did he——?"

"He seemed to get sober all in a flash. He said he'd behaved like a beast—because he thought no one cared."

"Men do, my dear."

There was a silence, and then Billy's voice lost its tiredness.

"Julie, are we silly fools? Does a man ever—change? Can one pull them out of the mud?"

"It depends."

"It's such a ghastly venture. I mean—when you care, and when you know that you are in it—or could be in it up to the neck. He makes something in me feel all tears."

Miss Lord was silent. She was silent for quite a long time. She was struggling with a memory, and forcing herself to say things, to uncover old wounds.

"You remember Frevick."

"Remember! Why—I never feel he is dead—somehow."

"Twenty years ago, Frevick was Isherwood, just that. And I——"

It was Billy's turn to be silent, profoundly and tensely silent.

"I—was a rather hard young person. I had a living to make. I had views, rather merciless views. Tom and I—— O, well, I was the sort of capable idiot who thought you could make people do things or not do things—by preaching at them. One can't, you know."

"Julie——! You dear thing."

"O, yes, I learnt my lesson a good many years too late. You get things by loving, not by scolding. It's so often the clever people who are the silly fools."

Again there was silence, and the shadow of the tree crept round and covered Billy's face. She sat for a while in the shadow, and then moved her chair nearer to Julia Lord's.

"Julie, you've done a great thing. But I want to ask you——"

"Well?"

"If you had known—I mean—if it could happen again, you'd risk it?"

"Yes."

"Even if——?"

"After all—life's not a cotton-wool affair. Life means taking risks."

CHAPTER XXXI

I

TOM ISHERWOOD walked very slowly up the last of the hill to "The Crater." He felt that he had no legs, or that the lower part of him had gone to sleep, but that the point that mattered was like the moonlight. What a night! The piper and the voices had gone past him up the hill-side, and everything had grown silent. He had the same kind of silence inside him, a wondering, astonished, sacred silence.

He opened the gate and went in, but he did not enter the house. He did not want to enter the house. It was like a little painted hutch in which a sick animal had been shut up, and he had escaped from it into the moonlight and the air. He wanted to stay in the moonlight, in the midst of this wonderful night. He remembered that he had left the wooden stool by the door, and he fetched it, and carrying it under one of the olive trees sat down. He was conscious of a sudden tremor of laughter, tender laughter. This stool, the first of his household possessions, a support for the weary, a stool for the penitent. But he felt neither weary nor penitent. Something in him had been restored, his sense of beauty, his belief in the essence of things, his faith in life as a process that did not lead to the pig-tub. In him a boyishness was reborn.

He sat and marvelled. Billy! That it should have happened just in that way! Would he ever forget those sudden words of hers and her way of uttering them? "I can't bear it." And he was conscious both of humility and exultation. He knew. No, by God, she would not have to bear it. He would see to that. She had spoken, and he would wash and be clean.

But his attention was caught by a sound in the valley below. It grew louder, and ascended; it was made by a noisy old car climbing on second gear from the Corso to the terrace where Strozzi's villas stood. It was the Marrish car. Isherwood sat and listened, and realized that he had forgotten Mrs. Marrish, Quelques Fleurs, and cigarette smoke and hot bath. Good lord! Something in him felt whipped to a new and naked fineness. No subterfuges.

The headlights of the car as it turned the corner threw their glare into the tops of the olive trees above his head. The foliage was effulgent for a moment, and then recovered the moonlight and the shadows. The car swept noisily past, its slack, worn gears screaming, and Isherwood's face had a sternness.

"Good night, my lady. For what we have received may the Lord make us sorry. My fault as much as yours."

He sat on. The car returned and helped itself with screeching brakes down the curves of the hill. The discords died away, and the silence smoothed itself out like water. Isherwood sat on. He felt that he could sit there for ever and ever, confronting the to-morrow, his to-morrow and Billy's.

He thought, "I must tell her about that woman. Pretty beastly, but it has to be done. Perhaps she'll understand, perhaps she won't. If it is to be a resurrection, let's be honest about burying all the nasty old skeletons."

But he did wish that he had not to tell her about Mrs. Marrish. Billy was so clean, and to have to begin by showing her this soiled affair seemed like damning yourself on the very first day. It would hurt her, and he realized that he was afraid of hurting her. Why tell? He had heard it argued that a clumsy conscience made a poor courtier, and that a woman might thank a man for leaving his past adventures with his bankers or his lawyer. Why be clumsy and over-conscientious and sesquipedalian? And yet——? Was Billy the kind of woman who would appreciate an accommodating cowardice, the consideration of a tactful and lying silence? She had courage. She was not the older sort of woman who expected life to be presented to her like a chocolate box with a pretty picture and a pink bow on the lid. Had not she used the word reality? Obviously it was his business to be real man to

her, and to prove—if she would suffer it—that he was capable
of other realities.

II

Miss Soulby had removed the cover from her typewriter,
and Billy was at her desk opening the morning letters when
Isherwood entered the office of the English Agency.   He
looked younger.   The slouch had gone out of his shoulders,
he had put on a newish suit, and his blue collar matched his shirt.
Also, he had visited the barber's on his way down the Corso.

But the transfiguration, stripped of its more crude externals,
showed itself in his movements.   They were more crisp and
more controlled.   Also he appeared less self-conscious.

"Good morning."

Almost he had the air of a man who had come in to see
Billy on business.   He stood in front of her desk, holding his
hat and stick.   There was no smile in him at the moment.

"Can I see you—on business?"

Looking up at him she understood, or felt that she understood.

"Yes.   I am free for ten minutes."

She turned to Miss Soulby.

"Miss Soulby, would you mind going into the library, and
waiting."

Miss Soulby's pince-nez glimmered.   She arose and disappeared, with her sloping shoulders and meek neck somehow
registering a protest.

Billy, with her elbows resting on the desk and a red pencil
joining her two hands, looked steadily at Isherwood.

"Won't you sit down?"

"No, I'd rather stand."

And he stood very still.   His face had an unwavering
seriousness.   He gave her the impression of a man who had
grown taut and firm in his clothes, and that the creases had been
pressed out of them.   His blue eyes had a severity, but not towards her.   Her feeling was that he had left all emotion upon
her doorstep.   He had not come in to her with a spongeful
of wine and hyssop.

L*

"About last night."

The pencil was under tension.

"Well, what about it?"

"I didn't thank you. I have come to thank you. But that's not all. When this sort of thing happens, a kind of sincerity flares up in me. Rather like that moon last night and the white walls. There's something about you that makes me most horribly afraid of slush."

Her eyes looked past him.

"Thank you."

"O, don't thank me for anything. I just want you to listen. I have to say these things or feel that I should be much more of a beast than I ever was."

"Were you a beast? Wasn't it——?"

And suddenly he looked fierce, just as she had seen men look fierce in the heat and striving of a game.

"No, don't make it easy for me—in that way. I want to wash and be clean. I want to burn all the old clothes. But to begin with—it wasn't only the stuff you get at the Ceres."

Her eyes fell. One hand rested on her writing-pad.

"O, I see."

"I let go. I don't ask you to understand just how and why a man goes with a woman. It may look like everything, and means nothing. But it happened. If you think I'm a beast for telling you this, well—there it is. I felt that I had to tell you."

She began to scribble figures in pencil on her writing-pad.

"That's your idea of thoroughness."

"It's my idea of thoroughness—with you. No subterfuges, all the cards on the table."

She seemed to reflect.

"It's a rather sound idea. By the way—I had a sort of affair three years ago."

"Here?"

"Yes. Though I didn't go quite so far—as you."

Almost her voice was casual. He looked at her brown head, and at the pencil scribbling nothings. He was a little whiter about the lips.

"Thank you.   I don't ask any questions."

"It was something and nothing.   I got over it."

"You mean to say——"

"The man's dead.   He was rather a rotter."

There was silence.   And then she put down her pencil, and looked at him, and her brown eyes were steady.

"So, that's that.   We are being very businesslike, aren't we?" She saw his face take on a kind of sheen.

"Exactly.   This—is—business.   Do you think I'm going to be content with an easy attitude—after the big thing you did last night, and the big thing you've done just now.   I'm going about with a scourge.   We spoke of realities."

She nodded.

"We did."

"That's it.   I've got to be a reality.   I've got to show you that I'm a reality.   No mere facile tosh.   I'm out to prove something.   Do you understand?"

Her eyes had a light in them.

"Perfectly.   I'm glad."

III

Sentimental people said of Stella Burt that she was like a Burne-Jones woman, "So mysterious, you know," but perfectly sweet when you got to know her, which nobody did save her husband, and to him her real mystery was apparent.   In his playful moments he would call her "Mother Eve," or hint at her reincarnations, for she had seemed to live in many centuries and places, Babylon and Thebes and Knossos, Argos, Rome, Seville.   But he would never have placed her in Paris. She could be so silent.   She would sit and look at people with her far-away eyes, and listen to their voices, and afterwards she would be able to tell Burt all manner of things about them, things that astonished him.   She seemed to see right down into people, into that something which is like water in a well, the intimate, dark mirror of self.

Few people knew Stella Burt in her garden.   She did not encourage them to enter her garden, and especially so in the early morning when she was cutting flowers.   She liked to be deliberate and to dream a little before she cut a particular flower. She would touch it softly with her fingers. "Pretty dear." They had eyes for her, rose eyes and pansy eyes, and the little peeping eyes of violets. She was not at all Marrish in her garden. Usually she wore an old black mackintosh, but above this dark sheath her little, graceful head was flowerlike.

Isherwood found her snipping roses, with a flat basket slung over her left arm. She made him think of Madame La Rêve with the dew upon her. She had the dew in her eyes.

He raised his hat, "I have come to catch your husband."

She looked at Isherwood and saw him as she might have seen the Isherwood of twenty years ago, but with a little grizzle of grey above his ears, and in his eyes that something which youth has not. She knew one of her moments of inward seeing. She saw right down into the deep well of him.

"You'll find him in his study."

She was aware of Isherwood looking at the roses in her basket, and his look had a kind of tenderness. There were very few men who could look at flowers in that way.

She said, "I don't think they mind it—really."

His consciousness was as quick as his smile.

"No. Not as you do it. They understand."

She picked up one of the flowers, glanced at it, and gave it to him.

"Good luck."

"Thank you. I don't deserve it."

He went in carrying the rose, and pausing in the hall as though he belonged there, tucked the rose into his buttonhole. He knew Burt's door; he knocked, having a feeling that other doors were opening to him.

"Come in."

He saw Burt's solid head and massive shoulders. The doctor held part of a little glass vase in his hand, its surface opalescent with the patina of age. A pipe stuck out from his laconic jowl. No wonder that some of the superficial people spoke of the Burts as "Beauty and the Beast." Yet his big hands could handle some fragile piece of glass as gently as his wife touched a flower.

"Sorry to be a pig, doctor."

"Why pig?"

"Rooting you out half an hour after breakfast."

"In my private sty or pig pound!   Look at that bit of glass, and the bloom of centuries on it."

He held it out to Isherwood who took it daintily and carefully into the cup of his hand.

"Yes, lovely.   Translucent mother-of-pearl on glass.   Are you going to illustrate it?"

"Would if I could.   I wish poor old Frevick——"

He looked at Isherwood's face and was silent, for he, too, could not help realizing Isherwood's new surface.

"Nothing wrong?"

"No."

"Nothing professional—then?"

"No, not exactly."

Isherwood replaced the remnant of a vase gently on Burt's desk.

"Not exactly.   But I want you to prescribe for me.   You might be able to.   I want a job."

The doctor's pipe had gone out and he relit it.   He smoked very big pipes, solid as himself.

"A job.   Well—why not!"

"Why not!   But what?"

"Any ideas?"

"O, some.   I think of taking seriously to Frevick's legacy. And then it occurred to me——   You can damn my cheek, if you like."

"How?"

"I have been wondering whether I could devil for you, sketch and illustrate.   I can do black and white work.   I don't want paying.   But when you go archæologizing I could draw things and make plans, if you would let me come along."

"It's an idea.   Well, why not?   I'm an absolute fumbler with a pencil or etching pen."

"Great.   It's awfully good of you, Burt."

"Not a bit.   I get a draughtsman for nothing.   I'll vet you for nothing as a protest."

Isherwood walked to the window, and stood with his back to Burt. He had a view of the hills, pinewoods, olive groves, little houses glimmering white, here and there a smother of fruit blossom.

"People are awfully decent. Fact is—I've pulled up my socks. Got to keep them up. Suspenders—you know. Work's that sort of thing."

Burt blew a little cloud of smoke.

"Better than anything in a bottle. I'm going out for most of the day on Sunday. I'm working up at Eryx on stuff that seems to link up with Mycenæ and Crete. Come along."

"I will."

IV

Mr. Jevens, feeling the need of adventure, and having driven his big Fiat within three hundred yards of Eryx, was constrained to descend from his chariot. The road, sufficiently adventurous, a series of loops slung along the rocky hill-side, died away suddenly in front of the chapel of St. Joseph, and the thread of the ascent was left in the hands of a mule path. Mr. Jevens took off his dustcoat and handed it to his Italian chauffeur.

"Better try and turn her here, John."

He had put the wind up his chauffeur, and a stiffish breeze blew over Eryx, and leaving Giovanni—whom he would call John—to turn the car on that narrow, rocky platform, he went on and up towards Eryx. Almost it was like scaling a stone ladder that leaned against the blue wall of the sky.

Mr. Jevens paused occasionally to get his breath and to look at the view. He could see Tindaro like a toy town, and forty miles of coastland laced with foam, and league upon league of wind-whipped sea. Mr. Jevens's thin face seemed to turn a sharp edge to the wind. He felt good, in spite of his trumpery chest. He had been climbing like this all his days, frail and indefatigable, leaving the stout, full-fleshed fellows behind him pottering about hitting little balls, or growing fuddled and suffused round card-tables. Mr. Jevens had a way of referring to that world as "Two B's and a G," which meant "Bridge, Bar, and Golf."

He arrived at Eryx, where the wind whistled over a jumble of rocks and cyclopean walls, and the sun brought out the lizards. It was indeed a citadel scraping the blue of the sky, and in a sheltered corner Mr. Jevens saw a man in an old brown suit and wearing a floppy hat, sitting on a chunk of stone and sketching something. It was Isherwood. The brownness of him had a tinge of gold. He was so intent upon his work that he did not see Mr. Jevens's lathlike figure inserting itself into the sunlight. Nor did he hear Mr. Jevens, for Mr. Jevens wore crêpe-soled shoes.

Mr. Jevens commented to himself on Isherwood.

"This architect chap. He's not so flat in the eye as I thought. Must have some drive to get up here. You don't get up here on alcohol and three no-trumps."

He picked his way towards Isherwood on his long, stiltlike legs. He had pushed back his panama hat till it sat on his head like a Corinthian helmet thrust back after the battle. He addressed Isherwood.

"Nothing much wrong with this observation-post, sir."

Isherwood laughed at him consideringly, and smiled.

"Not when you've got here."

Mr. Jevens, with his head on one side like a bird attentive towards a worm, carried the subject further.

"Yes, but the getting there, that's the great game. Not sitting in a drawing-room full of women and talking about it. Out by yourself, sweating, and puffing and blowing. What the devil for? Because you've got to. Something in you won't be satisfied with sitting still and talking."

He, too, sat down on a mass of sun-warmed stone, but as the man who had done his climbing and had arrived. He was observing Isherwood, and the texture of Isherwood's skin, and the clearness of the whites of Isherwood's eyes. A month ago this architect fellow might have been drinking too much and living the life, but Isherwood on Eryx had the eyes of a man who saw life steadily and saw it whole.

"What's that you're doing? Don't mind me asking questions?"

Isherwood pointed with his pencil to the remains of a wall,

the base of an archaic pillar, and two steps that had been worn by many feet.

"Sketching that for Burt."

"Illustrations for that book of his?"

"Possibly."

"That's one of the things I've never had a shot at, writing a book."

"Same here.   But it's only a difference of material, I suppose. Words, bricks, paints, figures, or bales of wool and cotton."

Mr. Jevens's sharp face showed an edge.

"That's new, for one of you artist people to include the arithmetic and the merchandise.   Most of you won't allow us that."

"Creation?"

"That's it.   We aren't all mere manipulators.   There's balance and form in business, the rhythm of your machines and your ships—you know.   It's a sort of building up."

Isherwood nodded, and continued to sketch.

"Lot of tosh talked about art and books.   After all, it's life one is after, and not to render the muddy skin of a highbrow clique.   I'm not much of a talker."

"Same here," said Mr. Jevens, getting up, and going to look over Isherwood's shoulder.   "Don't mind me, I'm just interested."

But he was more interested in Isherwood's right hand than in the sketch it was producing.   He watched the hand for a moment and thought "This chap's all right.   Nothing shaky about that.   Looks as though he could draw a straight line without a ruler.   No pose either.   Can't stand the arty-booky fellows who get on their hind legs.   Clever clowns.   A place like Tindaro is a regular monkey-cage.   Billy Brown's a good business woman."

He cleared his throat, a little self-conscious trick of his, like that of a public speaker in the act of rising with "Ladies and gentlemen" on his tongue.

"Ever thought of taking the job up—here."

Isherwood looked up and round at him.

"What job?"

"Designing houses."

"No, I hadn't. No scope. Though—of course—one might do it just for the fun of the thing."

Said Mr. Jevens drily, "Well, isn't that why we do things, just for the fun of doing them? My wife's obsession is watering the garden. Well, I just let her water it. Obviously."

CHAPTER XXXII

I

ON the wall of the office of her intimate self Billy had posted the notice "Business as Usual," yet there are varying ways of doing business, and the objective may enlarge itself. The facile phrase advertises the superficial. Risks must be taken, and partnerships are hazardous.

When Mr. Jevens had given her his views on a particular question she sat down at her desk and wrote a letter. On paper it appeared as the most ordinary of letters, an unadorned and practical product of "The English Agency," and yet, like an official declaration of war or the propounding of a policy, it presaged much interference with the affairs of men.

> "Dear Mr. Isherwood,
>
> I shall be glad if you will call on me to discuss a business matter that has arisen. Can you see me to-morrow, preferably about ten o'clock?
>
> Sincerely yours,
> B. I. Brown."

Isherwood found the letter waiting for him on returning from a day's work at Eryx. It left the romanticist in him unchallenged, for if Billy chose to be practical and abrupt, that was her method, nor was it unpleasing. It plunged one into fresh, cold water. Moreover, Isherwood knew that there were two Billies, and that the voice of the Billy of the English Agency was not the voice of the Billy whom he met in Julia Lord's garden. She varied her methods. She was both Billy and the woman of affairs, practical affairs. After his dose of Marrish a little ice in the cup was refreshing.

He smiled over her letter and put it in his pocket. Dear Mr. Isherwood! He supposed that there were young women who would have addressed him as "Dear Ishy," and certainly he preferred Billy's formality, the flower of her young dignity. Her smile never lost itself in lubberly laughter. Her sincerity was as abrupt as Eyrx with the blue of the sky behind it.

Possibly he murmured the words, "Business as usual," for was not three-quarters of life business, and the other quarter the cool of the day in your garden. Green grass and a hose playing, and the flowers drinking deep. Billy had deeps for a man to peer into. Raise the marble well cover and there were profundities. She was no shallow, pretty, neat-mouthed little Miss with a head like a smooth green pea.

But this business? He did not suspect its nature. Did Strozzi want to put up his rent? There was an unexpectedness about Billy. He bathed with her every morning, though his swimming was a leisurely affair compared with hers. Blue sea and yellow sand and the Island of the Triton! Did he realize that she adapted her swimming strength to his and curtailed her swiftness, and kept a watchful eye upon him? She convoyed him. In the sea and on the sands she called him "Tom."

They did not indulge in splurgings and splashings. They swam rather seriously to the Island of the Triton and sat on the rocks in the sun, and had not a great deal to say. But they looked at each other; they absorbed each other; they day-dreamed.

But always Billy had her brown eyes on an inward clock and upon the inadequacies of his sun-browned body.

"Time to go back."

Abruptly she would slip into the sea, and he would follow her. They did not trouble to wonder whether Mr. Sudbury Smith was busy with his telescope, for they were away and beyond the Sudbury Smith world and its lenses.

Perhaps Billy would realize Isherwood as being a little out of breath, but that he was none the worse for it. He held on; he had ceased to let go. The climb back to Tindaro, leisurely yet purposeful, had ceased to distress him. The impatience of youth was curbed in her; she had climbed to an understanding of life, and to compassion.

Isherwood was punctual.   The bells and clocks of Tindaro were tinkling and clanging when he opened the glazed door of the English Agency and saw Billy the business woman at her desk.   The cover had not been removed from Miss Soulby's typewriter, for Miss Soulby had been given a day off.   There was an Isherwood who was subtly amused, and an Isherwood who loved, and an Isherwood who felt like a lad calling upon his tutor.   He saw Billy both as Miss Capability Brown and as Billy, and the merging of her personalities resulted in no hard and chilly product, but exhibited a delicious and unexpected freshness.   She was on exhibition as the business woman.

"Good morning."

He laid his hat and stick on the table.

"I got your letter."

"Good.   Sit down."

Isherwood sat down.   He was impressed by her serious face, by her friendly formalism.   He felt that she was offering him a share in her pragmatism, and that her very seriousness was symbolical.   It piqued him.   It was so deliciously cool and unsentimental and real, like the sea they swam in, or the blue sky above Eryx.

He waited.   She drew a notebook towards her, and fingered a pencil.

"It is my job to interview you officially about a scheme the Agency has in hand."

His eyes widened a little.

"Oh.   How officially?   Am I——?"

"You know Mr. Jevens?"

"Slightly."

"I'll explain.   Some time ago I got the idea that Capo Moro was ripe for development.   It's an absolutely unique site, a second Cap Ferrat or Cap Martin.   But of course I hadn't the backing behind me, financially I mean, until I managed to interest Jevens.   Well, I have interested Jevens. He is going to finance us."

"You mean he is going to buy Capo Moro?"

"A syndicate is, and he is most of the syndicate.   I'm in it; so is Savelli, his Italian partner."

"To develop and build?"

"Exactly."

They looked at each other across the width of her desk. She was not smiling, and yet far back in her brown eyes he seemed to see a little glimmering light, like a light in the deeps of a house at night. He had a feeling of being poised on the edge of adventure. He guessed what was coming, and the lover in him stood still and waited.

"The point is we want one technical man, our architect and surveyor. Old Jevens is prejudiced in favour of someone who is English."

"And you?"

"Well, yes, somewhat. So what about it?"

He was suddenly and deeply moved. It was as though she had taken him up Eryx and shown to him a new world, a new Tindaro, a new self. And for a little while he was silent, looking at the papers on her desk, and aware of her as a waiting presence in this cool, clean room. Had she not been what she was he might have felt humiliated, but she was no more humiliating than a summer morning waiting upon love and life with clear and steadfast eyes. She was both an invitation and a challenge, a woman who could sit still and be silent and let a man get his grip on things.

He had to get a grip upon things. He rose and walked to the other end of the office, and looked at one of the posters on the yellow walls, and came back to her desk and stood looking at her.

"You're a rather wonderful person. But this—is not strictly business, is it? I mean, such personal references——?"

She gave him a little upward smile.

"Sentiment should not enter into business."

"No."

"But sometimes——"

"Yes, sometimes. Oh,—I'm stiff in the back all right—again. And you and Jevens think I'm capable?"

"Obviously."

"Thank you. And if I wasn't—I think I should have to be, even if I had to tear my heart out over it. But as a matter of fact——"

"Well, it's your job."

"Exactly."

He stood there looking at her as though he was only just beginning to see her as she was, neither as yesterday nor to-day nor to-morrow, but as Billy Brown, authentic woman, managing life and her Agency as her mother had managed her home. Modern woman emancipated, hostile to the male! What rot! And it occurred to him to think that the clever little journalists would write bright articles about Billy, and call her this and call her that, and get no nearer to the essential Billy than a printing machine gets to the soul of a creator. Certainly he did not see her in the saffron robe and shoes of the classic bride, or carried over the threshold by the bridegroom, nor could he picture her wired and whaleboned like her grandmother, but the body and the soul of her were catholic.

He said, "Well, this is about the best certificate of health I have had. Funny you should have given it to me. And yet it isn't funny. What we call chance."

"I agree with Julia. I don't believe in chance. One should have some sort of plan."

"Boss things instead of being bossed by them."

Her seriousness broke momentarily into what the older people would have called archness.

"Suppose I am a bit bossy! But not really. One has to get on with one's job. Though I can't stand women who are nothing but their job."

"Or men?"

"Oh, a man's rather different. I'm really rather old-fashioned in some ways."

He stood and looked at her.

"I think you are—what was the old word? Adorable? No, in these days that's not adequate. It's obsolete and also too recent. It doesn't go far back enough."

She smiled up at him.

"I'm antediluvian!"

"Not quite. A twentieth-century graft on a stock that came from Eden. But joking apart——"

He rested his hands on her desk.

"Thank you. As man to woman, thank you. Not much more to be said—is there? The proof of the pudding—and all that. I can't gas to you."

"I don't want you to."

"Business as usual, the job of living and going. But—by God—it isn't mere bricks and mortar. It's you—my dear, you from foundation to chimney-pot."

She scribbled something with her pencil.

"We'll do big things, Tom, or anyhow we'll live big. We —exiles!"

II

It was the season when Tindaro began to wear its halo of flies, and to close its shutters, and to realize itself as a southern town no longer sacred to the forestiere. The tables of the Café Ceres dwindled to a single row set back against the windows. Tommaso shed his waistcoat, and wore no collar, and mopped his head as well as the white marble. In the middle of May the Hotels Elyseo and St. George would go to sleep until the autumn, though the Hotel Flora panted and fanned itself through the hot season, and was shabbily at the service of a few Germans and Italians.

The sun blazed. The hill-sides put on the tawny coat of a lion. The road to the station was a ribbon of dust whenever a car passed to and fro.

But the Café Ceres continued. It would continue through all the summer season, with its little drinks and its flies and its tinkling orchestra. The same people sat there, the Cobbs and Botterels and Warners, and the strange women who seemed to grow more bleached and faded and red about the mouth. They sat and watched the other English going home, the taxis and cars and hotel buses rolling down the Corso full of prosperous people who would be seen at Ascot and Wimbledon and Henley. Yellow trunks and green trunks and black trunks, all nicely labelled, were going to that green island in the northern sea.

Isherwood, sitting at a big wooden table in the window of his living room, with one leaf of the shutters hanging open, saw a taxi go by on its way to catch the evening train. It contained Mrs. Marrish, bound for Paris and London, and other sensations, and as the dust raised by the car hung in a dun-coloured cloud, Isherwood laid his pipe on the table and watched the dust cloud slowly disappear. Rum thing life, so incidental and so transient, and full of Marrish if you were Marrish-minded! He smiled.

For he had not spoken to Mrs. Marrish since the day when he had sent her that rude letter, and he sat and reflected upon the shallowness of the physical intimacies. It was no more than taking a bath, a very shallow bath. And probably a woman like Mabel Marrish, with whom you had experienced the most intimate things of the flesh, was no more intimately yours than a public seat in a park. There was no more of her to be known.

To himself he said, "I rather thought such women made trouble. She might have done. Was it that she did not trouble?"

He picked up his pipe and relit it, and realizing that Mrs. Marrish and her world no longer mattered to him he forgot her. His consciousness was centred upon the table and its collection of papers and plans and reference tables, notebooks and bottles of coloured ink, and crayons and tracing-paper, and one of old Frevick's paint-boxes. Work. He sat in his shirt sleeves. The heat was tolerable behind the shutters. Tindaro lazed in the sunlight and the dust.

Presently he looked at his watch. Half-past six. He was to meet Billy at the tower on Capo Moro at seven. He pushed his chair back, put on a brown taffeta coat which lay on a chair, and stuffed a notebook and some plans in his pocket. After Capo Moro they were to have supper with Julia in her garden.

III

Mr. Jevens made a third at the tower. Isherwood had not expected him, but he had no objection to Mr. Jevens, who sat on a patch of scorched grass with his panama hat on the back of his head, and looking, in his brown drill shirt, like a piece of old sandstone.

Billy had climbed the tower, for it still possessed a circular stone staircase, and a vaulted roof. Sitting on the parapet she could look down on the world of Capo Moro and of men.

Mr. Jevens uncrossed his long legs, and looked whimsically at Isherwood.

"Well, Tom, your pockets look big."

He held out a hand for the rough plan Isherwood produced.

"My idea of the roads—in the rough. I ought to get my theodolite this week."

Mr. Jevens studied the plan, and then made a remark that had no apparent bearing upon the matter in hand.

"My wife has given up watering the garden."

But Isherwood was not paying any attention. He was looking up at Billy on her tower, and Billy was looking down at him, and Mr. Jevens, having observed them both, repeated his remark with an air of mischievous gravity.

"Isherwood, I was just saying——"

"What, sir?"

"My wife has given up watering the garden."

Isherwood's face was momentarily vacant.

"Indeed! Is that——?"

"The most portentous and significant event in Tindaro. It means——"

His smile was puckish.

"It means—Marlow. Another garden to water. It means that I shall have to compromise and go home—for four months. Compromise, my dear chap."

Isherwood's eyes dwelt on him with a glimmer of affection. Mr. Jevens was a rather lovable person. You got attached even to his panama hat.

"O, yes, compromise, sir. Especially with watering-cans."

His glance went skywards again towards Billy.

"I shall be hanging on here—for a couple of months."

"Yes," thought Mr. Jevens, "to someone's eyelashes. Obviously."

IV

Jevens's car was waiting for him below the Hotel Elyseo, and when their committee of three had looked at Isherwood's rough plans, and heard him on the subject of the road system most applicable to Capo Moro, Mr. Jevens said good-bye to them and walked up the lane to his car. He was liking Isherwood both professionally and as a man. The fellow had ideas. He had had the reputation of being a visionary person, but when he had taken Billy and Mr. Jevens to the top of the tower and had pointed out to them the lie of the land, and the dip of the strata, and given them his reasons for planning a loop-road to follow the line of the coast, Jevens had realized Isherwood's soundness. Such a road would be more easily constructed than a rectangular system carved out of the rocky plateau. The excavators would be working with the dip and cleavage in their favour, and such stone as would not be put to use could be tumbled into the sea. Also, a road looping the cape would give magnificent sites, and a lengthy frontage, and the higher ground could be left to be developed later if the scheme should prove a success.

Yes, Isherwood was all right. He had not let his imagination run away and play at building beautiful houses. He had begun with the roads, the water mains, the drains, and the electric cables, just as Mr. Jevens had begun his career in the subterranean realities of a London drapery store.

Meanwhile the two on the tower remained there for a while in the cool of the evening. At the end of the month the English Agency would close its doors until the autumn. Billy was going to Ealing, and from Ealing she was taking her mother to Scotland for a month. Julia Lord, who allowed herself to be absurdly limited in her movements by Frevick's little yellow dog, was travelling no farther than the Italian Tyrol.

Billy watched Isherwood folding up his plans and putting them back into his pocket. The figure of him seemed to have been carved anew out of the brown rock of Capo Moro. She realized that he had impressed Mr. Jevens and that nothing but clear, sharp type could leave an impression upon the Jevens mind. And she was happy. She felt that she could survey her scheme of things, as she overlooked Capo Moro from this tower.

She said, "Sound person, Jevens."

"Yes, sound because he can realize the difficulties."

"You impressed him."

His smile was boyish.

"Did I? But Jevens is not the most important person. When you are up in Scotland think of me on this tower. Splendid place for conning the whole cape. I'm rather glad about one thing."

"What's that?"

"We haven't got to turn out those peasant people, at least —not the ones who prefer to stay. After all—they do belong here, and I should loathe messing up their olive groves and vineyards. Plenty of space for us all."

"I'm glad you feel like that."

"You do, too."

"Yes."

He looked at his watch and remembered Julia Lord, but Billy was not quite ready to go. She had something more to say to him, and this tower was so much theirs.

"How long do you think of staying?"

"Oh, about a couple of months. I want to break the back of the surveying. I shall have to adapt myself to metres."

"Don't stay too long."

He looked at her quickly, and realizing that her face was lit by other lights than that of the sun, he withdrew his gaze.

"I shall be in England in July. It isn't only the work here, it's the proving. You understand that. I have to satisfy something in myself."

"Yes, I understand."

CHAPTER XXXIII

I

BILLY was catching the evening train, and Isherwood was with her in the taxi as it bumped and swayed down the road to the station. The heat of the day had passed, but over Tindaro a kind of dusty and tired stillness hung like the oppression of a thunder-cloud. Everything was grey with dust, the aloes and agaves, the cypresses, the olives, the hanging creepers. It was as though Tindaro had grown very old. Yet both sky and sea were vivid, the one a greenish blue, the other a dark amethyst.

They held hands in the taxi. They had little to say to each other. They looked at the sea and the hills, and the Island of the Triton floating like some ghost ship, and Capo Moro black as ebony against the afterglow.

"Don't work too hard."

The swing of the car round a sharp corner made her swing against him. Her hair and hat touched his cheek.

"I shall be al' right."

"Yes, but don't be silly. I stayed out here till August one summer, and I felt like a bit of dry string. Take your siesta, and tell Maria not to use too much oil in the kitchen."

His arm slipped round her.

"What a practical person you are."

"I'm something else, too. Practical people can care."

"And take care. I don't want a hair of your head altered."

As they walked together on to the station platform a star showed over the sea. And a sudden, indefinable sadness smote Billy. It seemed to her that a little chilly wind blew from somewhere, a ghost wind, reminding her of other nights when she had returned to Tindaro feeling lonely and exiled. She looked up at Tindaro, and in the gathering darkness she saw its

344

lights as she had seen them at her first coming, as a handful of sequins sewn to a black cloak, or as silver holes pricked in cardboard. They seemed to flicker. Nor was her chilly, restless wind imagining. Half an old crumpled newspaper, disturbed from its Tindaresque sloth, drifted along the platform and caught her feet.

Almost she shuddered. Absurd incident, absurd sensitiveness! She gave a little laugh.

"Isn't that just like Tindaro! Saying good-bye to you with a piece of old paper."

Isherwood moved the thing on with the toe of a shoe.

"It isn't good-bye. It's a rivederci."

She stood square to him. He was aware of her looking strangely and steadily into his face. Her eyes were big. Her look—somehow—was anxious, questioning, searching. And something in him understood.

Awkwardly, and with a feeling of vehement tenderness, he got hold of one of her hands.

"It's all right, Bill; it's all right. I'm not going under again. Do you think I could?"

And suddenly she put up her face.

"The train's coming. O, Tom, it's so much to me."

"Beloved."

II

In June, Billy looked at another sea, a sea colder and less blue. She bathed in it each morning, for the garden of the little Scotch hotel where she and her mother were staying sloped down to the rocks. Westward a whole fleet of little islands cruised like grey ships, sometimes seen, sometimes invisible, but always mysterious and a little sad. Though Billy's mother did not find them sad. She could sit for hours in a deck chair and feel the spell of those grey and green horizons, and the exquisite delight of having nothing to mend or to cook or to answer. Children brought your horizon down to the very doorstep, and though the house at Ealing had shed Irene and Ronald, Mary Brown's freedom was not yet.

She liked to watch Billy swimming, for Mary Brown had

never concealed from herself her preference for Billy, dear Billy once more, and watching the post for letters. Mary Brown had grown a little tired of her other children and now asked for that peace which passeth understanding, the peace of being yourself. She was not jealous of Isherwood. She had heard a great deal about Isherwood, and had neither been bored nor piqued, and when she saw Billy swimming in the sea, the rescuing of Isherwood had seemed inevitable. Billy was so strong. Yet Mary Brown, a very tired woman, had moments when she wondered whether a rescue could be lasting, and whether one submergence would not lead to others.

For in this Scotch garden, surrounded by the soft hills and the grey blue sea, she had a strange feeling about Billy. This western coast had a feyness. Its eyes, melancholy and grey blue, were as old as the hills, and sometimes as sad. The ancients might say that man is born to trouble as the sparks fly upwards, and Mary's feeling was that some women are born to loneliness. She herself had been a very lonely woman, in spite of a husband and in spite of children. The essential, intimate I in her had never been satisfied. Billy had come more near to her than any other living creature.

Perhaps that was why she felt about Billy as she did, and when Billy spoke of Tindaro and exile and the relativity of such a state, Mary Brown would be made to think of other forms of exile. Some people were born to loneliness, and she herself had been an exile in suburban London. A particular job might be thrust upon you; but it did not alter your apartness; you remained aloof in the midst of the crowd, seemingly busy and occupied, but your life had a kind of silence.

Yet Billy was happy, obviously and perhaps perilously happy. Sitting in a deck chair in that Scotch garden she read her letters and dreamed very practical dreams. Isherwood wrote to her with a touch of gaiety, and with the playfulness of the Englishman when he is very much in earnest. He headed his letter —"From the Tower." He had Capo Moro under his thumb. Maria was making him cool drinks, and he had found an intelligent lad to carry his theodolite and hold measuring-rods.

"I sleep daily and dutifully from twelve till three. The flies really are very considerate.   They attach themselves to your patent fly-papers.

"Yesterday there was a fire on the hills.   It burnt right through the night.   Rather splendid and rather sad.   I felt that we needed a super-Mrs. Jevens with an immense watering-can."

He was mapping his road and getting his levels, and marking out sites.   "I'm just about as brown as Capo Moro.   I swim every morning, and the Island of the Triton seems to have come much nearer.   No, I'm not jealous of your Scotch sea. Blessings on it.   My cresset is well alight on our Tower."

He was very vivid to Billy during those summer days.   She saw his eyes very blue in a brown face.   He told her that he went about in khaki-drill shorts and an old tennis shirt and a native hat.   She could picture the scorched hill-sides, and the fruited vines, and the oranges and lemons, and Julia Lord's garden all brown, and the shutters of the Agency covered with dust.   She was wise as to the heat and the flies and the dust.   But he was enduring.   His voice came to her cheerfully. It was the voice of a man.